UNFORGETTABLE YOU

The Lindstroms #6

New York Times Bestselling Author

Katy Regnery

writing as

Katy Paige

Please visit my website at **www.katyregnery.com**

Cover Designer: Marianne Nowicki

Editing: Ellie McLove

Formatting: CookieLynn Publishing Services

First Edition: October 2020

Unforgettable You: a novel / by Katy Paige—1st Ed.

ISBN: 978-1-944810-94-8

For real-life Summer.
Because she fought
and she won.

xoxo

Chapter 1

May Day

Maggie Campbell was drunk.

She was good and drunk and having a damn good time, but a frustratingly difficult time keeping her balance. The revelers from the annual Gardiner May Day celebration had somehow ended up at the Blue Moon Raccoon Saloon when the rain started pelting them from every direction. Everyone who'd been listening to the band on the high school football field had run for cover, and a sizable crowd had amassed at the local suds purveyor. After a few hours at the bar, Maggie and her friend Paul Johansson were definitely the worse for wear.

"Maggie, give us another toast!" demanded Maurice Evans, beer held high over his head, shaking in his unstable grip to shower him lightly with sloshes.

Likely owing to the fact that drunken Maggie had a strong, cheerful brogue and a cache of ribald toasts bestowed upon her young ears by her often-drunk Scottish father, she'd become a crowd favorite and they unplugged the jukebox every thirty moments or so to request another celebratory cheers. Of course, this meant that twice an hour, Maggie chugged a beer, the effects of which were affecting her aforementioned balance.

Maggie put her hand on her friend Paul's shoulder, bracing on the foot rung of the barstool, and held up her own full beer with her other hand. The crowd grew still as all eyes turned to look at the precariously-balanced redhead.

"May there always be work for your hands to do. May your purse always hold a coin or two."

She turned toward the door and then grinned back at the crowd.

"May the sun always shine upon your window pane…"

They chuckled with approval as she added,

"May a rainbow be certain to follow each rain. May the hand of a friend always be near to you and may God fill your heart with gladness to cheer you."

She beamed at the crowd, licking her lips as her beer teetered in her wobbly grasp and added with flair, "*Alba gu brath!*"

The crowd roared in approval, clinking their glasses together and chugging down their beers, none the wiser that they were all drinking to Scotland's long life. The jukebox was plugged in again and the raucous fiddles of Mumford & Sons thundered over the cheering of the crowd.

That's precisely the time the room started to spin.

Even Paul didn't notice as Maggie began to lose her balance, swaying as she finished her beer and lowering the hand that held the glass. Maggie closed her eyes for a moment, feeling the swirling start. Knowing she was likely to fall, she let her muscles go to jelly to lessen the impact. She certainly didn't have enough strength to stop herself.

She heard the screech of the stool's wooden legs as it skittered a short way across the floor and heard the hard clunk of her empty pint glass hitting the wooden bar. She looked down, as though in slow motion, to see Paul's horrified eyes, his arm flailing upward to grab her before she fell backward.

And then suddenly, a hard, warm wall slammed into her back and strong arms encircled her body. She let her head fall back until it rested on the flannel shelf of a shoulder, and she heard *his* voice, soft and urgent in her ear growl:

"I've got you, Maggie May."

His breath on her skin made her eyes flutter closed as she leaned back into him. When her feet hit the floor, he reached for the bar in front of them, caging her between his chest and the bar.

"You okay?"

His lips were so close to her ear, she trembled lightly, catching her breath. Every time he inhaled, his chest pushed into her back, which made it impossible to concentrate on anything else.

"Mags?"

The concern in his voice deserved an answer, so she took a deep, ragged breath and turned around, looking up to find familiar light blue eyes searching hers with worry.

Nils Lindstrom.

Over six feet tall and built like a lumberjack, Nils towered over her. He wore a plaid flannel shirt over a white T-shirt, both tucked into standard Levis that were a touch too tight in the front, showing a bulge along the inseam of his right thigh.

Her tongue darted out to wet her lips and her shoulders slumped with the wave of longing that crashed over her. Nils Lindstrom was one of her circle of friends, but—unbeknownst to him—he'd also pretty much owned her heart for the past four years.

He hooked a finger under her chin and drew her eyes up. "You going to be sick?"

She stared up at him, wishing for the thousandth time that he could see her as more than a friend.

Of course he would have been somewhere in the bar watching her make a fool of herself standing on barstools and yelling toasts in Gaelic. She reached up to wipe her lips with the back of her hand, feeling her already flaming cheeks heat up like a pagan bonfire. She was drunk, she'd almost face-planted into the bar floor, and now he was making sure she wouldn't vomit all over him.

Oh, for the love of—could she never, ever catch a break with this man?

"I'm fine," she said tightly, her accent more pronounced in her ears than usual. She turned her neck to her left to detach her chin from his finger.

Her friend Paul grinned at her sheepishly over Nils's arm. "Sorry I didn't catch you in time, Mags."

Maggie grinned at her drinking buddy. "No harm done."

"*Could've* been harm done." Nils's voice was thick with censure. When Maggie looked up at him, he was eyeing Paul with annoyance.

4

Paul Johansson was the best friend of Nils's younger brother, Lars.

"Wasn't Paul's fault if I chose to get up on a barstool and act like a drunkard."

She gestured to the bartender for another beer.

"Another, Maggie?" he confirmed.

"Lots of anothers," she answered, annoyed her words sounded so jumbled. Not that she minded, really, but she wondered how long Nils planned to keep her imprisoned between his arms. Must have been the beer that prompted her to ask him, "So, how long are ye' trappin' me here, Nils? Keen to babysit me t'night, are ye?"

His blue eyes captured hers, searching and intense, narrowing at her tone. "A *thank-you* wouldn't be remiss, Maggie May."

Maggie couldn't explain why his words got her back up, but they did. She didn't want to thank him for saving her. She wanted him to see her as a woman, as more than just a friend. She wanted him to kiss her. She wanted him to take her back to his place or over to hers and tear her clothes off. Preferably with his teeth.

"Thaaanks," she said slowly, licking her lips in a way she hoped was seductive, but they were so dry she re-licked them a few more times before catching herself. From the gaping look on his face, she was pretty sure she'd somehow managed to look more like a lizard than a *femme fatale*.

Nils stared at her lips for a moment then flicked his eyes to hers. His nostrils flared and his jaw pulsed once, twice, before he dropped his arms and turned to Paul. "Do a better job looking out for her."

Then he turned on his heel without another word, parting the crowd as he headed out of the bar.

***

Damn Maggie anyway.

She was going to get herself hurt if she kept carrying on that way. Well, she could just be Paul's problem for the rest of tonight. The last thing Nils needed in his life was a woman who took too many stupid risks. No matter how he felt about her.

The cold rain pelted Nils's face and the mountain air felt heavy in his lungs as he took a deep breath, his beat-up cowboy boots sloshing through the mixture of mud and puddle water as his long strides took him farther away from the bar where Maggie was making a spectacle of herself. He turned up the collar of his Shetland jacket as the rain slicked his blond hair to his head.

He pumped his fingers into fists repeatedly, trying to erase the imprint of Maggie's tummy when her sweater rode up as he caught her. He couldn't. He could still feel it. It felt like perfect, if perfect could be defined by soft, pliant, warm skin pressed intimately against his palm.

Abruptly he turned left, back toward town, away from the house he shared with Lars, toward Main Street, where the office of *Lindstrom & Sons* would be dark and empty. Maybe Nils could find some paperwork to do; the way his body felt, all charged up and hot, meant sleep would be elusive for a few hours at least.

And yes, damn it, from his office he could watch as

Paul helped her stumble home in an hour or so. Nils could make sure she got home safely. Maggie's Prairie Dawn Café and Bookstore, where she lived in an apartment on the second floor, was just a few doors down.

His phone rang in his back pocket as he crossed the bridge over the Yellowstone River, and he looked down at it. Jenny. His little sister.

"Heya, Jen," he said, still walking at a brisk pace.

"Heya, Nils!"

He smiled at the sunshine in her voice. A couple of years ago, Sam Kelley, a businessman from Chicago had spent a weekend in Gardiner, falling in love with his sister. She and Sam lived in Great Falls now, but he saw them—and their daughter, Erin—often.

"Why aren't you out with Paul and Maggie?" she asked.

"For someone who moved outta this town, you sure keep up with what's going on. Doesn't Sam keep you busy enough?"

"You're always such a grouch. Thought maybe you'd treat May Day like New Year's and move in for a kiss at midnight."

"Aw, Jen. Paul's not really my type."

His sister bellowed with laughter, and Nils—who'd felt annoyed a moment ago—joined her. Of all his siblings, Jenny was the biggest tease, and since she'd married Sam, she'd only gotten worse, blossoming into a right sassy thing.

"Let's hope he's not Maggie's type either," she said, all smart-mouthed.

"I think we all know who Paul's type is," returned Nils,

reminding Jenny of how she'd had to turn down Paul's advances once upon a time.

"Whew! Truce!" she exclaimed.

"Yeah, okay." Nils chuckled softly. She was a pain in the ass, but she was his only sister and he adored her. "Why are you bothering me anyway?"

"Like you have so many more pressing things to do. Bet you're in the office doing paperwork."

Nils unlocked the door of the dark office. He hadn't actually started the paperwork yet. "Nope. You're wrong. Was just over at the Blue Moon."

"Looking for a date? Hmmm. Maybe, um, Missy Branson can fit you in. Didn't you *visit* with her a time or two?"

Nils sighed. Missy Branson, who used to be Gardiner's resident good-time girl, hadn't worked at the Blue Moon for over a year. Though, to his embarrassment, Jenny was right—he and Missy had "gotten together" on occasion to scratch a mutual itch.

Damn Jenny's memory, that was years ago!

"So someone doesn't know everything, huh? Missy got married and moved to Billings year before last. Right after you. Has a little'un now. Looked happy the last time I saw her, back visiting her mama."

"Oh." Jenny was surprised enough to sound humble. "Oh, well. That's nice. Someone for everyone, I guess."

Except me, thought Nils. *That ship sailed a long, long time ago.*

"Still haven't told me why you're bothering me,

8

lillesøster."

"It's Pappa's sixtieth birthday on June thirtieth. I want to have a big party. Whole family. Lots of friends. *Smorgasbord.* Like Mamma would've done for him."

"That's nice, Jen." Nils hung his coat on the coat rack to the left of the doorway and flicked on the lights of the small office. Being the oldest, he felt a passing sense of guilt, like he should have been more on top of this. Truthfully, he hadn't even realized such an important milestone birthday was coming up. "We'd all come up there to you?"

"No. Pappa's home is Gardiner. I think we should have it there. And I already talked to Maggie. She said we could use the Prairie. What do you think?"

The Prairie Dawn was a great location for the party. Just like Maggie, it was a warm, unexpected spot in a western-style town that mostly catered to Yellowstone tourists, fishermen and hunters. With its copper bar, soft lighting, mismatched tables, and comfortable, shabby couches, it was a favorite Lindstrom hangout. The locals loved it and Maggie's coffee was the best to be found between Livingston and Jackson Hole.

"You mean, like, rent it out for a night?"

"Yeah," said Jenny. "We can all pitch in to pay for it, of course. I already talked to Erik and he said he and Kat will contribute and come down from Kalispell for a long weekend to celebrate. And since you and Lars live local, you can help Maggie."

Wait a minute. What? While Nils often found himself at the Prairie Dawn, drinking a cup of coffee or enjoying a muffin, he studiously avoided alone time with Maggie Campbell. He didn't trust himself not to make a move on her, so it was easier to leave her be.

"Paul will help, too," cajoled Jenny.

Great. Paul again. Paul who was practically joined to Maggie at the hip. As much as Nils enjoyed a fishing trip or hunting excursion with the high school principal, he hated how chummy he and Maggie were, and he lived in perpetual fear that their friendship would cross a line one day. Not that Nils was doing anything about it, but if he couldn't have Maggie, he sure didn't want anyone else to have her either because he was a...*selfish bastard.*

"Lars practically lives in the park, Jen. When he's not wildcatting." He turned on the coffee machine in the back of the office that made Gardiner's weakest and worst cup of coffee.

"Sorta thought he'd be better behaved once he lost his wingman."

"Erik getting hitched doesn't keep Lars from going after the Park Girls. Just gives him more to choose from."

"How come you never go after the Park Girls, Nils?"

"Who says I don't?"

"Seems like Erik and Lars always went carousing while you hung back, looking out for all of us. You don't have to be the big brother anymore, you know. You should be having more fun."

"I have plenty of fun, Jenny."

"What, working? Planning tours and going to church on Sunday?"

"Why are you giving me a hard time?"

"I'm worried about you. Maybe I got it wrong. Maybe you don't want to be with Maggie, but don't you want to be with someone?"

He winced at her words, cradling the phone between his cheek and shoulder as he carried his coffee cup over to his desk.

Want to be with someone? Of course. But it wasn't that simple. It would never be that simple. Once upon a time he'd been with someone and lost her and it had just about killed him. He set the mug on his desk and reached up to rub a spot on his forehead that still sported a mild bump after all these years. He didn't want to talk about these things with Jenny. He didn't want to talk about them at all.

"If I say I'll help Maggie with the party, will you hang up the phone and leave me alone?"

She sighed. "Will you?"

"Yes, *smärta i nacken.* You knew I would."

"If one of us is a pain in the neck…" she started, but she didn't finish the thought. Instead she offered softly, her voice warm and loving, "*Elsker deg,* Nils."

And that was why Nils—or any of his brothers, for that matter—would never be able to say no to Jenny. Because Jenny said *I love you* in their mother's voice, and Lord only knew how much they all missed her.

"*Ja,* Jen. *Elsker deg også.*"

"I'll call Maggie tomorrow and set everything up with her, and then you go over there and offer to give her a hand, Nils. And be nice. No grouchy-bear-Nils grudgingly offering

11

to help. You make her feel like you *want* to help, okay?"

"Anything else, Miss Bossy?"

"I'll get Paul and Lars to help, too."

"Like you could *keep* Paul from helping," muttered Nils.

"Paul doesn't like Maggie like that. He needs to find someone just as badly as you do. Come to think of it, Lars could use a good woman, too…"

He needed to hang up before she started marrying them all off.

"Hanging up, Jen…kiss Erin for *Onkel* Nils. Say hi to Sam…"

Jenny was still going on about possible eligible women in Gardiner when Nils softly tapped the red End button on his phone. Might be half an hour before she figured out she wasn't talking to anyone anymore. He grinned, taking a sip of coffee and cringing at the watery bitterness.

He didn't mind helping to plan a party for his father, and he was relieved that Jenny actually had a plan on the table. But working with Maggie? He pursed his lips. That was another thing. His heart sort of did a little leap, thinking about the time he'd need to spend with her planning such a large event…but it took a nosedive a moment later as he reminded himself:

You're not good enough for her, Nils. You're not good enough for anyone.

***

Maggie was grateful for Paul's arm around her shoulders as she stumbled through puddles and potholes, the cold rainwater splashing up on her jeans. She looked back at the

Blue Moon, sort of surprised to still see it so close. It felt like they'd been walking for a long time.

"Face forward, Mags. If you look back, you're gonna trip."

Oh, what did Paul know anyway? He was drunk. She decided to tell him so.

"Whaddaya know? You're drunk."

"Not as drunk as you," he answered under his breath, catching her around the waist as she stumbled and almost fell.

"Don' lemme fall," she said. "Wouldna he jus' love that? Big babysitter."

"No one wants you to fall, Maggie."

"I can fall over all the live long day, Paul. He canna tell me what to do and neither can you." Her words were so slurry, and so confusing. *Live long day*. What did that mean anyway? "Live long day. Live long day."

"Yeah. Live long day. Fine. I just want to get you home safe, Mags." Paul tightened his grip around her waist, pulling her against him.

"I shoulda fallen 'n love wit you," she mumbled, her boot heels occasionally scraping the pavement as she lurched forward then compensated.

"That wouldn't have worked. We're too good of friends."

"Friends! Ha! Ye're not listenin' to me!" She stopped walking, balancing herself before poking her finger into Paul's chest. "I'm a lass, Paulie. A *lass*! Even though we're friends, we need t'be clear on that point, boyo. An' you know what else, too? The way he looks at me sometimes? He should bed me or wed me, an'make no mistake. I know what I'm about."

He shook his head, looking supremely annoyed with someone. Maggie lurched around to see who he was looking at, but they must have been one fast walker, because they'd moved on by the time she managed to look. She swiped a limp hand in front of his face as he came back into focus. "I mean it."

"Yeah, you mean something, but damned if I can follow." He put his arm back around her waist and suddenly she was walking again. "It's okay, Mags. Just keep walking. Almost there."

"An' y'know wha'else?"

"No. What else?"

"What else is that—" *Ooo! The river!* "Look! I could jus' jump in and swim home, Paul."

"I don't think so, Mags. Little too cold for swimming."

"Yer no fun."

"That may be so."

"*I'm* fun."

"Yeah, you're usually pretty fun."

She caught the emphasis on "usually" and furrowed her brow. She stopped walking, pushing his hand away from her waist and poking him in the chest again. "*Always* fun."

Paul sighed loudly. "Sure, Mags. You're always fun. Especially right now."

She started giggling. "Thanks. Yer my bes' friend. Know that?"

14

He finally smiled at her, chuckling softly and shaking his head back and forth like she was making him tired. "I know."

He took her hand and dragged her limp arm over his shoulders, and then they started walking again.

"Hey, Paul."

Maggie looked up to see a blurry version of Nils Lindstrom approaching them from the front door of his office, which was just down the street from her café and apartment. Of all the bad luck. He was the last person she wanted to see.

"Need a hand?"

Maggie used all of her effort to turn her face from Nils to Paul. Paul nodded, looking relieved and tilting his head toward Maggie. "She started feeling tired and wanted to go home so we left, but I left my wallet at the bar. Can you take her the rest of the way home?"

"Ummm," said Maggie to no one in particular, staring at the pavement to steady herself. "I'm standin' right here. I can take *myself* the rest of the way home."

"No problem. I'll see to her. You go get your wallet."

"Yep," she slurred. "Go get yer wallet, Nils."

"No, not him, me. I'm going to—Aw, forget it. She's three sheets. Thanks, Nils. 'Night, Mags."

"'Night, Nils," she murmured, listening to his retreating footsteps.

Paul must have gone to work out somewhere for a few minutes, because when he gripped her waist again, his arm was stronger and bigger and he held her tighter than before, like even if she wanted to pull away from him, he wouldn't let her now. Like he wouldn't let her go.

She stared at the pavement, watching her boots as they moved along.

"Come on, Maggie May. Let's get you home."

"Only Nils calls me Maggie May."

"Yep. That's right."

"So, don' call me that, Paul. You should know better." Her words took a lot of effort, but she didn't want to think about Nils Lindstrom, about the way it had felt to be pressed against his chest in the bar. "Since yer m'best friend, can I tell ye somethin'?"

"Sure, anything."

"Y' know Nils Lindstrom?"

"Boy, you're in rough shape," said Paul, but he didn't sound exactly like Paul, probably because he was so drunk. In fact, he sounded a lot like Nils Lindstrom, all low-toned and grouchy. Tricks. Tricky beer mind games. "Yeah, I know him."

"Well, I'm gonna let you in on a lil' secret, laddie, and it's—"

"Maggie, I don't think you should tell m—"

"—this. We been cir'clin' each other for four-ish years, and I'm a'tellin' y' true. That man needs to bed me or wed me, Paulie. Anythin' else is puir wastin' my time."

"Is that right?" Paul's voice was deep and gravelly.

"Tha's right," she said, resolutely, tripping over a seam in the sidewalk. Paul hauled her up against his side, his paw-like hand tight against her hip. Since when were Paul's hands so big? "Paul! The beer ate your hands an' gave you bear hands!"

"Whew. Careful, now."

They were almost at the Prairie Dawn. Almost home. Maggie looked up at the dark sky littered with tears, and felt stars in her eyes.

"I wish I didna love him so well," she whispered to the heavens.

Paul's arm tightened around her as she whispered the words, but he didn't say anything until they got to her door. "Maggie May, where're your keys?"

She was leaning up against the wall beside her back door, but she felt so heavy and wobbly, she started to lean forward. Suddenly a hand was pressed into her abdomen, keeping her upright against the wall and a moment later she heard the sound of a key twisting in a lock.

"I hate it that you leave one under the mat. Anyone could…" Grouchy-voiced Paul kept talking about the unsafe practice of leaving keys under mats as she swayed and tried not to giggle at him. Then suddenly she was being carried up the flight of stairs to her apartment. The world swirled and her stomach rebelled and she closed her eyes, pressing her face into a warm neck that smelled of sandalwood and sweat. It smelled like Nils Lindstrom. It made her stomach calm down like magic.

"You smell like 'im, Paul," she sighed. "You smell like Nils. It makes me wan' kiss you."

How had she gotten to her bed? Had she taken her coat off or had Paul? He was pulling her boots off gently, first one, then the other.

"Gotta take your jeans off, Mags. They're soaked."

"Dinna get fresh…" she giggled in a singsong voice, her eyes still closed against the threat of spins.

She felt warm fingers graze her belly under her jeans as they unbuttoned the five buttons in her fly. The same fingers moved to her waist, peeling the jeans away from her skin and tugging them down over her panties. His fingers trailed lightly down the outside of her thighs as he pulled gently, finally freeing them from the curve of her ankle. His fingers hooked into the tops of her socks and he pulled them down until her feet were as bare as her legs. She heard a couple of drawers open and close and a moment later she felt dry, fuzzy socks being rolled onto her feet, and then her covers were pulled up and around her.

A warm hand brushed the bangs off her forehead, and then Nils Lindstrom's voice whispered in her ear—it was a cool trick that drunk Paul could sound so much like growly Nils—and the sound was like heaven.

"You need anything else?"

"Nah, I'm goin' asleep," she sighed, snuggling into her pillow. "Just dinna tell Nils what I told you, 'kay? He doesna like me that way. Doesna see me that way neither. Doesna matter. Ye're my best friend ever."

"It's okay," he said. She felt soft lips graze her forehead, brushing back and forth gently before pulling away. "'Night, Maggie May."

"'Night, Paul," she murmured, falling immediately into a deep sleep.

Chapter 2

"Nils! I've said your name three times, son," his father scolded him from the desk next to his.

"Sorry, Pop."

"Where's your head at today?"

Morning sunlight streamed into the small office, the cold rain from the night before long gone. But Nils's memories from last night were just as fresh as if he'd left Maggie's apartment five minutes ago. *That man needs to bed me or wed me… I wish I didna love him so well… It makes me wan' kiss you.* Nils took a shaky breath, wishing he'd never heard those things, wishing he didn't know what they sounded like in his ears.

He glanced at his father. "Don't know. Distracted, I guess."

"Feeling okay?"

"Oh, sure."

"I tell you what…how about you go get us two decent-tasting coffees from Maggie's place and when you get back, we'll discuss the McCarthy group coming in for the month of July."

"M-Maggie's?"

"Yeah. I'll have one of them lat-tays with cinnamon."

His father shoved his glasses up from the tip of his nose and turned his attention back to the files.

Nils stood up slowly, not sure he was ready to see Maggie after last night. She was so drunk, he doubted she'd have any recollection of the things she'd said to him, and yet they were seared on Nils's brain like a brand.

That man needs to bed me or wed me...That man needs to bed me or wed me...

Well, they lived in the same small town. Best to bite the bullet and smooth things over as soon as possible. Not to mention, he was going to have to work with Maggie on his father's surprise party. He couldn't avoid her forever.

He cleared his throat and pushed back from his desk. "Sure, Pop. I'll, uh, I'll maybe take a quick walk first. Get a little fresh air. Be back in a bit."

Outside, it was sunny, though cool for early May. Nils's favorite weather. He turned away from the Prairie Dawn and headed up the road, hoping to clear his head a little bit.

The first time he saw Maggie, working with her Aunt Lily at the Prairie Dawn, he'd been taken with her. Her strawberry-blonde head was bent over a cappuccino machine that was getting the full force of her frustration as she swore at it repeatedly in her thick Scottish accent.

"Ye keech sheepshagger of a—"

"Ah-hem," Nils had cleared his throat to get her attention, but hadn't prepared himself for the emerald green eyes that flashed up to meet his. He was rendered speechless by their sparkling depths, bursting with mischief and humor.

"Ya caught me cursin'," she said softly with an impish

grin. "This damned thing willna foam."

He knew he was staring at her—at her smooth reddish hair that curled softly against the milky skin of her neck, at the smattering of freckles over her nose, at her cherry red lips that spread into a bemused smile. She looked so much like...like...

"Yer starin'," she said, smacking the back of his hand lightly twice in quick succession. "Wake up!"

The combination of her skin touching his and her gentle command forced him back to reality.

"Sorry," he muttered. "You're new here."

She nodded, "Aye, that I am. I'm Lily's niece."

"From Scotland?"

"Aye, fresh from Glasgow. Ye ever been to Glasgow?"

She turned away and when she turned back, she'd placed a colorful mug of steaming coffee in front of him. He had no idea when he'd taken a seat on the stool in front of her.

"N-no. Never left Montana."

"Och! That's a shame. Scotland's lovely, though not so much Glasgow. It's a rough town. Gangs. Thieves!" She said this conspiratorially, then grinned again like she was making a joke. "What *you* want is Inverness."

"Is that what I want?" he murmured, as his heart thumped painfully behind his ribs.

Her looks were so familiar to him, but her accent kept throwing him. *This isn't Veronica. This isn't Veronica.* She'd folded her small, white freckled hands on the bar in front of him and he noticed she wore a Claddagh ring on the fourth finger of her right hand with the heart turned out.

"Aye! The Loch Ness monster, Urquhart Castle, Cawdor Castle…d'ye like castles?" Her bright eyes captured his, animated and expectant, as he considered her question. In all his life, no one had ever asked if he liked castles. He certainly didn't have a formed opinion. When he didn't answer, she answered her own question. "Of course ye do. Everyone likes castles."

A chuckle bubbled up from his throat and before he could stop it, it escaped from his lips. The male equivalent of a giggle. It sounded so foreign and so ridiculous, his eyes flew open and he rubbed his jaw with his hand, trying to get his head around this strangely familiar new girl who fairly sparkled with teasing energy.

"Ah! There 'tis. A wee smile. I knew you had one hidden somewhere behind all that sobriety." She rolled the "r" grandly, drawing out the sound like a purr, and stuck out her hand. "I'm Maggie Campbell."

He lowered his hand from his face, unable to wipe away his grin completely as he clasped her delicate fingers in his tanned paw of a hand. "Nils Lindstrom."

She cocked her head to the side, smiling at him for a brief moment before pulling her hand away, but not before he noticed a slight blush flush her cheeks. "D'ye know anything about fixin' coffee makers, Nils?"

And he couldn't help it. Though he had no business offering genuine smiles to pretty girls, he'd smiled at her again.

A cool breeze smacked him in the face and scattered his

memories. How was it possible that was four years ago? Where had the time gone? He pulled the dark brown corduroy collar of his barn jacket up around his ears, grateful for his cowboy hat.

Before Maggie's arrival in Gardiner, Nils had been quietly satisfied with his life. He didn't need much, and if he had longings deep in his heart for more than his life offered, he was able to ignore them. He lived quiet and alone, loving his family and avoiding anything more than an occasional short-lived fling. He'd had his chance for love long ago and destroyed it. He knew he didn't deserve a second chance; he'd come to terms with that truth long ago.

But after meeting Maggie that first day, a quiet battle had waged inside of him, and even as his mind won round after round, sometimes, just sometimes, his heart ached with loneliness, with the want of her. During those times, he'd leave Gardiner for a spell—lead a weeklong tour group in the park, visit Jenny in Great Falls or Erik in Kalispell. He'd physically remove his body from Maggie's proximity—until he could cope with being her friend and resolve that nothing more serious than friendship must ever transpire between them. For her sake, if not for his.

Mostly, being Maggie's friend was bearable, especially because she wasn't attached to anyone else. It made him a selfish bastard that he didn't make a move on her, but desperately hoped she'd remain unattached. If he truly cared for her, he'd want the best for her. He'd want for her to find a solid, responsible person to love her who didn't have demons at his heels. He'd want her to have the life he'd never be able to share with her, the children he'd never be able to give her. And yet every time he saw Maggie, *every* time his glance flicked to the Claddagh ring on her finger, seeing the heart turned out made him sigh softly with relief to know that her heart still hadn't been claimed.

Mostly, he just enjoyed the time he spent with her—the scraps of her warmth devoured gratefully and shamefully at the doorstep to his imposed loneliness. He lived for the evenings he played euchre with her, Paul, and Lars at the Prairie Dawn, for her smiles when he grabbed a cup of coffee before work and the sparkle in her green eyes for a few precious moments as she prepared it for him. One thing that had made his feelings for her easier was that aside from a friendship in which she occasionally teased him or colored when he caught her staring at him, she'd never implied that she had any special feelings for him. He could admire her from afar, wishing he had a right to her, but settling for the warmth of her friendship. He could convince himself that she was content with their friendship, too.

Until last night.

Last night had changed that.

It was impossible to tell himself that she only saw him as a friend now.

We been cir'clin' each other for four-ish years, and I'm tellin' y' true. That man needs to bed me or wed me.

He took a deep breath of cold mountain air, hating the surge of hope that followed the memory. Little did Maggie know that "bedding" her was his favorite fantasy. He imagined those green eyes rolling back in her head as he thrust his enormous length into her, making her writhe and tremble as he filled her. He imagined her small, pale body arching and quivering beneath him as he braced his weight over her. In his fantasies she cried out in pleasure. In his delusions she welcomed him, wanted him, took pleasure from him. In his desperate dreams she whispered she loved him as he held her against his pounding heart, as he vowed to never, ever let her go.

He growled softly, hating the way his body tightened, and forced the images from his mind as he had a hundred times before. But this time they wouldn't be banished completely as he recalled the softness of her skin under his fingertips as he caught her. Her hips and belly against his harder, larger frame as he trapped her against the bar. He ground his jaw, clenching his fingers in frustration.

*Bed me or wed me...bed me or wed me...*the words circled in a tantalizing loop in his head.

Bed Maggie? As much as he'd like to, he liked her too much to ever put *that* on the table. She wasn't some cheap piece of ass passing through. She wasn't a candidate for a cheap fling; Maggie was his sister's friend, a loved and respected family friend and since he couldn't offer her anything serious or respectable, he'd made a promise to himself not to make a move on her. *Wed Maggie?* He snorted. You only married someone if you wanted to build a life with them...a home, a family with children.

He might never forget Maggie's words to him last night, but as he turned back toward town, he fervently hoped that *she* would.

There would never, ever be a bedding.

There would certainly never be a wedding.

All they were able to share was friendship, and since Maggie's friendship was the brightest spot in Nils's melancholy life, he would protect it until it drained the last ounce of love from his pitiful existence.

***

Maggie fought not to rest her head on the copper bar in front of her.

Between the swirling in her stomach, the pounding in her head and the heaviness of her eyes, she actually considered—for the first time in her three years as sole proprietor of the Prairie Dawn Café & Bookstore—closing early. But she couldn't very well do that. She'd only opened thirty minutes ago and already lost all of the early morning traffic by oversleeping. She glanced at her watch. Ten o'clock in the morning. Ten hours of work to go. She rubbed her stomach and groaned.

She hated blacking out from drinking too much. She wasn't comfortable with missing pieces of a night, although she consoled herself that Paul was the safest possible companion in such cases. Her mother had relentlessly reminded her throughout her somewhat wild adolescence that her father had passed away from cirrhosis at a young age, and though Maggie might not have inherited his genes, she could still have a predisposition for over-imbibing based on his example. It's true that Maggie liked her drink; since high school, when she'd started sneaking beers with friends, she'd liked how it felt to be drunk. And it was May Day, for goodness sake! She shrugged defensively—she hadn't hurt anyone, now, had she? Of course not. She was only celebrating. She'd gotten home safely. And she was careful her occasional binges didn't get in the way of her business or friendships.

"It's harmless," she insisted aloud in a whisper, as she added cream to her coffee, her usual conviction missing from her voice.

If it's so harmless, why is last night sitting so funny in your gut? nagged the voice in her head that always plagued her on hungover mornings.

She reviewed the evening in her head to reassure herself. She and Paul had followed the crowd to the Blue Moon and settled in on their favorite barstools. She'd been cajoled to offer toasts over and over again, chugging her own beer with abandon every time. After the third or fourth, her memories were pretty fuzzy because she'd been good and stottered.

Sipping her coffee, she tried to remember more details. They'd drank beers, shouted toasts, danced to the tunes on the jukebox and—bollocks! She grimaced as she recalled what happened next.

"Oh, no…" she groaned.

Nils Lindstrom. Nils was there. Oh, Lord, Nils had saved her from falling flat on her face.

Aye. There it is, murmured the nagging voice in victory.

She'd acted like an unholy eidgit and Nils had come to her rescue. Resting her cheek in her palm, she felt her face soften as she remembered the feeling of his front pressed against her back, caging her against the bar as she regained her balance. But she gritted her teeth as she recalled his curt warning to Paul to "do a better job looking out for her."

And then he'd left. Walked away from her...like he always did.

Of course he did. Why would he stay and watch you play the drunkard for all the town to see?

And there it was again, as always: the crushing feeling that despite the way she felt about Nils Lindstrom—despite the way she'd felt about him for years—he simply didn't feel the same way about her. The sheer force of her feelings wasn't enough to make him see her as a woman, to make him see her as more than a friend.

Refreshing her coffee, she leaned her elbows on the bar and looked blearily out at the few patrons sipping coffee and reading books or newspapers as the mid-morning sun filtered in through the windows cheerfully.

Mismatched tile-topped bistro tables—more suited to the Amalfi Coast than a small bookstore in Montana— dotted the shiny hard wood floor. Several comfy chairs and two loveseats with cheerful, worn slipcovers invited patrons to enjoy their coffee while flipping through one of the bookstore's many available titles. Soft folk music by a popular new band played softly on the overhead speakers and the rich, warm smell of coffee beans and baked scones greeted every customer who entered the Prairie Dawn.

Maggie had inherited the café from her Aunt Lily, her mother's eldest sister, three and a half years ago when she passed away. Lily, who read about Yellowstone National

Park in a magazine and promptly left Scotland thirty years ago determined to find an adventure, had certainly found one. Upon arriving in Gardiner, Montana, she'd met Jock Henry, a local man who worked as a park ranger. Jock was twenty years older than skinny, fire-haired Lily, but he'd fallen in love with her at first sight. And once Lily set her sights on Jock? It was futile to resist. Lily Frazier was used to getting what she wanted, and Jock was the only name on her short list.

When Maggie was fourteen, she'd happened upon a shoebox in her mother's closet with hundreds of letters from Lily that illustrated, in great detail, her campaign to win the heart of Jock Henry. And Maggie was captivated. Utterly captivated. Not just with the story of how her aunt and uncle found their way to one another, but of the descriptions Lily shared of Montana, of Yellowstone, of Gardiner. And like her adventuresome aunt, young Maggie was determined to find an adventure of her own.

She'd even brought the letters with her when she ventured to Montana, hoping that Lily would help her put them in order—maybe even put them together as a book, a memoir. But by the time Maggie had arrived in Gardiner, Lily was too sick to do much but train Maggie to take over the Prairie Dawn. She was gone a few months later and Maggie had never mustered the nerve to talk to her aunt about her short, sweet love affair. Nor had Maggie looked at the letters since losing her aunt, keeping them carefully in a box in the top, far corner of her closet, unopened and untouched, as if in memorial.

The phone on the counter behind her rang way too loudly, and Maggie jumped, wincing when her head pounded in response. As she picked up the old-fashioned receiver, the curly yellow cord brushed against a pile of mail and the top envelope fell between the countertop and the wall. She sighed in frustration. Could absolutely nothing go her way today?

"Prairie Dawn," she growled into the phone, rubbing her forehead with her free hand.

"Ouch!" said Paul and Maggie grimaced.

"That's about the size of it, laddie."

"You hurting bad, Mags?"

"There should be a law that you can only have May Day on a Saturday. It's cruel and unusual when it falls on a Sunday."

"Why's that?"

"Because you have to go to work with a scorchin' hangover for the rest of the week."

She leaned back against the counter as Paul chuckled lightly.

"Masochist," she growled at him. "Why aren't you feelin' worse? You were as drunk as me!"

"Not even close. Nobody on the face of the earth was as drunk as you were last night, Mags. And don't call me names. I'm the good friend calling to check up on you. Making sure Nils got you home safely last night."

"Ha!" Her skin prickled. "That's not funny."

"I'm not trying to be funny."

"Wait. What?" Her green eyes flew open and her body

tensed, an uncomfortable feeling unfurling in the pit of her stomach. She had no memory of Nils walking her home. In fact, she had no memory of *getting* home, and certainly no memory of seeing Nils after he caught her from falling.

"What're you on about, Paul?" she asked, trying to keep her voice light. "*You* walked me home like you always do."

"Most of the way. But we ran into Nils at the Prairie and he finished the job. I'd left my wallet at the…"

Paul kept talking, but Maggie didn't hear a word of it. *Nils* had walked her home? *Nils* had somehow gotten her up the stairs and into bed? Her mind scrambled for memories, but came up blank. Suddenly her mouth dropped open and her face flushed hot as she realized: *I wore jeans and a sweater to May Day and I woke up in a T-shirt, socks, and underwear.*

"Paul. Paul! Stop talkin'!" Her heart thumped like mad and she tried not to hyperventilate as she got her mind around this information. "Are you sayin' that *Nils* put me…to bed?"

"That's a safe bet. I doubt you could've gotten there on your own. Maybe if you'd crawled—"

"But, I—" She whimpered before demanding: "Why?"

"I told you…We bumped into him on the way home. I had to go back for my wallet and he offered to give you a hand. Simple as that."

Her stomach flipped over again, but this time it had less to do with her hangover and more to do with that terrible sinking feeling that came from blacking out. She couldn't remember anything—*anything*—she'd said or done the night before. But she had that feeling…that sick, panicked feeling that she'd done something wrong or said too much.

The wages of sin, Maggie, said the mocking voice.

"Listen, the bell's about to ring. I just wanted to be sure—"

"Wait! Wait." She hated having to ask the next question, but if she didn't, she'd torment herself all day trying to put together the pieces. Did she owe Nils an apology? Had she ranted and raved at him? Made an ass of herself? "What was I talkin' about before we met up with him...I mean...what might I have said to him?"

"I have no idea. You weren't making any sense on our walk from the Blue Moon. You suggested you could swim home at one point. You insisted you were always fun while almost face-planting over a pothole." He paused and she held her breath. "You were talking about how life would've been easier if you'd fallen in love with me instead."

Her heart dropped. Not because of what she'd said to Paul, because of what it implied. It would've been easier to fall in love with Paul instead of...

Nils.

"Mags, are you asking me if you were going on about Nils? Sort of, I guess, but not really. Well, maybe just a little about how he doesn't see you as anything but a friend."

"Oh, Lord." Her eyes closed slowly, and she cringed. "I was, wasn't I? I was goin' on about Nils while you were walkin' me home. I was talkin' about him."

Paul paused before offering a soft, "You weren't making much sense. I promise."

She bent her head forward in misery, stopping just

short of banging it repeatedly on the bar. What in the hell did she say to Nils in those few minutes? And why did she have the feeling she'd regret it if she knew? Anger and frustration rose up inside of her, and she directed it at Paul.

"How could you let him walk me home? How could you do that?" she demanded, lowering her voice low as a patron turned to look over at her. She hissed, "I have no idea what I might've said to him. I could've—You know how I...I mean, you know that I—"

"Not to make your head ache any more than it already does, Maggie, but maybe you should think about easing up on the beer-chugging a little? I stopped at four and you were still going strong at six." He paused for a second to let her digest this reproach. "Listen, third period is starting. I have to go, but don't worry. I'm sure it's fine. You were so blitzed, he wouldn't have taken you seriously anyway, no matter what you said. Chill out and drink a lot of water today."

The phone clicked off and before Maggie could say another word, the bell over the front door rang to announce the arrival of Nils Lindstrom.

Chapter 3

He couldn't help his lips wobbling briefly as he suppressed a grin.

She looked awful.

He could tell how bad she was feeling—he'd been there before himself. But she squared her shoulders toward the door and lifted her chin a notch as he stepped into the warm, sweet-smelling café. So small. So full of spirit.

"Morning, Maggie," he began cautiously as he approached the coffee bar.

Does she remember last night? Does she remember what she said to me? Does she remember me kissing her forehead before I left?

"Mornin', Nils," she said without smiling, her green eyes more bloodshot than usual.

He gestured to her head. "How're you feeling?"

"A bit the worse for wear."

She held his eyes with hers as he sat down on a barstool in front of her. It was like she was waiting for something, bracing for something unpleasant, like a lecture or a bad surprise. Well, she wasn't going to get either. He didn't even know how to process what had happened between them last night, but if she had forgotten some of the details, it was probably for the best.

He flicked his gaze up to the chalkboard over her head, even though he'd memorized it long ago. *Damn, but this is awkward.*

"What can I get for you?"

"Two lattes. Please."

"Cinnamon for your pops?"

He nodded, looking back at her, his lips tipping up slightly. *Is she going to mention last night? Does she even remember last night?* She was acting so tense and cagey, he wasn't sure what to do, so he stayed silent as she turned to prepare the coffee.

"I'm thinkin' I owe you some thanks. For, er, last night." She glanced at him over her shoulder for a moment and he saw a blush creep up her cheeks before she turned back around.

"It's fine. You needed help," he said quietly.

She mumbled something incoherent then turned to him and placed the two steaming cups on the counter, pushing one closer to him before looking him straight in the eye and asking:

"But do we need to discuss how I woke up half-naked this mornin'?"

Nils choked on the sip of coffee he'd taken, sputtering and coughing, and Maggie quickly took the cup out of his hand. He took a deep breath and cleared his throat as she stood motionless before him, staring at him unflinchingly while the flush in her freckled cheeks deepened. The words "half-naked" had triggered an immediate reaction in his body, making his blood sluice hot and fast below his waist where it rushed to one place, increasingly rigid beneath his jeans.

In an effort to calm down, he released her eyes and his gaze lifted to her forehead where he'd brushed his lips gently across her skin before leaving her last night. It was a liberty he shouldn't have taken, but after what she'd said to him, the way he'd held her in his arms and readied her for bed, he couldn't help himself. It was a chaste, little kiss; even if she remembered it, he was sure she'd agree it didn't break any rules of propriety.

Still, he shouldn't have done it. In Nils's mind, in his heart, he'd crossed a line. Little though it was, it was still a kiss. It was still his lips caressing the sacred space of her face, touching her warm, soft skin, and breathing in the faint strawberry smell of her hair. It was the first truly intimate contact he'd ever allowed himself with Maggie and though he might try to banish the memory from his head, it was carving out its own steadfast, abiding place in his heart.

Quite simply, it couldn't be undone.

His face must have betrayed his thoughts in some part because she raised her eyebrows and widened her eyes as she placed his coffee back down on the counter.

"Nils…" she warned, reminding him she needed to know what had happened between them. "What exactly…happened?"

"Your, um, your jeans and socks were soaked. I didn't want you to catch a cold or get your bed all wet and muddy, so I…"

He could feel the heat in his cheeks as his words trailed

off, and he knew he was flushing as deeply as she.

For as much as Maggie and Nils had been friends for several years, he certainly hadn't spent any time in her bedroom, though his mind spent a good portion of every day wondering about it. Now that he knew it was decorated in white wicker and violets, his fantasies had a whole new reality to add to the mix.

"So, you took off my pants and socks." Her lips twitched and she couldn't suppress a small grin. "Did you peek?"

His fingers twitched as though remembering the soft, warm skin of her thighs as he dragged the denim down her legs, and he fisted them in protest. He bit down lightly on his bottom lip, looking down at the counter and shaking his head no.

But at the same time, he mumbled, "I might've. Just a little bit."

When he looked up, her face was a mixture of surprise, censure and...what? Merriment? Teasing? She was suppressing a smile. Was she *glad* he had peeked? The very thought made him harder, made his arms flush with goose bumps under his flannel shirt.

She turned her back to him, reaching to find two clean lids on the cluttered counter behind her. When she faced him again, her minxy little smile had faded.

"I didn't...I mean, did I—did I say anythin'? Anythin' especially awkward?"

That man needs to bed me or wed me... I wish I dinna like him so well...

He looked up for a second then flicked his eyes back down on the counter. He didn't trust himself to look at her. What was he supposed to say? Should he tell her what she'd said? No, he resolved, best not to open that can of worms.

"You thought I was Paul."

"Oh." She sounded worried.

"It was just a whole lot of nonsense, Maggie. Couldn't make out most of it."

"Oh." Instead of sounding relieved, she sounded a little disappointed. She shrugged lightly. "Well, thanks. For your help. I know I can be a handful...when I drink."

"You don't have to thank me," he said as she jammed the lids down on the cups in front of him.

His body was still on high alert, keeping all of the memories from last night pressurized inside. He needed to diffuse it before he did something stupid like touching her or telling her what she'd said. He'd promised himself long ago not to pursue Maggie and he wasn't about to reverse that decision now, not after staying strong for years. Best to make sure their friends-only status was intact.

"We're friends, Maggie. I'd always help a friend."

She winced and her eyes clenched closed for a moment, which made him feel like a bastard. He told himself it was for the best. She didn't know that anything beyond friendship was impossible, but it was. He'd never risk it. Never.

Still, he hated it that his words had hurt her. He tilted his head to the side and smiled at her gently. "That headache must be pretty bad. You have Advil?"

Her eyes flashed up at him and she looked frustrated, almost angry. "I have everything I need, Nils. Dinna worry about me."

"But I do," he blurted out. *Shoot! Shut up! You're going to confuse things!*

"What? You do?"

"Of course." *Back track, back track!* "We're friends. I think you drink too much sometimes, and it makes you reckless. And I'd hate to see any friend of mine—"

Her lips, which had softened a touch a moment before, tightened. "I told you. You dinna need to worry about me!"

She turned on her heel and headed to the end of the bar, where she took a metal hanger off a coat tree and started unraveling the wire, mostly keeping her back to him. He could tell she was in a bad mood and he knew he should pick up his coffee and leave. But damn it, he *did* care about her. A lot. A lot more than he should. He needed to smooth things over before leaving.

"Hey, Mags," he said, pushing off the stool and strolling down the bar toward her. "I talked to Jenny last night. She said something about us having a party for Pop here."

She didn't look up at him, grimacing as she wrestled with the hanger in her hands. "Aye. I talked to her yesterday, too. She was thinkin' late June. In a few weeks."

Battling the rigid wire, she grunted in frustration.

"Can I help you with that?" he asked.

She held out the hanger and crossed her arms over her chest when he took it. His strong hands untwisted it quickly and he handed it back to her.

"Thanks," she said, straightening out the rest of it until it was one long piece of mostly unbent wire. "I can manage the food and drink. She said somethin' about you and Lars being in charge of decorations and guests and such. I did some research yesterday and you know, at some of these parties, they have slideshows with pictures. You know, sort of a movie of the person's life." Her voice warmed up and she grinned at him. "Wouldn't that be nice?"

He nodded, feeling relieved. She still looked a little green, but her smile reassured him that they'd get over the speed bump of last night and everything—but a few new memories that he'd keep well hidden—would go back to normal. "Real nice. Maybe Lars and I can get our hands on Pop's old pictures without him noticing." He gestured to the wire in her hand. "What're you doing with that?"

"Oh. Some mail slipped behind the back counter. I keep meanin' to caulk the crack closed, but I keep forgetting."

Nils stepped behind the bar, following her to the place where several envelopes lay tangled in the cord of an old-fashioned push-button phone. He gestured for the wire and she handed it to him. "Here?"

"Yes. Thanks, Nils." She turned her attention to the other side of the bar where a customer ordered a Café Americano and two chocolate-chip scones.

A photo slideshow was a damn nice idea. Jenny had to know where Pop kept all the old albums from when they were kids, from when their mamma was alive. Heck, he might even be able to find some photos of their grandparents back in Sweden before they'd emigrated to Montana.

He fished the hanger down the crack between the wall and the counter and pulled it up to reveal a crisp white envelope. He read the return address as he placed it on the jumbled pile with the other envelopes: Marcona Electric. Huh. Wouldn't have been good to lose that one, he thought, thinking of Maggie walking into the café one morning only to find the power off.

He glanced over at her as she chatted cheerfully with an older couple from his church, her slim arms spread out over the copper bar. She was tiny compared to him; she barely came up to his shoulder fully straightened, with trim hips and a narrow waist.

On the other hand, he was like a grizzly bear, freakishly large and clumsy next to her spritely fairy-like build. He bit down on his bottom lip, forcing himself to look away from her. His eyes caught the electric bill again, and he decided to shove the hanger down the crack one last time, just to be sure no other bills had gotten lost.

He heard the sound of wire scraping back and forth as he toggled it, clean and clear, before snagging on something far over to the left side where the wall and counter almost connected. He pulled the hanger up and let it slide down gingerly against the wall again. Yep. There was definitely something back there. He shimmied the wire gently until he was pretty sure he found the corner of whatever it was and tugged up, listening to the muted sound of the wire sliding the item up against the back wall as he raised it up. Finally a dirty, mottled, brownish-gray corner of paper peeked out above the counter line and Nils reached forward with his absurdly beefy fingers to try to grasp it. No dice.

"Maggie," he interrupted, drawing her attention away from the couple. "Come grab this, would you?"

"Whaddya find?" She leaned over his arm and he tried not to groan when her small breasts brushed up against his coat sleeve. His body tightened and he fought the urge to move his arm up, flush against her chest, silently cursing that he had to be so attracted to her.

"Just pull it out," he growled.

She looked up at him and grinned, saucy. "Why, Nils!"

"I'm going to lose it," he muttered, not sure if he was referring to his tentative grip on the hanger, or his less tentative grip on his desire as she rubbed her breasts into his arm again, leaning forward to grab the dirty paper with her fingertips.

"Growly bear," she said softly, pulling back the envelope and flirting with him from under mostly downcast eyes.

He straightened, pulling the hanger out of the crack and thrusting it at her.

"You're welcome," he added sarcastically. "So, what is it? I guess it's not the electric company or your water bill since both are working…then again, with your stellar organization system over there, it could be—"

He turned back to her, surprised by the fraught expression on her face. Maggie stared at the filthy, crumpled envelope in silence, her eyes widening. She sucked in a breath, turning it over quickly and ripping it open.

She turned away from Nils as she unfolded the letter, but he heard her murmur, "No. Oh, no. Oh, God."

His adrenaline rushed like crazy from the look on her face and the tone of her voice. Without thinking, he reached out and put a hand on her waist to pull her closer to him, as though he could protect her from whatever was in that letter. "Maggie, what's happened? What's wrong? Tell me."

She took a deep breath and clenched her jaw once before looking up at him with a flood of tears brightening her eyes.

"My visa expired over six months ago. I'm here illegally."

***

The wrinkled paper trembled in her shaking hands.

How could she have missed this letter? How on God's green earth had it happened?

Maggie might not have the most comprehensive filing system in the universe, but for Lord's sake, she should have had a handle on when her visa was expiring!

Her heart pounded mercilessly in her chest as she skimmed the letter again, vaguely aware of Nils's warm hand encircling her wrist. She wished she could lean into him, turn into him and put her head on his shoulder, but she couldn't do that. Well, she could, but she shouldn't. It would mean something different to her than it did to him. In his eyes, they were friends. Just friends.

With that thought in mind, she took a step back from

him and tried to catch her breath as words and sentences popped out at her.

...inform you that your non-immigrant visa will expire within 60 days...failure to reapply may result in criminal prosecution...may be subject to a three-year ban upon reapplication for a United States visa...unauthorized residency by any foreign national may result...the Department of Homeland Security...

The letter fluttered from her hands and the room started spinning around her.

She was going to be deported. Or arrested. Or both.

Either way, her life in Gardiner, in Montana, in the United States, appeared to be over.

She turned away from Nils to face the back wall and braced her hands on the messy countertop. Humiliating tears streamed down her face.

What a mess. What a goddamned mess.

"Maggie. Maggie May," he whispered in her ear from behind, just as he had last night. She felt his hand touch her hip again and push her gently to her right, toward the end of the bar.

"Go back to your office. I'll take care of things for a bit."

She nodded, biting back a sob, and turned for the little office hidden behind a colorful yellow and red curtain. She pulled the curtain closed behind her and fell into her desk chair, laying her aching head on the desk.

It wasn't enough that she felt like death warmed over, or that she'd humiliated herself last night in front of Nils Lindstrom. It wasn't enough that he'd used the dreaded fword with her this morning repeatedly, consigning their blatant attraction to friendship once again. All of this would have weighed heavy on a normal day, but today was a catastrophic day. It wasn't enough that she *looked* scatterbrained and reckless, she *was* scatterbrained and reckless, and he'd had a front-row seat for the past twelve hours. She was about to be kicked out of the country she'd come to love. All because she hadn't been responsible enough to manage her own affairs and file the paperwork to renew her visa.

Through the curtain, she heard Nils greet some customers and tell them they had a choice between regular coffee or decaf coffee, but any other orders would have to wait a bit. She smiled through her tears, swiping her sleeve over her snotty nose. Levelheaded, rock-steady Nils had come to her rescue. *Again.* Her stomach flipped over at the thought of leaving him and she spun around to scramble for the little sink behind her desk, heaving once, but thankfully holding down the contents of her stomach. She took a glass from the shelf over the sink and poured herself water, sinking back down into her desk chair and opening the top drawer to root around for Advil. Her head was splitting open.

Then she sat back in her chair in a state of semi-disbelief and let the tears fall freely. She loved the little café she'd inherited from her aunt. She loved baking scones and other treats upstairs in her apartment and bringing them downstairs to sell. She loved the smell of fresh coffee beans mixed with books. She loved the friends she'd made—like

Jenny Lindstrom, Nils's younger sister, and Paul, who was like a brother to her. And Nils. Oh, Lord, how she'd miss his quiet brooding and longing looks. How she'd miss wondering every day if *today* would be the day his walls would tumble down and he'd reach for her, press his lips to hers, tell her that he wanted her—needed her—as much as she wanted and needed him.

She'd imagined it a million times: the café would be almost closed for the night and she'd have just finished putting the chairs on top of the tables and sweeping the floor. She'd be untying her barista apron when the little bell over the door would jingle, and he'd be standing there in the dim light. He'd catch her eyes with his icy blue ones and cross purposely to her, pulling her into his arms. *I can't hide my feelings for you anymore, Maggie May. I have to know...do you love me even half as much as I love you?* And she'd throw her arms around his neck, leaning her body into his and—

Her email pinged on the laptop before her, and she clicked twice on the space bar to animate the screen. *Need legal advice? The offices of...* She wiped her eyes, taking a deep, shuddering breath. Junk mail. Nothing but junk mail. Just—

Wait a minute. She stared at the words. Need legal advice? She took the edge of her apron and swiped at her wet cheeks again. Legal advice. Yes, of course! She pulled down the Yellow Pages resting on a bookshelf over her desk. Of course! She could talk to a lawyer, couldn't she? There had to be a loophole of some sort; she couldn't be the first person who'd ever let her visa run out. She flipped the pages to L and found the listings for two Gardiner lawyers. She called the first, Beck Westman, who she knew a little and who occasionally flirted with her over a cup of cappuccino, and made an appointment for that evening. Then, feeling marginally better, she splashed her face with cold water, blew her nose and stepped back out to the coffee bar where Nils had his elbows propped on the counter, staring down at her letter.

He looked up as she approached him, his eyes both worried and tender. When he looked at her like that it squeezed her heart; it made her breathless. It made her wonder, for the thousandth time, why he never made a move on her when his eyes said he cared for her as more than a friend.

"Feeling any better?"

"Not much. But I called a lawyer."

"Oh," he said trying to sound positive. "That's a good idea."

She shrugged, willing back the tears that threatened to shake her tenuous courage. She touched the letter. "Did you read it? Doesn't look good for me staying here, huh?"

He put his hands on his hips and faced her. "What do I know?"

"Thanks for taking over here for a few minutes."

She reached out and touched his flannel-covered forearm, swallowing as his ice-blue eyes looked into hers. It shocked the hell out of her when he reached out with both hands, placing them on her waist for the second time that morning and drawing her into his arms. Her eyes closed slowly as her cheek made contact with the soft fabric of the shirt covering his chest. She could hear his heartbeat, loud and solid, and she tried not to think of anything else—not last night and not this morning—just now. She tried to memorize the feeling of Nils Lindstrom's arms around her, of the way it felt to be safe and protected by his strong, burly warmth. His hands met and locked behind her back, and he lowered his chin until she felt it rest softly on the top of her head.

"I'm sorry," he murmured, and the low timbre of his voice vibrated against her head, making her shiver, making desire pool helplessly in her belly, warm and insistent.

"I'll get it sorted," she breathed.

"Want me to go with you?" he asked in a whisper.

"Where to?" she asked, half in a daze.

"To the lawyer. Just for...for moral support."

She didn't think. She gave him the only answer in her head, in a soft, strangled voice, full of emotion. "Yes."

His chin bobbed against her head lightly as he nodded and then his hands unclasped. He loosened his arms and she stepped back as she opened her eyes, willing herself not to fling her body back into the sanctuary of his arms and demand more from him than he had ever been able to give.

When she tilted her head up, she caught his eyes, brilliant and blue, shrouded with concern. "Thank you, Nils." She cocked her head to the side, offering him a small smile. "I feel like I'm endlessly sayin' thank you to you."

He clenched his jaw once, then twice, staring at her face, then turned away from her and quickly walked to the end of the bar and around it, zipping up his jacket. "What time tonight?"

"Six'll do."

"Then I'll see you at six." He held her eyes just a beat longer than necessary, watching her with that serious, worried expression. Then, without another word, he grabbed the coffees off the counter and left.

***

She cannot leave. She cannot leave.

She cannot leave Gardiner.

She cannot leave me.

The words were a litany in his head as he walked the short distance back to his office.

Though it would break my heart, thought Nils, *it'd be better for me if she did.*

He silenced the thought and remembered how good it had felt to hold her small body against his, almost shuddering with the intensity of his feelings. She was so much smaller than him, he'd had to draw his biceps against his own body to tighten his forearms around her. Like a little kitten, she'd nestled against him, her cheek against his pounding heart. Did she know what she did to him? Couldn't she tell?

But thinking of her that way invariably reminded him of another girl he'd known once upon a time, small and redheaded like Maggie. Carefree and young, though not so spirited. She'd only been a girl. A girl he'd loved like Maggie.

"Nils!" His father's voice snapped him back to reality and he glanced up to see the older Lindstrom standing in the doorway of *Lindstrom & Sons*, blinking in the bright sun.

"Took you long enough. Was about to send out the search party!"

Nils handed his father a coffee cup and followed him into the warm office, shrugging off his coat and hanging it on the coat tree by the front door.

"Nice and hot," his father muttered under his breath.

Nils's younger brother Lars sat at the small conference table in front of the left window, arranging bottled water and trail mix into hospitality bags. He looked up with an easy grin, gesturing to the cup in Nils's hand.

"That for me, *Største*?" asked Lars, using Nils's family nickname which meant "biggest," and had originally referred to Nils's place in the birth order, but was now—quite literally—an accurate description of his physique when compared to his two younger brothers.

Lars was slightly taller than Nils, but had an athlete's build which he kept toned and even. Though neither brother had more than an ounce of fat on their bodies, Nils's body was so dense, it almost appeared stocky. Tall, broad-shouldered and built like a Mack truck, he was a solid mass of muscled strength, whereas Lars's body type almost looked elegant in comparison.

Nils scowled. "Bite me, Lars. Get your own."

"Oh, that's nice talk," Mr. Lindstrom chided, raising his eyebrows at Nils. "Can't help but notice you woke up on the wrong side of the bed today, son."

Nils pulled a file off his father's desk and settled down in the chair at his own desk without responding.

"Want to talk about it?"

"Nope."

"Bet it has something to do with a certain Scottish café owner," said Lars, placing *Lindstrom & Sons* stickers on the aqua gift bags and grinning at Nils.

Nils was used to his siblings ribbing him about Maggie, but he really wasn't in the mood for it today, not after Maggie's troubling news. He squared his jaw and shot his brother a warning look, holding Lars's blue eyes until the younger man finally rolled his, chuckling, and looked away.

"Well," said Lars, "I guess I'd better get going. Flight comes in at noon, right Pop?"

"Noon, *Midten*," replied Carl Lindstrom, using the Norwegian nickname his late wife had bestowed upon his middle son. "Another TV group. Couple of cinematography people. They're scouting locations for one of those police shows."

"Got it, Pop."

Mr. Lindstrom looked up at Lars thoughtfully. "You're good with these flashy city types, Lars. Just had someone else call me from New York today. Magazine people who want to bring in a supermodel for a photo shoot. I'm thinking you should take the lead on that one, too, if they end up booking with us."

"When's that one, Pop?"

"End of the summer."

"Well, we'll see if it even happens, huh?"

"Sure. In the meantime, we got a lot of groups coming up. Good summer ahead."

Nils looked up to see Lars wink at him before heading

out the door.

A wave of envy broke over Nils as he watched Lars's easy gait, walking past the picture window toward the parking lot where they kept the airport van. Nothing ever got under Lars's skin. Nothing impacted his equilibrium or threw off his rhythm. Lars was about the most comfortable person Nils had ever met. He didn't have the kind of baggage that Nils had—no fiercely painful memories that assaulted him in quiet moments. Nils's younger brother was about as happy-go-lucky as any man he'd ever seen.

Nils, on the other hand, lived his life in a place of deep, secret sorrow. Externally, he knew people saw him as a stern and quiet man, aloof and cold, even. But inside, his heart bled with regret and self-recrimination, impenetrable to the affections of anyone outside of his immediate family and, it turned out, Maggie Campbell.

She was his type right down to her red hair and freckles. Her petite build taunted and drew him every time he was near her. And no, he couldn't have her, but he could watch her smile and listen to the faintly exotic, lilting melody of her accent. He could save her when her antics threatened to get her in trouble, or put her to bed when she'd had too much to drink. He could watch her treat the children in her shop to fresh-baked cookies, even though it both ripped out his heart and steeled his resolve when he saw her with them. His emotionally marginal life could be cheered by the one bright spot that he allowed himself: his unavoidable pleasure in Maggie's company.

He could never, ever allow himself to fall in love with

her because he could never, ever offer her a future...but somehow that didn't matter enough to look away. And it made his heart twist and strain to imagine losing her presence from his life.

"Ready to review these upcoming groups, *Største*? I was thinking I would take the McCarthy group in July while you hold down the fort here. You and Lars can split up the weekend trips and one-days. Give those magazine people to Lars. Plenty to keep us busy."

He looked up to see his father's gentle blue eyes, so much like his own, looking at him from over the top of his glasses.

"Sure, Pop. Whatever you think is best," he responded, half tempted—as he'd been innumerable times in the past fifteen years—to tell his father what had actually happened that horrible summer when his parents thought he was in Missoula participating in a forestry internship. But burdening his father wouldn't ease *his* heart. And knowing the terrible, unforgivable thing that had happened would only break his father's heart in half.

Chapter 4

"It's not good, Maggie," sighed Beck Westman from behind his desk, shaking his head back and forth as he re-read the letter. He swiveled in his chair and tapped a few keys on his keyboard, then looked at the screen, grimacing. "Did a little research today after we hung up, and unfortunately I don't think there's much we can do."

Maggie inhaled sharply and Nils fought the urge to grab her hand. Instead he spoke up from the guest chair beside her. "Is there *anything* she can do, Beck?"

"You know, I'm not an immigration lawyer, Nils. I deal mostly in property transfers and small-town legal affairs…family business and the occasional divorce. But from what I can tell, Maggie, you're in a pickle. I'm sure this wasn't a case of flagrant disregard for the terms of your visa, but USCIS will assume this was willful negligence. They sent you a warning letter as a courtesy and you still didn't renew that visa in time."

"It wasn't willful," said Nils in her defense, feeling annoyed with Beck. "She lost the letter."

"She'll have a hard time proving that since she has it in her possession. Worse, she's been operating a business for the entire time she's been here out of status." Beck rubbed his chin and shook his head at them. "You're going to have to go back to Scotland and reapply for a new visa, Maggie. They're unlikely to press criminal charges if you leave quietly."

"But I willna be able to come back! The letter says it'll be three years until I can come back. And this is where my life is. My café. My friends. My—Beck, please. There must be something you can think of!"

Beck sat back in his seat and Nils watched his eyes soften again as he looked at Maggie, an uncomfortable prickle tingling down his back as he recognized the look in Beck's eyes.

Damn it, how had he missed this?

Sure, he'd noticed Beck at the Prairie Dawn now and then, but everyone in town stopped by Maggie's café. Only obvious now, in the close quarters of his office, Nils realized with a sick feeling that Beck had a thing for Maggie. It made Nils want to sucker punch the handsome young lawyer in the face.

Finally Beck sighed and gestured back and forth between Nils and Maggie meaningfully, looking first at Nils then back at Maggie. "What's the deal here?"

"What do you mean?" asked Nils, an edge creeping into his voice.

"You two. You're here together. Are you...a couple? Dating?"

Why? You want to ask her out before she's deported?

"What business is it—" started Nils, leaning forward in his seat with narrowed eyes.

"What if we were?" interrupted Maggie in a direct

voice, sliding forward to the edge of her seat.

Beck tented his hands on the table before them. "Well…marriage to a U.S. citizen forgives any time you have out of status. You wouldn't have to renew your visa. You'd get married and your spouse" —Beck gestured to Nils loosely, still holding Maggie's eyes— "would file for a green card. Lots of forms, of course—you'd need to supply evidence and there could be an interview—but I believe you'd be issued a conditional green card in about six months."

Nils's jaw had all but dropped when Beck started speaking, the word "marriage" blaring like an air horn in his head.

Marriage. Marriage? What the hell—

"Conditional," whispered Maggie. "For how long?"

"Two years. If the marriage lasts for two years, you can apply for a permanent green card."

"Two years," Maggie repeated.

Nils's brain had finally processed the bottom line of Beck's suggestion: if Maggie married an American, she could stay. His heart sped into high gear, making him momentarily dizzy. Beck was suggesting that Nils marry Maggie.

The lawyer's gaze shifted to Nils but whatever he saw made him raise his eyebrows and shift his eyes quickly back to Maggie. "But Maggie…if they are suspicious that your marriage is fraudulent, it could go very badly for you. Any inconsistency could be grounds for suspicion. In law school they were very clear with us not to *ever* counsel a fraudulent marriage for the purposes of citizenship. We watched a video of a Stokes interview, which happens if you're suspected of marriage fraud, and it was brutal—they separate the spouses and ask individual questions you wouldn't believe. They employ confession and intimidation tactics. I don't know your...status. But unless you're legitimately together, I wouldn't advise you considering this route. I only mentioned it because you came here together tonight, and Nils seems very invested in your staying."

Nils looked up to meet the direct, brown eyes of his rival and nodded almost imperceptibly. Beck was right. He was invested. But marriage...

Marriage was impossible.

His face felt uncomfortably hot and he unzipped his jacket then fidgeted with the arms of his chair nervously. Were they waiting for him to say something? Was he supposed to suddenly get down on one knee and propose? His knee bobbed up and down and he finally glanced up at Beck who was studying him quietly.

He was about to shout, *I'm not marrying anyone today!* when he felt Maggie's hand on his.

He looked down to his left where her pale freckled hand covered his, and he surprised himself by quickly turning his hand over and lacing his fingers between hers. He didn't look at her, but held her hand tightly, and realized that the moment she touched him, his knee had stopped trembling.

Beck took a deep, resigned breath and stood up. "I'm sorry I couldn't be of more help. I guess you two have a big conversation ahead of you tonight, huh?"

"I guess we do," mumbled Maggie, and Nils tightened his fingers around hers.

"If you, uh, decide to...go for it? I can get you married up quick and legal. Just pick up a license up at the courthouse in Livingston first. I should probably add...since I'm your lawyer, I'm bound not to discuss your affairs, so your marriage could easily be kept a secret until you were ready to announce it to your families." Beck shrugged, looking at Maggie like he'd run all the way to the station only to see the taillights of the last train pulling away. "Anyway, it's just an offer....if you decide to go that route."

Nils looked down, adjusting his fingers between Maggie's and noticed that his hands didn't look monstrous entwined with hers. Her fingers were much smaller, of course—her tiny hand dwarfed by his tanned, rough-skinned mitt—but there was something protective and sturdy about his fingers laced through hers that somehow made it look okay, look almost *right*, and it made his chest ache.

There was so much going on in his head it was easier to concentrate on touching her, on the rush he felt from the contact of their fingers grasped together, on the solid, unexpected feeling of completeness that came from just holding her hand. It was easier to fool himself that just because it looked right and felt right, it *was* right. But it was an illusion, of course. He was the last person in the world who could make her happy. He just couldn't help how her touch made him feel, and he didn't want to let go of it quite yet.

They stood up at the same time, and Nils half expected

Maggie to drop his hand, but she didn't. She kept her palm flush against his, and it made his heart flutter with possessiveness and yearning. He stuck out his free hand, offering it to Beck, but he held hers tightly so she couldn't do the same.

"Thanks for seeing us, Beck," said Maggie, softly.

Beck's gaze lingered on Maggie's face, flicking briefly to her lips before finding her eyes again.

Nils saw sympathy there, but want, too, and he tugged Maggie a little closer to him until he could feel the heat of her body by his side.

"Good luck, Maggie," said Beck. "I hope you...figure it out."

"We'll figure it out," said Nils quietly, a restrained warning in his gruff voice.

Then he turned and pulled Maggie gently toward the door.

***

The feelings Nils was rousing in her body were so distracting, when she should be concentrating solely on her legal problems and Beck's unexpected solution to them.

It's just that he was so strong and sturdy beside her, she wanted to trick herself into believing he would somehow keep her safe, that by holding her hand, he was offering her his protection. Which he wasn't, of course. He was just being a supportive friend. She frowned, wanting to pull her hand away, but not daring to break the warmth of the contact. Lord, but she was weak for this man.

As they walked toward his car, she could feel the

tension mounting between them. She glanced up at him, at his chiseled jawline and handsome angular face that gave away so little. She sensed there was a lot going on inside his head; she could feel it in the way he gripped her hand, in the way his jaw clenched and released repeatedly. The casual observer would be forgiven in mistaking his stern countenance for apathy, but after years of watching Nils Lindstrom, Maggie knew better. Just as his jittery knee and red cheeks had given him away when Beck suggested a green-card marriage, his stern silence was betraying him now. He was trying to figure out what to do.

"Are you cold?" he finally asked, gesturing to her open jacket with his free hand.

"No." She took a deep breath. "I'm a bit gobsmacked."

"Does that mean baffled?"

"Somethin' like it."

It also meant astonished and confused.

Her life was moving too fast and she wasn't ready for it. She was still a little hungover from last night and her visa had expired, of course, but distracting her most of all was that something had shifted subtly in her relationship with Nils since last night, and she sensed that shift was sweeping them away to murkier waters than they'd navigated in the years they'd known one another. He'd undressed her last night, held her in his arms this morning and here they were now, holding hands as though they had a right to. Before last night, they'd never touched each other, almost ritualistic in their avoidance of crossing an invisible line that lay between them. Now that it had been crossed, they couldn't seem to stop reaching for each other.

Maggie swallowed nervously. The word *MARRIAGE* hovered between them about as subtle as a purple elephant on a rhinestone leash. They needed to talk about it, even if they both only dismissed it as nonsense. She pulled back as he steered her toward his car.

"Could we walk a bit, Nils? Instead of driving home?"

"It's a little ways back to your place."

"I dinna mind if you dinna mind. I could use the air. I'll drive you back for your car in the mornin' if you like."

"Nah, I don't mind coming back for it later." He shoved his keys back into his pocket and as they started back toward town, he readjusted his grip on her hand, making a shiver run up her arms as their palms fused together again.

She sighed shakily. "That was—"

"Intense."

"It's a…daft idea…that you and I…"

He was quiet beside her.

She cleared her throat. "He must have thought that we were—I mean, *I'd* never ask you to—"

"I know," he murmured. His profile looked square and stern as the streetlights bounced off the planes of his high cheekbones.

"Thank you for going with me," she said.

"Anytime."

She scoffed bitterly, more at the situation than at him. "Anytime I'm about to get deported, you'll join me for a legal consultation, eh?"

"What're friends for?" he asked lightly.

Friends.

She winced in the darkness, clenching her teeth together. She thought about flexing her hand open to release his, but she didn't. They walked in silence for several more minutes, their boots scuffling along the sidewalk.

"A green-card marriage," she said softly beside him, more to herself than to him.

He stopped them for a moment, turning to face her. "It's cold out."

She kept her eyes trained on his, but he kept his down, staring at their hands. Finally he unlaced his and moved his fingers to the front of her coat, pulling the sides together, his big fingers needing an extra second to manage the little white zipper. As he zipped it up, his eyes lifted to hers, and she almost gasped from what she saw there in the light of the dim streetlamp. Such longing, such sadness, such regret.

What happened to you? she wondered, as she often had before. Why was there such deep sadness behind his blue eyes?

"I wish…" he started, his fingers still holding her zipper, the warmth of his hand touching her chin as his stricken eyes beseeched hers for understanding. "I wish I could…"

A wave of anger and frustration overcame her, making her nostrils flare and her jaw clench. In that moment she realized how much she wanted him to do this for her— marry her. Yes, for the sake of a green card, but also because she loved him. She wanted him, and she didn't care how she got him, so long as he ended up hers. *How pathetic,* she thought bitterly with a heap of self-loathing. He was ready to push her away, and all she wanted was to stay with him.

She stepped back from him and lifted her chin in fury and hurt, in defiance of everything unspoken that existed between them, everything that he refused to acknowledge. She tried to swallow back the heartbreak as she realized that, for the first time she could remember, Nils Lindstrom wouldn't be swooping in to save her. His eyes said it all: this time, she was on her own…and it made her heart ache like someone had reaching into her chest and squeezed it.

"Dinna worry yourself, Nils. I can take care of myself," she said in a low voice, hating how contrived the lightness sounded in her own ears. She shoved her hands into her pockets, staring up at him with all the courage and bravado she could muster. "Just so you know, I plan to ask Paul to marry me."

Then she stepped around him and continued walking home on her own.

***

She might as well have punched him in the throat. As she made her declaration, Nils inhaled a huge breath of cold air so fast, it burned his lungs and his words came out in a wheeze as he whipped around to follow her.

"*Wh-what?* Now, you wait a goddamned minute! What the hell are you talking about?"

"I'm not leavin' Montana. I dinna see any other option."

"If you go back to Scotland, you can renew your visa and still come back in—"

"Three years!" she scoffed. "Didn't you hear? It could be *three years* before they renew my visa. And who's goin' to run my business in the meantime?"

"It might not be three years. It might just be a few months. You can hire someone to manage things until you get back." *And I'll be here when you come back. And everything can go back to normal.*

"You think I have that kind of money? To hire someone indefinitely while I sort out my legal affairs?"

"You can lease the business."

She stopped in her tracks, whipping around to face him. "It was my *aunt's* business. I'll not sign it over to someone else. Even temporarily."

Heat seeped into his face as desperation overcame him. "Lars and I can help—"

"Dinna be ridiculous. You haven't the time. Besides, I'd never ask my *friends* to—"

"You're *not* marrying Paul," he thundered, seizing her eyes with an anguish he could only remember feeling once before in his whole life.

Losing her to Scotland for a few months was one thing. Losing her to Paul was another.

He couldn't explain what was happening inside of his body—the despair, the freakish fury, the ludicrousness, the single, searing thought that he might have to murder Paul. He reached out to put his hand on her waist to pull her closer to him.

"Nae!" She stepped out of his grasp, her accent ramping up with her agitation, as it always did. She started walking again, talking over her shoulder. "Ye have no say in this, Nils. We're *friends*, but I dinna let my friends tell me what I can and canna—"

He sped up and blocked her path, his body like a wall before her.

"Maggie," he begged.

She stepped forward deliberately, her breasts pushing up against him, her eyes narrow and challenging as she looked up at him. She was a full foot shorter than Nils, but she was holding her own and if he wasn't so upset about her unthinkable suggestion to marry *Paul*, he would've admired the hell out of her.

"You're *not* marrying Paul," he repeated in a growl, reaching forward to grasp her arms.

"*I wish...I wish I could...*" She used his halting words to mock him, but the tears flooding her eyes betrayed her.

"I won't let you do it," he rumbled.

"Won't *let* me? Ha! It's not for you to say, laddie..." she protested, poking a finger into his chest before stepping around him to start walking again on her own.

Nils knew full and well that Maggie and Paul were only friends, but every cell in his body revolted against the possibility of Maggie marrying Paul. He couldn't let it happen. Even on paper, he couldn't watch it happen without a fight.

You'd get married and your spouse—Nils—would file for a green card.

Beck had said it so matter-of-factly. Like it was possible. Like it could actually happen. Nils clenched his teeth so hard, his jaw ached. They should have set Beck straight that there was nothing between them but friendship. Because regardless of the feelings that snapped and popped like static electricity between him and Maggie, they *were* only friends. Until last night, he'd never touched his lips to her skin. Until this morning, he'd never held her in his arms. Until this evening, he'd never held her hand.

And yet, from the moment Beck had made the suggestion, deep inside, the fantasy had taken root. Maggie as his wife. Maggie Lindstrom. His wife. *His.*

It was such a slice of heaven to imagine it: Maggie belonging to him, coming home to her every night, waking up to her sweet face every morning, a child with her red hair—

Stop right there! No! No children. Absolutely not.

He *couldn't* marry Maggie. He couldn't marry anyone. Marriage meant sharing a home and a bed. It meant families entwined and—God forbid—the possibility of children. It meant pain. It meant definitely hurting her and probably losing her. Veronica's face appeared briefly in his mind and he winced. He couldn't risk Maggie. He wouldn't.

He sucked in a boatload of air, exhaling a long puff of misty breath into the chilly evening, and forcing himself to calm down. *A green-card marriage. A green-card marriage.* His hands had fisted tightly by his sides, but as he mulled over the words "green-card marriage," they started to relax.

This wouldn't be a *real* marriage. It would be a *green-card* marriage just so Maggie could stay in Montana. That's all. He took another deep breath as his heart stopped racing. He'd never end up hurting her as he had Veronica because they wouldn't actually *be* together. It's not like they'd ever live together, let alone sleep together. No, of course not. He'd just be giving her his name, allowing her to stay in Gardiner. Heck, nobody even needed to know about it; they could get quietly married, she'd get her green card, and they could get quietly divorced in two years. Maggie could stay in Gardiner and no one would end up getting hurt.

And most importantly, in the end, they'd stay friends. She'd still exist here, in his life. Nothing had to change.

"Mags! Maggie!"

He was pretty sure she sped up a little when he said her name. "You can't tell me what to do!" she threw over her shoulder.

"Maggie, stop!"

He reached out and grabbed her hand as it swung back, holding it firmly but gently, until she stopped and turned around. Her face glistened in the moonlight, pale and freckled and covered with tears, and seeing her so sad made his heart squeeze with a panic that had nothing to do with what he was about to ask her. He couldn't bear to see her so upset and know that he—partially—owned some of the blame. He hoped his next words would fix that.

"I'll do it. I'll do it instead of Paul."

"Dinna do me any—"

"I want to."

"Oh, stop it! You dinna want—"

"Yes I do."

"No. You dinna want to! I saw your face in Beck's

office. I saw your face when you zipped up my coat."

"Twenty minutes ago a lawyer suggested we get married. Could you maybe give me a minute to get my head around it? Christ, woman! It might be for a green card, but it's still a marriage!"

She took a deep breath and relaxed her shoulders. Her eyes darted down to where he stroked her palm with his thumb, furrowing her brows as if surprised to see he was holding her hand again. They both watched his thumb slide back and forth for a moment before slowly looking back up at each other.

When her bright, shiny eyes caught his, Nils Lindstrom was pretty sure that Maggie Campbell—in that moment when he was asking her to be his wife, even if it was just on paper—was the prettiest thing he'd ever seen. Ever. In his whole life. His heart swelled with feelings so deep and true, his eyes stung.

"Let me do it," he insisted softly. "Let me do it for you."

"Why?" she sobbed.

He shrugged, offering her a careful smile. "Because I want to."

Her eyes widened.

"What are you sayin'?" she asked, her voice unsure and hopeful and nervous all at the same time.

"I'm just—all I'm saying is…don't marry Paul." His fingers laced themselves through hers again so naturally, it was as though they'd done so for a thousand lifetimes. "Marry *me*."

"I need to know *why* you're doin' this." Her eyes searched his face. "And don't say it's because we're friends, because I'm friends with Paul, too."

He swallowed. After last night, he knew what she wanted to hear, and part of him wanted to tell her. *I want you. I need you. I'm crazy about you. I care so much for you, I can't get you out of my head and if you're going to be anyone's wife—even if it's on paper only—you're going to be mine.* But, if he did, he could never take it back. He'd only be confusing things between them further. He'd be giving her the hope of a real marriage when it was something he'd never be able to offer her. Instead he cocked his head to the side and shrugged.

"I like helping you. I like...*you.*"

"That's all?"

"Plus, Beck saw us together. It was his idea and he's the one who'll marry us. If he's ever called to testify as to the legitimacy of our marriage, he can say we were together from the beginning. The story will play better if it's me."

She flinched, her eyes glistening and crushed in the moonlight, and for a brief, insane moment, he had an urge to take it back and tell her the truth. But that wouldn't be fair, so he forced himself to stay silent. He clenched his jaw and swallowed, moving back to his position beside her and tugging her forward to resume their walk.

They crossed over the Gardiner Bridge, which spanned the icy cold Yellowstone River, and Nils gave her the time and space to figure out her answer. His heart thumped with each step they took, hoping she would say yes to his proposal. He couldn't give her his heart, but in this one way he could offer her something she wanted, he could keep her safe, he could do something important for her. If she'd let him.

He paused at the middle of the bridge, holding on to the railing with his free hand and looking at the rushing river below.

"So, what do you say, Maggie May?"

Her outside hand gripped the cold railing like his, but her inside hand was still braided with his between them. Her answer was soft and a little broken, but clear in his grateful ears.

"Okay."

He turned to look down at her upturned face and felt a smile burst across his face. He felt like taking her cheeks in his hands and kissing her. He felt like taking her back to his place and making love to her all night. He felt like laughing. She was saying yes to being his wife. Even if it was only on paper. She was saying yes. He brought her knuckles to his lips and brushed them softly, whispering against them, "Yes?"

"Aye." Her eyes were wide and surprised as she watched him kiss her hand. When he raised his head, she gave him the impish grin that he loved almost more than anything else in the world, her eyes finally twinkling for him over rosy cheeks. "Yes."

Chapter 5

Five days later, Maggie left the Prairie Dawn in the capable hands of her assistant, Bethany, crossed the street to sit on a picnic table overlooking the Yellowstone River, and waited for Nils to pick her up.

It was finally warming up again, so she unzipped her parka, leaning back on her hands and letting the high sun bathe her face as the river rushed furiously below. About thirty yards away, an elk sauntered by slowly, occasionally grazing on the brown and green grass and pointedly ignoring her.

Again she experienced the wave of gratitude for Nils Lindstrom's clumsy, unromantic proposal, gratitude for facilitating her stay in this untamed place that had come to mean so much to her. Gardiner would be her home now—would *always* be her home—and Nils had made it possible. Whatever unarticulated feelings lay between them, her thanks would never be ambiguous. He had saved her bacon, and it was another reason she loved him.

For the better part of three years she'd loved Nils Lindstrom, but Maggie wasn't the sort of girl to throw herself at an unwilling suitor, and for all of Nils's kindness toward her, he'd never given her a solid indication that he saw her as anything more than a friend. Despite the fact that she'd joined his family for Christmas dinners and Easter brunches. Despite the way he watched her as they played euchre twice a week with Lars and Paul, or the way he always seemed to swoop in and look after her when she was in a jam. And though she *sensed* his affection for her went deeper than friendship, he was careful to always, *always*, remind her that they were friends and he didn't see her romantically.

And yet.

When he'd held her close on Monday morning and wound his fingers through hers as they walked home from Beck's office? She had almost fooled herself that they were actually going somewhere. Again, when he convinced her to marry him instead of Paul, she wondered if jealousy could have possibly played a part in his proposal, rather than friendship. And while she'd taken a day or two to savor the deliciousness of the notion, she'd been forced to abandon the fantasy because Nils had insisted—in no uncertain terms after euchre last night—that their status quo as friends remain unaffected.

After they'd finished their game and Paul and Lars had said goodnight, Nils had stayed behind to help her turn the chairs up on the tables. They'd worked quietly in the dim light without speaking, their shared secret buzzing like an electrical current between them.

"Maggie," he'd said as she took the broom out of her office and started sweeping. "Can we talk about tomorrow?"

She leaned on the broom handle and looked up at him. He stood tall and impossibly beautiful in the center of the room with his hands on his hips. The dim light caught the light blond of his hair, and she longed to cross to him and reach up to catch one of the locks on the back of his neck and thread it softly through her fingers. His icy eyes were stern, as usual, but he bit his bottom lip, and she couldn't help the way her gaze darted to it, staring at his lips for a moment before catching his eyes again.

"Of course." She gestured to the loveseat beside him. "Do you want to sit?"

He sat down on the faded floral slipcover, taking up more than half of the settee, and when she sat down beside him, her hip grazed his. He flinched, but Maggie didn't move away. She liked that she affected him. She wanted her body on his radar.

"Walk me through it," he said in a low, gravelly voice.

She wanted to put her hand on his arm, but decided against it. Since Monday he hadn't reached for her or touched her again, and the thought that he might pull away from her was enough for her not to risk it.

"You pick me up here at noon. We go up to the courthouse in Livingston. Dinna forget your birth certificate and driver's license. We complete the application, I pay the fifty-three dollars and we're back in time for our five o'clock appointment with Beck."

When she glanced at him to her right, he clenched his jaw twice, staring down at his lap where his hands were clasped between his spread legs. He nodded once, curt and businesslike. "Okay."

She wondered if sharing some more details would help

him feel easier about it. "Beck's secretary, Emma, will be there. To witness."

"Emma Branson?" asked Nils, raising his eyebrows as he looked at her.

"Yes. And Emma's daughter. Um, Missy. She's visitin'. Beck understands that we want to keep everything quiet and he thought Missy would be a good person to witness because she goes back to Billings on Sunday."

"Missy Branson," said Nils quietly, looking away from Maggie as his face reddened perceptibly.

"No. That wasn't it. Missy...uh, Flynn. Flynn, I think."

"Right," said Nils, shifting away and losing contact with Maggie's hip.

"You know her?" asked Maggie, a little bit intrigued and a little bit jealous that any woman's name got this big of a reaction from Nils.

"Yeah. She was, um...well, we sort of, um, I mean we occasionally, that is...well, she's married now. It doesn't matter."

"Was she a—a high school girlfriend?" She hated the hopeful tone in her voice.

"No. We, uh, spent time together, uh, later."

"How much later?" This was surprisingly unpleasant news and Maggie couldn't keep the slight edge out of her voice.

In all the time Maggie had known Nils, she never remembered him dating anyone, and she certainly would have remembered. It was strangely upsetting to think he'd had a girlfriend at some point while she'd known him, and she'd been none the wiser. Aside from the overwhelming jealousy that was making her stomach flip over again and again, it meant he *did* date. He just didn't date her.

"A few years ago."

"Before I moved here?"

"Around that time."

"She was your girlfriend?"

"Not exactly." His voice was low, like he was getting annoyed with the questions.He looked at her askance, giving her a warning look, but she couldn't help herself.

"Who was she to you?" she whispered, hating the quasi-demanding tone she heard in her voice. It reeked of jealousy she didn't have a right to. Their marriage would be a business arrangement. Where he spent his private time was none of her affair…and yet, and yet, oh, God…she couldn't help the pain that twisted her heart at the mere thought of *her* Nils sharing his body, his bed, with anyone but her.

"That's enough, Maggie."

"Please tell me," she whispered, not even sure what she was begging him for.

His eyes had been trained on his lap, but now he looked up at her, and she saw the familiar longing in his eyes. His blush spread to his neck and he looked away from her, shrugging. "She was a…a friend. With benefits. And no strings attached."

"Oh." Maggie's breath came out in a rush, which was strange because she didn't realize she'd been holding it. Her cheeks flushed hot as she understood his meaning. They'd had an *arrangement.* "Oh. I—you and she were…"

He looked up at her again and Maggie swallowed, surprised by how much it bothered her that Nils had slept with this Missy, no matter how long ago. Tears pricked the back of her eyes as she absorbed the fact that while he wasn't interested in dating her, he'd had his *needs* met by someone. She blinked twice and stood up, circling around the loveseat to grab the broom and move it slowly to the sounds of Van Morrison singing "Tupelo Honey" softly on the overhead speakers.

It made no sense that she felt like crying. He owed her nothing. He'd never promised her anything. Even their "marriage" was an agreement between friends. She had no right to feel so sad, but she did. She couldn't help it.

"We were just friends who occasionally..." His voice trailed off as he watched her from where he remained seated on the loveseat. "And I ended it when—"

"It's none of my business," she forced herself to answer, looking away from him, staring at the floor like sweeping it was the most important thing she'd ever done in her entire life. You're being stupid, Maggie. He's a man. Men have needs. And apparently this Missy had been there to meet them.

Why couldn't it have been me? the voice in her head demanded, and she shrugged it off. She knew the answer. *He doesn't see you like that...never has, never will.*

He sighed loudly, standing up and putting his hands back on his hips in a gesture that was nervous, defensive and sorry all at once. "One other thing. I just need to say this...to be sure we're on the same page..."

Maggie stopped sweeping.

"What we're doing tomorrow? The green-card marriage? It doesn't change anything between us, Maggie. It can't. We're still just friends." He used his thumb to swipe at his bottom lip and his eyes bored into hers with intensity and determination. Hidden behind that show of strength, she saw a little bit of sadness, too. "It's an agreement. It's a contract. That's all."

Her chest tightened and her heart pounded with the force of her feelings.

Part of her wanted to cross the room, throw her arms around his neck and kiss him—pour her feelings into that single action and try to convince him that there could be so much more between them if he'd only try to see her as something more than his friend, if he could only see her as he'd seen this Missy woman. Her eyes burned and she looked quickly away.

He pressed on. "I need to know that you understand that."

"Understood."

"I'm glad to do it, I just…"

"Please stop. I said I understand." She clenched her jaw twice, looking at the small pile of dirt on the ground. When she could be sure she wouldn't cry, she lifted her gaze, slamming her eyes into his. "And I'm grateful to you."

He took a deep breath and sighed, zipping up his jacket. "See you tomorrow?"

It took all of her strength to offer him a small smile. "Tomorrow."

Van Morrison was singing "Crazy Love" as she watched him leave. She crossed the room, locked the door and dimmed the lights to almost dark. She knew it wouldn't do for the whole town to see her tears as she swept up the rest of the floor.

It was exasperating that despite the baldness of his words, by the next morning, they still hadn't gotten through to her heart. Either her heart was a total glutton for punishment or the stupidest heart ever born, because when she looked at herself in the mirror this morning, that wayward heart had leaped with joy and she'd whispered, "I'm getting married today," to her reflection. All she could think was that by tomorrow, nothing in her life would have materially changed except for one very small detail: she'd be married to Nils Lindstrom. By the end of tomorrow, the man she loved would be her husband. Her *husband*. Hers.

And deep in her heart, a part of her—a small, foolish part of her—admitted that it had partially accepted his proposal because she hoped that what would begin tonight as a marriage on paper only might, over time, find its way toward authenticity—that being so legally bound to Nils might somehow help him make the leap from friendship to love. In light of his feelings, it was a foolish and dangerous hope, but nonetheless it thrummed desperately with every beat of her heart.

And now here she sat, waiting for him to pick her up so they could get a license and say their I do's. She looked down at her watch, shifting on the picnic table to make sure Nils wasn't looking for her yet.

While she had a few extra minutes to herself, she gave herself a stern talking-to. She had no right to expect anything of him. She had no right to feel anything when he mentioned an old girlfriend. She had no claim on him, and even today, when she looked into his eyes and repeated her wedding vows, she wouldn't have any real claim on him. She'd sooner die than repay his kindness with unfounded expectations or jealousy. So despite her own wishes and the love she bore for him in her heart, she was determined to be his friend. If that's what he wanted than she would shove her feelings to the side and, at least outwardly, be a good friend to him. She was committed to giving him whatever he wanted.

She twisted again to see Nils approaching from the street. He wore his usual barn coat unzipped over a navy-blue plaid flannel shirt with a gray T-shirt beneath. Both were tucked into worn-out blue jeans that hugged his muscular thighs and covered the tops of his scuffed cowboy boots in frayed denim. He was slightly bow-legged and all man.. Her mouth watered as he neared.

"You ready?" he asked, his lips tilting up slightly.

"Are *you*?" she teased.

"As ready as I'll ever be, Maggie May." He surprised her by putting out his hand and helping her down from the top of the picnic table, but she couldn't help the wave of disappointment when he dropped it quickly.

Stop it now, Maggie. Friendship. That's what he wants.

"Nils," she said, putting her hand on his sleeve to stop him from starting back to the car. He turned to her and she looked up at his face. "I meant what I said last night. I'm grateful to you. I'll always be grateful."

He glanced down at her hand, then back into her eyes. "I asked you to marry me instead of Paul. No one's forcing me to do something I don't want to do."

"I know that," she whispered. "But you're still doin' it. Swoopin' in and savin' me again."

"Gotten kind of used to it." His eyes searched her face and his voice was soft and kind. "I don't mind."

She swallowed. She had promised herself she'd get this next part out and she wasn't going to chicken out now. "And what you said last night? About nothin' changin'? Well, I'm all for it. I'm lucky to have a f-friend like you."

She stumbled over the word "friend," but otherwise she'd said her piece. Withdrawing her hand from his arm, she walked over to his car.

***

Four and a half hours later, as they approached Gardiner after the painless procedure of obtaining an official marriage license in Livingston, Nils wondered why he couldn't shake the sinking feeling he'd had since he picked her up. Her words: "I'm lucky to have a *friend* like you" had left him feeling so damn sad, he was sinking deeper into melancholy as the afternoon wore on.

Last night when they'd been alone in the Prairie, it was his last chance to reconfirm that their arrangement wouldn't muddy the waters between them, mostly because he'd woken up yesterday morning with the sort of hope he had no right to. As he'd shaved and brushed his teeth looking at his reflection in the mirror, he hadn't been able to keep the elation out of his heart: *I'm marrying Maggie tomorrow. By the end of the day tomorrow, Maggie Campbell will be my wife. My* wife. *Mine.*

The very thought had almost knocked the wind out of his lungs and made him giddy and ridiculous, staring at himself with a dopey, almost drunken, grin. It hadn't taken him long to sober up and realize all over again that he was only offering her his name for legal purposes and they were about as far from a real marriage as two people could get.

"She's not your wife," he told his stupid face. "She's not ever going to be your wife. Not in any way that actually matters."

The grin had faded as he reminded himself of Wednesdays and Sundays at the Prairie Dawn. One Wednesday evening and Sunday afternoon a month, Maggie converted one corner of the little café-bookstore into Little Café on the Prairie story time. Parents from miles away brought their children for the free, homemade shortbread and tart lemonade that Maggie made with real lemons. But mostly, they brought their children to bask in her loving warmth and to listen to Maggie's magical voice read fairy tales and legends for an hour or so.

The first time he'd stumbled across children's story time, he'd backed up toward the door to leave, but just like all of those beautiful, eager, young faces, Nils had been captivated by Maggie's lilting accent and found himself leaning against the doorway, listening to the story about a princess who wanted to be a regular girl. At one point, Maggie had lifted her eyes from the story and caught his, stumbling over the next few words and blushing before composing herself and resuming the story with gusto. The small café was bursting with other adults, mostly parents ordering coffee from Maggie's teenage helper, or quietly listening to the stories from a respectable distance behind the children. Nils was probably the only unattached adult in the room, so it made sense that his watchful, relaxed presence would surprise her.

As she started each story, she'd ask for a volunteer to sit on her lap and help her turn the pages and every little hand would shoot up in the air, fluttering and waving to be chosen. And that child would nestle against her, close to her melodic voice and encouraging smiles. She knew all of their names and welcomed new children every week. Sometimes the stories ended after an hour, but one Wednesday she chose a longer book and not one child stirred until the story was over, almost two hours later. She loved those children and there was no doubt that they loved her.

After that day, any fantasy he'd had about making a move on Maggie had died. Of course a woman as warm as Maggie wanted children of her own one day. The pain of this realization—of knowing he could never give her what she wanted—had forced him to firmly place Maggie in the "friend zone." And there she'd stayed. All the way up to today. Today. Their wedding day.

And yet.

The longing he felt for her—the deep, uncomplicated love he bore for her— had never stopped growing since the day the roots had planted themselves deeply and permanently in his heart. Even now, as she sat beside him in the comfortable quiet of his car, he ached from wanting what he couldn't have.

"It's a strange day. Here we are, license in hand, about to get married," she said, turning to him, a teasing grin softening her words. "I never pictured my weddin' day like this. No white dress, no tuxedo. No friends nor family. No bonny flowers or cake or…bagpipes."

"Bagpipes?"

"Aye. Bagpipes. If we were marryin' for real, there'd be bagpipes. In the mornin' as I dressed. As I made my way t' the kirk. As we walked back down the aisle. And later, on the kirk green as we stuffed ourselves with cake. Lots of bagpipes."

"You miss Scotland, Maggie?"

She shrugged. "I didna live in highlands, Nils, in lovely Inverness."

"Where they have the castles," he said, remembering their first conversation.

"Aye. The castles. And lochs. And monsters." She chuckled beside him and his lips tilted up for the first time all afternoon. "I lived in Glasgow, a modern city, in a flat with my mum and brother and aunt and cousin, all together in one small space. It was cramped and a little drab. Everyone worked too hard and made too little. When Lily invited me here, I jumped at the chance to come to the States."

"And you've never gone back."

"Nae. I love my mum and Ian, my aunt Janet and

cousin Graham. But…"

"Your life is here," he finished for her.

"Aye." He felt her eyes on him, soft and warm. "Aye. Thank goodness for Lily."

Nils realized that in all the years he'd been playing cards with Maggie and stopping into her shop for coffee, she hadn't talked much about her life in Scotland. Now he found himself rapt with interest, wondering about this woman who'd left everything behind to come to Montana.

"I didn't know your aunt very well. But she and my mamma were friendly. They both loved books. Your aunt started a book group and my mamma attended it for years."

"I'm verra sorry I never met her."

"She was a good woman. A lot like Jenny."

"Then she was a *verra* good woman."

They passed the sign indicating Gardiner was only five miles ahead and Nils felt Maggie shift in her seat. He wondered if she felt as nervous as he did, and damn but he wished he could grab her hand again and hold it, but he had promised himself not to confuse her anymore. All that touching on Monday was like a gateway drug and he was perilously close to becoming addicted. He glanced at her quickly, at the red pillow of her lips, wishing things were different. Wishing for bagpipes and cake and flowers. Wishing for her to have more than a green-card wedding to a man who couldn't love her the way she deserved to be loved. Wishing for *anything* to make today just a little bit more special for her.

Suddenly he had an idea.

Without a word, he jerked the wheel and pulled into the parking lot of the small grocery store to his right, found a space, and left the engine running. Maggie looked over at him, surprised.

"Give me a sec, okay? I have to grab something."

While the young woman in the bakery section wrapped up the two white-frosted cupcakes in a white box, he downloaded the first song that came up on iTunes when he searched for bagpipes. Then he quickly paid for his purchases and returned to the car.

"What in the world?" asked Maggie, looking pointedly at the small bag in his hand, the whisper of a curious smile on her pretty lips.

"How much time do we have?" he asked her.

She glanced at her watch. "Twenty minutes."

"That's just enough!"

He put the car in gear, backed out of the parking lot and took a right onto Main Street. After crossing the bridge, he turned the bend and headed for the Roosevelt Arch, the gateway to Yellowstone. He pulled up beside a picnic table and cut the engine, opening his car door and stepping out without a word.

Maggie joined him a second later, looking at him with wide, worried eyes. "Is this cold feet? Because you dinna have to do this. I can just—"

He'd already pressed play on his iPhone and her face changed as she realized that the strains of bagpipes surrounded them. He offered her his hand and helped her up on top of the picnic table, placing the white grocery store bag on her lap, and then stood back a step to watch her face.

"Bagpipes," she whispered and her green eyes, glistening and tender, held his for a moment before she opened the bag and pulled out the little box, looking inside at the little white cupcakes side by side. She bit her lip as a tear snaked its way down her nose, finally resting on her lip. He couldn't help himself. He stepped forward and swiped the droplet away with the rough pad of his thumb.

"Cake and bagpipes," he said softly. "I know they'd come after the wedding if you were home in Scotland, but we're not doing anything in the right order anyway."

She was still staring at the cake box, but now she raised her eyes. She reached out with both hands and placed them on his cheeks, as tears coursed down her own. As she pulled him gently toward her, he was powerless to look away or pull back from the stark emotion in her eyes. When they were almost nose to nose, she tilted his face, then leaned forward and brushed her lips against his cheek.

His held breath released with an almost inaudible sigh into her hair, and his eyes closed for a second as his brain memorized the feeling of Maggie's lips touching his skin—at once the most erotic and most meaningful touch by anyone in all of his adult life.

Her breath was warm on his cheek as she whispered. "For all my livin' life, I will never forget you did this for me."

The urge to lean his forehead in the warm, sweet-smelling curve of her neck, to pull her small body against his and savor the warmth of her, the goodness of her, was so overwhelming, it physically hurt him to pull back. But he did.

Holding on to the last shred of his self-control, he did.

She reached up to swipe the back of her hand over her cheeks, sniffled, and then offered him the most brilliant smile he'd ever seen.

"By the way, this song is called 'Highland Cathedral.' Proper weddin' music. Of every tune in the whole world you *could've* chosen, somehow you chose the right one." She chuckled lightly, her face bright with happiness as she raised the white box on her lap. "Cupcake?"

Chapter 6

Beck glanced at the license again then lifted his troubled gaze to Maggie.

"You sure about this, Maggie?" Nils had excused himself to use the men's room and she and Beck were left alone for a moment. "I don't mean to pry, but...I don't remember you and Nils being a couple. Recent, huh?"

"You could say that. And yes. I'm sure."

She and Nils had agreed not to include Beck in their charade, but allow him to believe they were an actual couple. It seemed safer just in case the immigration people ever questioned him about the legitimacy of their marriage.

"You just...I mean..." Beck stumbled over his words, finally sighing as he looked up at her. "I think I sort of hoped..."

Maggie had sensed for some time that Beck was interested in her—he came in frequently for coffee and lingered at the bar, looking for reasons to chat with her, his eyes often drifting to her lips or her chest in the course of conversation. He wouldn't be a bad catch either; only a few years older than she, country lawyer, not bad looking. If her heart hadn't already been attached to someone else, she may have even encouraged him. For a moment she wished that her heart had been taken with Beck. How much easier would it have been to love someone already attracted to her, already interested in her?

"Beck," she said gently, "it's always been Nils for me."

He nodded slowly. "I can see that. I guess my question is…has it always been *you* for *Nils*?"

Huh. They weren't fooling Beck one bit. "Does that matter?"

"In this case? I hope not." He rubbed his chin. "If they ever suspect…"

"We'll cross that bridge if we come to it."

"I want you to know…no matter what, Maggie, I'm here for you. Legal advice, friendship…*more* than friendship—whatever you need…"

Her eyes widened. "*More* than friendship? Beck, I'm gettin' married today."

"That's why I wanted to say it now. Before." His warm brown eyes reached out to her across the desk. "I'm just trying to say that if you ever need anything, Maggie, anything at all, I hope you know that I would—"

"You'd what?" asked Nils, who had slipped quietly back into the room.

Beck looked up, his cheeks flushing with surprise. "I—I was just telling Maggie that if she ever needs anything, I'm here for her."

Maggie twisted in her seat to look back at Nils, who stood in the doorway of Beck's office, taking up every inch of space. His Arctic eyes narrowed at Beck momentarily before he glanced at Maggie. She smiled at him and his face softened, though he didn't smile back. "I'll look after Maggie."

"That's good," said Beck, a hint of challenge still lingering in his voice. "Lucky man to call her your *wife*."

Nils looked back at Beck with hard eyes, but to Maggie's relief he didn't wince or grimace. He nodded once and then hooked his thumb toward the waiting area. "Should we get started? Missy's car just pulled in."

Beck got up from his desk, gesturing to the door, and as they left his office, Maggie felt Nils's hand on the small of her back. Possessive. She fought the urge to lean back into his hand, reminding herself his gesture was more for Beck's benefit than hers.

A slightly overweight, tall, blonde woman stood next to Emma Branson's desk with her back to Maggie, and Maggie stiffened instinctively, bracing herself to meet Nils's ex-lover. She didn't want for her face to betray her with a petty, ridiculous show of jealousy over a man who really didn't belong to her, regardless of what they were about to do. As they approached, Missy turned around, and Maggie was instantly disarmed when she saw that her rival was holding a small child in her arms, a little girl who looked around one year old.

"Oh!" Maggie exclaimed, smiling at the blond-haired, brown-eyed baby. "She's so bonny!"

Missy grinned at Maggie proudly, readjusting the child in her arms and straightening the little pink hair bow on top of her head. "This is Josephine. Joey. Joey, meet Maggie. Maggie's getting married today."

"Hello, Joey!" said Maggie, reaching out a hand to Joey, who grasped on to her finger with surprising strength.

Maggie smiled at the baby, but her glance flicked back up to Missy's face just in time to see her lift her gaze and focus over Maggie's head. Missy's face softened with tenderness and her voice was soft and warm when she added, "She's marrying Nils."

Nils's hand dropped from Maggie's back as he sidled up beside her, leaning forward to kiss Missy on the cheek. It made Maggie's stomach lurch and she fought the urge to yank on his arm and pull him away from this other woman, this intruder who'd touched her man's body, known the weight of it over her as she loved him, as she shared something with him that Maggie longed for so desperately.

"You look good, Missy. Marriage agrees with you."

"I'm lucky," she said, giving him a small, wistful smile. Her bright blue eyes seemed misty when they returned to Maggie's face. "I hope you'll be as happy as I am."

"Thank you," answered Maggie, trying to control her feelings before she embarrassed herself.

Anyone could sense the bond between Nils and Missy.

It was the specific intimacy shared by people who'd given and taken the most intimate parts of themselves with one another.

He'd touched this woman's body, run his lips over her skin, maybe looked into her eyes as he fused his body with hers. The way he'd kissed her on the cheek was so natural with none of the halting awkwardness apparent when he touched Maggie. His voice was so tender as he spoke to her.

It made Maggie's heart clench and her stomach roll over. Was it possible he still had feelings for this Missy? Was *she* what stood between Maggie and Nils? It made Maggie want to burst into tears and run from the room to see his connection to this beautiful, buxom blonde woman.

And she may have…if she hadn't suddenly felt Nils's fingers reach gently for hers, clasping her hand in his and then rotating his hand to lace their fingers together. She looked down at their hands first then lifted her gaze to his face where he clenched his jaw, still looking at Missy, as though telling her something.

Missy stared at their hands in amazement. "Oh!" A lovely smile spread across her face, brightening her already pretty features as though she was seeing something beautiful or miraculous. "Nils," she breathed with wonder in her voice.

Nils cleared his throat awkwardly. "Can we get started, Beck?"

"Of course. Let's go into the conference room. It's just a little bigger and we can sit around the table in there."

Maggie took a seat next to Nils, puzzling over the odd exchange that had just occurred. What had made Missy so happy? That Nils and Maggie were holding hands? Why did such a simple act make her look so amazed? So surprised? Maggie's curiosity was piqued, and—if she was honest—it bothered the hell out of her that this woman knew his secrets, knew far more about him than Maggie feared she ever would.

***

He shouldn't have grabbed Maggie's hand, but he felt her whole body tense up beside him as he kissed Missy on the cheek and he wanted to reassure her—to let her know that whatever had existed between him and Missy was long gone. She deserved that much.

But, Missy, who was the only person in the world to whom Nils had ever confided the details of the tragic summer he lost Veronica, had jumped to conclusions as he reached for Maggie's hand. Wrong conclusions. Part of him longed to set her straight, *No, Missy.. Maggie and I are just friends. You know as well as I do why we can never be more than friends.*

And heck, he liked touching Maggie. It calmed his frayed nerves for his skin to be flush with hers. The closer they came to saying their wedding vows, the more his stomach flip-flopped with second thoughts. Maybe he should have let Paul do this for her. But what if he started noticing sunnier smiles between them? What if their fingers started touching more frequently, more deliberately as one of them dealt the cards for euchre? What if one day he realized that what had started as a green-card marriage had somehow become a real marriage before his eyes? He couldn't bear it. He'd want to die. So, selfish bastard that he was, he'd practically forced her to choose him.

She pulled him down in the chair beside her, leaning toward him to whisper in his ear. "Are you okay?"

"Just fine."

"You seem nervous."

She was so close to him, suddenly he didn't feel

nervous. He felt electric with her breath brushing his ear for the second time in an hour. He felt like bellowing at Beck and Missy to get the hell out and pinning Maggie to the conference table, biting her ear and running his tongue along the freckles on her jawline, making her whole body bow into him as he kissed her until they both saw stars.

"Just remember. Two friends. One green card."

"Yeah." *Friends. Yeah, right.*

She drew back and tilted her head to the side, smiling at him reassuringly as she squeezed his hand.

Beck had taken the seat across from them, flanked by Emma, who was holding her granddaughter, and Missy, who smiled back at Nils knowingly. He pursed his lips and looked away.

"Okay, folks, we're going to get started." Beck opened a glossy paperback to a bookmarked page, smoothing it flat on the table before him. "This is a standard civil ceremony. No bells and whistles. Just your basic wedding vows. Unless you wanted—"

"Sounds good," interrupted Nils.

"And you have the ring?" asked Beck.

"The ring?" squeaked Maggie.

"You need at least one," explained Beck.

"Well, I…" Maggie slipped her hand out of Nils's and laid it on the table, looking down at the gold Claddagh ring on her fourth right finger. "It's an Irish weddin' band."

"Perfect," said Beck, holding out his hand. "Can you slide it over to me? I promise I'll give it back in a second."

As Maggie drew the ring down her finger and pushed it

lightly across the table, Nils's heart fluttered. The ring that had always assured him she was free would now remind him that she was his wife. *That man needs to bed me or wed me...* He drew a shaky breath. This was real. This was happening. He was actually *marrying* Maggie.

Beck cleared his throat before beginning. "Okay. Here goes. We are gathered here in the sight of God and the presence of these witnesses to join together this man and this woman in Holy Matrimony, which is an honorable estate and is not to be entered into lightly or inadvisably, but reverently and discreetly." He paused, looking up at Nils, then Maggie. "Nils and Maggie, have you come here freely and without reservation to give yourselves to each other in marriage?"

"Yes," said Maggie.

"Yes," said Nils.

Beck nodded and looked back down at the book. "I require and charge you both to remember that love and loyalty alone will prevail as the foundation of a happy and enduring home, which will be full of joy and will abide in peace."

Nils listened to the words, discomfort uncurling in his gut and making his chest feel tight as he thought about the words "happy and enduring home." He glanced at Maggie, at her freckled face, and wished he could take her hand again, be soothed by her warmth, be reassured that what they were doing wasn't wrong.

Beck interrupted his thoughts by looking up at him. "Nils Lindstrom, will you have this woman, Maggie

Campbell, to be your wedded wife, to live together in the estate of matrimony? Will you love her, honor her, and keep her in sickness and in health and forsaking all others so long as you both shall live?"

Nils cleared his throat, looking briefly at Maggie's profile again, knowing in his heart that despite his inability to share Maggie's bed or be a real husband to her, it didn't change the fact that he would love her and honor her for the rest of his life. He knew that if she was ever sick, if she ever needed him, he'd race to her side. He knew there would never be another woman who could possibly threaten the claim she had on his heart. He knew that he wasn't lying when he answered, "I will."

Under the table, her fingers touched down on his thigh, scrambling lightly against the soft denim, searching for his hand. Without giving it a moment's thought, he gently covered her hand with his.

"Maggie Campbell," asked Beck, "will you have this man, Nils Lindstrom, to be your wedded husband, to live together in the estate of matrimony? Will you love him, honor him, and keep him in sickness and in health and forsaking all others so long as you both shall live?"

Her voice was soft and clear. "Aye. I will."

"Okay, Nils," said Beck, sliding the ring back across the table to Nils. "You're going to put this ring on the fourth finger of Maggie's *left* hand and repeat after me."

Nils took the tiny band between his fingers and shifted in his chair to face Maggie. Her face was pale and serious as she held out her left hand, which trembled, suspended, between them. He lifted his other palm flush to hers and carefully slid the gold ring onto her finger, pushing the little gold heart closer and closer to her own heart. He shouldn't have raised his eyes to hers, but he did, and her bright green eyes captured his, holding them hostage as he repeated after Beck, saying the words that would make her his wife.

"I, Nils…"

"I, Nils…"

"…take you, Maggie…"

"…take you, Maggie…"

"…to be my lawfully wedded wife."

"…to be my lawfully wedded wife."

He kept repeating after Beck, lost in Maggie's eyes, helpless and undone by the simple fact that he meant every word he said.

"To have and to hold from this day forward…"

"…for better, for worse…"

"…for richer, for poorer…"

"…in sickness and in health,"

"…to love and to cherish…"

"…until death do we part."

Love and cherish until death. Until death. There was no fiction in the words he'd spoken, and though he'd live his life without the warmth of her legs tangled with his every night as he slept beside her, at least he wasn't a liar. Yes. He would love and cherish Maggie Campbell for the rest of his pitiful life.

"Okay, Maggie. Because you don't have a ring for Nils, I'm going to ask that you please remain holding hands as you say your vows. I, Maggie…"

Only once did his eyes slip to her lips, to watch her say the words "my lawfully wedded husband" which leveled him for a moment as he realized—on some level, paper or not—he'd just crossed the threshold from belonging to no one, to belonging to someone. It made a shudder pass through his body and he looked back into her eyes for reassurance.

She claimed them with a calm, tender certainty, repeating the rest of the vows in her sweet, musical voice. Nils searched her face for discomfort or unease, but he saw no trace of either. Just warmth and openness, and when she said "to love and to cherish" a bolt of something impossibly pure and true made his eyes burn with emotion. The way she said it, it was almost as though she meant it.

"All right. Now, by the authority in me vested by the laws of this state, I pronounce you husband and wife."

Maggie's eyes widened just a touch at those words and Nils watched as her lips tilted up a tiny bit in wonder.

Beck cleared his throat. "Uh, Nils. You may kiss your bride."

Nils jerked his head to look at Beck, whose eyes narrowed briefly before looking down at his book again.

Damn it, Nils hadn't anticipated this. It had simply never occurred to him that he'd have to kiss Maggie in order to make things official. He turned back to her and watched her eyebrows knit briefly as her tongue darted out to wet her lips, and aw, hell, that little move was his undoing. She started to shake her head, but Nils was feeling too emotional, too invested in what had just transpired between them, to pull away from her now. He reached for her face, cupping her cheeks reverently as he leaned toward her. He tilted his face and closed his eyes as his lips touched hers.

He didn't expect for her to make a small sighing sound in the back of her throat, or lift her hands to flatten them on his chest, which swelled with love for her. On one of those fingers was the ring that made her his wife, and it made him bold and possessive. His tongue darted out to part the seam of her lips, and his heart kicked into a gallop as her fingers curled into the fabric of his shirt, her nails grazing his chest through the layers. Her lips opened softly beneath his and he touched his tongue tentatively to hers, a shudder of pleasure taking his breath away before he realized she was gently but firmly pushing against his chest. She was pushing him away.

The faint sound of clapping snapped him back to reality and he drew back from Maggie, staring at her as she panted lightly, her chest rising and lowering quickly, her eyes dilated and uncertain. Her cheeks were flushed and her lips glistened as he stared at them in shock. He winced as he met her eyes again. God damn it! He'd kissed Maggie. Kissed her. Crossed a major line. Damn it. Damn, damn, damn!

"To the new Mr. and Mrs. Lindstrom!" said Missy, smiling even more knowingly than before as she clapped quietly with her mother and Beck. "Congratulations!"

***

Maggie was having trouble taking a good, deep breath.

It wasn't like she was some untried virgin. Maggie had had several lovers in secondary school and at university. She'd even had a quiet fling with a cute tourist when she'd first moved to Gardiner. But she'd never, ever experienced the maelstrom of feelings that Nils's kiss had awakened in her. My God, how was she ever supposed to see the world in the same way ever again? And more importantly, how was she ever supposed to look at him like a *friend* again?

She turned to Missy and gave her a weak smile, hoping she didn't look as off kilter and emotionally overloaded as she felt. Maybe it was just the surprise of it. Maybe that was it. For so long she'd longed for Nils to see her as more than a friend. From the moment they walked into that conference room, the energy between them had changed, and when they stared into each other's eyes and recited their wedding vows, she'd almost felt like they were actually marrying each other, not just saying vows that would lead to a green card. Would it be crazy to hope that the mere act of saying the words had opened his heart to her? Because that's how his kiss had felt. It hadn't felt like an official gesture to seal the deal or allay suspicion. It had felt...real.

Missy had circled around the table to give Nils a hug, and she turned to Maggie with her arms open. Maggie stared at the attractive woman for a moment, then gave her a quick embrace as her eyes started to burn with so many different emotions: jealousy of Nils's bond to Missy, confusion over the intensity of the marriage ceremony, hope that their wedding had opened a window into Nils seeing her as a woman, and not just a friend. She needed to take a moment for herself before the tears started to fall in front of Nils, Beck, and the Branson women.

"I-uh, thank you, B-Beck. Excuse me," she muttered

quietly, pulling away from Missy and rushing from the room quickly to use the ladies' room.

She closed the door of the small, single bathroom behind her, placing trembling hands on the sink in front of her as she looked at her reflection in the mirror. A strange feeling passed through her as she heard the words *Maggie Lindstrom* whispered in her head. She was Nils's wife now. Regardless of their arrangement to keep the marriage a secret and continue to live their independent lives, something fundamental had changed between them. She meant every word she'd said to him when she had repeated the vows after Beck: she loved Nils and she would love, honor, cherish and keep him forever. For as long as he would let her.

She reached up gingerly and touched her lips with her fingertips, marveling at the gentle possession of his kiss, the way heat had pooled in her belly, then below, signaling that she was ready for far more than a kiss from Nils. Her toes had curled in her boots and her fingers had grasped the fabric of his shirt as her world spun on an axis made up of the space shared by her lips pressed against her husband's on their wedding day.

A wave of hope made her eyes burn with fresh tears as she wondered if it was possible that Nils could feel the same way she did. He couldn't have kissed her like that—with that much unrestrained emotion—just for show. Every cell in her body told her that he cared for her just as much as she cared for him. She took a deep breath and ran her fingers through her reddish-blonde hair, pushing it behind her shoulder and smiling at herself. If it was possible, she intended to find out.

After that kiss, she would ask Nils if they could test the waters of "more than friends," hoping that today was just the beginning of something special.

She turned the knob and walked back into the waiting room.

"Ah, Maggie. You okay?" Beck searched her eyes with that worried, disappointed look that was starting to annoy her.

"Of course." And she was. For the first time in years, it felt like her dreams had a chance of coming true. That kiss had meant something. She just knew it.

"I need you to sign this for me." He smoothed his hand over her marriage certificate and Maggie took the pen, signing Magaidh Lioslaith Campbell with a flourish.

"Maga…" Beck looked up at her, unable to navigate the tongue twister.

"It's still pronounced Maggie. My da just felt strongly about the traditional spellin'."

"And Lio…"

"Lioslaith. Like the English name Leslie. That was my Aunt Lily's full name. I was named for her."

"I see," he said softly, then nodded, a grim expression chasing away his grin as he offered her his hand. "I hope it works out for you, Maggie Leslie. Remember…remember what I said, okay?"

She smiled at him as she shook his hand. "Thanks for everything, Beck. Is Nils still in the…"

Beck gave her a tight smile and nodded toward the conference room. Maggie walked the short distance to the door but stopped by the entrance to the room, taking a deep breath and gathering her courage to make a move on Nils. The rumble of his soft, deep voice made butterflies flurry in her tummy, and she leaned her head against the door frame for a moment, listening unobserved to the low timbre of his voice.

"...I swear to you, you've got it wrong," he said, and Maggie swallowed uncomfortably, straightening.

"I know what I saw, Nils. You never looked at me that way. You look at her the way Lucas looks at me."

"No, Missy. You're wrong. I mean it. There's nothing there. Nothing. She's just Maggie. We're friends and I'm doing her a favor. That's all it is."

"Could've fooled me."

"You *know* me, Missy. You know that I'm not looking for—"

"Yes, but I thought maybe—*finally* you were able to..."

"No." His tone was harsh. "No. Never."

"But the way you touched her...the way you kissed her...Nils, it looked like—"

"Good. Because it needed to look real. But it wasn't. It was just an act. For your mom...and Beck. Just in case they ever have to testify, they can say that to the best of their knowledge it was a legitimate wedding. We're just friends, Missy. She's not special to me. Not like that."

Missy's soothing voice answered, saying something about hoping he would give himself a second chance at happiness one day, but Maggie wasn't listening anymore. She was dizzy and the blood had drained from her face. Her chest hurt like he'd sucker punched her in the sternum. All of it had just been for show. The vows, the handholding, the kiss. It had been an act and nothing else. There was no hope for a future together. She clenched her jaw in an effort to stave off the impending tears and braced her hand on the door, making it creak softly, and drawing Missy and Nils's eyes to where Maggie had been standing.

Nils's eyes met hers and she could tell he was processing the fact that she had overheard everything.

"Maggie…" he said softly, his voice low and tight with regret.

She backed up into Beck, whom she found at her shoulder. Turning, she lifted her glistening eyes to his kind brown ones. "Drive me home?"

Without waiting for him to answer, she turned on her heel and walked out of the office, away from Nils, away from her husband, away from the friend who couldn't seem to stop breaking her heart.

Chapter 7

Over the next month, Nils made a concerted effort not to go anywhere near the Prairie Dawn.

His father and Lars started making the daily coffee run, and he thanked all that was holy neither his father nor his brother pried into the reason for his reluctance to visit the café. They seemed to understand that whatever had happened between Nils and Maggie wasn't trivial, and even Lars's usual teasing was kept to a bare minimum.

Maggie hadn't even asked for Nils to come by and sign the various forms to start the process for her green card. She'd had her young barista, Bethany, drop them by his office one day with yellow sticky notes in Beck's handwriting, indicating everywhere he needed to sign.

Being away from her, however, had the unfortunate result of keeping her foremost in his mind. At every free moment of the day, Nils relived the kiss he'd shared with Maggie. He'd lie in bed, his body aroused almost beyond bearing and touch his fingers to his lips, remembering the soft pliancy of her mouth beneath his, the way her tongue had tentatively touched his. Some nights, it took every ounce of his strength—of his honor—not to rush from his house, stride through town and walk into that café to pull her into his arms. He fantasized telling her that he'd meant every word of their vows, that he loved her, that he needed her, that his body wanted her so badly that he could barely think straight since he'd married her.

Married her.

And that was the other thing. The other reason he stayed away from her: he couldn't stop thinking about her as his *wife*. As someone who belonged to him. And until he could actually see her as his friend again, it was best he stayed away. He'd already confused things between them by kissing her after their wedding vows. Kissing her like he was actually kissing his wife.

It killed him that he'd hurt her right before she rushed out of Beck's office. Did he feel bad about denying his feelings for Maggie in his conversation to Missy? Yes. He felt like a bastard. But, even in the split second he considered running after her, he knew it was for the best that she believe their wedding vows were meaningless to him.

He didn't know why he'd protested his feelings so vehemently to Missy. Maybe because she was the only person in the world to whom he'd ever told the truth. Only Missy knew that something inside of him had died with Veronica on that operating table in Missoula. Only Missy knew how culpable Nils was in everything that had happened to that poor girl, though she'd tried over and over again to convince him that it wasn't his fault. Missy's intentions were good, but Nils knew better. It was *all* Nils's fault and the least he could do was make sure that it never, ever happened again.

And so his life moved forward in quiet agony, missing Maggie, staying away from her, throwing himself into work and reliving every moment of his wedding day, until somehow a month had passed.

He woke up bright and early on the first Saturday in June, checked the calendar on his phone to reconfirm it was a rare Saturday with no tours booked, and laced his fingers behind his head. A Saturday of leisure stretched out before him. Only one thing was certain: the day had to start with Swedish *våfflor*.

After showering and dressing, he whipped up the batter and checked his cabinet looking for *sylt ligon*, ligonberry jam, grimacing when he realized he was out. Maybe Lars had some. He slipped down the back stairs and knocked on his younger brother's back door. One benefit of sharing a two-family house with his brother was that Lars kept his kitchen much better stocked than Nils did.

Lars answered the door looking tousled and satisfied, wearing only his boxer shorts and holding a mug of coffee. He likely had a Park Girl over, per usual. Lars broke into a grin as he opened the door.

"*Morgon, Største*," he said with a twinkle in his blue eyes. As always, Nils was struck by how carefree and uncomplicated Lars's life seemed in comparison to his own. Though he tried not to resent this, deep down, he did. Not to mention, Lars had about the most active sex life Nils could imagine, which added salt to the wound.

He scowled. "*Har du sylt ligon?*"
Do you have ligonberry jam?

"Maybe. But only if you're sharing *våfflor*."

Nils peeked his head past Lars's shoulder, expecting to see a half-dressed woman prancing about his apartment begging for another round. He wasn't in the mood to be teased with his brother's bounty over breakfast.

"*För två, inte tre.*"

For two, not three.

Lars flashed his white teeth at Nils, chuckling quietly. "She's long gone. She was meeting her girlfriends at seven for a hike."

Lars padded to the kitchen, returning with a jar of red jam, and Nils glanced at his little brother's bare torso. "Then get dressed and come up."

Ten minutes later the brothers sat across from each other at Nils's kitchen table in silence, drinking good coffee and filling up on waffles.

Finally Lars shoved his plate to the center of the table and twisted his wrist to look at his watch. "We're going to be late if we don't get moving."

"Late?" Nils gave his brother a look. "For what? We don't have a job scheduled for today. I checked the—"

"For Maggie."

"Maggie," he repeated, her name rattling him more than it should. "What are you talking about?"

"Pop's party? Ring a bell? Jenny's gonna have your hide if you back out now. She's counting on you to come up with a slideshow of photos or something."

"I'm sorry, but I think I'd remember if our *lillesøster* was coming to town."

"Jen's not..." Lars smiled at Nils, nodding his head indulgently. "When's the last time you checked your email?"

"Oh, just yesterd—"

"Not your Lindstrom and Sons account. Your Yahoo email that your sister uses now and then to email you when she's scheduled a meeting about your father's surprise birthday party?"

Oh, hell. Never. "Been a while."

"So you haven't gotten any of her emails? None?" Lars grinned as he slapped his leg and stood up, taking the empty plates to the sink. "Boy, are you in trouble."

Nils threw back the rest of his coffee, grumbling. Jenny, he could handle. She may throw her weight around here and there, but she was still his little sister. But Maggie? He just wasn't ready to see her yet.

"Why don't you head over there, *Midten*? Let me know what the girls say. Tell me whatever they need. You know I'm glad to help."

Lars turned around and faced his older brother, leaning against the sink with his arms crossed over his chest. For once he didn't look playful. His face was a mixture of concern and disappointment, and for all that Lars's carefree ways and life on a silver platter needled at Nils, he loved his younger brother. Disappointing him wasn't a pleasure.

"I know what's going on, Nils," he said quietly, his voice laced with sympathy.

Nils's heart started hammering, though he took pains not to reveal his surprise. How in the hell had Lars found out that he and Maggie were married? He tried to remain impassive. "That so?"

"You've been avoiding the Prairie for weeks. I know how much you like her. I mean, I assume you did, the way you got all red-faced around her and couldn't spit your words out to save your life. I know how much it must be bothering you."

Nils sat forward in his seat, brows furrowed in confusion. "How much *what* is bothering me?"

"That Maggie's dating Beck Westman." Lars turned back to the sink to run hot water over the plates. "But it's a small town. You can't just avoid Maggie and the Prairie forever. I reckon you have to move on."

"Um." Nils rubbed his jaw with his hand, trying to—at least partially—conceal the fierce riot of emotions inside. "What the hell are you talking about?"

Lars faced his brother, cocking his head to the side and searching Nils's face. "Maggie and Beck. They're…dating. I mean, I think they are. They're together a lot. And Beck took over your seat at euchre when you stopped coming."

"Maggie," growled Nils, "…and Beck."

"Yeah. I thought you knew. I thought that's why you were avoiding her. Because it didn't work out for you two and she started dating B—"

"I didn't know," Nils whispered, his right forefinger rubbing the bare fourth finger of his left hand, the same spot where she wore a Claddagh ring, heart in, that he had slid on her finger four weeks ago. On their wedding day. He felt heat flush his face and as he picked up his coffee cup, his fingers curled so roughly around the handle, it snapped off in his hand.

Lars cringed. "Sorry I had to be the one to tell you. Mind now, I've never seen them kissing or anything. Just all smiley and familiar when we're playing cards and I saw them having dinner together a time or two at the Cowboy Lodge when I filled in at the bar, so I just

assumed—"

"It's fine," said Nils, his voice tight and cold. As cold as his heart, which had no right to feel betrayed, but he couldn't help it that he did. She was *his*. Beck would be lucky if he didn't end up with Nils's fist shoved down his throat by the end of today.

"But, Nils? No matter what sort of issues you got going on in your love life? This is Pappa's birthday party. You got to step up and help out, or you'll regret it later. You're coming to that meeting with me today."

"No worries, little brother," said Nils, standing up to throw the broken mug in the trash and run his bleeding hand under the faucet. "It's about time I stopped by the Prairie."

***

Maggie was ninety-nine percent sure that Nils wouldn't be at the meeting this morning, but the way her belly fluttered and her hands shook told her that that single percent chance was wreaking havoc on her nerves.

She'd barely seen Nils since their wedding day—the day he'd played bagpipes for her at the Roosevelt Arch and kissed her like she meant something to him, tricking her into believing for one brief, toe-curling moment that he might actually be marrying her for her heart, not just doing a favor for a friend.

She's not special to me. Not like that. Not at all.

How many nights had Maggie cried herself to sleep with those words circling in her head? For years she'd held out a ridiculous hope that Nils Lindstrom would suddenly cultivate the sort of feelings for her that she'd long harbored for him. Well, over the past month she had come to the conclusion that it simply wasn't going to happen. He was a good man—a good friend—and she would always be grateful for the way he gave her his name and facilitated her citizenship. But a year and eleven months from now, when she could quietly divorce him and sever any remaining connection to him, couldn't come fast enough.

In the meantime, sympathy and companionship had some from an unlikely source: Beck Westman.

When Beck had driven Maggie home after her wedding, he'd ended up staying for hours, keeping her company as she drank herself into oblivion, spilling out her heart. He'd sat beside her on the couch as she cried and raged about Nils not loving her back. He'd offered her his handkerchief and his shoulder and helped her into bed after her fifth or sixth glass of wine.

Maggie knew that Gardiner was buzzing about her and the handsome, eligible lawyer; they'd dined a couple of times at the Cowboy Lodge and met for drinks at the Grizzly. He'd stopped by the Prairie with all of the green card forms, staying late to help her fill them out, and took care of putting them in an envelope so Bethany could take them to Nils. He was, increasingly, a fixture at the Prairie, and had filled in for

Nils at euchre for a month now.

"I'm here for you," he often said. "Whatever you need."

What Maggie needed was a friend, and she'd been more than clear with Beck that her battered heart needed a break from romantic thoughts and hopes. She needed to get over Nils Lindstrom after so many years of longing and fantasy. She knew it would take a while, if not years, but Beck always touched her arm or swept her bangs off her forehead gently and assured her with a confident smile. "I'm not going anywhere, Maggie Leslie. I'll be whatever you need."

Part of Maggie felt a little guilty accepting Beck's support and kindness, because regardless of his words, she sensed that he wanted far more than friendship from her. But every time she turned around, there he was, with his encouraging smiles and suggestions to grab a beer or a bite. As long as she'd made herself clear, there couldn't be much harm in accepting his friendship, could there? Besides, it wasn't just her. He was becoming friends with Paul and Lars, too. He was filling a chair that had been left willfully vacant.

The little bell over the door jingled and Maggie's head whipped up to find Paul sauntering over to the bar. She smiled in greeting as her shoulders relaxed and she released a shaky breath.

"Morning, Mags."

For the hundredth time she thought to herself that she needed to find someone nice for Paul. "Heya. Coffee?"

"Please. Black." He settled himself on a barstool and looked around the buzzing café. "No Lindstroms?"

"Not yet. I'm sure Lars will be here soon."

"Nils, too," said Paul carefully, watching her.

"I doubt it," Maggie said cheerfully, placing his coffee on the counter before him. Paul knew that something had happened between her and Nils, and while Maggie hated that she couldn't share the whole green-card wedding with Paul, she knew it was better to keep him in the dark. Anyway, Nils had insisted on it, too, and she felt compelled to keep the secret.

"It's his pop's birthday. He'll be here."

Maggie shrugged lightly but her stomach flipped over uncomfortably. The little bell jingled again, and her hands fisted then uncurled as Beck walked through the doorway with a broad smile and a small plant in one hand, housed in a colorful ceramic planter.

"Mornin', Maggie Leslie," he said in his usual greeting, winking at her.

"What do you have there?"

"Lavender. I saw it at Arnold's and thought…" His cheeks colored as he placed it on the bar. He was always doing this—bringing her thoughtful little gifts. On one hand, she loved the attention, but it also worried her that Beck wasn't listening when she said she couldn't handle more than his friendship in her life.

She took the little plant and slid it to the middle of the bar, leaning down to breathe in the tiny purple flowers. "It's lovely, Beck."

Beck sat down next to Paul. "How's school?"

"We're getting there," said Paul. "About six weeks left

'til summer break, but spring fever has set in with a vengeance."

Maggie grinned. "Have your hands full, huh?"

"I've got kids making out in the bathrooms, behind the field house, in empty classrooms, behind the stacks in the library…you name a place, I'm finding them."

Beck faced Paul, eyes twinkling. "And what do you do when you, er, find them?"

"I tell them to go to class."

"Once you pry their lips apart?" asked Beck, winking at Maggie.

She gave him a tight smile, turning around to pour him a cup of coffee.

The only lips that passed through Maggie's mind were Nils's, with an unrelenting regularity. The way he'd cupped her face, the pads of his thumbs had stroked her cheek as his lips had descended to touch hers, warm and certain and—

The bell over the door jingled again and Maggie didn't need to turn around to know she'd find him standing there. She could feel it, just as she always had. She sucked in a breath, wishing she could still her trembling hands. Clenching her jaw, she turned, unable to stop her traitorous heart from leaping with pure joy to see his face again.

***

Nils couldn't have looked away from her if he tried.

If someone had thrown sand in his eyes, he still would have kept them open, burning like fire, to drink in the sight of her. Her bright eyes glistened fiercely, and as her little chin lifted just slightly, he felt the corners of his mouth twitch upward. Good God, he had missed her. How had he managed to stay away for so long? How would he manage it again after today? When all he wanted in the whole world was to vault over the bar and take her into his arms where she belonged, and never, ever let her go.

Lars stepped around him, jostling his shoulder and snapping him back to reality. Maggie cleared her throat and turned her back to him, working at the counter. He finally dragged his eyes away from her and they settled, disagreeably, on Beck Westman, who sat perched on a barstool like he owned the place.

Paul and Lars were already in conversation, so Nils nodded coolly to Beck. "Heya."

"Nils. Been a while."

Yeah, thought Nils, *since I married the girl you're dating, you dickhead.*

"Got all my forms?"

"Yep. Sent 'em in weeks ago. Hopefully she'll hear something soon."

Maggie turned around then, and Nils stared at her face from where he stood behind Beck, but she didn't look up and wouldn't acknowledge him. Not even to say hello. She gestured to an open table in the back of the café and directed her comments to Lars and Paul. "Why dinna you all get started? Bethany isn't here to take over yet. I'll join you once she gets here."

Look at me. Look at me and let me know you've missed me as much as I've missed you.

She didn't. Her arms were flat on the bar and she

looked straight ahead at Beck instead, clenching her jaw, before resetting her expression and offering him a wink and a bright, intimate smile. Nils knew the one, damn it. She'd offered it to him often enough.

Beck reached out and put a hand on her arm. "I don't open my office until noon on Saturdays. How about I help out until Bethany gets here? And after your little pow-wow, I'll take you out to lunch, Maggie Leslie."

Paul and Lars stopped speaking, turning in unison with wide eyes and gaping jaws to stare at Beck and Maggie.

Beck didn't look at either of them or at Nils behind him. He kept his eyes trained on Maggie. "What do you say?"

I say…if you don't take your hand off my wife, I'm going to be tempted to break it.

Nils could practically feel the steam coming out of his ears as he watched Beck making a move on Maggie right in front of him. He seethed quietly, staring at Maggie's face until she finally lifted her eyes to his, holding them fast.

"I'd just love that, Beck," she said softly, her eyes flat and angry as she stared at Nils for the first time since he'd walked into the café. After a beat, she looked back down at Beck, sitting in front of her, and smiled.

Nils took a step forward, reaching up to pull Beck off the stool and smash his fist in the lawyer's face, but he suddenly felt Lars's hand firmly on his arm. Lars moved himself quickly between Nils and Beck, putting his other arm around Nils's shoulder and ushering him in the direction of the table.

"Why don't we get started, huh, Nils?"

Beck turned his head and scoffed lightly, looking at Nils with a mocking half-smile before sliding off the barstool and walking slowly around the bar. Lars tugged Nils forward and he was pretty sure he heard Paul mutter, "Guy has a goddamn death wish" as he followed closely behind them.

"Get off me, Lars," growled Nils between clenched teeth.

"You stay cool, brother. It's not your business who she dates."

"You don't know what you're talking about."

"I may not have all the pieces to this puzzle, but here's what I know...that guy's a lawyer. You clock him? Oh, I'll back you up. You know I will. But we'll both be arrested and charged with assault."

"It'd be worth it."

"*Stanna, Største,*" Lars said in a low, direct tone. "*Jag vet att du är arg. Ta det lungt.*"

Stop...I know you're angry, but take it easy.

Nils shrugged off his brother's arm around his shoulder as he lowered himself into a bright yellow chair, never once taking his eyes off Maggie, who giggled at something Beck said as she pointed out the various coffee-making apparatuses.

"Stop managing me."

"Stop acting like someone who needs to be managed." Lars rolled his eyes at Paul. "This is going to be real fun."

"Do you all want anythin'?" Maggie called to them from the bar.

Nils glanced over at her. *Yeah. For you to stop encouraging that dickhead. How about that?*

"Coffees?" she asked again, the slightest challenging smile on her lips as she checked out Nils, then looked back and forth at Paul and Lars. They both nodded at her, so she filled up two mugs and, balancing three in her hands, hers included, made her way to the table to join them. She set theirs down in front of them and without sparing a glance at Nils, folded her hands on the table and turned her body toward Lars to her left.

Nils, sitting to her right, could barely stand it anymore. He banged his elbows on the table and cleared his voice. Nothing. Not even a glance.

"So," she said pleasantly. "I talked to Jenny this mornin'."

"Oh?" asked Nils.

"Mmm," confirmed Maggie, her body still facing Lars. "And she asked for us to split up the duties a little bit. She said she'd take care of the guest list and invitations. I'll handle the food and get Bethany to help out servin'. Lars, she asked if you could keep your father busy on the day of the party...take him into the park or somethin'. Bring him here on time for the surprise."

"No problem," said Lars.

"Paul, are you willin' to buy the liquor and help me set up a bar that afternoon?"

"Sure."

"Jenny and Sam'll reimburse you whatever you spend."

"Aw, I don't mind. I'm glad to help do something for

Mr. Lindstrom."

She bent her arm at the elbow and cupped her face with her hand, smiling at Lars. Nils stared at the gentle curve of her neck as her fingers thrummed lightly against her cheek. "And someone needs to do the slideshow."

Lars looked across the table at Nils. "Maybe you could do that part?"

Nils dropped his eyes from Maggie's neck—which he was torn between wanting to kiss and wanting to wring—and nodded at Lars. "Wish Jen was here to help me, though. Girls have a better eye for that sort of—"

"Maggie will help you," Lars blurted out. "Won't you Mags?"

"Oh. I..." She dropped her elbow and straightened in her chair a little, casting a brief, annoyed glance at Nils. "I'm sure that Nils is perfectly capable of—"

"Nah. He's right," said Lars. "It'll need a woman's touch. I guess we could ask Jenny to come down a few days early to give a hand, but with baby Erin and all..." He let his voice trail off.

"Fine," said Maggie, bristling. She turned her head and caught Nils's eyes and he tried to keep the hurt off his face, but he was pretty sure he didn't succeed. In her eyes, he saw plenty of hurt of her own and he hated himself for putting it there. "I'll help. For your *pappa's* sake."

"Great," said Lars. "Come over tomorrow for Sunday Supper. I'll keep Pop busy making the meatballs and watching the game while you and Nils root around in the attic. We'll come up with some reason you two should be up there."

While you and Nils root around in the attic.

After a month away from her, he was going to be all alone with her in his parents' attic looking at old photos. Tomorrow couldn't come fast enough. And while he should have told her no, or at least told Lars to knock it off, he couldn't. After a month of going through the motions in his stagnant life, he felt alive again. He needed her in his life. He had to figure out a way to have her there.

"Well, I guess it's a date, then," he said quietly, staring down at his hands and trying to conceal the wild leaping in his heart.

Maggie raised her coffee to her lips and agreed sourly, "I guess it is."

Chapter 8

As Maggie pulled into Mr. Lindstrom's driveway, she tried to calm the fierce flurry in her stomach. For heaven's sake, she'd been to the Lindstrom's house a thousand times before. Just never when she was married to one of his sons. And never when she was about to spend time alone with that son after a month-long cold freeze and the most awkward party planning meeting ever.

His words to Missy on their wedding day had been so incredibly painful to her, so embarrassing, she could barely think about them without cringing. But then he walked into her café yesterday morning and those ice-blue eyes may as well have been as green a spring grass. He was jealous. Spitting mad, ready-to-hit-Beck style jealous. And she'd never admit it to a soul, but she loved it, because just like that, the game wasn't over. As far as Maggie knew, jealousy only came about if you wanted what somebody else had, which made her question what he'd said to Missy because it didn't add up. If he wasn't interested at all in Maggie, if touching her and kissing her and playing the bagpipes for her was all just an act, he wouldn't care if Beck was interested in her, right?

She'd purposely batted her eyes at Beck and made a show of accepting his lunch invitation. She'd directed all of her attention to Lars, despite Nils clearing his throat and shifting in his seat to get her attention. It was pure weakness to agree to Lars's suggestion that she help Nils, but if she was honest, she was spoiling for a fight. Nils had hurt her with the things he'd said to Missy—really, really *hurt* her—and if nothing else, she intended to tell him so today to his stupid, handsome face.

She parked her car and took the little plaid tin of shortbread off the passenger seat, glancing at her face in the rearview mirror. She'd put on a little eyeliner and mascara, though she wore neither very often, and a little bit of lip gloss too. She pursed her lips, watching them glisten. She'd spruced up for Nils's benefit, of course. When a woman's about to tell off a man, it's in her best interest to look good.

She swung her legs out of the car, the frayed cuffs of her jean-clad legs brushing the top of her western-style boots. She adjusted her long-sleeved, black, scooped-neck T-shirt that rode the line between casual and sexy, tugging it down a touch until it revealed her modest cleavage. Then she pushed up the sleeves to her elbows and bared her heavily freckled, toned forearms. It had taken her over an hour to wash and blow-dry her thick strawberry-blonde hair, but damn if it didn't bounce around her shoulders like a shampoo commercial—a nice change from the bun she always wore, that always had two or three pencils sticking out like spikes.

She climbed up the porch steps. The front door opened before she could knock, and suddenly Lars was standing there grinning at her.

"Heya, Mags," he whispered.

"Heya, Lars. I brought shortbread. Why're we whisperin'?"

He took the tin from her and kissed her on the cheek. "Pop fell asleep in front of the TV. You know how to get up to the attic, right? Nils is already up there."

She nodded. More than once she'd opened the attic door by mistake en route to the bathroom in the early days when she'd been a new guest to Mr. Lindstrom's house.

"Go on up." He put a finger to his lips. "And shhhhhh."

She winked at Lars and tiptoed through the living room that had picture windows looking out at the park and mountains beyond, past Mr. Lindstrom snoring in his recliner and through the dining room to the back stairs.

"Hey, Mags!" hissed Lars, coming up behind her. "Don't kill each other."

She rolled her eyes at him. "No promises."

"What happened between you two?" he asked, placing the tin on the kitchen counter.

The smell of Swedish meatballs in brown sauce drifted out into the hallway and made her mouth water. It was Mrs. Lindstrom's recipe and the Lindstroms kept it heavily guarded. She had a fleeting thought that she was a Lindstrom now, too, and she should ask for it, then shook her head at such silliness.

"It's complicated."

"You dating Beck? Like, for real?"

"Does it matter?"

"Yeah. It matters to him. A lot."

Maggie gave Lars a sad smile and shrugged. "Would you hate me if I asked you to stay out of it, Lars?"

Lars took a step back, brows furrowing as he crossed his arms over his chest. "Don't hurt him."

"Hurt *him*? Yeah, right!" she said, Nils's words to Missy flitting through her head.

She wondered if it was a bad idea to come over here today. She thought about turning around, getting in her car, and going home.

"I know he's gruff," said Lars, hands on his hips, eyes concerned. "But he'd do anything for someone he cares about and it's a short list. You're on that list. You know that, Mags?"

Maggie dropped his glance, looking down at the tips of her scuffed boots. She'd bought them two months after she'd arrived in Gardiner. A few days after meeting Nils and the rest of the Lindstroms. Years ago.

The Lindstroms had been like family to her ever since. Right down to one of them offering her his name and protection when she needed it. Her face flushed and colored with shame. Yes, Nils had hurt her feelings, but he'd never promised her anything. All he'd ever been was good to her, and her attitude was ungrateful.

Lars's words softened the edge she'd arrived with. She twisted her Claddagh ring. She hadn't taken it off since the day Nils had put it on. Even on the mornings her eyes were red and puffy from crying, she'd left it on.

"I know I'm on that list," she answered quietly.

Lars cocked his head to the side and smiled at her before slipping back into the kitchen. "Then go easy on him."

Maggie trudged up the stairs, turning left on the landing and opening the second door on her right. The old wooden stairs creaked as she climbed up into the attic, her sweaty hands slick on the polished wood banister.

"Lars? That you?"

She held her breath for a moment, all of the confidence she arrived with ebbing from her body, siphoned by the tone of his voice so near to her.

"I-It's me." She cringed at the tremor in her voice.

Nils peeked his head around the doorway at the top of the stairs, and it took her eyes a moment to adjust to the dim light, but she could make out the blondness of his hair as some stingy light filtered in through a round window behind him.

"Heya, Maggie May," he said in the gentlest voice she'd ever heard, as he stared down at her.

Oh, Lord. She stilled between two steps and took a deep breath as every feeling she'd ever had for him came rushing back, covering her like mist, until she was saturated with love for him, as bright and shiny as the day she'd married him.

This is too hard, too complicated, a voice inside her head whispered, but she hushed it.

"Heya," she answered, resuming her climb. "Findin' anythin' good?"

"Some," he answered, not moving.

When she was two steps away from him, she paused,

looking up, still holding his ice-blue eyes with hers.

"What you said to Missy hurt me," she blurted out in a whisper.

He swallowed. "I'd erase it from your ears if I could."

"Did you mean it?"

He stared at her sadly and then shook his head slowly back and forth. "No."

Tears sprang into her eyes at the sound of that sweet, single word and she longed for him to open his arms to her, to bury his hands in her hair and crush her lips with his. Instead she asked timidly, "No?"

"No," he repeated, frowning. "It wasn't all an act."

"Oh," she murmured, her head whirling from this information, desperate for clarification. What wasn't an act? Saying the wedding vows? The kiss? The feelings between them that he wouldn't acknowledge? All of it?

"Maggie, I…" She watched his tongue dart out and wet his lips before he bit the bottom one, shaking his head again. "But I still can't do anything about it."

"Oh," she breathed again. "Why not?"

"I just can't." He winced, looking intensely sad and frustrated and regretful.

That's not enough. I need to know why. I need to know why you think this can't *happen, so I can figure out a way to* make *it happen!*

"I don't understand."

"I'm sorry. I just…I can't. But I care about you. Your friendship's important to me."

She nodded briefly, ignoring the ache in her heart caused by his words. Someday she would figure out why.

Someday she would figure out why he wouldn't let himself be with her and she'd do something about it. But for now, it just felt so good to be around him again, she nodded again, letting it go.

***

"What about this one?" he asked her, as they sat side by side on the dusty floor against an old steamer trunk, passing photos back and forth to each other from boxes they'd found in an ancient bureau.

Maggie looked over and giggled at a picture of Jenny sticking her tongue out, thumbs in her ears and fingers waggling. "Och, she'd nae be so pleased to have that one suddenly appear on the screen!"

He looked sideways at Maggie and grinned. Whenever she was drunk or comfortable, her accent was just the slightest bit stronger, and he loved it. After their initial awkwardness on the stairs, they'd settled into a comfortable rapport, and man, it felt good to be around her again. Like sunshine after a month of rain. Like forgiveness.

But feeling good around Maggie had never been the problem. Feeling good had always pretty much come naturally. It was "what comes next" that had always led Nils to personal quagmires.

"Look at wee Erik!" she exclaimed, her shoulder brushing against his as she leaned toward him, showing him the picture.

It was sweet torture to be sitting so close to her. He could feel the warmth of her body next to him, the smell of her strawberry shampoo. His eyes couldn't stop flicking to the neckline of her low-cut shirt, black against her creamy freckled skin. And every time one of them moved, they touched. Their shoulders, their hips, their legs. It was all he could do not to haul her up on his lap and kiss her until she was writhing against him. He cleared his throat, taking a deep breath and drawing up his knees to hide his growing erection.

"Erik?" he asked weakly.

"Or is this Lars?"

"Nope. You were right. Erik. All ready for his first ski run. Man, he was scared."

"Why? Did he fall?"

"Amazingly? He didn't. He was a natural from the start. Pop sure was proud of him." Nils put the picture in the slideshow pile and scooped up another handful of photos to sift through.

"Now I know this is you, but who's this next to you?" Maggie chuckled beside him.

Nils glanced over at the picture Maggie was holding up and sighed, taking it from her fingers. He was about ten years old in the picture, holding hands with a little girl who came up to his shoulder. She had a wreath of daisies on her head and a shy half-smile on her face. "That is Maisy McKintrick."

"Maisy?"

"Mm-hm. Miss Maisy. My first love."

"Your *first*? Have there been loads since? Hoards?"

"Don't you hear them all beating a path to my door at night?"

"And here I thought it was a stampede of buffalo comin' out of the park for a wee visit to town, but nae. Just your dainty admirers."

"They plague me to no end."

"Maybe you should tell them you're married."

A quick current of energy buzzed in the small space between them as though her comment was a live wire, wild and sparking, separating them, but fascinating all the same. He swallowed, eyeing her carefully.

"Ha," he said finally, in a flat, low tone.

"Ha," she answered, smirking at him, all dry and sassy and adorable. Her big green eyes twinkled with mischief and he felt a smile take over his face even before he chuckled.

"I made you laugh," she said with quiet triumph.

"You've always been able to do that."

She stared at him for an extra beat before looking away. Anxious not to spoil the mood, he nudged her hand with the picture.

"It was *Midsommardagen*. Ten minutes after that picture was taken, she tried to kiss me behind my folks' house, and I refused. She told me I was stupid, stomped away and never gave me a second glance."

"Pushy little thing," said Maggie, her lips tilting up in amusement as she put the picture in the back of the pile.

"It was complicated."

"Complicated? At ten years old?"

"Her brother was my best friend."

"Ah. I see."

"Not that I don't appreciate a woman who knows what

she wants."

"Is that so?"

He didn't know what to say in response, sensing that they were drifting into murky waters. She shifted a little to face him, plucking the photo from his fingers. "But you liked her. And she liked you. Maybe he would have understood." She paused, glancing at the photo before looking back up at him with her wide green eyes. "Maybe you should have just…leaned in."

The last words were spoken so softly, they hovered between them like a breath, like a spell or a dare. Nils felt his body leaning in, just as Maggie had suggested, her strawberry shampoo daring him to make a move. He tilted his head just slightly so his lips would touch down flush on hers, and felt his eyes starting to close. What he wouldn't give to be able to pull her into his arms, pliant and warm, her lips softly open and—

Wait, no! You can't do this! The voice in his head bellowed for him to stop. *You just got back on level footing with her. You can't mess this up again!*

His eyes flew open and he jerked back. "Sorry," he murmured, his heart pinging like a hammer on anvil.

"Um…it's fine," she answered lightly, lowering her chin. She took a deep, ragged breath, her chest heaving up and down rhythmically. "So…so it, um, it didn't work out with Miss Maisy?"

"Nope." He cleared his throat. "Although she did get that kiss."

"From whom?"

"Lars."

Maggie gasped, her eyes shocked and teasing at once. "Your brother stole your girl!"

"She turned to him for comfort." He shrugged, trying to look pathetic, trying not to grin. "Plus, in fairness, I guess she wasn't mine by that point."

"I dinna know what's worse...that she was such a fickle lass, or that Lars made a move so quickly." "Can't blame Lars. It's just his way. She probably sidled up next to him and took him by surprise."

He lowered his knees and turned his attention back to the small pile of photos still in his hand. When she didn't say anything, it took Nils a moment to realize she was staring at him—staring at his bowed head beside her. When he looked up, her eyes were compassionate and searching.

"You'd forgive him for anything, wouldn't you?" she murmured.

"Lars?" He stared at her, mesmerized by the softness in her eyes.

"Aye."

"He's my brother."

"You love them so much. Lars and Erik and Jen. And your da."

And you, Maggie. You're on that list, too.

He bit his bottom lip, unable to look away from her. "They're my family."

She made a small sound in the back of her throat then nodded at him, looking away quickly. "It's just so lovely."

The sadness in her voice made him pause.

"You know," he said, pulling two pictures from his parents' honeymoon in Stockholm from the batch he was holding and placing them in the slideshow pile. "I barely know a thing about your family. You never talk about them."

"Oh, well…my family isn't exactly like yours."

"What's that mean?"

"You're all so lovin' and close and we're…not."

"There's got to be more to it than that," he insisted, nudging her leg gently.

She sighed. "My da passed on ages ago. He was a big drinker which made for an unpredictable childhood. He wasna violent, but he wasna much good for anythin' either. My mum was one of three sisters and once my da passed, we moved in with her younger sister, Janet, my aunt. I have an older brother, too. Ian. And then there's Janet's son, Graham. That's all of us, I guess."

"How old is Ian?"

"Three years older than me. And Graham's about ten years younger."

"You group them together? Your brother and your cousin?"

"Aye. I guess I do. We all lived together in the same flat for years. I took care of Graham while mum and Aunt Janet worked, so…"

"You didn't resent it? Caring for a younger cousin?"

"Resent it? Och, no! I loved it! It's probably why I love children so much, all that time I spent tendin' to wee Graham. He was a charmer then, for sure."

Why I love children so much. Nils winced, reminding

himself of why he could never make a move on Maggie, why it was best that they remain friends. He could never give her what she wanted.

"You were close to him?"

"To Graham? Aye. To me mum and Ian and Aunt Janet? I love them, but…" She handed him a photo of his parents looking young and vibrant, his mother holding a baby as his father held the hands of two little blond boys. "…we aren't close like you and yours. More like we were just…sharin' space. Ian's married now and settled, thank God. We feared he might turn out like da for a while there."

The way she described her family—so disjointed and cold—tugged at his heart. His childhood had been full of warmth and love, while hers had been uncertain and frightening, her closest relative a cousin ten years her junior. And yet, it was Maggie who offered warmth and cheer to him, while he was helpless to offer her anything but friendship. It didn't seem fair. She deserved better. She deserved stability and love. It made him wish—for the thousandth time—that things between them could be different.

"Graham's still a hellion," she added distractedly as she passed Nils a baby picture of Jenny. He put it absently into the slideshow pile, more interested in learning more about Maggie than sifting through pictures.

"What does that mean?"

"He hangs about with some shady characters. It scares my aunt to death. Me too. I've told her over and over again to send him here to me for a while."

"Here? You mean, come live with you here?"

She looked up at him. "Sure. It'd be good for him to get away from the city, from his... *friends*."

She said the word with such derision and disgust, he had to ask. "What about his friends?"

"Street riff-raff."

"Like. . . drug dealers?"

"I dinna know for sure." She sighed. "Good chance, I guess. There are loads of gangs in Glasgow. I dinna know if he's definitely joined one or not, but if he hasn't, it's just a matter of time."

"Christ, Maggie. He sounds like a handful. Is he coming?"

"I dinna know. Maybe. No plans yet."

"Don't take this the wrong way, but I'm not sure it's a good idea...you taking on some wild teenage kid on your own."

"He's my cousin." She looked up at him and grinned. "You worried for me?"

Nils shrugged, but the answer was yes. He didn't like the idea of her troublemaking cousin coming to stay with her. He didn't like the idea of anything entering her space that could threaten her safety or happiness. Most of the time, he didn't like himself for that very reason.

"Well, I hope he does come here," she said. "He could use the change. The country would do him a lot of good."

"If he does, promise you'll let me and Lars take him under our wings. Keep our eyes on him. Whip him into shape."

"Ah, just what Gingy needs. A lesson in pickin' up Park Girls from the notorious Lindstrom brothers." She smirked, handing Nils a picture of Nils, Lars, and Erik in front of the *Lindstrom & Sons* touring van, their arms around each other's shoulders, looking tan and blond and impossibly handsome.

"Gingy?"

"A nickname. On account of his red hair."

Nils glanced at the photo, biting his bottom lip so he didn't grin at her. "Picking up Park Girls? Now you're talking about Lars and Erik."

"Not you?"

"When have you ever seen me with a Park Girl?" Nils shook his head, putting the photo in the slideshow pile and straightening it.

"Just because I've never seen it…"

"No, Maggie."

"What, never?"

"Not for a long time."

Her wide eyes locked in on his and a smile spread across her face. It made him blush as he realized what they were talking about—him having sex with some anonymous girl. Did she think about things like that? She had used the words "Bed me." Damn, she *did* think about him like that. It made his breathing change as his blood rushed south again.

"That's not for me, Mags."

"What *is* for you?" she asked softly.

You are, if I could have you.

He had to diffuse this conversation before he did something stupid. He swallowed nervously, turning to her,

"Didn't you hear? I'm married."

"Ha," she said softly, just as he had before, turning away from him. But her smile hadn't faded during the exchange, which made him ridiculously happy for no good reason.

"Anyway, you'll let me know if he comes? Graham? Gingy? So I can give you a hand?"

"Aye, I'll let you know."

But he wondered if she actually would. He worried that maybe she'd ask Beck to help since he was around all the goddamned time and so goddamned amenable to being whatever Maggie—*his* goddamned legal wife—required.

He cleared his throat, reaching for another pile of photos from the box on top of the trunk. "You, uh, you got all the papers signed? For the green card?"

"Mm-hm. Beck is very efficient."

"That ain't all."

She turned to him with pursed lips. "You've no reason not to like him."

"That's not what I hear," he answered in a low, sarcastic voice, narrowing his eyes.

"Och, look at you, growly bear!"

"It's not funny, Maggie."

"I never said it was."

"We're supposed to be married...I mean, Beck, of all people, shouldn't be sniffing around..."

"He knows it's a farce, Nils. He overheard every word you said to Missy."

Nils hissed, shaking his head. "Damn it."

"He's been a good friend to me. Besides—"

"A *friend*," Nils interrupted.

"Aye, a friend."

"*Just* a friend?"

"Not that it's any of your business, but aye, *just* a friend. There was a lot of paperwork and he walked me through all of it. And we had drinks a time or two. And—"

"And *what?*" he asked harshly, imagining Beck's hands on Maggie's body, imagining his hands around Beck's neck.

"We needed a fourth for euchre, for Lord's sake! He was kind enough to fill in," she said, huffing with attitude.

"Kind enough…" muttered Nils. "He wants to get into your pants!"

"Well, at least someone does!" she yelled back at him.

His jaw dropped as he stared at her. He could hear his heartbeat in his ears, furious and thrumming, as she stared back at him, thin-lipped and perturbed. His body had just started to calm down and damn if it didn't go on high alert again, because inside her pants was a destination that made him lose his mind with want.

"Maggie…" he started, his voice dangerously low.

"I shouldn't have said that. What happens inside my pants is—I mean, my pants and who goes into them isn't your concern…I mean, bloody hell, we shouldn't be discussin' this. It's none of your—"

"I'll be back for euchre on Thursday," he growled, interrupting her through gritted teeth. Talking about what happened inside of her pants was pushing him to the brink of his endurance. Not to mention, he was solidly against

Beck visiting there, no matter how selfish it made him.

"Huh. Just goin' to show up and expect to join us again?"

"Pretty much. My brother. My friend. My…" He gestured at her and the word "wife" hung between them, but he didn't say it, although he held her eyes, daring her to contradict him. "…*seat.*"

"Just come and go as you please, aye?"

"We needed a break. We had it. We're back to normal now."

They were anything but back to normal and they both knew it.

"Fine," she responded in a breathy voice, shifting away from him slightly. "Best get there early, though. And you can be the one to tell Beck."

"No problem," he said. It would be a pleasure to let Beck know that his card-playing services were no longer required. While he was at it, he might suggest that Beck stay the hell away from Maggie. Weren't there any other goddamned lawyers in Gardiner anyway? Old ones with gray hair and bushy eyebrows and yellow teeth?

"Two more pictures of your parents' honeymoon in Sweden. Looks like heaven. Have you been?"

"No," he answered, still annoyed with the whole Beck situation, hating like hell that someday, someone would take her away from him. Well, when that day came, he'd make damn sure the guy was good enough for Maggie, or else. "You?"

"Nae. I've been all about Scotland, of course, and to

England. And to Ireland, though I dinna remember it. And here."

"You've seen a lot more of the world than me, Maggie May."

"Where would you have gone?" She blushed and looked away. "If you'd really been married with a honeymoon and all?"

"Where would *we* have gone? You mean, theoretically?"

She shrugged. He'd had the fantasy about a million times since their wedding. It was almost a relief to verbalize it. "I'd have taken you to Sweden. To Åre, where my grandparents came from."

"Here?" She waved the pictures at him. "Skiin' at Åre? I've never skied a day in my life."

"But I'd teach you! All Lindstroms have to ski and since you're a Linds..." His face felt hot as he stopped himself, biting his lower lip, and taking the photos from her. "Anyway, that's where my folks went on their honeymoon. Erik and Kat went to England."

"I know. Kat kept me hostage at their weddin', askin' me every possible question," said Maggie, the affection for his brother and sister-in-law evident in her voice. "He's mad for her, isn't he?"

"He's mad for her," agreed Nils softly, watching her as she sifted through photos, tucking one into the back of the pile. For the next twenty minutes or so, they were quiet, working efficiently to sort through the remaining photos.

Nils glanced at her thoughtfully as she separated the pictures into two piles, evaluating each image for its merit or worth.

She was an anomaly, Maggie. She was a good businesswoman; he knew that. Her café ran smoothly and he knew for a fact that she turned a profit. And yet she didn't get her visa renewed on time. She fostered herself so easily to others: to him and his family, to Paul, to the children who came for story hour, to Beck…and yet her relationships with her own family members seemed so strained. She didn't make sense, and watching her as she took a moment to glance at each photo, he realized that he liked it that she didn't necessarily make sense. It kept him guessing. It kept him wondering. It kept him wishing he had a lifetime to figure her out.

"And who's this now? She looks a wee bit like me!" She held up another picture, and as his eyes shifted from the top of her sweet-smelling head to the teenagers in the photo, the room started spinning.

Veronica.

It was a picture of Veronica. Of him with his arms around Veronica in front of an archway of red and green balloons at the senior Christmas formal.

It was like the wind had been knocked out of him as he stared at the picture. It had been over ten years since he'd seen her picture and in no way had that time lessened the strength of his guilt, the gnawing, inescapable regret.

Her bright eyes were heavily made up and her pink lips tilted up in a tentative smile. Her reddish-blonde hair was styled in a high ponytail and her emerald green dress shimmered, the same color as his tie and cummerbund. That was the night...*the* night...

He felt dizzy and put his hands to his cheeks surprised to find them so hot.

"Nils, are you okay?"

"No, I...I need some air, I—" He pushed himself up from the floor as pictures scattered around him and half staggered over to the round window, wrenching the rusted latch open and pushing the bottom half moon forward to let in a rush of cool air. He rested his palms flat on the unfinished wooden wall on either side of the window frame and took a deep breath.

Jesus, she was so young. So goddamned young. And beautiful. And trusting.

And—in the end—terrified.

He took another breath, bowing his head forward. He had no business being married to Maggie, having the sort of feelings for Maggie that he did. He didn't have the right to be with anyone. He didn't have the right to love anyone or be loved.

He felt her hands on his back, tentative fingertips at first, then flat palms that rubbed gently from his shoulder blades down to his waist and up again. He suppressed a groan, fought against the throbbing longing to turn around and drag her up against his body, hold her, take comfort from her. *Take, take, take.*

"I dinna know what just happened," she said softly behind him. "That picture...upset you? She was someone special?"

He took one last deep breath, pushing back from the

wall and turning slowly to face her. "Aw, Maggie," he murmured, his voice thick in his ears. "If only I..."

Her eyes were stricken and concerned as they searched his face and her hands reached up to cup his cheeks gently.

"What, love?" she asked tenderly, her thumb stroking the stubbled skin of his jawline, soothing and heady at the same time. "What is it? I—"

"Nils? Son? You up here?" Mr. Lindstrom's voice from the foot of the stairs made them jerk back from each other.

"Uh...yeah, Pop."

He rubbed his palm over his lightly sweating forehead, putting his hands on his hips as Maggie stood helplessly beside him, still thoughtfully inspecting his face with knitted brows. His father's footsteps got closer.

"Maggie up here, too?" Mr. Lindstrom asked from the top of the stairs, eyes squinting as he adjusted to the sun shining into the dim, dusty room from the half-opened window in front of him.

"Lars told Maggie she could have some of Mamma's old cooking things. Pots and pans and such." Maggie looked at Nils in surprise and he gestured to a small pile of cooking ware in a neat collection by the mouth of the stairs.

"Maggie May," said Carl Lindstrom affectionately. "Can't think of anyone who should have them more than you."

Nils watched as Maggie's fingers went to the ring around her finger. She twisted it nervously.

"Promise you'll use them to make me a batch of shortbread?"

"I brought you some today," she said, and Nils noticed the tremor in her voice. She stepped forward to give his father a quick kiss on the cheek before heading to the stairs. After collecting the pots and pans in her arms, she gave Nils one last look before starting downstairs. "Thanks for them. I'll be off, I guess."

"You're not staying for dinner, Maggie?" asked Mr. Lindstrom.

She stopped on the second stair, turning around and picking through the dusty, hazy late-afternoon light to find Nils's eyes.

"She can't, Pop," said Nils in a low, controlled voice, staring back at her.

"S-sorry, Mr. L," she said quickly, holding the pots closer to her chest as she started back downstairs. "Not today."

Chapter 9

It didn't surprise Maggie that Nils started coming back into the Prairie regularly again. For all that their attic date had ended on an uncertain note, she had sensed his relief that their break from one another was over. Maggie felt the same way. She had missed him, and knowing that he hadn't meant the hurtful words he'd said to Missy changed her heart.

But in the days following their time in the attic, her mind circled endlessly around their conversations, trying to put together the puzzle of Nils Lindstrom, trying to understand him. What stumped her the most was his reaction to the prom picture; she'd never seen him so stricken, so shaken—the way he'd started sweating, his eyes staring at the image as if he was looking at a ghost. After hearing the ill-fated story of Maisy McKintrick, she knew that Nils wouldn't pursue her if there was a complication between them.

Who was the girl in the picture and why did Maggie have a growing suspicion that *she* was the complication? Was she an old girlfriend? Yes, she must have been. Their body language in the photo said that they weren't on an awkward first date; they meant something significant to each other. Not to mention, Nils's reaction to the picture had been so intense—almost devastated. Had something happened to her? Something dreadful? Whoever she was, Maggie was determined to figure out why she elicited such a strong reaction from Nils. But it would have to wait a bit. For now, she just wanted to figure out how they could live in a small town, be secretly married to each other, and still manage to spend time together as friends.

She was wiping down the bar on Thursday evening when Nils walked into the café, a big, teasing grin on his face as he winked at her and headed to their usual euchre table. She glanced at her watch and couldn't help but chuckle. He was two hours early for their game.

"So," she said, "back as promised."

"You did say to be early."

"Two hours? That'll do."

"It's my seat."

Maggie glanced around the room. A young high school couple was canoodling on the window seat between the bookcases and two off-duty police officers shared coffee at a table in the center of the room. It wouldn't get busy again for an hour or so, when the after-dinner traffic started. She took a seat across from him, grinning.

"And what exactly are you planning to do for two hours?"

"I like the view here," he teased, then shrugged. "I brought my Kindle."

"And what're you readin'?"

"Nothing exciting. There's this guy...Bill Bryson. He walked the Appalachian Trail a few years back then wrote a book about it. Called..."

"*A Walk in the Woods!*" said Maggie. "One of my bestsellers!"

She got up and reached for a dog-eared copy of the paperback on a nearby shelf, gazing down at the image of a bear head with the woods behind. She placed it on the table before him.

"That's the one."

"You work as a tour guide. You're always in the park. Why would you read somethin' like that in your free time?" she asked.

"I like what I like, Maggie May. Parks and tours. Hey, by the way...that reminds me. I have a tour this weekend, but my dad's hosting a little *Midsommardagen* supper at his place on Sunday night. Outdoors. Wanted me to tell you you're invited."

She grinned. "Lars already told me."

"Figures."

"I'll be there. But..." She tried not to look too disappointed. "...you won't be?"

"We'll see how fast I can make it back to town. I've been trying to pick up a little extra slack since Pop's got a long haul coming up in July—four-week tour. I'll be there, eventually, but I'll be a mess. Dusty from the trail. They want hiking."

She looked down quickly. He'd just described the beginning of her favorite fantasy...that he walks in the door of her apartment on a Sunday night, tanned and dirty from two days in the park, and without saying a word, she takes his hand and pulls him into her bathroom where's she's lit twenty tiny candles that flicker and fill the room with soft, romantic light. She kneels before him to unlace his muddy boots and takes her time undressing him, loving the clank of his belt buckle hitting her tile floor, the red dust floating from his clothes to cover the white basin of her sink. Once he's naked and hard as rock with wanting her, she pulls her dress over her head and slowly unhooks her bra. He makes a low sound in the back of his throat when her panties land softly on top of his jeans and she takes his hand, pulling him into the shower, which is hot and—

"Maggie? Mags?"

"W-What?"

"Where'd you go?"

"Oh, I, um…yes, you'll be dusty on Sunday night."

He screwed up his face at her, shaking his head. "I'll stop home and shower quick first. Or grab one at Pop's place. Did you hear anything I said after that?"

She looked into his blue eyes, her fantasy still vivid, making her stomach flutter like it could happen…someday. She smiled at him weakly.

"Where are you today?" he asked softly.

"Right here," she said, putting her palms on the table and pushing up. "Can I bring you a sandwich?"

He reached out and placed his palm over her hand, the rough warmth of his skin shocking and exhilarating because since Sunday she'd been longing for him to touch her again. She stared down at his hand covering hers, feeling her heart kick into a gallop.

"Mags, you okay?" The playful tone he'd used for most

of their little visit was replaced by a light, but sincere, concern.

She pulled her hand out from under his and nodded. "I'll make you somethin' to eat."

Turning back to the coffee bar, she wondered how much longer they could go on like this…how much longer they'd need to deny themselves what they both wanted, what they both needed, what already belonged to them.

***

Beck had taken it pretty well, thought Nils dryly as he shuffled the cards for the final hand. He glanced up to catch Beck at the bar, eyes narrowed, sipping his coffee and lingering like he had a reason. Nils had to hand it to his rival: Beck didn't give up easily. It was something that Nils actually respected in another man and he fleetingly wondered if he and Beck could have been friends if Maggie didn't stand between them.

But she did. She did.

And more and more, Nils was worried. He couldn't seem to stop thinking of her as belonging to him. His mind insisted on calling her his wife, regardless of the secret, sham status of their arrangement. And he knew he was wrong to block Beck from making a move on her, but he couldn't seem to help it. For the first time in fifteen years, he started wondering if he had any other options, if there was any possible way to share his life with someone, to—

"Deal, Nils, for God's sake! Those cards don't need more shuffling." Lars nudged him with his elbow.

"Anyone need a refill?" asked Maggie, and all three men

nodded yes. She balanced their cups and headed up to the bar as Nils watched her surreptitiously between flicking cards to the four spaces at the table.

Once behind the counter, she leaned forward and giggled at something Beck said. Nils's nose flinched in a sneer and he cleared his throat.

"I may have been wrong about them dating," said Lars, picking up his cards.

"I don't think they are," added Paul.

"Might be time for you to do something about her, though," said Lars gently, a thread of serious in his generally playful tone.

"Shut up, Lars."

"You know." Lars folded his cards in his hand and rested them against the table, zeroing in on his brother with uncompromising eyes. "I've tried to figure you out for years...I mean, you watch every move she makes; it's clear you like her. And it's not like you don't get with a Park Girl from time to time. Hell, you've even had girlfriends before. I remember that chick you dated in high school, Ver—"

"Enough," growled Nils, flattening his palm on the table with a loud slap.

"Let it go, Lars," advised Paul, as Maggie rejoined them.

"What're you boys fightin' about? Whatever it is, there's an end to it," she said, sliding their coffees across the table. "The party's in less'n two weeks. Where're you takin' your pop that day, Lars? So we can set up?"

"I was thinking that the park wouldn't be enough," he answered. "We need a real diversion."

"Hearts," bid Nils, still shaken that Veronica, who'd only lived in the shadows of his mind for years, had stepped into conversation with Maggie in the attic and now with Lars over euchre. It was like her spirit was bearing down on him, demanding something from him, or at least refreshing his memories to shame him away from Maggie, reminding him that he didn't deserve the sort of happiness she could offer him.

"So, what'd you come up with?" asked Paul. He glanced at his cards. "Pass."

"Clubs," answered Maggie, looking at Lars.

"There is only one diversion in the whole world that'd make Pop drop everything," said Lars, grinning. "I promised Jenny-girl we'd babysit Erin. We're taking her to Old Faithful and then to Mammoth Springs. Her first trip into the park with *Morfar* and *Onkel* Lars. My only worry is getting him back out again once he starts showing her everything!"

Nils nodded in approval at his little brother. He had to hand it to Lars. It was the perfect distraction. Like every other Lindstrom man, their father was crazy about that little girl; if anyone could keep his attention occupied, it was definitely Erin.

Nils was distracted by Maggie, whose shoulders were shuddering as she stared at her cards, desperately trying to hold back her giggles.

"Maggie, what's so funny?" Lars's brows were knitted together as he watched Maggie warily.

She erupted into gales of laughter, finally looking up at all of them with tears in her eyes. "She's in a car seat! She's six months old!"

"Jen said she likes car rides," Lars grumbled.

"Oh, I'm sure she does," said Maggie, still trembling with laughter. "But, more to the point…do you and your da like changin' diapers? Babies dinna like cold bottles either. Where're you goin' to find warm water in the middle of the park? Canna use the geyser water, Lars!"

"Diapers and bottles? Damn it," said Lars, grimacing before gathering his cards in his hands and throwing them into the center of the table. "I'm out. I got a phone call to make."

He grabbed his jacket and they heard him exclaim, "Jenny! It's Lars! What the…" into his phone as he walked out of the Prairie Dawn.

"I think Lars is about to get schooled in babies." Paul watched him go and then turned to Maggie with a grin. "I should go, too. We have the graduation rehearsal tomorrow and I'm still working on my speech."

"Another year down, huh?" asked Nils, gathering the cards. Looking around, he realized the café had mostly cleared out over the couple of hours they'd been playing, although Beck still lingered at the bar, looking at a newspaper.

"Thank God," sighed Paul. "I'm running out of steam. Summer can't come fast enough."

"You goin' to let me try to find you a nice lass this summer?" asked Maggie.

Paul cringed, looking over at Nils for help. Nils smiled at his friend then looked away, shuffling the cards before straightening them into a neat deck. Lord's sake, Paul and his brothers had given him a hard time often enough about Maggie. Turnabout was fair play.

"Aw, Maggie. No offense, but you're a terrible matchmaker."

"One time! One time, I tried to set you up with—"

"One? Try three! And all awful dates!"

"Well, there aren't that many women to choose from. Plus, I think you're a wee too picky."

"Picky? The last one had shingles, for Chrissakes! And that's all she talked about. No dates! No more." Paul rolled his eyes, pushing away from the table and throwing on a windbreaker. "I mean it. Nils, tell her I'm serious."

"He *seems* very serious, Maggie."

"He doesn't know what he needs."

Nils smiled at her and shook his head back and forth, shrugging at Paul.

Paul smirked at Nils. "Oh, you're lots of help. Thanks for nothing." Then to Maggie, "I mean it. NO MORE."

"We'll see…" said Maggie in a singsong voice as Paul headed out the door grumbling about people needing to mind their own business. "I love teasin' him."

"Do you set him up on bad dates on purpose?"

"Tsk!" she scolded, touching her fingers to her chest in mock outrage which was ruined by her lips quivering with another round of giggles. "Would I ever do somethin' that devious?"

"I think you're lowering the bar so that when you present someone marginally appropriate, he gives it a shot."

"How rude! You certainly have a low opinion of me," she teased.

"Not at all," he said, looking up at her. "I know that women can't stand to see a bachelor."

"It's in our nature to pair you all off."

Nils nodded, looking at her, the irony of their situation making the air suddenly thick and meaningful between them.

Her cheeks finally flushed and as she took a sip of her coffee, he stared at her for an extra beat, at her pink freckled cheeks and delicate strawberry-blonde eyelashes.

Tonight had felt so normal, so much like the easy, teasing relationship he'd always shared with her, he'd almost forgotten about the green-card marriage. His longing for her, familiar and throbbing like a constant ache, was something he could handle, something he'd handled for years. It was the circumstance of marrying her that had confused things in his mind. And as he stared at her, he realized that his feelings for her were so deep and so possessive, he wasn't going to be able to hold out against the strength of them much longer. The overwhelming urge to reach out to her—to touch her, to take from her, to be with her, to belong with her—was so alive inside of him, it felt like heat, like his blood was on fire with the force of it.

"Tonight was fun," she said softly, tilting her head like all of the Lindstroms and grinning at him. "But it's time to close up. Give me a hand?"

"What about him?" he lifted his chin, gesturing to Beck, still installed at the bar.

Maggie took a deep breath and sighed. "Give me a

minute."

He watched the sway of her slim hips as she walked over to Beck with a gentle smile on her face. He knew the one...he'd seen her give it to men before. She was going to let Beck go. She was going to tell him—with her eyes and lips and the soft finality of her words—that he didn't have a chance. She was going to tell him to go and when he asked why, she was going to look over meaningfully at Nils who could offer her...nothing.

The moment Maggie had started toward him, Beck had looked up and trained a toothpaste commercial smile on her. She'd essentially blown him off all night to play euchre with Nils, but Beck had waited. He liked her. He must *really* like her.

And that's when Nils felt it: a feeling so sharp and bitter, he wanted to fight it, but couldn't, because his heart whispered these words:

If you love her, get out of the way.

Let her be with Beck. He's smart and successful. He's been kind to her. He's proving himself worthy.

You have no right to stand in the way of her happiness.

It ached and twisted to acknowledge the truth, but he knew it was the right thing to do. Before he lost his will, he jumped up from the table, heading for the door. As he got there, Maggie called out. "Nils! Wait! You're not leavin'?"

He heard the disappointment in her voice, the confusion. It made his heart clench with profound sadness, but in a strange, unexpected way, it also felt good to do the right thing. It felt good not to be selfish. He stopped with his hand on the door handle, fixing an easy, polite smile on his face and looking up at her.

"Beck can give you a hand."

"But…" Her face twisted and she held out her hand toward him. The hand he'd held. The hand that bore her wedding ring.

It took all the strength he had to nod once to Beck, holding on to his smile, and damn if Beck Westman didn't seem to understand completely, his narrow eyes relaxing as he nodded slowly back at Nils.

"Sure, I can give you a hand," he said. "'Night, Nils."

"'Night, all."

Without looking back, Nils stepped out into the cool evening, his heart breaking a little more with every heavy step that took him away from her.

***

"Well, Beck Westman! What a surprise!" greeted Mr. Lindstrom, approaching Beck and Maggie and extending his hand in greeting. "You've come with our Maggie, have you? How nice. Um, welcome! Welcome to *Midsommardagen* supper."

Maggie smiled gratefully at Nils's father as she leaned forward and accepted a kiss on the cheek. "I hoped you wouldna mind."

"More the merrier at *Midsommar*, Maggie May," he said thoughtfully, catching and holding her eyes. He was dumb like a fox, Mr. Lindstrom. He knew something was up. Putting his arm around Beck's shoulders, he led him toward the table that held a metal tub of beverages icing in the middle. "You like Swedish beer, Beck?"

Paul sidled up beside Maggie, elbowing her in the ribs. "Really?"

She shrugged, having a hard time meeting Paul's glare. "He wanted to come."

"You want to get him killed?"

"So dramatic," she said, rolling her eyes and taking in the festive setup on Mr. Lindstrom's front lawn.

Four picnic tables had been pushed end to end to end and covered with white paper tablecloths. Jelly jars lined the table acting as both decoration and paperweights. Half contained yellow and blue wildflowers cut from Mrs. Lindstrom's *Midsommar* garden and the other half had votive candles set in sand on the bottom of the jars. They weren't lit yet, but later the glow from the jars would create a warm and intimate atmosphere for everyone seated at the picnic tables for supper once the sun finally started to set.

Maggie looked to her left, toward the park where the mountains were backlit by a sun that still had two hours of daylight to share, and saw a massive bonfire built on the edge of the front lawn, ready to be lit after dinner. Comfortable chairs and blankets were scattered around the ring of heavy stones welcoming guests to linger until the sun came up.

Closer to the house, she could hear merry Swedish folk music and noticed the massive grill set up with Lars at the helm, the smell of grilling meats and sausages making Maggie's mouth water. There would also be herring, herring, and more herring, of course, potato salad, Swedish cheeses, various breads, and smoked salmon. And always for dessert, Kringla cookies in the shape of eternity symbols with fresh strawberries and whipped cream.

Midsommardagen was—hands down—Maggie's favorite annual event, and no one did it better than Carl Lindstrom.

She did a brief perimeter search for Nils, but her heart dropped traitorously when she didn't see him.

"Dramatic? *I'm* being dramatic?" asked Paul, poking her in the ribs. "You've *met* the Lindstrom brothers, right?"

Aye, she'd met them.

And when she'd watched one of them—the one she was married to, in fact—walk away from her on Thursday night to leave her with Beck, something inside of her had snapped.

As the door swung closed behind Nils, she'd fixed a bright smile on her face and invited Beck to be her date tonight, a decision she wasn't regretting...yet.

"Tall? Blond? Stubborn? Aye. Rings a bell." She took a deep, shaky breath and sighed. "Is he here?"

"Not yet. Tour ran late." Paul pursed his lips at Maggie, furrowing his brows as he looked at her. "Are you going to tell me what's going on with you two?"

"What do you mean?"

"Maggie, it's *me*."

"Paul, it's *complicated.*"

"You two have been weird for a month now. Then it seemed okay on Thursday night— back to normal. Now you show up here with Beck. I can't figure out what's going on, but my male intuition tells me it's going to end badly."

Maggie looked over at Beck in his sharply creased khaki pants, a yellow sweater tied casually around his shoulders. He looked out of place, yet his body language was easy as he tipped back his beer, chatting with Mr. Lindstrom. For the hundredth time, she wished she could fall in love with him. How she wished her heart wasn't already taken.

"Dinna be ridiculous. Nils and I are just—"

"Friends? Like hell."

"Ask him yourself. Friendship is all he wants from me. He's made that clear more than once."

"Maybe that's what he says…but it's certainly not what I see."

"Please, Paul." Maggie put her hand on Paul's arm, looking up into his blue eyes beseechingly as hers watered with longing and despicable, implacable hope. "I canna bear it."

Then she turned away from him and smiled at Beck, who popped the top off a Swedish beer, holding it out to her with a grin.

***

Eight-thirty.

Nils glanced at his watch as he drove under the arch, back into Gardiner, headed for the Best Western where he'd drop off his group of five. Looking straight ahead, he could just make out the glow of his father's bonfire as the sun started to set on the horizon.

Bonfire already started. He frowned. He'd be good and late to the festivities.

Maybe that was for the best, though. Less time with

Maggie. She was probably sitting there right now on a picnic bench between his dad and Lars, waiting for him to show up. How was he supposed to withstand those hopeful, disappointed green eyes?

Honestly, Nils was at a loss about what to do except stay away from her. He knew she had feelings for him, and after admitting that he hadn't been honest with Missy, she could assume he did, too. But he'd also been clear with her that a future was patently impossible, so she really had no choice but to move on, right? And Beck seemed like a good man. He had a good job. Didn't have a reputation for womanizing. And damn if he wasn't persistent, hanging around her for weeks now. At least *he* could offer her something.

Nils pulled into the motel parking lot, stopped in front of the reception area, and exited the van to open the sliding door for the Parker family. The mother and three teenage children hopped out, thanking Nils and chattering about the hot tub as they hurried toward their room. Mr. Parker stopped in front of Nils for a moment, extending his hand.

"Excellent tour, Nils. Thank you."

Nils smiled politely, shaking hands with the man he'd just spent the better part of two days and nights accompanying through the park.

"My pleasure, Mr. Parker. I hope you'll consider us again if you return to Yellowstone. My brother is an ace at ferreting out the wildlife. Sorry we didn't see much today."

"We saw plenty. And I don't have any plans to be back this summer, but we have some friends heading west in two weeks. I think I'll give them your name. Have time on your schedule in July?"

"Absolutely, sir. My father's got a group for the whole month, so we're down a guide, but between me and my brother, we'll take care of your friend."

"Name of Callahan. From Boston."

"Callahan. I'll keep an ear out for them, sir."

"That's just fine, Nils." He put his hand into his back pocket and pulled out his wallet, taking out a hundred dollar bill and folding it before offering it to Nils. "Thanks again."

Nils took the tip and nodded once before saying goodbye and turning back to the van. He checked his watch again. *Eight-fifty.* He turned the van back toward his father's place, steeling himself for Maggie's pleading smile even as his mouth watered for cold beer and herring.

***

Maggie smiled with the rest of the guests as Mr. Lindstrom recalled last summer's *Midsommardagen* celebration at the Triple Peak Lodge when Jenny had announced the news that his first grandchild was on the way.

"There's naught better in the world than a granddaughter, folks!" He raised his glass and thirty other raised arms joined him in toasting. *"Skål!"*

"Were you there?" asked Beck softly, turned slightly to face her in the candlelight, as other guests resumed their dinner and conversations. "Last year?"

Lars, Paul, and Mr. Lindstrom had just walked the length of the tables with lighters, picking up the jelly jars and lighting the votives. Candlelight cast a warm glow over the festivities, as guests filled up on the bounty offered at the extensive *midsommarbord*, or *midsommar* table.

"I wasn't," said Maggie. "I was invited, but I was also short-staffed at the café…and they're kind to me, the Lindstroms, but I horn in enough."

"I doubt they see it that way," said Beck, placing his beer bottle back on the table and grinning at her. "I can't imagine anyone getting tired of your company. Especially me."

Her cheeks flushed at his compliment. "You're sweet to me, Beck."

"If you'd give me a chance, I could be more than just sweet, Maggie Leslie."

Maggie shivered lightly and Beck's hands went immediately to the knot on his sweater to offer it to her. "You chilly?"

"I'm okay."

He put his arm around her shoulders, pulling her closer to him. "If you won't take my sweater, at least take my body heat."

She swallowed, feeling eyes on her. When she looked up, Paul and Lars stared at her from across the table. She nestled a little closer to Beck in response to their censure and her heart jumped a touch when his fingers curled over her shoulder with a tiny bit of pressure. He was so kind to her, so reassuring. With a full belly and a slight buzz from the three or four beers it had taken for her to loosen up, she almost felt cozy enough to close her eyes.

Except the bright lights of an approaching van made

them open just a little bit wider as her heart dove, danced, somersaulted, and cheered, pumping faster and faster as she realized that Nils had finally arrived. Her lips tilted up and she lifted her head from Beck's shoulder, taking a deep breath and sitting up straighter.

He's here! He's here, cried her heart in glee, and she had to place her hands on her knees to keep herself from standing up and running to his side.

Mr. Lindstrom and Lars leaped up as the headlights brightened the party then released it back to darkness. Maggie watched as Nils swung his body out of the driver's side door, accepting a hug from his father first, then his brother. The three men talked by the side of the van for a moment, and Maggie strained her ears to distinguish Nils's voice from his father and brother, her eyes riveted on his tall, solid body as he finally headed toward the table in the dusky light. His jeans looked rumpled and worn and she could tell that his white *Lindstrom & Sons* polo shirt was covered with dust. Muscles deep inside of her body clenched with longing, her shower fantasy running through her mind like a tease. And then—suddenly—there he was, sitting down at the table where his brother had been sitting diagonally across from her, tilting back a bottle of beer as Mr. Lindstrom handed him a clean plate.

He thanked his father over his shoulder, then, starting at the end of the table, he carefully scanned the guests in the flickering candlelight until his eyes found and rested on Maggie, where they stopped. Where they stayed.

His lips parted slightly, softly, as he stared at her, first her eyes, then dropping to her lips, then his gaze dipped lower to the low scoop neck of her Swedish blouse, one that Jenny had given to her years ago for her first *Midsommardagen* dinner with the Lindstroms.

Maggie's heart pounded like a tribal drum, flushing her face with arousal as she stared back at him. His face was tan and rugged after two straight days in the park, and his almost-white blond hair seemed slightly redder from trail dust. His white teeth peeked through the pillows of his lips as he grinned at her, and without meaning to, she smiled back, her fingers reaching up to brush over her lips, seeking the imprint of their wedding kiss. His wide blue eyes stayed fastened on hers as he picked up his beer and tipped it back, and she watched, transfixed, as his throat worked to swallow it, the taut, corded muscles clenching and relaxing.

But as he put the beer back down on the table, something in his face changed. His smoldering eyes narrowed and shifted to her shoulder, lingering there for an extra moment before whipping his face back to hers, an angry question furrowing his brows.

"How was the tour, Nils?" asked Beck from beside her, his hand massaging her shoulder gently.

Maggie's eyes widened in realization—Good God, she'd forgotten that Beck had his arm around her!—and it was like watching a spell break and shatter before her eyes. Nils's eyes shuddered closed before her and he looked down at his plate, reaching for a platter to fill it.

***

"It was fine," he muttered, but his stomach was churning.

Even as he'd left them alone in the café on Thursday night, he was wholly unprepared to see them together, Beck's arm around her like they were a couple, like they were out on a date, which he guessed they were.

Nils took a deep breath and reached for the smoked salmon, his voracious appetite ebbing away as the ache in his heart slowed the galloping excitement that had started the moment his eyes had landed on her face.

He couldn't help his kneejerk reaction, but he tried to reason with himself and calm down. *It's for the best. It's for the best. If you can't give her happiness, let someone else try.*

He spooned some of the salmon onto his plate and when he replaced the dish, Paul was nudging him with a platter of grilled meats. "What else do you want, Nils?"

Maggie. I want Maggie. That's all I want. The words swam aimlessly, fruitlessly in his head and he couldn't even look up at Paul, quietly picking a few things off the platter that plopped inelegantly onto his plate.

"Can you pass that cheese plate down here?" asked Paul, swapping out the meats for the cheeses.

In a matter of seconds, Nils's plate was piled with his favorite Swedish foods, some of which he waited for all year, but his mouth tasted like sawdust and his appetite was gone. He took another swig of beer and looked up again to find the two spaces that Maggie and Beck had occupied were vacant now. He twisted his neck toward the fire and caught them walking—with Beck's goddamned arm still around her shoulders—toward the fire ring where the flames licked the sky and sparks dotted the landscape like low-hanging stars.

"She showed up with him," Paul offered softly.

Nils tucked into the plate of food, barely tasting anything.

"Have they kissed?" he demanded in a low, anguished whisper without thinking. He had no idea what made him ask this question, and suddenly he wasn't even sure he wanted an answer. He didn't trust himself not to rush Beck and beat him bloody if the answer was "yes."

"No," said Paul. "Not that I've seen."

His shoulders relaxed and he took another bite of food then pushed the plate away. "I'm taking a shower if Pop asks for me."

Paul nodded as Nils swung his body out of the bench, grabbing his beer and casting one last look at Maggie and Beck sitting side by side on a blanket by the fire.

Good, he thought, clenching his jaw so tightly it made his head ache. *Beck'll be good for Maggie.* He stalked toward the front porch of his father's house, his boots pounding loudly against the three steps. *This is what I wanted, right?*

He practically ripped the screen door off its hinges opening it. It slammed into the porch wall then whipped back to slap the doorframe as he beelined through his father's living room to the stairs. He took them two at a time, turning right to the room he had shared with Lars and Erik growing up. He and Lars both kept a change of clothes at their father's house, and he yanked the dresser drawer open, grabbing clean jeans, boxer shorts, and an old navy-blue and orange t-shirt that read "Go Broncos!"

It was only then that he noticed his hands were shaking.

He backed up against the bed, tugging his dirty polo shirt over his head, then bent his neck, his palm coming up to rest on his forehead as his elbow braced on his thigh.

"Damn," he snarled softly, rubbing his forehead as though he could erase the image of Beck's arm around Maggie's shoulders.

***

Maggie's heart felt brick heavy sitting next to Beck by the bonfire.

He was trying his best to make conversation with her, but it was no use. She could barely give him monosyllabic answers. To see Nils's face—full of unguarded joy—slip into cold darkness on a dime had taken all of the fun out of the celebration and all she wanted to do was go home.

He had practically *thrown* her at Beck on Thursday night, yet tonight he'd looked almost murderous at the sight of Beck's hand on her shoulder. He was hot and cold, attracted to her, yet keeping her at arm's length. She didn't understand him, and she'd had just about enough of his mind games.

Her eyes welled with tears of frustration and sorrow. She swiped at them then pushed up from the blanket. "Beck, do you mind if we get goin'?"

He stood up beside her, dusting off his hands on his pants. "Whenever you're ready."

The lump in her throat was so thick, she worried she'd cry when she said goodbye to Mr. Lindstrom and Lars, but she couldn't very well leave such a nice dinner without saying thank you.

"I'm just goin' to go inside and use the bathroom first," she said.

I'll splash some cold water on my face, give myself a firm talking-to, then come downstairs and say my goodbyes.

She looked over at the long table that sat mostly in candlelight, still lined with dinner guests. Nils would still be eating his dinner. She took a deep breath and turned toward the house. Stomping up the steps, she opened the screen door too forcefully and it slapped against the wall of the porch then flew back and slammed shut.

Calm down, Maggie.

Rubbing her burning eyes, she walked quietly through the living room and dining room, to the stairs beside the kitchen. As she headed upstairs to the bathroom, she looked at the pictures on the wall: Nils and Lars grinning in snowsuits with goggles perched atop their blond heads; all four Lindstrom children sitting on a boulder somewhere in Yellowstone; Jenny on her wedding day, Erik on his. About two steps from the top, she reached out and gingerly touched a photo of Nils holding Erin against his chest as he sat in a recliner, his eyes closed as the tiny infant dozed.

"You came here with Beck."

Her head whipped up to see Nils standing at the top of the stairs.

Oh...my...God...

His chest was bare and his jeans were unbuttoned and unzipped to reveal the plaid cotton of his underwear beneath. Her mind went utterly blank as she stared at the V of exposed muscle that tapered from his waist to his hips, pointing effortlessly to his—

A small sound escaped from her throat and she bit her lip, forcing herself to look away. Flicking her eyes up to his face, she felt herself exhale, the first indication that she'd been holding her breath as she ogled him like a stripper. She must have swayed, because his free hand snaked out to grab her wrist, tugging her gently up the remaining steps until they stood facing each other in the dim light of the upstairs hallway.

"You brought Beck to *Midsommardagen*," he growled.

She could barely breathe, but her spirit rallied to put together a response.

"Isn't that what you wanted?"

His fingers tightened around her wrist as he stared at her, and she wished she could still the wild fluttering of her heart, but she was surrounded by him; he smelled of sweat and sun and fresh air. She dropped her eyes to the solid wall of his chest, tan and smooth, his nipples prominent and hard against the contour of muscle. She was surprised to see two crosses—one slightly larger than the other—tattooed over his heart with the date 2001, and she longed to know the story behind them, to reach out and trace the shape of them, to press her lips to them and rest her head against them so that his heart could beat under her ear.

His thumb stroked the soft skin inside of her wrist and when she glanced down at his fingers against her skin, she noticed the red dust of the trail on his corded forearms. She licked her lips and her insides leaped with want, as her fantasy cycled through her mind, coming to life before her in startlingly beautiful detail.

When she looked up at his face, his eyes searched hers, his lips pursed into a tense line. And then his head was bending softly toward hers, his lips closer and closer.

"Nils," she sighed, stepping closer to him, ready to fall into him, to wrap her arms around him and succumb to whatever he could offer, whatever he was able to give.

But, at the sound of her voice, he froze, his eyes refocusing on her face as he drew back with a grimace.

"I never wanted any of this," he choked out in an angry, tortured voice. "None of it."

"Any of what?" she asked in a whisper, stepping toward him again, her breasts brushing his chest through the thin linen of her blouse, her neck tilted back to hold his eyes, daring him to finish what he'd almost started.

He winced and then shook his head, releasing her wrist like he was surprised to find himself still holding it. He swallowed, staring at her for one more second before stepping around her to walk into the bathroom and close the door behind him with a decisive click.

Maggie raised her hands to her flaming cheeks, rooted in place, her brain overloaded by the image of half-naked Nils. He'd almost kissed her. This time she was sure of it. *What did it mean?* He pushed her into Beck, but fought his will to kiss her. She touched her wrist gently with the fingers of her other hand, as one thought circled relentlessly in her head: *How much more will it take for you to surrender to me?*

Chapter 10

After their electric meeting in Mr. Lindstrom's upstairs hallway, Maggie had to admit, she was both excited and apprehensive about seeing Nils again. Excited because she felt him caving to his attraction to her, apprehensive because she knew if he did, they'd have a whole new set of problems to solve together.

That there was scorching chemistry between them was undeniable. Ever since the morning after he'd helped her to bed, she'd felt it. It had only increased through his offer to marry her, taking their wedding vows and working together on his father's party. Every time they were near each other, they practically set off sparks from the strength of their attraction.

Yes, he *said* he only wanted to be her friend, but all the while she watched him fight their attraction to each other with every ounce of strength.

She thought about Nils, who he was, what she knew of him. Over the years she'd learned actions spoke louder than words with Nils. They always had. Before his short speech on the attic stairs, he'd never admitted that he cared for her aloud and yet he was always there for her—when she was drunk and needed someone to walk her home, when something broke at her shop and needed fixing, for God's good sake, when she'd needed someone to marry her for a green card. He'd showed her how much he cared about her before he'd ever said the words.

So, what is he showing you now? she asked herself.

She thought of his eyes as he caught hers on Saturday night, the joyful, hungry way he'd captured her face, followed by fury when he'd noticed Beck's hand. The way he'd seized her wrist on the stairs, holding it as he bent his head to kiss her before stopping himself. He'd done the same thing in the attic. Stopped himself. That was it. He kept stopping himself from touching her, being with her, loving her, giving them a chance.

Why? Why wouldn't he give into it? Why did he deny himself when it was so clear he had feelings for her?

As she sorted out her thoughts and feelings over the week following *Midsommardagen*, she became more and more certain that there was something—or someone—significant standing between them. It was the reason he kept nudging her toward Beck. It was the reason he kept her at arm's length.

She rinsed out the plunger from the French press she used for decaf espresso, lazily running her hands over the slick stainless steel as she ruminated. Friday afternoon summer sun streamed into the windows of the quiet café. Should she confront him? She grimaced as the words formed in her head:

*I know you want me as much as I want you...*Yuck. No. Too self-assured.

I know your mouth is sayin' you only want to be friends, but your eyes are sayin' you want—Ugh. No way. It sounded like the worst pickup line ever.

I know you almost kissed me on the stairs at your dad's house... What if he looked at her in shock and denied it all as he had to Missy? How would she bear the humiliation? She shook her head in defeat.

Man of action. He's a man of action. The words circled in her head and suddenly her eyes widened and she knew the answer to her conundrum even before the idea solidified in her head. Of course. The key to cracking Nils wasn't conversation, it was action. And if *he* wouldn't make the first move, that only left one option...

"Hey! Where do you have to go to get a good cup of coffee around here anyway?"

Maggie looked up, her thoughts scattering and a smile taking over her face to find Jenny Lindstrom Kelley standing in the doorway of the Prairie, holding baby Erin in her arms.

"Right here!" she exclaimed, hurrying around the corner of the counter and running to embrace her friend. "Och, Jen! It's good to see you! And here's Erin, so bonny!"

Jenny was as tall and blonde as ever, her long hair braided back into a tail and her slim body totally recovered from Erin's birth six months ago. Maggie raised her eyes to see Sam over her shoulder. *Damn, but some girls have all the luck.*

"Heya, Maggie," he greeted her affectionately, his brown eyes sparkling.

"Heya, Sam. How's it feel to be a father?"

"Like a duck to water. Don't know what I ever did

without these two troublemakers."

Jenny turned to look at her husband in indignation. "Troublemakers? *We're* the troublemakers? *We* weren't the ones dating supermodels and—"

He chuckled at her. "Weather girls. Get your facts straight."

Jenny grinned back at him then turned to Maggie. "Want to hold her?"

"Of course I do! Give her to me!"

Jenny carefully transferred the sleeping infant from her arms to Maggie's, smiling at her friend once the baby was settled. "Mind if I make coffee for me and Sam?"

Maggie looked up, blissful with the weight of Erin against her, her own heart longing for one of her own someday. Someday.

"You remember where everythin' is?"

"I spent many an evening here crying into my coffee, Mags. I think I do."

"Who was she crying over?" asked Sam, winking at Maggie.

"A *troublemaker* who blew into town from Chicago," Jenny said, over her shoulder as she headed around the counter.

Maggie edged carefully into a barstool, staring down at Erin's perfect little fingers with paper-thin fingernails that clutched the blanket wrapped around her. Maggie leaned down and breathed in the singular scent of baby, closing her eyes to savor the moment. She barely heard the bell over the door ring.

"Nils!" exclaimed Jenny, running back around the counter to launch herself into her older brother's arms. "You got my text!"

Maggie looked up to watch the reunion, Nils's face breaking into a delighted, unguarded smile. Jenny was someone on his short list, just like Maggie.

The realization boosted her fragile courage and she'd take whatever extra she could get. She'd already decided what she needed to do. She just needed to figure out when.

Maggie turned to Sam, who stood beside her, and nudged him. "Take her for me? I'll make the coffee."

Sam gently took Erin back, but not before Maggie lifted her eyes to find Nils staring at her as she cuddled his niece. Several emotions passed across his face: hope, happiness, awe...and finally, regret. He looked away, back at Jenny, who stood before him.

"Got here safely?"

"As you see," she answered. "Erik and Kat here yet?"

Nils shook his head. "Erik said not to expect them until dinnertime or later. Something about stopping to pee every half hour, but damned if I know what he's talking about."

Jenny chuckled softly as Maggie took four colorful mugs off the shelf and started filling them with coffee. "Kat's seven months pregnant with twins, Nils. Have a heart."

"You know I don't understand a lick of that women's stuff, Jen."

"Someday you might," said Jenny, and though Maggie had her back to them, she felt Jenny's eyes boring into the back of her head. She wished, for a moment, she could give the younger woman a good smack on her backside. The last thing Maggie and Nils needed this weekend was more teasing.

"*Mamma* always kept that lady business between you and her," Nils retorted, sitting down at the counter. When Maggie turned around, his cheeks were bright pink with embarrassment.

"Always wondered if that was a mistake," mused Jenny, taking a seat beside him.

"Jenny, give him a break," sighed Sam, rolling his eyes good-naturedly at his wife.

"Always liked you Sam," said Nils, taking the coffee from Maggie, his eyes seeking hers across the copper bar. When his finger grazed hers it sent a jolt of heat through her whole body. "Always liked you a lot."

She kept her eyes locked with his for an extra beat. Her decision was made:

The next time they were alone together, she would make her move.

***

Nils had to return to the office after coffee, but they had all agreed to meet back at the Prairie at eight o'clock to start setting up for the party. In the meantime, Jenny and Sam had gone back to his pop's house to settle Erin for a nap. His pop had agreed to babysit for her this evening so that Jenny and Sam could have a "date night," which was good. They didn't want him suddenly showing up at the Prairie Dawn looking for a cup of coffee and ruining the surprise.

The hours went by slowly as Nils waited for eight to roll around. He fielded one call from the McCarthy group, who wondered if they could get started tomorrow instead of Sunday, but with the party tomorrow, Nils insisted the tour would need to start on Sunday as planned. They reconciled all of the June accounts and reviewed all of the July tours that Nils and Lars would be taking care of single-handedly while Pop took care of the McCarthys for the entirety of July. His father headed home at six o'clock and even though Nils was anxious to get out of the office and itchy to see Maggie, he dreaded the inevitable war that waged inside of him every time he did.

Damn, but his attraction to her, which he didn't think could possibly get any stronger, had strengthened since their wedding, and he was having a tougher and tougher time fighting against his longing for her, the sharp ache of want that accompanied every meeting now.

The only thing that managed to squelch his passion were memories of Veronica, but even those recollections seemed to be losing their vibrancy, their hold on him. And he was desperate to keep them alive, because without them—without the potent reminder of how he'd destroyed someone's life, of what he'd lost—he'd be in jeopardy of making the same mistakes again. The very thought of Maggie meeting Veronica's tragic end twisted his heart so painfully, it left him breathless. Better to have her safe and fight against his feelings than be weak and give in to them.

The buzzing of his cell phone broke his trance, and he looked down at his desk to see a text message from

Maggie.

Any chance you can come early to finish the slideshow?

He took in the neat, quiet office with one sweeping glance. **When?**

Now? I have the pictures scanned, but need your help captioning them.

He grimaced. Without Jenny and Sam there as a buffer, he worried about being alone with Maggie. His self-control was running on fumes. But, his conscience tried to convince him otherwise: *She's done all this work for your pop's party. The least you can do is give her a hand when she asks. Stop being a selfish ass.*

I'll come over in 10 min, he responded.

Gr8. I'll say good-night to Beck and close up now.

Nils felt his lips purse and his eyes narrow as he stared at the text. Beck. Goddamned Beck. Jealousy made his cheeks hot as he closed up the office in double time. The mere thought of Maggie with Beck was enough to reduce Nils to a caveman who wanted to throw Maggie over his shoulder, lock her in his bedroom and have his way with her, whatever the goddamn consequences. The thought of Beck made Nils reckless.

He grabbed his phone and shoved it in his pocket, hurrying to the Prairie and vaulting up the stairs to Maggie's apartment where she was already waiting for him without a sign of Beck. An hour later they were still working through the slides, putting them in order and captioning them.

Torture. That's the only word he could use to describe the close proximity of her body to his as they sat side by side on her living room floor with her laptop open on her lap and a throw pillow on his. He'd grabbed the pillow from the couch behind them as his dick turned to stone in the first five minutes of sitting beside her.

Her strawberry shampoo, light and taunting, made his breath catch every time she moved her head slightly, and every time she bent her elbows to type, she grazed his waist. It was becoming more and more painful, and yet if he left her side, he wouldn't be able to look at the pictures with her, defeating the whole point of him being there in the first place. Best just to struggle through and get out of there as soon as possible.

"And this one?" she asked, turning her head slightly to catch his eyes with hers. She moved her leg slightly and it brushed against his.

He tried to hide the way his body tensed and purposely stared at the photo and not her. "Oh, yeah. That's Jenny and Pop entering the father-daughter fish-off at Upper Slide."

Maggie's fingers flew across the keyboard as she typed the caption then clicked on the next photo, wiggling her hips just enough to graze his. His breath hitched for a second. *Was she doing it on purpose?*

"Is this you?" Maggie asked softly, staring at the screen, touching it gingerly with her fingers.

Nils leaned his head to the side a little, careful not to touch hers, but she leaned hers at the same time, and her soft hair caressed his cheek. He held his breath to see if she'd draw away, but she didn't. His whole body felt like a finely tuned instrument, ready to be touched, ready to be played. He glanced at the picture, trying to ignore her, ignore his body, ignore his lust and raging hard-on. *Look at the picture. Look at the picture, damn it.*

It was a black and white photo of a little boy who smiled down at the baby on his lap.

"Me and Jenny-girl," he responded.

"How old were you?"

"I was six. She was new."

"New?"

"Mmm. She'd just come home. I think I was pretty sure she was *my* baby. Prettiest little thing I'd ever seen."

"*Your* baby?"

"My little girl. My *mamma* had stressed that little girls needed their big brothers to look out for them and since I was the biggest, I was pretty sure she meant me and only me. I walloped Lars and Erik good whenever they got too close that first year."

"I didn't know you felt that way…a-about babies."

He flinched, sitting upright, pulling away from her.

"Nils?" she asked softly in that musical voice he loved so much. She tilted her head to look at him with her wide green eyes, and he clenched his jaw.

He couldn't stand much more of this. He couldn't.

"I won't."

Damn it, he was so distracted by her, the words had tumbled out before he could stop them, before he even realized his mouth had formed them.

"Won't what?"

"Have children," he murmured, running a hand over his jaw, which felt hot and tight. "Have a family."

"W-what? Why not?"

"It's just not possible."

"Oh. Were you…sick? As a child? I've heard that the mumps can—"

"It doesn't matter why. I just can't," he sighed, adjusting the pillow on his lap and wondering if she always kept her apartment so damned hot. And why the hell had he opened his mouth?

"I didn't know," she said softly.

"How would you?"

"But you love children! You loved baby Jenny and I've seen you with Erin."

"I don't have anything against them," he said, but it was a lie.

She was right. He loved children.

He thought of Erin, and his chest tightened with longing and regret. Of course he wished he could have one of his own. He rubbed his eyes, wondering what had come over him that he should blurt out a very personal truth so baldly, as if he'd wanted her to know.

And then something occurred to him: maybe he did.

Maybe he wished he could tell her his terrible secret. Maybe he wanted her to know the reason she shouldn't be with him, why they never had a chance. Like most women, she'd want children of her own one day and he wouldn't be able to give them to her, which is why, as much as it wrecked him, she should be with someone like Beck, someone who could—

"Did you know I was adopted?"

"What?"

He turned to her, shocked to learn something so seminal, so significant, after a friendship of almost four years. It scattered all of the other thoughts from his brain and he stared at her face, only inches away from his.

"I was adopted from a convent in Ireland when I was four months old. My parents had Ian, but couldn't seem to get pregnant again and my mum always had her heart set on a little girl. So, they adopted me." She reached out and touched the back of his hand gently, her small fingers curling until they caressed the skin of his palm. Every nerve ending in his body suddenly concentrated on the patch of skin owned by her touch. "There are so many ways to have a family, Nils. Dinna lose hope."

For a moment, he forgot about his fierce physical longing for her, distracted by her generosity, her kindness, her warmth and hope and spirit and selflessness. His eyes started burning as he looked down at their hands, her wedding ring catching the dim light in the quiet apartment.

He squeezed her hand gently before letting it go. The truth is, he'd lost hope a long, long time ago, and she'd feel differently, he was sure, if she knew the whole story.

***

Damn. Damn. Damn.

She'd been intentionally touching him, teasing him,

working up her courage to make her move, and then suddenly her whole plan had gone out the window because he was sitting beside her telling her something real, something crucial. And now—as he drew his hand away from hers—she felt him closing up emotionally again. What secrets, she wondered, were trapped in his head? And how in the world could she gain access to them? Fix them?

She turned back to the computer, but the screen swam before her, unfocused as her thoughts distracted her. His choice of words was interesting. He'd started with "I won't" before changing his words to "I can't." So which was it?

"Can't" would mean he was impotent or sterile and unable to have children. But Maggie had noticed a significant bulge under the zipper of his jeans more than once. It couldn't be impotence. Sterility, then? Mumps? Or an injury that had done permanent damage? Either way, it sure would explain some of his behavior. The way he kept her at arm's length, the way he wouldn't indulge in any discussion of a future, but would still have an affair with someone like Missy. That he wouldn't want to deprive her of motherhood fit perfectly into the picture she had of him. It made sense that Nils would be protecting her. It made sense that he would put her happiness before his.

And yet all she wanted out of life was to be the person who offered him happiness, who would brighten the darkness behind his wary eyes and soften the edges of his gruff, hard shell. Maggie just about lived for the moments she managed to make him grin, the times he suddenly chuckled at something she said. Watching his face soften as he talked to her did something to her head, to her heart, to her body, and she yearned for him to love her with the ferocity she knew he was capable of. It made her single-minded and determined to find out why he refused to love her. To have children.

An interesting point bubbled up to the surface of her frustrated thoughts. "Won't" implied that although he was perfectly capable of fathering children, he chose not to. Why not? Not because he didn't like them. He'd adored his baby sister, and Maggie had seen him several times with Erin, holding her carefully with his massive hands like she was breakable.

"Spit it out, Maggie May," he said quietly beside her.

"No, I…" she sputtered. "I dinna have anythin' to spit out."

"Liar."

"*Won't* or *can't?*" she asked in a rush. "Children. You won't? Or you can't?"

He looked at her, his face in agony as he spoke with a soft, firm finality. "It doesn't matter."

"It matters to me," she murmured, trying to figure out her next move.

His eyes were hypnotizing, hungry, and wary, drinking in her face, but shadowed with regret. She couldn't look away. She didn't want to look away.

"It shouldn't," he breathed.

"It does," she whispered, inching closer to him. His breathing was fast and ragged, and his shoulder brushed the tip of her breast as she leaned forward, making heat flood to her belly in waves, pooling there, making her breathless with longing.

"Please, Maggie," he begged, his voice so low, she could almost have tricked herself into believing it was in her head alone.

Her heart kicked into a gallop and she took a small gasping breath as she leaned forward, touching her lips to his. She felt the shocked jolt of his body as the laptop slid from her lap, clunking onto the floor as she twisted slightly to press her chest against his and reached up to cup his face in her hands.

As though he'd finally realized what had happened between them, he growled into her mouth, grabbing her hips and lifting her effortlessly over his thighs where she straddled him, pushing forward until her chest was flush with his and her knees ground into the couch behind him.

His rough hands slid up her back, bunching her shirt as he clasped her against him, his tongue invading her mouth with a primitive urgency, demanding hers. She surged forward on his lap, grinding against him, feeling his erection pushing against her, utterly massive and throbbing against her belly, pleading for release. It made her moan to think of him thrusting that hugeness into her body, rising to meet him, stretching to accommodate him. The strangled sound from deep in her throat seemed to make him even wilder, his rough fingers slipping under her shirt to slide up the hot skin of her back, unfastening her bra like he did it twenty times a day.

"Oh," she gasped, her fingers pushing into his short

hair as his lips deserted hers, burning a path from her mouth to her jaw to the soft skin under her ear where he lingered, moving his lips in nibbles and licks that made her writhe helplessly on his lap, pushing her sex against his again and again.

Just as his teeth grazed her earlobe, his thumbs found her nipples, and the sharp pleasure of both sensations made her arch her back, rubbing against him while her back bowed. He reached up for her neck, cradling the back of her head and gently forcing her back to him. His lips found hers and he groaned into her mouth as his thumbs brushed her nipples relentlessly into hard, aching points, making her run hot and wet as she moved her hips rhythmically against his rigid length, sucking on his tongue and—

"Maggie? Are you home?" Jenny's voice from the other side of Maggie's unlocked front door made them jerk back from each other, eyes wide and dilated, mouths glistening, cheeks pink, panting like they'd just run a mile.

His fingers slipped from her breasts, but his arms closed around her like bands of steel, as he rested his forehead on her chest.

Her heart thundered in her ears as she tried to process what had just happened between them and—Oh, my God!—Jenny was right outside her unlocked door knocking lightly. If she twisted the knob, she'd find them wrapped around each other, breathless and—

"Jen, uh…" she said in a trembling voice. "Just give me a…second…"

Nils tilted his head up and the agony she perceived in

his eyes made her breath catch, but before she could process his feelings, he leaned forward and pressed his lips against Maggie's lingeringly, brushing his lips back and forth gently like his sister wasn't standing right outside the door. Like he had one last chance to kiss her and get it perfect for the rest of his life. Then, without warning, he leaned back, sliding his hands up under her arms and picking her up off his lap to set her down beside him. He moved his hands quickly out from under her top and she snapped into action, adjusting her bra and smoothing her shirt. She glanced down and her nipples were like headlights, high beams, beaded and proud against her shirt.

"Nils and I were just, um, finishing the uh, the slides for…"

When she looked up, Nils was staring at her chest from where he sat catching his breath a few inches away from her. He looked wild, feral, utterly destroyed, staring at her with such hunger it made her tremble.

She gaped at him, needing an extra moment to talk to him, to understand what he was thinking, to figure out what would happen next, but there was no time. He ran a hand through his hair, hefting himself up onto the loveseat and crossing a leg over his knee to conceal his arousal. She tried to catch his eye as she stood up, but he refused to look at her, totally focused on the front door.

She picked up her laptop and put it beside him, swiped the back of her hand over her glistening lips and stood up to answer the door. As she got there, she looked back at Nils one final time. His face was severe, furious and hard, as though in pain or bitterly disappointed.

Maggie turned the knob and opened the door. Jenny grinned at her from the hallway. "Still had my key for the downstairs door."

"Ah," said Maggie, trying for a smile but failing. She turned quickly back toward Nils, who sat as still as a statue.

"Sam's downstairs, ready to get started." Jenny slid past her into the apartment. "Slideshow all ready?"

"Just about," said Nils, gesturing loosely to the laptop beside him.

"You look all sorts of grumpy," Jenny said to her brother. "I hope you're being nice to Maggie, Nils."

Maggie's face flushed hot and she didn't trust herself to look at him or wait to hear his reply.

"I'll meet you two downstairs in a minute, okay?"

She headed for her bedroom. She needed to splash some cold water on her face—heck, maybe she needed a cold shower—before meeting them downstairs.

She looked back as Nils stood up and followed Jenny out of her apartment, catching his anguished eyes just for a moment before he ducked out the door and she lost sight of him.

***

He helped with the decorations for an hour or so, careful to stay away from Maggie, then made an excuse about needing to discuss business and headed directly for his father's house.

He found his father on the living room recliner, Erin in the crook of his arm having a bottle in the dim light.

"Why *Største*! I was sure you'd be helping Jenny and

Maggie set up for my surprise party tonight!"

Nils couldn't help grinning as he sat down in front of his father on the edge of the trunk that doubled as a coffee table. Their broad knees almost touched as Nils leaned forward on them. "Doesn't anything get past you?"

"Not much."

"They'll be crushed if they find out you know."

"Then we won't tell them, eh? When Lars said we should take a six-month-old into the park to 'show her around,' I sort of started putting things together."

"And here we thought that was such a good plan."

"You don't know babies, Nils. Poor little Erin saddled with *Morfar* and *Onkel* Lars for a day in the park? *Stackars lilla kex*." *Poor little biscuit.*

"Who caved and spilled the beans?"

"Oh! No one! But, Paul was at Liberta's Liquors buying up Aquavit like it was going out of style. Maggie closed the Prairie Dawn early tonight. Jenny's in town. Erik should be here in an hour, even though his wife should probably be on bed rest with those two little'uns kicking around inside. A man knows when his kids are up to something…"

Nils nodded, the grin fading from his face as he summoned the courage to pose the question he'd come here to ask. "Pop…"

"Nils. You got the weight of the world on those shoulders." Carl put the bottle on the table beside him and wiped the milky drool from the corner of Erin's mouth, hefting her gently onto his shoulder to pat her back rhythmically.

Had he ever been that small? Nestled safely on his father's shoulder? Or had he always been this freakishly enormous human being?

"It doesn't scare you? Her?" He gestured to his niece whose little feet sticking out of her jammies curled into one another as she settled onto her grandfather's shoulder.

His father looked at him thoughtfully from over his glasses. "Scare me? I had four."

Nils looked down at his hands—huge mitts that he clasped in his lap. His voice was soft when he asked, "What if you'd lost one?"

"Would've wanted to die, I reckon." He patted and rubbed the little back on his shoulder, trying to coax a burp. "Your *mamma* miscarried once, and it just about leveled us."

Nils's eyes whipped up to find his father's. "What? I had n-no idea!"

"Yup. Between you and Lars. She was about four months along, so we'd just told everyone at Thanksgiving. But your mama took a spill on the ice two weeks later, and…"

"She lost it."

"She did."

"I don't remember."

"You were barely two."

"*Jag är ledsen, Pappa.*"

He said he was sorry softly, his own heart straining with its own secrets, its own private pain.

"When she came home from the hospital, crushed and sad, she went straightaway to your room, Nils. Pushed the blond hair off your little forehead. Watched you sleep for hours."

Erin let out a little erp, and Mr. Lindstrom chuckled quietly, resettling her into the crook of his arm, touching her pouty little lips gingerly with the cloth again before turning back to Nils.

"You gave her the strength to move on, to try again. *You*, son. Her *Største*."

Nils stared at his father's glistening light blue eyes, a mirror image of his own, overwhelmed with feelings of regret for his parents, for himself. He didn't know what to say, but he swiped at his eyes, glad he'd come to his father's house, glad to know this little piece of family history, despite how sad it made him feel for his parents. In the strangest way, it made him not feel so alone.

But a voice in his heart reminded him that as sorry as he was to hear about his father's loss, his own overshadowed it. It steeled his resolve to do what he knew had to be done.

"Pop," he started softly. "The McCarthy group. I want to take it. And I'm glad to take them tomorrow afternoon like they asked."

"*Gode Gud!*" His father looked up from Erin's blonde head, brows furrowed. "That's a month-long tour, Nils. Why would you want—and it means you'll…you'll miss the party tomorrow."

"I've done three week tours before. Four can't be so different. And, Pop," he looked away from his father, desperately hoping his father would understand, "I'm so sorry about the timing with the party and all, but I just feel like…"

"Don't worry about the party. I don't care about that. And it's not your skill I question, Nils, but your motives. Why d'you suddenly want this group? Why do I feel like you're running away from something?"

"I need to get away for a while, that's true. I need to get out of Gardiner. I need…space. From something."

"I see. No other options?"

"I'm afraid not. The sooner, the better, Pop."

"You won't let yourself have her," his father murmured softly. "Maggie May."

"*Jag kan inte.*" Nils shook his head sadly. *I can't.*

"Nils…son, I wish you'd tell me why. I see how much you care for her, how much she cares for you. You'd get along well together. Why can't you—"

"Please, Pop," Nils whispered, standing up from the trunk. He leaned forward and pressed his lips to the white hair on his father's head, holding his cheeks gently. "Please don't ask. Please, just…"

When he drew back, his father nodded sadly. "It's all yours, then. We'll spend some time early tomorrow morning going over the itineraries. Why don't you call over to the Best Western? Let them know you can leave tomorrow afternoon? Mr. McCarthy will be happy to hear it."

"I'm sorry to miss your party, Pop."

"Doesn't bother me a bit, son."

Nils wished he could smile at his father, but he couldn't. He knew he was doing the right thing for him and Maggie. He knew that he couldn't repeat his behavior from tonight, but he also had to face the fact that he was helpless around her. He hoped that four weeks apart would lessen the pull between them, and hopefully give her a chance to solidify things with Beck. When he came back, she'd be taken and Nils would be strong again, and they could find their footing as friends if it wasn't already too late. But at least they could finish out their farce of a marriage so Maggie could get her green card, and once she was settled with Beck, he wouldn't be tempted to make a move on her again. He'd let her go. Once she belonged to someone else, he'd have to.

"*Største.*" As Nils turned to leave, his father's voice stopped him. "I know you're running away from something. I know you been running for years. I always hoped you'd come and talk to me about whatever it was, but I can't force you to tell me what weighs so heavy on your heart. I just need you to know that when you're ready to talk, I'm ready to listen, son."

Nils turned at the door and tilted his lips up briefly in a vague facsimile of a smile, then turned to go. The thing was? He'd never be ready. Never.

Chapter 11

One month later, Maggie was in a better place than she'd been on the night of Mr. Lindstrom's party, though if she thought about it too hard, she still trembled with panicked embarrassment when she thought about Mr. Lindstrom's face the night of his party, informing her that Nils wouldn't be coming, that he had, in fact, left for the park with a group that afternoon.

"Left Gardiner," she'd repeated, utterly blindsided. "For a month."

"I'm sorry, Maggie," he'd replied softly.

"Left for a month. Instead of comin' to your birthday."

His blue eyes were profoundly sympathetic before he was distracted by one of his other children.

Her eyes had burned so sharply with tears, she'd kept her head down as she made her way through the crowd of people, heading out the back door of the café and running up the stairs to her apartment where she'd collapsed on the floor against her front door.

That kiss had been like a collision, like a force of nature mixed with fate: magnetism, gravity, inevitability...perfection. Once their lips touched and he had hauled her onto his lap, there was no turning back. Maggie's life had flashed before her eyes like a home video stuck on fast forward. In every fiber of her being, she knew that she'd been living her whole life to arrive at that moment with Nils Lindstrom: the end of their friendship, the beginning of their forever.

Except it hadn't been a beginning for Nils. For Nils, who'd taken the first possible opportunity to leave Gardiner—for a month, no less—it must have been a mistake. A *massive* mistake. And the pain it caused for her to realize this incredibly humiliating truth was so white hot and overwhelming, she could do nothing but weep. There she'd sat on her apartment floor, ruining her pretty silk blouse—one she'd ordered a while ago and saved for a special night like tonight, when she and Nils were finally finding their way—as the music from the party drifted up from the café below.

Beck was the one who'd come to find her, knocking gently and asking her to let him in. He'd sat beside her on the floor against the door. He hadn't touched her; somehow, he seemed to know that she only needed a friend in that moment, and Maggie would be forever grateful for his kindness to her.

So grateful that when he'd asked her out on a proper date a week later, she hadn't been able to say no. So grateful that when he'd put his arms around her and kissed her at the end of the night, she didn't have the heart to tell him that his kiss paled to gray next to the scorching red of the one she'd shared with Nils, but her face must have said it all, because he hadn't tried for another kiss after that.

As the weeks wore on, Maggie examined that kiss with

Nils more clearly, concentrating less on her bruised feelings afterward, and more on the act itself. No man could have faked that kind of passion, that level of heat and attraction. Nils wanted her just as much as she wanted him—of that she was utterly certain.

But she could also say with certainty that she was finally starting to accept the fact that Nils Lindstrom's issues might be unfixable. After four years of hope, a green-card marriage and a kiss that made her world tilt on its axis and spin, Maggie had to begin reconciling herself to the idea that as much as Nils wanted her on a carnal, visceral level, he might never allow himself to have her.

As for her feelings? They hadn't changed. She couldn't just shut down four years of longing, but despite the fact that she wanted him, she needed to start letting go. She wasn't willing to wait forever for him to work out his problems and make space for her in his life. She was already twenty-nine years old. Not that she was old, but she wanted a family and children someday, and if there was one painful reality that she'd had to accept, it was that Nils had a big problem with kids. And since having kids was something non-negotiable in Maggie's future, a future that included Nils seemed less and less likely.

So, she worked hard during their weeks apart to ignore her love for him and even buried it, systematically and deliberately, in the deepest depths of her heart until she could bear the conscious loss of it. Her anger at his abrupt departure and humiliation at his rejection helped her make it easier to let him go.

A month had gone by and Maggie quietly promised herself—and her fragile dignity—not to pursue him ever again. There was a strange strength that came from admitting defeat and accepting the truth, and Beck's friendship and obvious attraction to her cushioned the blow. Maybe Nils didn't want her, but someone else did.

"Hey, Maggie Leslie," said Beck with a happy smile, walking into the Prairie after hours, slipping onto his favorite barstool at the far end of the counter.

"We're closed," she said, returning his smile.

It was Friday evening and they had a date scheduled for dinner tomorrow night, so she was surprised to see him, but not bothered. He hopped off the stool and reached for the doorknob, pushing the lock in, before returning to his seat with a "there you go" grin. As much as she didn't feel romantic about Beck, she did have legitimate feelings of affection for him and looked forward to his company. He was good-looking, successful and kind, and she knew from their conversations that he wanted kids someday. Perhaps, she thought, her feelings could grow into something more.

"Coffee?"

He nodded. "And a scone. I've earned it. Thought I'd cheer myself up by coming to see you."

"Tough day?"

Beck looked around to reconfirm that the café was empty. "Remember the Sparrow divorce? I was telling you about it?"

Maggie nodded, leaning forward. She quite liked hearing about Beck's various cases, though she was sworn to secrecy on the details of them.

"Mrs. Sparrow just keeps making things difficult."

"What is it this time?"

"The family cat. Myrtle."

"They both want it?"

"She doesn't. He does. She doesn't want him to have it. She's trying to say that her niece gave them the cat, and the cat should go back to the niece instead."

"Is that true?"

"The niece wrote a letter asking for her cat back. I guess *her* cat gave birth six years ago and Myrtle was one of the kittens. Hank Sparrow doesn't have a bill of sale or receipt to prove they bought her."

"So he's goin' to lose his pet?" Maggie put a scone on a small white plate and poured Beck a cup of steaming coffee.

"I don't know yet. Maybe. Probably. It just seems so darned mean spirited."

"Aye. It is, but…"

"Yeah, I know. If Hank hadn't cheated on Francine, he'd have an easier time of it."

"He humiliated her," said Maggie. "He turned his back on her."

"But what good does it do to punish him now? They've split up. They're divorcing. Why not part as friends?" he asked.

"Maybe she *can't* be friends. Maybe she wants to know why she wasn't enough for him. Maybe she wants to hurt him for hurtin' her." Maggie paused when she realized her fingers had curled into tight fists and were biting into her palms. "Maybe the niece *should* have the cat."

Beck looked at Maggie carefully for a moment, searching her face before looking away. He took a bite of the scone then looked up and grinned. "Good batch."

She let her fingers unfurl, won over by his compliment. "I used coconut oil."

"Whatever you're doing," said Beck, his eyes holding hers tenderly, "keep doing it. It's certainly working for me."

She reached forward to dust a crumb off the corner of his mouth and he stilled, but she heard his breathing more pronounced on the exhale, as though he'd been holding his breath while she touched him.

His longing for her passed across his handsome face and it made her wince. "Beck, I—"

Beck shook his head, like he was shaking the moment away, and looked down at his plate. "It's okay, Maggie Leslie. You haven't made me any promises."

His goodness moved her, as it always did, but she stopped herself from reaching out to touch his hand. She was careful not to lead him on. "You're so kind to me, Beck. I dinna deserve it."

"Maybe I'm a glutton for punishment, but I keep hoping that if I stick around long enough, I'll wear you down."

"Well, you never know," said Maggie, giving him a playful smile.

"You mean that?" His face was serious, his voice low.

Her cheeks flushed when she looked at his face. Somehow their conversation had taken an unexpectedly serious turn. "I canna predict the future, Beck…"

He tilted his head to the side, as if seeing something important for the first time and wanting to examine the details of it. "But you're not…*against* it? Me? *Us?*"

"I'm just not ready to jump into anythin', as you know. But, *against* it? No, Beck. I'm not against it. If it happens…someday."

"Maggie," he said tenderly, staring at her for a long, intense moment before his face brightened. "You give me hope."

Without warning, he leaned over the bar to press his lips against hers. Just a soft touch. She closed her eyes, willing her body to feel something, desperate to want this good man who could offer her love and security. But the familiar emptiness washed over her as he pulled back. She opened her eyes to look at him, and his brows furrowed.

She knew he could see it all over her face—the disappointment, the fizzle.

He turned his attention back to his scone and took another bite as she finished wiping down the counter in awkward silence. "Oh, I almost forgot…" He turned around and rifled through the messenger bag he'd hung behind him on the back of the chair. "This came today. Must have sent it to me because of the return address. I think it might be your temporary papers."

He slid a white envelope across the bar to her, his eyes bright with anticipation.

Maggie picked up the envelope and looked at it. The last time she'd received a letter from USCIS it had informed her that her visa was expired and used words like "deportation" and "Homeland Security." Of course Nils had been with her and his sturdy, calming, supportive presence had made everything better. She couldn't help the butterflies that flapped their tiny wings nervously against the walls of her belly. She pushed it back toward Beck.

"You open it. I'll refresh your coffee."

"Scaredy cat." He took his unused knife from beside his plate and made a slit in the top of the letter, then withdrew it and unfolded it. Maggie poured his coffee, watching his face. His brows quickly furrowed together, and he swore softly. "No. No, no, no. *Damn* it."

"What does it say?"

"I'm sorry, Maggie. I'm so damned sorry." He placed the letter on the bar and turned it to face her. "You've been flagged."

***

Nils had to admit it, as much as he loved Yellowstone, he'd had just about enough after almost a month away from home. Today was Saturday and that meant that four weeks had somehow come and gone. He looked around at their last campsite. Only three more tents to put away and then he'd go find them down by the river where his customers were spending their last morning fishing. He'd be back in Gardiner by dinnertime.

The McCarthy group was made up of five retired couples who'd ventured north from a tony neighborhood in Scottsdale to immerse themselves in the wonders of Yellowstone for four straight weeks. And Nils could verify it:

they'd seen just about everything. They'd fished and hiked, cooked over an open fire and slept under the stars. They'd seen all the wildlife the park could offer, done some horseback riding and spent a few luxury days at one of the resorts. Of the twelve campgrounds in Yellowstone, they'd spent four nights in six, plus three nights at the Lake Yellowstone Hotel about a week ago, which was the last time Nils had enjoyed reliable wi-fi. The first thing he'd done after settling the folks into their accommodations was check his phone. He'd scrolled through quickly to find emails waiting from his father and Lars, Erik and Jenny and Paul.

He had no right to the disappointment that washed over him as he realized there was no message from Maggie. He hadn't really expected one, had he? He certainly didn't deserve one.

He collapsed the second-to-last tent, put the sticks in the drawstring bag and rolled the nylon into a tight ball. They'd be headed back to Gardiner today and Nils couldn't wait to sleep in his own bed again, take hot showers every day and cook his food on a stove. He'd grown a wild and wooly beard that he'd shave off first thing before heading into town to see his father and Lars, and…and…

Maggie. Maggie again. Always, *always*, his mind circled back to Maggie in a never-ending loop of longing. He had been sure that four weeks away from her would cool his feelings. It turned out he was wrong. If anything, he missed her with such a gnawing, all-consuming ache, it amazed him every day that he didn't abandon the McCarthys and their friends and zoom back to Gardiner to beg her forgiveness.

But even as his feelings for her grew stronger and stronger, he knew the chances of her forgiving him when he'd ditched her after a kiss like that, were—in her words—*not bloody likely*.

That kiss was seared on his brain and while he was away from her, it had been his constant companion. He'd relived every detail, examined every nuance of how she felt in his arms, pressed up against him, sucking his tongue into her mouth as her nipples beaded into little pebbles. He wondered how she would have tasted if Jenny hadn't interrupted them—would her skin have been as sweet as her lips?—and every night he dreamed of her. He dreamed of how she'd look as he thrust into her waiting warmth, moving slowly, stroking her, teasing her, taking his time giving her pleasure and finally feeling the walls of her sex clench around him like a vise as she cried out his name in surrender.

He woke up sweating and rock-hard every morning, jumping into whatever lake or river was nearby to assuage the effects of his dreaming before his clients woke up. But every night she returned to tease and taunt him, as he fell asleep to the memory of her eyes, dilated and tender.

More than anything, Nils regretted the hasty choice he'd made that night in kissing her back. He'd destroyed their friendship by kissing her and any chance of a relationship by leaving her. Despite the fact that he didn't deserve her, he *wanted* her and the only thing he'd ever see in her eyes again was scorn.

Which sucked, because for the first time in years, the high walls that Nils had kept between him and Maggie seemed to be crumbling. He couldn't fight or deny his feelings for her anymore. That kiss had shredded the last of his self-control and there's no way he'd be able to be around her anymore without reaching for her, touching her, wanting her.

As far as he could tell, he had two choices: leave Gardiner or try to figure out a way to be with her. And most days that's where his thoughts ended, since he couldn't conceive of leaving his home, and as much as he wanted to be with Maggie, he wasn't quite ready to figure out how. He'd have to offer her a commitment. And when you're already married and one of you loves children, that's where the commitment would invariably lead. Somewhere he couldn't go.

He rolled up the last tent and stuffed it into the corresponding nylon bag, then hopped up on the roof of the van to finish repacking the roof pack. The sun beat down on his face and he glanced down at his arms, five shades darker than he'd been when he left. And he was leaner, too. He'd probably gained five more pounds worth of muscle since June. He could feel it on his body, hard and tough, and he didn't need it, but it still felt good.

He moved some of the camping equipment around and managed to stuff all of the tents into the corners of the pack, finally zipping it completely before sliding down the windshield to sit on the hood of the van for a few minutes. He was ready to go, but he may as well give the McCarthys a bit more time before they'd have to say goodbye to Yellowstone. Before he had to return to his real life.

Even with so much time for thinking, it still surprised him that Maggie hadn't been the only woman on his mind. As though a floodgate had been inadvertently opened, for the first time in years, he allowed himself to remember Veronica, to think about her not just as a victim, but as the girl who he'd loved so desperately. It was strange to find how vividly his memories had been preserved, and it was a revelation to find that some of them—most of them, in fact, aside from the final few—were good. Really good. He'd almost forgotten how they'd met, how the pretty redhead had teased him mercilessly in biology for three weeks, finally asking him out over a frog dissection.

"Nils Lindstrom," she'd said softly, wearing light green plastic goggles that deepened her dark green eyes. "I get the feeling that if *I* don't ask *you*, we're never going to get this show on the road."

His stomach had leaped as he realized the possible meaning behind her words. "What show?"

"The Nils and Veronica show."

"Oh." Shyer-than-shy Nils Lindstrom noticed pretty girls, of course, but hadn't quite mustered the courage to ask one out yet. He hung back, playing sports and drinking beers with his buddies on the weekends. Asking a girl out on a date made him feel dizzy and terrified. It wasn't that he hadn't fantasized. He did, of course. Daily. And mostly about Veronica Olsen, the pretty transfer student spending her senior year in Gardiner with her aunt while her single mother completed a one-year tour in Afghanistan.

"So, what do you say?" She'd put her hands on her tiny

hips and looked up at him, giggling as she pointed to her goggles. "You can't say no to *this*, can you?"

As far as Nils was concerned, Veronica Olsen in light green biology goggles was the loveliest thing Gardiner High School could ever offer. He stared at her, shaking his head back and forth lightly.

"Nope," he'd muttered as his stomach flipped over and a wave of anticipation and lust washed over him. "I can't say no."

She'd giggled again and he'd carried her books after class, spending every waking moment falling in love with her until the Christmas formal.

It was no wonder his face had collapsed when Maggie showed him the photo of him and Veronica from that night. *That* night. The night they'd lost their virginity to one another.

They'd agreed to get a motel room, even ditching the dance early because they couldn't keep their hands off each other, couldn't wait to consummate their love. They'd undressed slowly, both of them aware of the gravity of their decision, then kissed and touched each other, whispering confident, tender I love yous as they fell back upon the motel room bed.

The act itself—which didn't have the finesse of subsequent encounters—had been perfect in its own way: an act of innocence, an act of love. He'd come too quickly, she'd bled a little, and they realized way too late that they'd forgotten to bring the box of condoms that Nils had dutifully purchased the day before. But with the foolish invincibility of horny teenagers in love, they'd spent the rest of the night making love to each other, insatiable, irresponsible. Over the ensuing weeks, they found every possible way to be together, sneaking into bedroom windows, making out in the flatbed of his father's truck and under the bleachers at school, even in a tent overlooking the Yellowstone River during one memorable weekend in the park. And they'd always been careful, using condoms after that first night, not that it made any difference by then.

A hawk cried loudly overhead, and Nils took his phone out of his back pocket. One p.m. He slid off the hood of the van and stretched, then headed toward the river. It was three hours back to Gardiner. At least. They should get a move on.

As he walked purposely toward the river, he let himself savor the good memories for another moment, remembering her hair spread out on the pillow beneath, the touch of her innocent hands on his untried body, the way she'd murmur his name as her body clamped and shuddered around him. It was a relief to remember the months of good times they'd shared after so many years of only recalling the bitter end.

Nils felt like he was finally saying goodbye to Veronica, like maybe he'd be able to heal and move on. Maybe he'd even know that sort of love and completeness in his life again.

But no matter how hard he tried, the old familiar sorrow would intrude when he thought of her final moments, of *their* final moments. Of the blistering loss not just of his first love, Veronica, but of their tiny, infant son,

Jens.

Losing them both had broken his heart, shattered his spirit and scarred his soul. Moreover, his culpability in her tragic end made him remember the promise he'd made to himself only hours after she'd gasped her last, terrified breath: no matter what, he would never, ever let it happen again.

He swiped at his eyes as a dark cloud passed over the sun. Was it possible to honor the promise he'd made to Veronica, but still make room for Maggie in his life? Damned if he could figure out how.

***

Maggie left Bethany in charge downstairs for the Saturday afternoon lull and trudged up to her apartment, heavyhearted. She needed to call Mr. Lindstrom. She needed to find out if Nils was definitely coming back today.

Last night, after Beck had told her they'd been flagged, she'd stared back at him in dumbfounded shock. In the weeks since she'd sent in the forms, it had never occurred to her that they'd be flagged. It simply hadn't crossed her mind.

"W-why? Do they—do they give a reason? What do you mean, flagged?"

"When you filled out the forms, you listed separate addresses...and worse, you signed your name 'Maggie Campbell,' not 'Maggie Lindstrom.' You've been called in for a Stokes interview."

Maggie Lindstrom. She wished that hearing him say it didn't make her heart twist with longing, not when she'd come so far in placing distance between her feelings for Nils and her life. She hadn't signed her name that way, because regardless of their sham marriage, that's not who she was. Not really.

"What happens next?" she'd asked in a daze.

Beck turned the letter back around and scanned it. "You and Nils have to be in Billings on September fourth for an interview with USCIS."

"S-so, you'll make a list of questions for us and we'll answer them and exchange them and memorize the answers. Then we'll be all set. That can work, right?"

"It's not a bad jumping off spot, but no, it won't work." He rubbed his jaw and sighed. "This is bad, Maggie. This is what I was worried about from the beginning." He shook his head back and forth. "I'm going to be straight with you...I know how you feel about Nils. Hell, you know what I think of the guy. I'd like nothing better than for him to move to Timbuktu and never come back to Gardiner again."

Maggie looked down at the counter to conceal her feelings from Beck. She knew that she should agree with everything Beck was saying, but through a thick layer of hurt and anger, the idea of never seeing Nils again sat like acid in her belly and she hated herself for her weakness. She should hate him for kissing her and leaving her, for giving her such hope, then hurting her so profoundly with his rejection. She wanted to hate him. She longed to hate him.

"But the people who will be interviewing you are psychologists. They've been trained to ferret out frauds. To pull this off, you're going to have to appear married, Maggie. Like a real married couple. People who read each other's expressions and know each other's secrets. You have to know what kind of toothpaste he uses, and he needs to know when you last had your period." He cringed at her, tapping on the letter with his index finger, his face worried and serious. "I'm sorry to be crude, but those are the sorts of things they could ask. You're going to need to know those things about each other and you're going to need to appear as though you're married. *Really* married, not fake married."

"Oh, my God," Maggie murmured.

"I'm sorry, but you're going to need to spend a lot of time with him to pull this off."

"How much?"

"A lot. Enough so that you can pass for married. Or you'll be deported. And he'll go to jail for fraud."

"Oh, my God. This is such a bloody mess," her stomach rolled over with nerves and fear. "I think I'm goin' to be sick."

She rushed to the little sink in the backroom and braced her hands on the basin as the realities of the situation sunk in. Nils, for whom one kiss was such a grave mistake he'd left town for a month, was now going to have to spend a month getting to know every detail about her. And Maggie, who'd been rejected, who'd just started accepting the reality that she and Nils could never be, was going to have to figure out how to *look* deeply in love with him while somehow keeping her true feelings out of the equation.

She ran the water and splashed her face, wondering if she should just get on a plane and return to Scotland. *There is no way this can possibly work. No way.*

She felt Beck's hand on her shoulder and turned to meet his worried eyes. "I have an idea."

She swallowed, blinking her watery eyes quickly to keep from crying. "An idea?"

He pulled her into his arms, and she tensed at first then allowed herself to relax against him.

"Let me help you, Maggie Leslie. Okay?"

***

Maggie stepped into her apartment, remembering the simple details of Beck's plan. She would send Nils a text when he returned today telling him she needed to see him and asking him to meet her at Beck's office. Beck had suggested that he coach them through the questions for a few days to set a businesslike tone, and that they could then continue to meet in the conference room at his office to both ensure privacy and guarantee a chaperone. The idea had immediately appealed to her. They may have to spend time together, but meeting at the law office with Beck within shouting distance made it feel safer, like informational exchange sessions, keeping the muddied waters of feelings and attraction at arm's length.

Maggie picked up the phone and dialed *Lindstrom & Sons*.

"*Lindstrom and Sons*. Lars here."

"Lars, it's Maggie."

"Maggie! Good to hear your voice! Haven't seen you much lately."

He was referring to their erstwhile Thursday euchre nights, which Maggie had canceled indefinitely after Nils kissed her and ran screaming for the hills. She wasn't in the mood to spend much time with the Lindstroms. She'd been avoiding all of them, even in Nils's absence.

"I know. I've been so...busy. And my cousin's comin' to visit in a few weeks. Been gettin' ready for him."

"Huh. I had no idea."

There was an awkward silence that stretched between them for a minute before they spoke at the same time.

"I was wonderin' when—" she started.

"So, Nils'll be back by—" he said.

"What?" she asked.

"Nils is coming back today. Don't know when, but by nightfall, I reckon."

"Is that right?" Maggie said, trying to keep her voice neutral.

"Longest tour he ever took," said Lars. "Hey, I probably shouldn't ask, but—"

"Don't, Lars. Best if you don't," she said. She'd gotten the information she called for. "I have to go. Say heya to your pop for me, aye?"

"Sure, Mags."

She hung up the phone quickly before he could ask her anything else and sat back on her couch, sighing. It had taken her a week to be able to look at her couch without seeing herself on the floor in front of it straddling Nils's lap, grinding herself against him as he kissed the daylights out of her. Her eyes burned suddenly, and she bit her lip, forcing herself not to cry. She was going to have to spend time with him—a lot of concentrated time—and she couldn't exactly dissolve into tears every time she recalled the hot sweetness of that kiss and how awkward it must have been for him afterward.

She took a deep breath and then stood up and went to her bathroom. She splashed her face with cold water and looked up at herself in the mirror, feeling the tears recede. Her jawline was severe and her eyes dull, but that didn't matter. All that mattered was that she needed to learn everything about Nils Lindstrom over the next five weeks, or she'd be deported, and he'd go to jail. And although her lips turned up in a slight smirk at the prospect of Nils in handcuffs being led away, her amusement was fleeting when her traitorous insides went hot as the image developed in her head, complete with his gorgeous chest bared and lying on her bed while the handcuffs bound him to—

No. No, no, no. No more Nils Lindstrom fantasies. Absolutely not. No more.

To distract herself, she took her phone out of her back pocket, pulled up a text box and typed a quick message to Nils. Without overthinking her words, she pressed send and pushed the phone back into her pocket.

It didn't matter that she'd loved him for years. It didn't matter that he'd sent her years of conflicting messages. It didn't matter that they'd held hands and even kissed. It didn't matter that they were legally married. It didn't even matter that while she might propel her life forward through sheer force of will, she might never actually leave her feelings for him behind. None of it mattered.

"Only one thing matters. If you don't want to be

deported, you're just goin' to have to figure out how to work together," she told herself curtly, reminding herself to lean into her anger if she felt weak for him, to remember the scorching humiliation of his surprise departure. All they had to do was sit in a conference room for a couple of hours every night and learn everything they possibly could about each other. She wasn't a good actress, but she could do this; her life depended on it. Anyway, it was only for five weeks, and then they'd never have to be in a room alone together ever again.

***

Nils's belly fluttered with anticipation as the van lumbered along under the Roosevelt Arch, past the high school and around the bend toward Main Street. He was almost home. About fifteen minutes ago, his phone had started buzzing like crazy as it finally found a signal and emails and text messages started loading one by one. They were probably from his siblings and father, but he teased himself, played a game with himself as he got closer and closer to the Best Western where he would drop off the folks in his tour. Maybe one of the messages would be from Maggie.

She'd send him a breezy, flirty text letting him know the kiss was water under the bridge and they could go back to being friends. They could still play euchre every week; she'd still join his family for holidays. He could still orbit around her, still know her warmth and affection, still enjoy her teasing smiles…and friendship.

He passed the Prairie Dawn, staring out the window for a glimpse of her, and then took a deep breath as reality shut down his ridiculous fantasies. There was no way to go back. He'd killed their friendship a month ago when he left for Yellowstone.

No, he thought, even before that: when he'd pulled her onto his lap and shoved his tongue in her mouth and his hands under her shirt on the floor of her apartment.

No, he corrected himself. Earlier than that: the moment he kissed her at their wedding. That little kiss had changed the game.

Or maybe even before, when he insisted that she couldn't marry Paul and he'd held her hand and insisted she marry him?

Nope. It was even before that…

And then he knew. He knew the exact moment his friendship with Maggie had died, and he was mortified to discover it had been his choice alone.

"Thanks for everything, Nils!"

He pulled into the hotel parking lot and said goodbye to the McCarthy party, distractedly accepting hugs and tips and smiling numbly as his mind reeled.

Once they'd taken their luggage and waved goodbye, he got back into the van, staring at his white-knuckled hands on the steering wheel as he finally took responsibility for what had happened between him and Maggie.

May Day. That night. He had pushed her hair softly away from her forehead after taking off her pants and putting warm socks on her feet. Then he'd bent down and pressed his lips to her forehead. That was the moment. That was the moment he'd crossed a line and turned a corner.

And he could see clearly now, although he hadn't realized it at the time, that every ensuing decision he'd made after that kiss on her forehead was actually a charge upon her heart. While he thought he was fighting *against* his feelings, his actions had actually been fighting *for* them. His words may have begged her for friendship, but his heart and his body kept crashing into her, right up until the moment he'd hauled her onto his lap and kissed her like his life was ending.

All this time he thought he'd been pushing her away, and maybe he had been, half-heartedly, with his words. But the undeniable truth was in his actions: he *wanted* her—to feel her lips under his, to touch her body, to love her, to be with her. He was desperate for her, and his feelings weren't going away. Which begged the question again: Was it possible to make room for Maggie in his life?

Maybe. Maybe it was time for his brain to surrender to his heart and start figuring out a way for them to be together, despite his past and his hang-ups and his fear of hurting Maggie as he had Veronica. Maybe it was time to forgive himself, to figure out a way to give himself a second chance at love. There had to be a way to be with Maggie without breaking his promise to Veronica and baby Jens. There had to be.

His phone buzzed again and without thinking he picked it up, shocked to see Maggie's name flash up on the oncoming texts banner. His heart leaped so hard, he raised a hand and pressed it against his chest as his thumb swiped at the screen to bring up her message.

I'm sorry to bother you. Believe me, I'd leave you

alone forever if I had my way, but

we've been flagged by NSCIS. Please meet me at Beck's office at 8:00pm Sunday night.

He winced as he read and re-read the text. *I'd leave you alone forever.* This was Maggie, whose sunny smiles and teasing ways were the brightest spot in his life. This was Maggie, to whom he was married, the woman who owned his heart, to whom his soul cried out. This was Maggie, whom he'd love every moment of every day until the day he died. And goddamn it, he'd finally started clearing a path to her, only to find out she wasn't waiting for him anymore.

His heart ached with sorrow and frustration, and he swallowed painfully, turning the key and pointing the van toward his dark and empty home. As much as he'd tried to prepare himself for her scorn, now that he was faced with the probability that he'd lost her, he had no idea how in the world he'd be able to bear it.

Chapter 12

Maggie shifted in her seat for the tenth time, checking her watch before looking up at the conference room door again, ears straining to hear the front door open and the sound of Emma Branson greeting Nils.

Beck glanced up from the two stapled packets in front of him and turned slightly so that his knee nudged hers.

"You okay?"

"Perfectly fine," she answered crisply.

She had dressed with studied casualness, but the careful observer would notice that her hair was down, she was wearing light makeup and her linen blouse was a little dressier and dipped a little lower in the front than the t-shirts she wore almost every day.

"Tonight's just about going over the process and setting up your meeting times. It's going to be okay."

"Sure," she agreed. She rubbed her sweaty palms on her jeans then folded them on the table as she looked at the lone chair across the table from them.

"Maggie. I'm right here and I'll stay for as long as you need me. It's going to be okay. I mean it." Beck reached over gently and covered her hands with one of his. "I promise."

She heard the front door open and she was sure the sound of her heart was audible to Beck, it was so loud in her own ears. Her eyes were riveted on the conference room door, which swung all the way open and then...there he was.

She gasped softly, drinking him in after a month apart. He stood tall, taking up the entire doorway, eyes locked on Maggie's. He'd changed since leaving: his hair was almost white from so much time in the sun and his face was clean-shaven, but there was a fairly prominent tan line where a beard would have been until recently. He was altogether darker, harder and bigger, somehow, though that might just have been her heart seeing perfection because it was him. He wore creased khaki pants and a Sunday dress shirt in the same light blue as his eyes that made them seem ten times brighter than usual. Her lips twitched because she realized that he'd dressed up and—*Oh. My. Good. Lord.*—he looked delectable.

Beck's hand squeezed hers, bringing her back down to earth and reminding her that when Nils left her a month ago, it was Beck who'd been there for her. She flipped her hand over, pressing her palm against Beck's and lacing her fingers through his, without dropping Nils's eyes. She watched his glance flick to their hands, then back to her face. He didn't wince or grimace or show any other sign that he was bothered, but the arm behind his back dropped to his side where a bouquet of wild flowers wrapped in cellophane hung dejectedly beside him.

"Oh," she whispered, looking at them for a moment, then back up Nils.

And then the strangest thing happened.

Instead of growling or frowning at her, his face

softened as he watched her. The tenderness he'd always tried so hard to conceal was etched into every line of his tanned face. It made her body tingle. It made her want to cry.

He finally stepped forward, pulling out the chair across from her with his free hand and set the flowers on the table in front of her before sitting down.

"Nils," said Beck in a measured voice.

"Beck," said Nils, dropping Maggie's eyes to look at Beck. His eyes snuck a quick glance at their joined hands, then back up to the lawyer's face.

"Glad you could make it tonight."

Nils slid his eyes languidly to Maggie and purred, "Thanks for inviting me."

"Should we just get down to it?" asked Beck. "Here's what's hap—"

"Heya, Maggie May," said Nils, tilting his head to the side, totally ignoring Beck, still holding her eyes with his unbelievably beautiful blue ones.

Her stomach flip-flopped in riot, making her sex clench and her breath quicken. He was so bold, so direct, staring at her like her body was a place he'd visited, a place he'd spent time. It made her hot and uncertain, because it was so unlike him. Which made her realize that there was something else different about him, though she guessed she'd be on the short list of people who noticed. His eyes. His eyes that were always so hard and wary were…easier, somehow. Though not carefree, they were decidedly less tortured than usual.

"Welcome home," she said softly, still trying to figure out the differences in him, wondering what had engineered them.

And then the second strange thing happened.

His lips curved up into a grin. Then they passed a grin and segued into a smile. A *sexy* smile, accompanied by a low chuckle.

Now, Maggie had known Nils for four years. He didn't do sexy smiles. That was Lars's department. Or Erik's. For Lord's sake, even Paul's now and again. But, Nils? No. His grins were occasional and even when she managed to wheedle one out of him, they didn't quite reach his eyes, which almost always maintained their stony reserve. But not this one. This one backed up the heat behind his eyes, making her breathless, making her want to rip her clothes off and offer herself to him on top of the conference table. Her mouth watered and her throat went dry and she swallowed nervously. She looked down at the table sharply to see her fingers playing with her Claddagh ring, twisting it around and around. When had she unlaced her fingers from Beck's and pulled her hand away? She had no recollection.

She looked up at Beck beside her and his eyes were cool and a little hurt. "Now that we've all said our hellos, should we get started?"

Maggie glanced at Nils and he shrugged, his massive body relaxed and easy in the smallish conference room chair. With a confident smirk he nodded, "Sure, Beck."

***

Beck pushed a packet toward Nils, launching into his plan to get them up to speed on each other's personal history by September fourth, just in time for their Stokes interview.

They each had a thirty-page packet of questions to fill out that detailed all manner of information—their childhoods, friends, and family, job history, education history, religious beliefs, and general interests. Beck walked them quickly through the packet, explaining that they needed to be honest and thorough in their answers. He said they'd have three days to fill out the packets and asked if Nils could meet that deadline.

"All of these questions," he asked. "By Wednesday?"

"I'm afraid so," said Beck. "Starting Wednesday night, you're going to need to start studying. After you've absorbed the information, you're going to have to start spending time together, casually, conversationally, so that this information feels organic."

Nils glanced at Maggie, whose knuckles had whitened around her pencil when Beck said the words "spending time together." He could tell she was thrown off by his appearance, by the flowers and especially by the smile he'd pilfered from his brother's arsenal. He didn't want her off kilter, but it was better than anger and far better than scorn.

As Nils and Lars had unloaded the van last night, Nils had paid extra attention to Lars's way of moving. His smiles and grins and intonation. When Nils finally got upstairs to his place last night, he took a long shower, thinking the whole time, "What would Lars do?" and the pieces started coming together.

Lars would charm her. Lars would wear light blue—like he always did around new girls—and he'd bring flowers. Lars would keep his voice playful and offer a few of those wink-

'n'-smile sunny grins that girls loved so much. He'd smirk and stay calm and generally just ooze relaxed confidence. And while Nils didn't necessarily feel the sort of relaxed confidence that Lars owned so effortlessly, he realized that his time away from Gardiner had been more productive than he'd originally thought. Sorting his feelings about Veronica had taken a measure of weight off his shoulders.

"Mr. Westman?" called Emma Branson from the doorway of the conference room, hand held over the phone.

"Yes, Emma?"

"Mrs. Sparrow's on the telephone for you. She's…um, well, she's yelling some angry words, and I just, well, land sakes, I don't know what to…" Emma's free hand fluttered around her neck and she looked down at the cordless phone like she was holding a snake.

"Send her call through to me in my office," said Beck, looking annoyed. He stood up, giving Nils a hard look. "Please bring Mr. Lindstrom and Miss Campbell some pencils. And—and coffee, if they want some. I'll, uh…" Beck looked at Maggie from the doorway behind Nils. "I'll be back as soon as I take care of this."

"Take your time," said Nils, glancing at Beck from over his shoulder before turning his gaze squarely on Maggie.

Maggie gave Beck a weak smile as he left the room and Emma bustled in with a cup of pencils. "You want coffee?"

"Sure," said Maggie. "I'll take a cup, Emma."

"Sure," said Nils, giving Emma a Lars Lindstrom-style smile. "Me too. And thanks, Emma."

Emma simpered, blushing and reaching up to pat her

tightly curled gray hair. "Oh, well, I'll just..." She turned and headed out the door, closing it with a quiet click.

Maggie reached forward and grabbed a pencil, keeping her eyes down as she started filling out her questionnaire.

She was angry and hurt. He could tell that. What he didn't know was how serious she was with Beck. That handholding had made his spirits take a dive, until she'd pulled her hand away and Nils had watched Beck's face change quickly from smug satisfaction to hurt annoyance. Whatever was going on between them, it wasn't solid yet. Which had made Nils practically sigh with relief. He wanted Maggie in his life. He still had to figure out how to get her there.

He reached for a pencil, tapping it on the edge of the table as he read through the first page of questions:

Where were you born?

What year?

What do you know about the circumstances of your birth?

Were your parents married at the time?

Nils rolled his eyes. Why was Beck giving them these questions in a packet like a test? Couldn't he and Maggie learn the answers just as well if they were sitting across from each other at a restaurant while he occasionally rubbed his leg against hers under the table?

"Keep makin' that racket and I'm leavin'," she ground out and the sound of her voice surprised him.

"Maggie," he said gently, cajolingly, still channeling Lars. "We don't have to meet here. Why don't we ditch these questions and go to the Blue Moon? I'll buy you a burger and you can tell me all about where you were born."

"I dinna think so," she said without looking up at him.

"This is silly. I know you're mad at me but—"

"Mad at you?" She snapped her neck up and furious green eyes met his. "I'm not mad at you, Nils."

Then she looked back down at her paper, using her pencil like a dagger on the page.

"Oh, well that's a relief, because I could have swor—"

"I think you're a first-class jackass and I wish I had married Paul that night. Or Beck, for that matter. Yes, Beck. He's such a good, fine man. But, mad at *you*? No. Not a bit." She whipped the finished page up and tucked it under the rest, attacking the next set of questions with gusto.

"Maggie, can we talk about what—"

"No, Nils. The time for talkin' is long gone." Her pencil made a scratching noise as she answered the questions like a woman on a mission. Her lips were tightly pursed and her posture—erect and uncompromising—probably felt as uncomfortable as it looked.

He looked back down at the page, clenching his jaw and willing "growly bear" Nils not to make an appearance.

"Park was beautiful," he said, tapping the pencil eraser lightly against the packet, tilting his head to get a better look at her eyes, but they were downcast, and he couldn't make them out. "Group was nice. Had a lot of time for thinking."

"Good for you."

"Want to know what I was thinking about?'

"Not in the least. Not one bit." She rubbed the back of her neck for a moment and Nils actually considered getting

225

up, circling the table to stand behind her and rubbing it for her. But he didn't. He'd never seen her this angry. Never.

"Don't get the wrong idea. I was—"

"The *wrong idea*?" She flashed her eyes up at him, throwing her pencil on top of the packet and slapping her hand on the table. "Let me be clear. I couldn't give a handful of shite what you were thinkin' about, laddie. I'm verra sorry that ye're stuck doin' this with me, but all ye have to do is answer a handful o' bloody questions. That's all. I dinna want to know about yer bloody group or yer bloody park or yer bloody thoughts about the mistake you made kissin' me that night. So, pick up your pencil and answer the feckin' questions so ye dinna have to suffer my company any longer than need be!"

Emma had probably been knocking at the door for several moments, but they hadn't heard her through Maggie's tirade. "Everything okay in there? I got the coffee."

Nils gave Maggie a hard, humorless look, then stood up and opened the door for Emma, who glanced nervously between them, finally setting the cups down on the conference table.

As she walked out, Beck walked back in, brushing past Nils to go to Maggie, taking stock of her flushed cheeks and rigid posture. He rounded the table to sit beside her, putting his arm around her stiff shoulders. He gave Nils a menacing look as he shook his head back and forth, his hand rubbing her upper arm like he had a right to touch her.

"What's wrong with you? Haven't you hurt her *enough*?"

Staring back at Beck's furious expression, Nils felt

ashamed. He had, of course. He'd been hurting her for years. But he wanted to change that.

"I'm sorry," he said softly, still holding onto the door he'd opened for Emma. Maggie didn't even glance up at him. He reached for the packet on the table and picked it up, nodding at Beck while Maggie stared wordlessly at the table. "I'll have them done by Wednesday."

Then he turned and strode out of the conference room, away from Beck, away from Maggie, all alone.

***

By the time Beck drove Maggie home, she wasn't stewing anymore. She was embarrassed by her outburst. Not that Nils didn't deserve it, but Maggie liked keeping a cool head. It made her cheeks flush with heat when she reviewed her short speech.

"I guess that didn't go so well," said Beck, as he pulled up in front of the Prairie Dawn, letting the engine of his BMW idle as he turned to her. "I'm so sorry I had to take that phone call. I promised I wouldn't leave you alone with him and—"

"No, Beck," she reassured him. "You've been so great to me. Please dinna apologize. How's Francine Sparrow?"

"Still angry. We're not getting anywhere. It's almost like she's holding on to her anger to hold on to Hank. The longer she throws roadblocks into the mix, the longer it'll take to finalize the divorce."

"Then she'd be wise to let go. Hank Sparrow is a philanderin' ass."

"More and more? I think she loves him. In spite of

what he did. I don't think she can turn off the way she feels about him, no matter how much she wishes she could."

"More's the pity for her, then."

"We can't help who we want, can we?"

He leaned over to kiss her goodnight and without thinking first or meaning to, she drew back quickly, hitting her head lightly on the window in retreat. The movement was instinctual, and therefore definitive, and Beck's face fell as he processed what it meant.

"Sorry," she whispered. "I didna mean to—"

"Sort of knew it would turn out this way."

"What way?"

"When he got home."

"N-no! No, Beck. No. I'm through with him. He—he left without a word, he doesn't want me l-like that—he's an overgrown man-child who canna even—"

"Maggie." His eyes were kind and resigned. "Francine Sparrow can't turn off the way she feels about Hank, no matter how much she wishes she could." He paused and then continued, his voice measured and sensible with an underpinning of regret. "The day you married Nils, you told me, 'It's always been Nils for me.' Remember that?"

She bit her bottom lip. Hard. Hard enough to taste blood. Then whispered, "Aye."

"That hasn't changed has it?" He tilted her chin upward with his finger. "Please be honest with me. I think I've earned that."

She couldn't seem to make the words, so she stared at him, feeling miserable. *No, it hasn't changed. I tried so hard to hate him and all it took was one meeting for all of those feelings to rush back again. I can't hate him, and I'm so confused I could cry.*

"Maggie? Has that changed? Because this is me giving up. If you don't want that, say something right now. Tell me to hold on. Tell me not to walk away. Tell me not to give up hope."

Her eyes filled with tears as she looked up at him. "It hasn't changed."

"Thanks for being honest." He swallowed uncomfortably, dropping his finger from her chin and nodding. "That's what I thought."

"I'm sorry," she murmured.

"I'm not," he said, offering her a regretful smile. "It was nice to hope again. It's been a long time. A long, long time."

"I hope you find someone, Beck. You're such a good man."

"He doesn't deserve you," he mumbled.

She leaned over the bolster between them and kissed his cheek then drew back, making sure it was okay.

"*Now* she kisses me," he said with a sad grin.

She giggled through the last of her tears and wiped the wetness from her cheeks. "Friends?"

"Absolutely. I wouldn't have it any other way."

She waved as he pulled away then took her keys from her pocket and walked around the café to the back door that led to her apartment. She could make out a shadowed figure sitting on the stoop with his head hunched over his knees, and her muscles tightened in a fight-or-flight response until she noticed the shock of whitish-blond hair illuminated by her front door light.

Nils looked up as she approached, shifting his position slightly to rest his elbows on his knees and stare at her from the meager pool of light.

"What're you doin' here?" she asked, putting her hands on her hips in an annoyed stance and wishing her stomach would stop fluttering like crazy every time she saw him. It was hard to look indifferent when your whole body responded to someone like she responded to Nils.

He stood up gracefully, picking up the questionnaire that had been sitting beside him.

"Need to talk to you."

The easy-going act he was putting on at Beck's office was more stilted now, but his eyes still looked far more relaxed and less hooded than she'd ever seen them. Maybe he *had* done some serious thinking, because she could see that he was different. He was lighter, somehow. Something had changed.

"What about?"

"Maggie, give me a break," he deadpanned, his blue eyes searing in the dimness of her porch lamp. She held up the questionnaire. "This is bigger than you and me."

"Fine." She flicked a glance at her front door, remembering the last time they were alone in her apartment. Better to have a wide copper bar between them. "I'll open the café. We can sit and talk…for a minute."

Without waiting for his answer, she turned and headed to the front of the building, unlocking the door, and flipping on the lights as he followed behind.

"Do you want coffee?" she asked over her shoulder.

"No, don't go to the trouble."

"It's a coffee shop. It's not trouble. Do you want a cup or not?" She walked to the end of the bar, feeling slightly easier as soon as the familiar barrier stood between them.

"Sure. Decaf."

She switched on the coffee maker and measured out the grounds, trying to calm her pounding heart with the mundane tasks that filled her regular days. She felt him behind her as he pulled out a stool and settled himself on it. His questionnaire hit the bar lightly, but she still didn't turn around.

"Maggie, it's not going to work," he said quietly.

Her heart, which had been cantering, kicked into a gallop. Was he refusing to go to the interview? Did he want to surrender to the federal government and confess their marriage was fraudulent? Didn't he understand that she'd be depor—

"I can't learn all this stuff sitting across a conference table from you in some lawyer's office, who happens to be the guy you're dating. With him breathing down my neck, I'm either going to punch his lights out, or use all of my energy not punching his lights out, but either way I'm not going to absorb anything."

Her tightly bunched shoulders relaxed, and she closed her eyes for a moment, exhaling. He wasn't trying to get out of the interview. She thought about telling him that she and Beck weren't seeing each other anymore but decided against it. Jealousy was a good motivator for Nils, and she needed him motivated. Taking a deep breath, she turned around, trying to keep her face impassive and expression hard. "What do you suggest?"

"We need to spend time together." He shook his head, looking down at the counter. "I know that spending time with me sounds pretty awful to you. I know I hurt you when I left. I didn't mean to, I just...I couldn't—I wasn't ready for..."

"I never offered you anythin'," she said, her cheeks blazing hot as she turned around to pour two cups of coffee into brightly painted ceramic mugs. She took cream from the mini fridge by her legs and put in the amount that he liked. She swirled it and placed it on the counter in front of him.

"I know that." He exhaled loudly, picking up his cup and wincing at the heat as he took a sip. "I'm not good at this."

"You were sayin' we need to spend time together."

"Yeah. I think...I mean, I wasn't that great at book learning. You know, just learning a bunch of facts from a book or a—a questionnaire." He swiped disdainfully at the packet on the bar in front of him. "I don't want to go to jail. I don't want you to be deported. I did a lot of reading on the internet last night after I got your text. This Stokes interview? It's hardcore, Maggie. We need to appear married. Really married. Not green-card married."

She took a tentative sip of her coffee then leaned her elbows on the counter, looking up at him as he continued.

"And we're not going to look married by memorizing a bunch of facts. You can read that my mother died of cancer, but I think you'll answer the question totally differently if you've seen me talk about her death. You can read that my favorite food is meatballs, but it's a hell of a lot different if you learn to make them and share a meal with me."

She tilted her head and pursed her lips. "We've talked about your mother lots and I've seen you eat meatballs a hundred and one times."

"Then you. You lost your father and I don't even know how. I only just found out you were adopted. I don't know how you feel about that. I want to know. I mean, I *should* know, um, for the interview. And I'm not going to learn it by reading the words 'I felt sad when my dad died.' on a form. They're going to know we memorized facts. They're going to know we're lying."

Nils wasn't given to long speeches and this was one of the longest that he'd ever made that Maggie could recall. Again she wondered about the changes in him, the relaxing of his countenance, the loosening up of his communication, the way he could hold her eyes without flinching.

He sighed before continuing. "I wish I could say that we don't have to be friends, but we do. Married people are friends with each other. I wish I could say that I'd never touch you again, but married people touch each other, especially newlyweds." He paused, looking at her gravely. "We need a truce. Just for the next few weeks. We don't have time to be mad at each other and sort out all of that stuff from before I left. We need to do this. Just do it."

"A truce?"

"So that we can figure this out together. Not with Beck.

You. And me."

He picked up his mug again and took another sip. She could tell he was finished speaking for now and he would patiently wait for her to respond.

She took a deep breath. What he was saying made complete and total sense, of course. They didn't have time to process what had happened between them—they had to figure out, minimally, how to be friends again, and fast. He was right—they needed an immediate truce, no matter how hurt she was, no matter how much she wished things had worked out differently between them.

"Okay." She sighed, rubbing her sweaty palms together. "How does this look? This *truce*?"

"Well, we were going to meet at Beck's every night and exchange personal facts about each other, right?"

She nodded, trying to keep the corners of her mouth from tilting up.

"So, we still meet every night. Seven o'clock. Your place. Whenever I don't have a tour."

"And when you do?"

"Get Bethany to run the café. Come with me."

Her eyes widened. "No! I canna do that, go cavortin' all over Yellowst—"

"Maggie? My wife would occasionally go on tours with me. It's a fact. And I've got one next weekend. Friday afternoon to Sunday afternoon."

She huffed. Going on a tour with him was different from meeting for two or three hours over dinner. It meant spending a whole day together, possibly even sleeping—

She placed her hands over her cheeks. "Separate tents?"

He shook his head. "No. It'll be the best possible opportunity for us to practice on other people. You can have your own sleeping bag and I'll put my back to you, but..."

"But we'll have to share."

He shrugged. "Like a married couple."

Like a married couple.

She studied his face, considering the easy way he'd just said the words, words he could barely touch before he left. Before she'd yelled at him in the conference room, he mentioned he'd done a lot of thinking while out on tour. About what? What had he thought about that had relieved some of the perpetual burden he'd always carried on his shoulders.

"What happened to you?" she murmured.

"What do you mean?"

"You've changed."

"Maybe a bit," he conceded without a fight. "I did—"

"—a lot of thinkin' in the park," she finished. "About what?"

He seemed to turn this over in his head for a moment, staring at her briefly then looking away as he used to. But instead of keeping his eyes from hers, he surprised her, by looking back up again quickly. "A lot of things, Maggie May. I'll be at your place tomorrow at seven. We'll learn everything about each other that there is to know."

He put his hand out to her—his big, calloused, tan hand that would make electrical currents trail up her arm like lightning hitting a tree branch the second she took it. She

235

knew this and stared at it for an extra second, wondering if she had the strength to bear the heat, or if she would combust the second they touched.

"A truce," she replied.

Then she reached out, touched him, and let herself be electrified.

Chapter 13

After they shook hands, Nils left the café quickly, sticking around only long enough to agree that tomorrow night it would be his turn to make them dinner. He'd gotten a lot of what he wanted from Maggie without much of a fight and he didn't want to press his luck any further. Since he had the rest of the week off after the long tour, he could be at her place as early as five o'clock to prepare it. She'd given him a key with tentative approval, requesting Swedish meatballs.

"Wait a minute," she'd added as he headed for the door, "I'll try to get Bethany to come at five. If I dinna get anythin' else out of this marriage, I want that recipe. Dinna start until I get there, aye?"

He'd tried one of Lars's moves and winked at her from over his shoulder, nodded once, and shut the door behind him carefully.

After sleeping in long past his normal five a.m., and showering leisurely to enjoy every drop of hot water on his body after weeks of going without, he headed to Arnold's for groceries.

Swedish meatballs could be made, he supposed with derision, with frozen meatballs and brown sauce from a packet, but that's not how Britt Lindstrom had made hers and it's certainly not how she'd taught her children to make theirs.

He strolled through the spice aisle, picking up nutmeg, allspice, and ginger, then over to the baking goods where he chose a small bag of white flour, brown sugar, black pepper, and salt. He chose fresh ground pork and beef from the butcher case and a Vidalia onion from produce. Finally he picked up a carton of eggs, heavy cream, butter, and sour cream. He doubled back for egg noodles, whispering "*Jag är ledsen, Mamma*" because he knew full and well that meatballs should be traditionally served with mashed potatoes, not noodles. He couldn't help it. Nils was a man who loved his noodles.

He paused then, wondering if he should get something for dessert and realized, with some surprise, that he had no idea what sort of dessert Maggie liked best. He could learn that tonight.

He felt his face soften, thinking about her eyes last night when he'd walked into the conference room at Beck's office. Oh, she'd been furious with him, but she couldn't keep her eyes off of him either. And it had done something to his insides; he'd already resolved to figure out a way to make space for Maggie in his life romantically, but hearing her soft gasp? Seeing her eyes track down his body like a full blown body scan? It had set his blood on fire, made him harden and flex inside, but it had also reassured him.

She was still...winnable. She wasn't lost to him, and his relief was fierce.

But Beck had certainly thrown a wrench in his plans.

Nils couldn't quite figure out their relationship, because if she was with Beck, she wouldn't have looked at *him* like that, would she?

He decided to skip dessert and headed to the checkout line, which snaked all the way back to the produce area with housewives doing their Monday morning shopping. He didn't mind. He nudged his cart up slowly, still thinking about Maggie. It didn't matter if she was with Beck or not. He intended to make his feelings known over the course of the next few weeks. Thanks to their truce, he'd have her all to himself, every day, every night, and he would show her, he would wear her down, he would win her back. But first, he needed to find out—as subtly as possible—how she felt about adoption. Not *being* adopted, though he cared about that also, but adopting children...someday, of their own.

Sometime on Sunday night he'd realized that adoption was the loophole he'd been looking for. *There are so many ways to have a family, Nils.* That's what she'd said when she revealed her own history to him. Would she consider adopting children? Would she give up the chance to have her own biological children in order to be with him? Was it possible? Maybe it was. Maybe it was even fate that Maggie, herself, had been adopted, because it might make her more amenable to the idea. Children, now the most significant stop-gap to them being together, might not have to be the wedge between them after all. They could still have a family together if adoption was an option.

Which left only one, final wedge: If he told Maggie the awful truth of what had happened to Veronica and Jens, would she still want him? Would she still be able to love him?

He pushed his cart forward and offered a friendly wave to a friend of his father's, still mired in thought.

He'd never know unless he took the risk of telling her. Not tonight. Not right away, of course. He had weeks to re-secure her affection for him and hope that it was enough. Enough to love him in spite of the terrible tragedy of his eighteenth summer.

"All good, Nils?" asked Palmer Jones, as he scanned items and carefully bagged them.

"Good enough," answered Nils, offering a polite smile to the white-haired proprietor of the store, whom he'd known for most of his life.

"I'm guessing meatballs tonight, eh?"

"That's the plan."

"You Lindstroms ever going to share that recipe?"

Nils chuckled lightly. "Only with family, Palmer."

Family. Like his pappa, his sister and his brothers. Like Paul, for all that they weren't blood. And family like his *wife*, like Maggie.

***

No matter how hard she tried to think about something else, all she could think about throughout the day was five o'clock. She'd make a cup of coffee and check the clock. Reconcile bills and check the clock. Place an order for more paper cups and filters and check the clock. There was no escaping the moment the hands would align, and she'd exit the back of the café to find Nils on her doorstep again. She glanced at her watch for the umpteenth time: Four forty-five. Her shoulders bounced up merrily with anticipation as she watched Bethany, who was a senior at Gardiner High School and had been recommended by Paul to assist her over the summer, handily make a tray of cappuccinos.

"Hey, Beth," started Maggie, untying her apron. "I'm goin' to need a bit of help throughout August. Might spend a weekend or two in the park and I was thinkin' of leavin' early in the evenin's. You have a friend who could help pick up the slack? I'll make you assistant manager and give you the keys and a wee raise too, so you'd be in charge when I'm not here."

Bethany's big blue eyes widened, and she grinned, nodding at Maggie. "Would you mind my sister, Miss Campbell?"

No matter how many times she asked the teen to call her Maggie, Bethany insisted on calling her boss Miss Campbell. Maggie had a passing thought that Mrs. Lindstrom would be more accurate, but shushed it. "Not if she's just as responsible as you. What year is she?"

"She'll be a junior, but she just turned seventeen. Her name's Summer."

"Have her stop in tomorrow, aye? I'll be off now."

Maggie shoved the folded apron under the counter and popped into her tiny office at the end of the bar, looking at herself in the mirror. She took a brush and lip gloss from her desk and brushed her hair, then swiped some goop on her lips so they glistened. Frowning at her reflection, she wiped the goop off. She wasn't trying to look sexy, was she? A truce didn't mean she'd forgiven Nils for kissing her and leaving. A truce didn't mean he had true feelings for her and even if he did, it didn't mean he was ready to acknowledge them. Tonight wasn't a date. It was reconnaissance. That's all.

He wasn't waiting for her at her back door, as she'd predicted. She found him in her kitchen, dwarfing a chair at her kitchen table with his massive body that wore banged-up, frayed jeans. They probably felt as soft as they looked, and even from behind she could see that the white T-shirt he wore was going to show off his assets in front like a Greek god. Her fingers twitched, remembering the feel of those hard muscles under her palms as he kissed her. She sighed lightly to herself, wondering how she was going to make it through a night with him, let alone four weeks.

"You're here."

He turned in the chair, revealing her *Cosmopolitan* magazine in his hands. "I didn't hear you come in. I thought I'd…do some, you know…research."

Maggie's lips tilted up, catching the cover story in bright pink. "On how to please your man in bed?"

"Do you read this?" he asked, a little wide-eyed.

"Faithfully."

"Maggie May, it's…explicit."

She felt the heat in her cheeks, but this was part of who she was and the whole point of these evenings together was to get to know one another, right? "I read romance books, too. The dirty kind."

She dumped her purse on the kitchen counter and turned to face him, raising one eyebrow in challenge.

"I didn't know," he said softly. "Did you read that one about, um, fifty shades…"

"*Fifty Shades of Grey*?" she asked, amused that he knew about that book at all. She sat down across from him at the table feeling sassy. "You bet. All three."

"What was your favorite scene?" he asked, placing the magazine on the table and leaning toward her.

She looked down at the table and chuckled lightly, thinking that this was totally unchartered territory. She and Nils had always enjoyed polite conversations at the café and over euchre, and even though those conversations sometimes touched on their families or feelings, they'd never discussed anything remotely sexual, for all of the tension that existed between them. When she looked up, the searing heat in his eyes made her mouth water, made her smile fade a little, made the muscles between her thighs contract a lot.

"In the first, second, or third book?" she asked in a low voice.

"The first."

"The elevator scene," she murmured, placing her hands flat on the table before her, inches away from his.

"Mm-hm. In the beginning. I liked it, too."

"You liked…" Maggie's mind grappled with the meaning behind his words. "You mean, you…"

"Ask me *my* favorite part."

She was still trying to get her head around this conversation, let alone the fact that Nils had actually read *Fifty Shades of Grey*. The sheer intimacy of it, of knowing they'd both read the deeply sexual books, made her breath catch. Who had he thought of as he'd been reading? Her heart raced and her breathing quickened, shallow, like soft panting in her head.

"What was your favorite part?" she asked, wondering if he noticed the slight tremble in her voice.

"In book one?"

"Y-yes."

"Their first time."

"Th-their—"

"He tells her: 'You are mine. Only mine.' Remember?"

"Yes," she murmured.

Maggie's breath was so fast and short now, she knew he could hear it, but she didn't care. She couldn't look away from him. Couldn't look away from the ice-blue eyes that were so scorching hot, she wondered how she hadn't burst into flames. Wondered how in God's name she'd ever look at those eyes again without remembering him quoting Christian Grey.

Suddenly he grinned at her, flicking his glance to the groceries on the counter and gesturing with his chin. "Meatballs?"

She blinked twice. And just like that, her shoulders relaxed, and she started giggling for no reason at all. Except for this: she was happy. For the first time in months and months and months, she felt happy.

"Meatballs," she agreed, smiling up at him.

***

He couldn't think of another way to get out of the conversation. It's not like he'd intended to launch into a conversation about his occasional habit of reading highly sexualized romance novels, but that was the whole point of the next few weeks, right? It's something his wife should know...plus, once her cheeks had colored, he hadn't been able to resist. She looked so cocky and adorable, challenging him, wanting to prove to him that she was so naughty. He couldn't resist shocking her right back.

As they unpacked the two bags of groceries, her hip brushed against his and he sucked in a quick breath. Damn, but he wanted to reach out and pull her up against him, especially after that charged conversation. But, demanding too much from her too fast could destroy the tentative truce between them. He needed to bide his time.

"I thought you only read those travel books...like *A Walk in the Woods.*"

"Hand me a bowl. Big one. For mixing," he said, unwrapping the white paper from the ground meat. "I don't date much. I don't go out much. I like TV, but there's only so much you can watch, and Gardiner doesn't have a movie theater. Not to mention, books are good company during overnights in the park. So, I read. A lot."

"All kinds of books, too," she replied, with a touch of sass in her voice.

"I read the three in that series, yes. I didn't buy the first one. I sort of stumbled across it. I was already at the airport one Saturday to pick up folks when they announced that the flight I was waiting for would be three hours late. I went back to the van to wait it out, and found the book shoved between one of the seats and the window." He shrugged. "I had nothing else to read, so…"

"Three hours later, you were addicted."

"You got a spatula?" He nodded. "Addicted. Yeah. Pretty much. I know that lots of folks criticized her writing, but I sure liked those books. They kept me hooked."

Maggie rummaged through her drawers for a spatula and handed it to him, watching carefully as he mashed the two lumps of meat together.

"Here's the trick, Maggie May. You ready?"

She hopped up to sit on the counter beside the bowl. "Ready."

"First of all, you have to stop calling them 'Swedish meatballs.' No one with the surname Lindstrom would call them that, okay?"

"Okay," she nodded.

"Repeat after me: Svenska Kottbullar."

"Svenska Kottbullar."

The sound of his Maggie speaking in Swedish made an unexpected smile break out across his face, but he looked down quickly so she wouldn't have the pressure of seeing how freaking pleased it had made him. He reached for a small bowl that had been resting on her counter.

"What's that?" she asked, and when he glanced at her, her nose was turned up.

"Bread crumbs and cream. Been soaking since I got here." He dumped it into the bowl with the meat. "Now watch. We mash up the meat and bread crumbs and add egg, sugar, and spices."

"How much of each?" she asked.

He looked up at her. "Like, how many teaspoons?"

She nodded.

He had no idea. He'd watched his mother make meatballs as a child, and learned from watching. He knew how long his mother's hand paused over the bowl with a cylinder of salt or a small bottle of nutmeg, but he had no clue of how to translate that to amounts.

"We don't cook like that," he instructed. "You have to watch. That's the only way to learn."

"Svenska Kottbullar," she said softly, as though testing the words out on her tongue.

Her tongue. Damn it, why'd his brain have to go there? He felt a bead of sweat begin at his hairline and make its way down his face.

"Tell me something in Gaelic," he said to distract himself.

"Okay," she answered, swinging her leg beside him.

It was bare and tan and smooth. He wondered how often she had to shave it to keep it that smooth and suddenly he didn't trust himself not to touch her, so he threw the spatula in the sink and plunged his fingers into the bowl as he'd seen his mother do a million times before.

"Tha an t-acras orm," she said softly.

The sound of her words, soft and rolling and slightly exotic, made his whole body respond. His fingers curled and kneaded, grateful for something to do, for something to grab and touch.

"Means?" he ground out.

"I'm hungry." She reached over, placing her hand over

his, sliding it over the slick mess of ingredients on the back of his hand, through the threads of his fingers. "I'll do it. You must have something else to do?"

She'd knocked the wind out of him the second her skin had touched his. He stood motionless at the counter staring at her hand resting on top of his in the center of the chrome bowl.

"Maggie," he started, but she reached for the bowl with her other hand, pulling it away from him, onto her lap. His hand hovered motionless over the counter, cold and goopy, bereft of hers. He cleared his throat. "Can I use your bathroom?"

"Of course. You know where it is, right? Same place as it was in Jenny's apartment."

"I know. I remember from the night when I—"

He looked up and his eyes slammed into hers, finishing the sentence in his head…took your pants off and kissed you for the first time. He watched as realization passed over her face too and her cheeks bloomed pink.

"And I'll just keep kneading this?"

"Yeah. I'll, uh, I'll be right back to slice the onion."

He washed his hands quickly and sat on the edge of her bathtub, willing his body to calm down, his heart to stop racing. He noticed a pink bottle beside him and caught the black writing: Strawberry Italian Soda. Twisting off the top, he inhaled deeply, and goose bumps sprouted up along his tan, corded arms. He'd know that smell anywhere. It was Maggie's smell. It was the smell that had haunted him for four straight weeks in Yellowstone. The smell he'd looked for in his mind as he fell asleep and made him hard as stone as he awoke every morning. He turned the bottle over.

Damn you, Philosophy shampoo. You don't know what you've been doing to me.

He wanted her. He wanted her like he'd never wanted anyone or anything in his entire life, he thought as he carefully screwed the top back onto the bottle and set it back down on the little corner shelf. But, he had a marathon in front of him, not a sprint, and tonight was just the opening lap. Not to mention, for all that she had shared her love of dirty books and touched his hand as she took the mixing bowl from him, it was possible she was still seeing Beck.

He clenched his fists together, remembering them at Midsommardagen, all cozy by the fire. Then again, she'd kissed him, Nils, a few days after. Talk about mixed messages. What was the deal with them? She wouldn't see much of Beck in the evenings over the next few weeks, but Nils's stomach lurched as he imagined Beck stopping by on his lunch break, secreting Maggie up the back stairs and having his way with her before returning to his goddamned office. Nils winced, grinding his jaw until he feared it would pop. He couldn't take it. He couldn't bear not knowing.

He hopped up and strode back into the kitchen where he found Maggie standing at the counter slicing up the onion.

"What next?" she asked cheerfully.

"We sauté the onion in butter. Add it to the meat. Shape the meatballs. Brown them. Bake them. Are you seeing Beck?"

Her face jerked up and the knife clattered down on the cutting board. She turned to face him. "What?"

"Beck Westman. Lawyer. Short. Funny looking. Are you seeing him?"

She pursed her lips, but her eyes were laughing as they locked on his, damn her.

"He's not exactly a Lindstrom, but he's not short either. And I think most girls would agree he's not funny lo—"

Marathon not spr—Oh, screw it.

Nils reached out and grabbed her waist, pulling her to him, her body against his body. He tried to control his breathing, but he was losing the battle because yanking her into his chest had released a burst of her shampoo scent and pressed her breasts against his body and he was helpless to do anything but lean his head down and catch her bottom lip between his.

***

Aside from the quick kiss at their wedding, it was the first time he'd ever really initiated a kiss between them, and Maggie's knees went to jelly. As she slumped, she felt his arms lock around her waist like steel and she leaned back against his arms as he leaned forward, tilting his head to capture her lips again. That's the moment when she stopped thinking about anything but this confusing, addicting man holding her in his arms. That's the moment she knew she was ruined, forever, for anyone but him.

Her hands slid slowly up his chest until she touched the hot skin of his neck, where she rested them, the heat from his tanned skin making them tingle and tremble. He sucked on her top lip, nipping it gently as he turned them slightly so that her bottom was pushed up against the drawers under the counter. He released her only to put his hands on her waist, lifting her effortlessly onto the counter before reaching up to hold her face, gently, tenderly, the pads of his thumbs pressing into the skin of her cheeks as his fingers threaded through her hair. Her fingers skated down his forearms, touching the hard contours of muscles and veins, lingering at his elbows, and finally dropping to his hips where they slipped under his T-shirt and curled into the soft, worn denim of his waistband.

His fingers deserted her face and sank into her hips, pulling her to the edge of the counter so that he fit perfectly into the apex of her thighs and she sighed into his mouth as she raised her legs, sliding them up his jeans and locking them around his back.

He kissed a trail from her lips, tracing her jawline to her ear where he took the tender lobe between his teeth while sliding his rough hands up the soft skin of her back. She arched against him, gasping at the sensation of her tender skin held lightly between his teeth, while his fingers spanned her body from spine to breast.

Her core started to vibrate. Wait a minute. The vibration that she thought was internal was…external? She leaned back from Nils, glancing down at the pocket of his jeans that was flush against her inner thigh.

"Nils," she breathed. "Your phone."

"What?" he panted.

"Your phone. It's vibrating. It's ringing."

251

"No," he said, lowering his lips to hers again.

She pushed gently against his chest, regaining her senses as she murmured against his lips with breathy urgency, "Answer your phone."

"No," he mumbled, pressing feather-light kisses along her jaw. Her eyes closed again, and she moaned softly, letting her fingers play with the bristly hairs on the nape of his neck.

"Could be...important," she murmured.

"Impossible."

"Why?"

"Because nothing's more important than this."

As his tongue found hers, his hands slid down her back, over her jean shorts, squeezing her ass lightly as he pulled her closer. His phone had quieted, but a second later, it vibrated against her inner thigh again, an almost unbearably erotic sensation as she tightened her legs around him, stroking his tongue with hers as his fingers flexed and relaxed, over and over again, making her gyrate lightly against him.

"Damn it," he exclaimed, pulling back from her, and shoving his hand in his pocket. He put the phone to his ear, staring at her intently. "What?"

She touched her fingers to her lips, wiping lightly as he kept his eyes locked with hers, listening to whomever was on the phone. As Maggie started scooting forward to hop off the counter, Nils used his free hand to press down on her bare thigh and keep her there.

"It was only three nights at the Yellowstone Inn, not four."

He glanced down at his hand, which he slid forward, under the frayed edge of her cut-off shorts, gently, experimentally. She looked down at his hand and waves of hunger kept her frozen, unmoving, as his index finger found the fold where her thigh curved into her pelvis. Her breath hitched as his finger glided under her panties.

"Four. No, I mean three. Listen, can we do this tomorrow?"

"Oh," she gasped, eyes closing as she braced her hands on the counter behind her and leaned her head back against the cabinets. Her breathing quickened as his finger explored her soft folds, finally finding its mark and stroking the small, slick bud of her sex.

"Tomorrow," he repeated in a low, strangled voice.

Her eyes were closed, but she heard his phone hit the counter as his finger continued its brushing, rubbing caresses. She bit her lip, listening to the sounds of her breathing as the unbelievably sweet pressure mounted, pooling in the spot he stroked with a more rhythmic, less teasing, cadence.

"Jesus, Maggie, you're so wet."

His words were so hot and so unexpected, her fingers curled on the countertop behind her as she panted, the hot air almost painful on her lips until he licked them, wetting them, plunging his tongue into her mouth for her to suck on just as she tipped over the edge of sanity, convulsing, trembling, falling apart against his hand that slowed its motions, following the arc of her orgasm. Finally, he withdrew his finger, reaching for her and pulling her into his arms to kiss her gently, tenderly, until the fierce throbbing subsided. His lips brushed against hers, soft and cool, a soothing zephyr after the explosion of heat she'd just experienced.

She felt him lean away and she opened her eyes slowly through a fog of latent arousal, to find him staring at her, his expression so intense, so full of emotion, she held her breath as she stared back at him.

For the first time since she'd known Nils Lindstrom, she saw love looking back at her, and she never, ever wanted to look away.

***

Feeling Maggie climax against his hand was the most erotic, arousing thing he'd ever experienced. But surprisingly, as much as he knew their chemistry would be mind-blowing in bed, he wasn't in a rush to get her there. He'd known that he loved Maggie for a long time, but being with her physically was changing that love from a distant longing to something more real, more solid, more undeniable. Something substantial had just shifted between them. He wondered if she felt it, too.

"Are you okay?" he asked.

"Aye," she said softly, letting her legs drop slowly from around his waist.

"That was intense."

"Aye," she said again. She leaned forward, staring at her hands in her lap.

"Do we need to talk about it?"

She shook her head no, so he put his finger under her

chin and lifted it, giving her a small, reassuring smile. "Tell me you're hungry."

"Tha an t-acras orm," she said, luminous green eyes staring up at him with uncertainty.

"Maggie," he said. "Ask me anything."

"Why did you always say you just wanted to be friends?"

"I didn't know how to do this." He stepped away from her, taking the cutting board of chopped onions and moving them closer to the stove. "Frying pan?"

She hopped down from the counter then squatted in front of the cabinets to get one for him. He plopped a bit of butter in the skillet and set it on the stove to melt.

"What does that mean? You're a grown man, not a wee lad."

"I've got history, like anyone else."

She sat down at the table to watch him work. "Tell me."

"Let's start simpler and work up to it."

"I need to know somethin' first."

He pushed the onions into the pan with the back of the knife and turned to face her, folding his arms across his chest.

"Was that a one-time thing? What just happened?"

"God, I hope not," he answered.

"In twenty-four hours, we've gone from not speakin' for a month to agreein' to play at being married, to…that," she said, a blush deepening the already pink color of her cheeks.

"I don't know any other way to do this. To make it look real, it has to feel real."

He was pretty sure she winced as she looked away.

"What about when the truce is over?"

Aw, hell, that's not how he meant it. What had just happened between him and Maggie had zero to do with the goddamned truce. And even more than merely feeling real, he wanted it to be real. Over? He didn't ever want it to be over. Frankly, he hadn't even thought in terms of it ever being over. As far as he was concerned, their marriage started forty-five minutes ago when she walked in the door after work. Getting to know each other? Figuring out how to be married? Eventually telling their families? Details they'd hash out together over time.

He looked back at her, trying to be brave. It was entirely possible that this was only a one-month temporary arrangement for her, and that Beck would be waiting for her on the other side. And even as that made his heart ache, he comforted himself that he had a month to make her see they were right for each other, to try to find compromises that would let them be together. For now, pressuring her wouldn't get him anywhere.

"I guess we can walk away," he said softly. "If one of us wants to."

She nodded, biting her lower lip before looking down. It was on the tip of his tongue to say, *But it won't be me. It'll never be me. I'm in this for the long haul. I'm in this forever.*

"Then I guess we should be careful. With our feelin's."

"I guess so," he responded.

He gulped quietly, miserably, as he stared at her downcast face that had been so enraptured in his arms just minutes before. His eyes watered as he turned around and stirred the onions, moving them around in the pan so they wouldn't burn.

Chapter 14

On Thursday night, they sat side by side on the couch in front of Maggie's TV, watching her favorite movie, The Quiet Man, which Nils had never seen before. His mother and sister's tastes had tended toward high-brow British movies, while he and his brothers, when they actually watched a movie, opted for action.

An old John Wayne romance wasn't something he'd been likely to come across, but he had to admit, it was pretty good. American man, spirited Irish woman with red hair...he glanced over at Maggie, who sat on the other side of an enormous popcorn bowl, with a perpetual smile on her face and her feet tucked up under her butt. She wore a pair of skimpy pajama shorts that she changed into almost every evening after work—that tortured him for the entirety of their date—and a low-cut sweatshirt that left just enough to the imagination to keep things on the painful side of interesting.

Especially since they'd barely touched again since Monday night's kitchen make-out session.

As if by tacit agreement, they'd concentrated on their questionnaires, not writing in the answers, but asking the questions and talking about them. He'd learned that she never knew her birth parents. Never went to find them. She'd been born in what she called a Magdalene House, a convent-like institution, and assumed her biological mother had been an unwed teen. She also assumed she was from Kerry, since her adoption papers had listed the institution address there, but other than those few bits of information, the rest of her early history, aside from her birthday, was unknown.

"And you were happy? Your childhood?" he'd asked her over grilled burgers and potato salad on their second night.

"I guess. My mum and da loved me. In their own way. As best as they could anyone. As much as they did Ian, anyway."

He sensed she wasn't finished, so he sat patiently, giving her the time and space to finish her thoughts. She sat staring at her food, her brows creased and worried.

"What else?" he asked.

When she smiled, he recognized it—from his vault of friendship knowledge—as her melancholy smile, the smile she forced for the benefit of someone else.

"Another time."

She'd left off talking about her brother. Perhaps the shadows across her face belonged to him. He prodded gently. "And Ian? You mentioned once that you're not close?"

She shrugged lightly. "He was older, maybe a little resentful of his adopted wee sister. Now he's married and settled north of Edinburgh with a family of his own. I barely see him."

"And your, um, mum?"

She grinned at his use of her vernacular. "She was a hard worker. Most kids are raised by their mum while their da goes to work. But, my da went to the pub and my mum went to work. She kept food on the table and clothes on my body, but..."

"But what?"

"I dinna think life turned out the way she wanted it to. She loved my da, you know, when they were young. Even when they adopted me. Even when I was a little girl. He was a gentle drunk. He could make her laugh, even three sheets to the wind. It got worse, though. He died of cirrhosis at forty-three, leavin' her alone with a little girl and a rowdy teenager."

"I'm sorry."

"Me too," she murmured.

"Do you miss him?"

She shrugged again. "I didn't know him very well." She looked down, lost in thought for a few moments and he watched as a tentative smile spread uncertainly across her face. "He sang to me. Bawdy songs that he shouldn't a'taught me. I remember every one of them."

He reached out and covered her hand with his, and when she looked up there were tears brightening her eyes. For the first time for as long as he could remember, he felt the silent communion he'd always suspected that committed couples experienced. He felt the pain of her loss, that terrible loss of potential when someone you love dies. All of the things that weren't, and now, could never be. He related to it. He understood it. He reached out to her to let her know that from now on, he'd own some of it for her, if she'd let him.

After a moment, he drew his hand back and as she dabbed at her eyes with her napkin he asked, "And Graham? Your cousin?"

"Wee Gingy." She'd smiled then, nodding her head and chuckling. "He's a big handful of trouble and no mistake. I told you he's comin', right?"

"No!" exclaimed Nils. "When?"

He'd done a quick calculation that a troublemaking younger cousin would throw waves into the waters of their nightly dates. He knew it was selfish, but he wanted every possible moment he had with Maggie while their truce was in effect.

"Oh, a few weeks. End of September, I think she said. My aunt called a week ago and said she'd finally booked a ticket for him to come. He's finishin' a carpentry course and tryin' to keep his nose clean 'til it's over with. He'll come for the fall and build me a deck for outdoor coffee and dinin'. Nice, aye?"

Nils had nodded, but he quietly promised himself to keep an eye on her wayward cousin.

They'd discussed other details of her childhood; where she went to primary and secondary schools, what subjects she liked the best and the names of her two best friends "back home": Fiona and Becca, with whom she still spoke on the phone monthly.

Throughout all of it…their dinners and conversations, even when they talked about something sad, he felt the underlying tension between them. He felt it when their hands brushed against each other washing the dishes or setting the table. He felt it when he reached for her hand and she didn't pull away. He felt it every night when he headed to the door, his feet like cement as he forced himself to leave her without touching her, without holding her, without kissing her goodnight, without making love to her in her bed which teased and taunted him every time he passed it en route to the bathroom. He certainly felt it now. He was supposed to be watching The Quiet Man, but with her warm, wonderful body only inches away from his in flimsy pajamas that drove him crazy, it was almost impossible to concentrate on the movie.

He shifted uncomfortably in his seat, throwing his arm over the back of the couch, but his hand barely reached her shoulder, and he couldn't slide over next to her with the swimming-pool-sized bowl of popcorn between them. He glanced down at her legs, feeling his body tighten. Her legs had been the focus of his ardor ever since the night in May when he'd pulled her jeans off, his knuckles skimming the soft skin as she lay almost passed out on her bed. He ground his teeth together then forced his eyes back to the screen. As distracting as she was, it was important that he knew the plot of her favorite movie. In fact, he'd looked up some trivia online before coming over tonight. Maybe to impress her. Just a little.

"This is only the second of five movies that paired John

Wayne and Maureen O'Hara," he commented nonchalantly, lowering his useless arm and reaching for a handful of popcorn.

He felt her look over at him, but kept his eyes trained to the screen.

"Is that so? I had no idea! You did some research, did you?"

"I did."

"What were the others?"

"Rio Grande, McClintock, Wings of Eagles, and Big Jake."

"Never heard of any of them, which means The Quiet Man was the best of the bunch."

"They were Westerns."

"Do you like Westerns?" she asked, her eyes sparkling in the ambient light of the TV.

This is how it was. Talk a little, ask a question. Talk a little, ask a question. Always learning more about each other, always aware that they needed to cram years of knowledge into the space of a month. Mostly he was okay with it. Unless he remembered their conversation over onions on Monday night. Predictably, the more time he spent with Maggie, the more his feelings deepened, the more agonizing the thought of their "truce" ever ending.

He shrugged, reaching for another handful of popcorn. "I don't have anything against them."

"But action is your favorite," she reconfirmed.

"That's right," he said, grinning at her.

"Especially Indiana Jones."

"Right again."

She grinned back at him then shifted her attention once again to the TV, giggling as Michaleen Flynn walked into the newlyweds' cottage to find their bed broken.

"Impetuous! Homeric!" the actor exclaimed in an amazed whisper.

"Homeric," she repeated in a soft voice full of laughter, moving her hair off the shoulder closest to him.

Drawn by the scent of strawberries suddenly wafting in his direction, he looked over, transfixed by the curve of her neck where it met her shoulder—the smooth, white skin, covered in freckles. He wished he could lean over and kiss every one of them. Touch his lips to her skin over and over and over again until she—

"Aren't you watchin'?"

"Yeah," he murmured, flicking his eyes from her shoulder to her legs and then back up to her lips.

"Not me. The movie," she scolded.

He took a deep breath, unable to keep the frustrated expression off his face. When he exhaled through his nose, he felt like a rutting bull, like Maggie was a female in heat and he had to have her, or some critical law of nature would be violated. Swallowing, and slightly petulant, he looked at her legs again before turning back to the screen.

Shorts that short should be illegal and people in fake relationships should practice making out more.

"Nils?" she whispered.

"Hmm?"

"You're doin' that thing where you clench your jaw."

"Leave it alone, Maggie."

"Why do you do that? What does it mean?"

"Nothing."

"Tell me. We're supposed to get to know each oth—"

He whipped his face to her, his self-control at its bitter end. "It means I'm sitting next to you watching a movie and every time you move I smell your hair which makes me look over and check out your legs which are ridiculously long for such a short person and make me remember what it felt like to have them around my waist, which makes me remember you sucking on my tongue while your body fell apart against my hand on Monday night. Damn it, Maggie, I want you! All the time. Every minute. This is torture. Christ, can't you see that?"

Her smile had faded halfway through his diatribe and her eyes were wide as she stared back at him. Then—if her goal was to keep him at arm's length—she made a mistake. A big mistake. She dropped her glance to his lips and licked her own.

Watching her do that was like being shocked by a live wire. His blood raced, hot as lava, to one place and his breath was short and furious as he stared back at her. He needed to leave. Now. Right now. If he didn't, he was pretty sure she'd be on her back beneath him in the space of a hot minute.

"I'm sorry. I'm—I'm gonna go. I'll read what happens in the movie online. I'll be back tomorrow."

As he started to stand, she reached out and placed a hand on his thigh keeping him seated. With her other hand, she picked up the remote from the armrest beside her and turned off the TV. She stood up in front of him, her body silhouetted by the ambient light from outside, and held out her hand to him.

"Dinna go," she whispered.

He looked at her hand in desperation. "What are you asking me?"

"To stay."

"Overnight?"

"Overnight," she confirmed softly, but he listened carefully to the word and—damn it all to hell!—her voice wavered.

He was grateful for the darkness which concealed his disappointment. Before this moment, he knew he wanted to have sex with Maggie, of course, but the reality had never felt as possible as it did right then. And yet, that waver said more than her actions. That waver told him that while she might be ready to sleep with him, chances were, she wasn't. And in that instant, he knew, in both his heart and his aching groin, it would be a mistake for them to add the possible confusion of sex to their relationship.

When they finally did sleep together, he wanted them both to be sure.

He took her hand and stood up, but as she turned toward her bedroom, tugging his hand lightly, he pulled her back toward him and brought her hand to his lips. He let them rest softly over the warm skin on the back of her hand, breathing her in, hating what he had to do. He closed his eyes, cursing himself for the biggest fool that ever walked the earth…the woman he loved, the woman he wanted, the woman who was, in fact, his wife, was asking him to lie down beside her, and he was about to say…

"No, Maggie May. Not tonight."

"What?" she asked, confusion making her delivery high and sharp.

"There is nothing I want more than to wake up next to you. Nothing. But nothing about the way we've gone about this has been in order. We went from friends to married, and now we're learning about each other and it's—"

"Stop talkin'. Stop…talkin'. Are you sayin' no?"

"I'm saying that I don't want you to regret it."

She pulled her hand away with more force than needed, stepping back from him and putting her hands on her hips.

Daaaaaaaamn. Her angry stance. She was pissed.

"You need to go home. Right. Bloody. Now."

"Maggie," he started, "you have to know—"

"You have to know I want you out of here. Now."

"I just don't—"

"…want to sleep with me. I know. I heard. Let's not rehash it."

She marched to the door, throwing it open so hard it banged loudly into the vestibule wall, making a small dent. She stood there, furious, with her hands still on her hips while she waited for him to leave.

"I'm trying to do the right thing," he gritted out, stalking to the door. He stopped inches from her and turned. "You actually think I don't want you?"

He put his hands through her arms, pulling her roughly

against his body, running his hands down to her ass, which he shoved forward roughly so her pelvis was forced up against his crotch. Her eyes widened as she made contact with the rigid thickness of his erection. "This isn't about me not wanting you. You can go ahead and assume I want you every passing second, every millisecond, every nanosecond, and every little space in between. There is literally no moment left when I am not dying. Of want. For you."

Her mouth was lightly open in surprise as she stared up at him. "Then why...?"

"Your voice wavered."

"W-wavered?"

He loosened his grip on her, sliding his hands up under the flimsy material of her low-cut sweatshirt. Just as he had suspected all night long, she wasn't wearing a bra, and his body tensed, remembering the way her nipples had beaded under his thumbs when he'd kissed her last month. His hands splayed out over her skin and he stared longingly into her eyes.

"When you said 'overnight.' Your voice wavered."

"Oh," she breathed, leaning into him. "It did, didn't it?"

"Mm-hm," he said, feeling drunk from the sensation of her body pressed up against his as his fingers kneaded her back and her hands skimmed over his T-shirt, meeting at the back of his neck.

He leaned down, letting his forehead touch hers, roll softly against hers, breathing deeply and loving the closeness of her, the sweetness of this woman in his arms who he loved more than anything. His eyes fluttered closed and he nuzzled her nose with his, touching his cheek to hers, before feeling her breath, warm and ragged, on his lips. He tilted his head slightly to capture her lips with his.

Like every other time they kissed, it was an explosion, a chemical reaction, a force of nature. He backed her up against the open door behind her, sliding his hands to her hips to lift her and groaning into her mouth as she wrapped her legs around him. She wound her hands through his hair, frantically sucking on his tongue, small, breathy moans of pleasure making him rock-hard as he stroked his tongue against hers again and again.

Knowing he had to leave, he gentled their kiss, feathering kisses down her neck and finally resting, panting, in the hollow he'd been so taken with before as he sat beside her on the couch. He savored the feeling of her much smaller body pressed intimately against his, knowing the memory would haunt his dreams all night long. He closed his eyes and rested his lips on her skin, against her pulse, the relentless throbbing of her heart.

After four years of wanting her and watching her and wishing for her, here she was—finally, finally, finally, thank you, God—in his arms, wanting just as much from him as he wanted from her. And like a geyser, bubbling with heat and demanding release, he felt the words rise up from the depths of his soul:

"My wife," he murmured against her neck. "Mine."

She stiffened slightly in his arms and he leaned back, releasing her gently. Her feet slid down his thighs to hit the floor and she looked up at him with heaving breasts, searching his eyes warily.

"Truce," she whispered, low and deliberate. A reminder.

He took a deep breath, staring back at her. He shouldn't have said it, shouldn't have called her his wife in such an intimate way, but it's not like he'd planned it. It came from a place deep inside, far stronger and more pure than his conscious mind. And in spite of the caution in her eyes, he didn't want to apologize for saying what was true, or cheapen it by saying he'd only gotten carried away.

He forced himself to smile lightly at her in a way he hoped was reassuring and kissed her tenderly on the forehead. "Pick you up tomorrow? Noon? Pack for camping, Miss Maggie."

Her face was inscrutable as she nodded once, backing into her apartment and closing the door between them.

***

Maggie looked at the Roosevelt Arch in the side-view mirror as it got smaller and smaller. She'd just had one of the most surreal experiences of her life.

Nils had picked her up at the Prairie half an hour ago, and they'd headed directly to the Best Western to pick up his clients, a family of five, the Skinners. While Nils called their room from the hotel courtesy phone, Maggie had waited beside the van, letting the sun bathe her face while she tried not to freak out about tonight's sleeping arrangements, which included her. In a tent. With Nils. She opened her eyes when she heard his footfalls striding toward her. He leaned beside her against the van.

"They'll be here in a second," he said quietly. "Hey, um, Maggie…"

Shielding her eyes with her hand, she turned her face to look at him. He held up his left hand, which sported a simple gold band on the fourth finger. "It was my grandfather's. My father gave it to me years ago because I'm the oldest, and I thought, well, as long as you don't mind, maybe I should wear it this weekend…"

She stared at the gold ring, the way it caught the sun, glowing as he held it out before her eyes…and found she didn't know what to say. Over the last few days, things between them were feeling a little too real for comfort. How was she supposed to protect her heart if she started to believe that their truce was actually making way for a real marriage between them? How would she go on living in Gardiner if he wanted to go back to friends—as was his right—the day after the interview?

Smiling lightly, she shrugged. "It certainly fits you. Your grandfather must have been a big man, like you."

His eyes lingered over her lips for a moment and she could feel the sudden flare of heat between them. It made her suck in a breath wondering if he'd suddenly reach for her as he had last night, but something over his head captured his attention and he stepped away from her.

"Welcome, folks!"

She watched his tall, muscular body cross the parking lot gracefully, purposefully, reaching out his hand to take the backpack on the mother's back and tousling the hair of a school-aged boy. Her heart swelled with sudden, unexpected pride, watching him go to work. She'd never seen this side of him before.

The Skinner family consisted of Mrs. Skinner, Mr. Skinner, and three sons, aged nine, twelve, and sixteen. Maggie straightened as they approached the van, pasting a nervous smile on her face.

"Folks, this is my wife, Maggie. She's coming along for the ride this weekend."

Before Maggie could process the jolt of confused pleasure she got from his words, Mrs. Skinner stepped forward, offering her hand to Maggie. "How nice not to be the only girl with all of these boys."

Maggie chuckled softly, shaking hands. "Sure you dinna mind, Mrs. Skinner? Havin' the ol' ball and chain along for the ride?"

She cringed inwardly at her awkwardness, but the older woman grinned at her, dropping her hand. "It's Danielle. Dany. And of course not. Not at all. Nils tells us you're newlyweds?"

"Aye. We were married in May, Dany."

"Still in that period of adjustment, huh?"

"You have no idea," Maggie answered, catching Nils's eyes over Mrs. Skinner's head. "I should give my, my, er— that is, Nils might need a hand. You'll pardon me?"

Nils ushered the Skinner's into the air-conditioned van, then slid the door shut and turned to Maggie. "Weird?"

"Pretty surreal," she agreed.

"Think we'll manage by September?" he asked. "To own it?"

"We've got three more weeks to get it right." She shrugged and tugged at the bag he held by his side, which had five bottles of water for the Skinners' ride. "Let me be useful. I'll hand these out. You get their stuff packed in."

"Bossy little missus I've got."

She'd grinned at him, then, and winked. Only later she realized it was the first time he'd ever made reference to their marriage without ruffling her feathers. It felt strange that she was getting used to it, getting used to the circumstance of being called "wife." And good. It felt really good, too good, even…until she remembered the words he'd whispered against her neck last night right before leaving: My wife. Mine.

A shiver of pleasure went down her spine before she could stop it, and she looked over at Nils, in the driver's seat to her left, wondering if he had any idea how deeply those three words had affected her. There were only three others she could think of that might possibly affect her more.

He caught her staring and winked at her, reaching out his right hand to her. She clasped it, entwining her fingers through his like she imagined a brand new wife would do. He drew her hand to his lips and kissed it gently before releasing it with a lopsided grin as he refocused his attention back on the road. Her stomach fluttered in response and she quickly looked out the window, catching the arch again in the side-view mirror, no more than a small dot now.

She wouldn't dare ask him after only a week, but was there any chance that his feelings for her, like hers for him, were coming into sharper focus now? Any chance that, like her, the playacting was feeling more and more real because more and more it wasn't acting? After last night, she didn't question his attraction to her anymore. Physically, he wanted her as much as she wanted him—that was clear—but, emotionally, he hadn't opened up to her very much. He didn't share his feelings for her, or tell her what she meant to him. It was hard for her to know if his actions were the result of their truce or backed up by actual, growing feelings for her.

And there were so many unasked questions and obvious problems between them that impeded any genuine progress toward happily ever after: Was he or was he not able to father children? On Tuesday night as they'd discussed her adoption over burgers, he had sensed that she had more to say on the topic of her own adoption, and he was right. What she wanted to say was that the deepest longing in her heart was to have biological children of her own someday. She'd never smiled into a face that shared her exact eye color or the funny dimple in the center of her chin. No one had ever told her brunette mother how much she and her redheaded daughter looked alike, because they didn't. When she looked at the faces of her parents and brother, there was no special recognition of her blood in communion with theirs. She was just Maggie, the adopted child, all alone.

She sighed, opening the cap of her own water bottle, and taking a swig as her thoughts weighed down on her. In the back seat, the Skinners were already exclaiming about the views as they trundled along the Grand Loop headed for Old Faithful. After a visit to the geyser, they'd head to Madison

Campground where Nils and Maggie would set up the campsite and build a fire while the Skinners obtained a fishing license and tried their luck.

In the rearview mirror Maggie caught a look at the three boys, all towheaded and blue-eyed in the back seat, and her heart clutched with longing. Maggie loved Nils with all her heart, but even if his feelings were changing from fake to real, it would take nothing less than his everlasting love for her to consider giving up her dreams.

***

Several hours later, after setting up the tents and cooking dinner over an open fire for the Skinners, Nils and Maggie sat around the campfire roasting marshmallows with the boys. Danielle and Tom Skinner snuggled on the ground against a log, sharing a blanket to ward off the cool evening air. The boys exclaimed as their marshmallows caught on fire and watched the tiniest embers take flight as bright orange sparks trailed up into the sky.

Maggie sat beside Nils on a log and he glanced down to catch her trying to stifle a yawn behind her hand. She'd been a huge help today, making his job twice as fast and ten times as fun. He'd teased her when she put the wrong rods together for the boys' tent and when she realized what she'd done wrong her freckled face exploded into cheerful giggles and she told him, "I've never built a bloody tent before, for goodness sake!"

All day he'd wanted to pull her up against him, hold her, touch her, kiss her, but he'd been careful to be reserved. He was working, after all, and it was already a risk to have

Maggie here with him. He'd have to field all of the incoming calls at the office over the next few days once he returned to Gardiner just in case Tom Skinner called with questions or to thank him. He couldn't risk anyone mentioning "Nils's lovely wife, Maggie" to his father or brother.

He and Maggie had agreed not to tell his family about their little arrangement. His father, an old-fashioned man who held marriage in the highest possible regard, wouldn't understand and would be very disappointed in them for misusing the institution. It was best for them to keep it all silent, until...until...

He glanced down at her again, watched her poke her marshmallow stick in the dirt pensively, and couldn't help himself—he put his arm around her shoulders, pulling her into the curve of his side, delightful shivers running down his arm as some stray hairs from her bun brushed his bicep. He leaned down and pressed his lips against her soft, reddish hair, smoothed back in a bun, and closed his eyes for a moment, wishing that he'd done things differently, wishing he'd had the courage to date her properly and ask her to marry him in some romantic way that would have appealed to her. It's not that he wasn't grateful for how they'd ended up here together, but his Maggie deserved better. She should have had better than a green-card marriage and a reluctant groom. She deserved so much more than this.

He tightened his arm around her, feeling ashamed of himself, and yet the sweetness of Maggie was that she took what he offered, meager though it was, and rested her head against his shoulder, sighing in contentment. How in the world would he earn someone as wonderful as Maggie? How could he change the past and prove to her that he was worthy?

When he looked up, Tom Skinner was watching them from across the fire.

"Remember the first few months, Dany?"

His wife nodded against his shoulder, smiling at them. "Of course I do. We fought like cats and dogs. Nothing like these two."

"What'd you fight about, Mom?"

"This and that. How your father hung his shirts on the floor. That he'd forget to call me when he was running late for dinner. That he never put the cap back on the toothpaste. Silly stuff."

"Had to make up a lot…from all that fighting," said Tom, and Danielle turned to peck him on the lips which received a loud moan of disgusted protest from their sons.

"Just wait," said Tom. "You'll be just like me and Mr. Lindstrom one day. Head over heels for a beautiful girl who ties you up so tight in knots, the only way to untangle is to tie the knot with her. Tell 'em, Nils."

"Oh, uh…"

Maggie looked up at him, then, on the verge of laughter, her eyes bright and merry from the light of the fire. He could've looked at her forever. He'd never seen anything as beautiful as Maggie Lindstrom. Not ever. Not in his whole life.

"You can't think about anything but her," he started softly, staring into her eyes, speaking low against the snaps and crackles of the campfire. "All the time. As you're walking to work. When you walk home. All through the day you're thinking, 'Maybe I'll run into her. Maybe she'll smile for me. Maybe this time I'll work up the courage to ask her out.' And when you do bump into her, you can barely put words together because your heart's about to beat out of your chest, and you know—you know—that if she'd give you a chance, if she'd just give you a chance, you could be everything she wanted, anything she wanted...just for a chance to be with her..."

***

Halfway through his monologue tears had filled her eyes and they streamed down her face now as she stared up at him, searching his eyes fiercely for answers to unasked questions. Was this true? Was this how he'd felt all of these years? Was it possible that he'd loved her quietly at the same time she'd been falling in love with him?

"Do you hear that?" Danielle Skinner demanded, elbowing Tom in the side. "Enjoy it, Maggie. You won't hear words like that after twenty years together!"

Maggie swiped at her cheeks, looking at Danielle and chuckling softly. "He's a smooth talker, my—my, uh, my husband."

"I'll say." Danielle winked conspiratorially at her. "Boys! Time for bed!"

After groans of "Mom, do we have to?" the Skinner boys threw their roasting twigs in the fire and politely bid goodnight to Nils and Maggie.

"'Night, dear," said Danielle knowingly to Maggie as

she followed Tom to their tent. As the Skinners' tents brightened colorfully from lantern light, Maggie realized she and Nils were alone.

"You don't have to stay up," he said softly. She could hear the uncertainty in his voice, and it occurred to her that he probably hadn't meant to say as much as he did, or that he was unsure of how she'd respond to it. Or—her heart twisted a little—maybe it wasn't true at all. Maybe it was all part of their truce to act married.

"What's left to do?" she asked.

"I'll throw sand on the fire. Pack up the food tight. Fold up the blankets. Fill up the water jugs. You go on to bed." He hadn't looked up at her and her brows furrowed, wondering what was wrong.

"It was beautiful," she whispered. "What you said."

After a long moment he looked up at her and his eyes were fraught with emotion as he whispered back. "It was true." But he looked away quickly, frowning at the fire. "Maggie, I can sleep out here. Under the stars. I'm not a stranger to it. You can...have your privacy, if you want."

She stared at his bowed head, wondering what in the heck was going on inside of it. No, she didn't want him to sleep outside. She wanted him beside her. Though her nerves had gotten in the way here and there, all day she'd been waiting for the moment that they lay down side by side in the little green tent at the far corner of the campground. And now he was backing out. All because he'd shared a little too much emotion.

She glanced at the Skinners' tent and grabbed his

shirtsleeve, yanking him into the darkness on the other side of the van.

"Why?" she whispered angrily, her fingers curling into a fist with a bunch of his shirt trapped within. "Why are you offerin' to sleep on the ground?"

He shook his head, looking miserable.

She bent her head, trying to catch his eyes. "You asked for a truce and I agreed. You backin' out of that now?"

"No, I just..." He covered her hand with his, rubbing it gently until it relaxed and she released his shirt to lace her fingers within his. His eyes were regretful in the dim light. "You deserve so much better, Maggie May."

"Better than what?"

"Than me. Than this. Than a green-card marriage to a—"

"Stop it!" she demanded in a fierce whisper. "Stop it now."

She stepped closer to him and her breasts brushed against his chest. She stared at the light blue polo shirt in front of her, tightening her grip on his hand and relieved when he tightened his back.

"We're not rewritin' history here, Nils Lindstrom. I was in trouble. In big trouble, and my friend—my dear, carin', concerned friend—came to my rescue. Like he always does, again and again. When my cappuccino maker breaks or my mail slips behind the counter or I'm about to fall off a barstool and crack my head open. He comes to my rescue, and I am..." With her free hand she reached up to stroke his cheek and he tilted his head, leaning into the gentle pressure of her hand. "…I am grateful for him. I'm grateful for you. I've messed up your whole life, and you've—"

He closed his eyes and tilted his head slightly to press his lips against her palm, making her gasp lightly.

"I've what?" he murmured, his breath hot on her hand, his voice thick and low.

"You amaze me," she whispered.

"I want to deserve you," he said softly.

"Then come to bed," she responded as his lips moved hypnotically against her skin, nibbling, sucking, licking until she thought she'd faint from the simple pleasure of it. "Hold me while I fall asleep. That's all I need."

His lips brushed tenderly against the inside of her wrist and he locked his eyes with hers for a long moment and then nodded, stepping back. "I'll be there soon."

She dropped her hand from his face, unlaced her other hand from his, then turned and walked away from him into the darkness.

Chapter 15

When she woke up the next morning, he was gone, probably up early to make a fire and get breakfast started, so Maggie snuggled deeper into her sleeping bag. By the time he'd finally entered the tent last night after straightening up the campsite, she'd been mostly asleep in her own sleeping bag, but he'd wrapped his arms around her, bag and all, pulling her against his chest, into his safe, warm embrace. Even through the material and down of two sleeping bags, she could feel his heat, his strength, his protective tenderness surrounding her. And even though her intent had been to talk and make-out until dawn, her heavy eyes had overruled her intentions and within moments she was asleep.

The second night ended almost identically, and though she didn't actually remember him coming to bed, she loved waking up in his arms. Or she would have loved it if she hadn't felt so totally and completely miserable. There was a reason for her heavy, tired eyes and unbelievable willpower when the man of her dreams was snuggling behind her in the small space of a shared tent: she was coming down with something and from the way she felt, she knew it was going to be a whopper.

Her throat was on fire and her muscles ached. Her head

felt three sizes bigger than usual and she couldn't breathe through her nose. She flipped onto her side to face Nils and his "good-morning" smile quickly turned into a look of concern.

"You're really flushed."

"I dinna feel well," she confessed, trying to enjoy the feeling of his arm slung over her hip, but distracted by how beat-up her body felt.

Nils reached up and felt her forehead. "You're hot."

"What's on the agenda for today?" she asked in a gravelly, nasal voice.

"Not a lot. Mostly just a slow ride home. Maybe stopping at Hayden and one of the boys mentioned Tower Falls. Tour's meant to end by early afternoon, same as it began. But I'll cut it short. I'll tell them we need to go straight back." He crawled out of his sleeping bag and pulled on his jeans.

"No," Maggie mumbled, the "o" sound in "no" ending with a light wheeze. She looked at his rumpled undershirt and realized, fleetingly, he had been sleeping beside her only wearing his underwear. She took a second to mourn how incredibly unfair it was that she hadn't been able to enjoy that circumstance. "It's your job. I'll, uh, I'll tough it out. I'll stay in the van and rest when you make the stops."

"Maggie May...you look terrible."

"Thank you," she said, triggering a coughing attack.

"And you sound like a seal."

"A seal? Oh, no. Croup," she croaked. "Croup sounds like seal barking."

"Croup? What the hell is that?"

"I can't have croup. I'm a grown-up." She closed her eyes and laid her arm across them, wondering how the hell she was going to get herself dressed, packed, and into the van when she was feeling as weak as a kitten.

"I wish I had a signal," Nils griped, looking at his phone before shoving it back in his pocket. "This croup. Is it serious?"

"It's a childhood disease. Like mumps or measles. Gingy had it. Years ago. Barkin' cough, flu-like symptoms. I remember."

"And do you recall the course of treatment? Hospital or home?"

"Home. But there was medicine, I think. I'm pretty sure." She tried to take a deep breath, but her lungs felt so tight it started another coughing attack.

His hand may have been resting on her arm for a while, but she wasn't sure. "I don't like this, Mags. What can I do?"

"Water?" she rasped.

"God, of course!" He kissed her forehead then hurried out of the tent. She heard the hush of voices as he shared morning greetings with the Skinners.

A moment later he returned with a bottle of water and knelt beside her as Maggie raised her head. She'd be lying if she said it didn't take effort. She took several gulps, enjoying the relief as the cool liquid slipped down her fiery throat. He offered her a couple of Advil and she swallowed them gratefully.

"Nils, dinna cancel the tour. I'll get dressed and get in

the van. I'll sleep in the front seat."

"And cough your brains out the whole day? Feverish? Maybe with chills? Maybe needing medicine?" He shook his head. "I don't think so."

"Please. I'm strong. I'll be—"

"Mags, it's done. It's already done." He reached out and brushed the hair from her forehead tenderly. "When I got you the water, I told them you were sick and I wanted to get you home. And they wouldn't have it any other way."

A tear slipped out of her eye as relief washed over her. As much as she would have tried to sleep in the van, it would have been a terribly long morning when all she longed for was her own bed. Still, he'd lose income, and it would be her fault. Messing up his life. Again.

"I'm sorry," she sobbed. "I'm such a bloody nuisance. Sick and—"

"That's enough." He cupped her cheeks with his hands, stroking away her tears with his thumbs. "You're not a nuisance. You're wonderful. You're also sick. I'm taking you home and putting you in bed and making you soup and staying with you until you feel better."

She inhaled sharply, surprised by the conviction in his voice, the smooth delivery of his words, almost like he meant them, like they were real. Her lungs wheezed and she started coughing again.

He dropped his hands from her face as the coughing subsided. "Rest a while. I'll send the Skinners out to do a little hiking and fishing while I break down the camp. I'll come wake you up when it's time to go."

He pressed his lips to the top of her head then stood up hunched over in the low tent as he headed for the opening.

"Nils!" she rasped.

He turned and looked at her with one hand holding the flap open. The sunlight filtered in behind him, making him look like a god, ethereal and strong and totally irreplaceable.

"Thank you," she whispered.

Then she let her eyelids flutter closed, her mind holding on to the image of her strong, beautiful, young husband bathed in a pool of morning light.

***

After he dropped off the Skinners at their hotel, Nils intended to take Maggie directly to her apartment. Damn, but she wasn't looking good. She was slumped down in her seat, and aside from the occasional barking fit, she'd barely made a sound all the way back to Gardiner.

When they reached the hotel, Nils had pulled Mr. and Mrs. Skinner aside. "I'll refund the money for the final day, folks."

"Thank you, Nils," replied Tom. "But there's plenty of time for that. You tend to that pretty bride of yours."

"I'm awful sorry about it all. If you need anything else before heading back to the airport tomorrow, I hope you'll call my cell phone instead of the office."

Danielle took the card with his personal number on it and gave him a hug. "We loved everything we saw on Friday and Saturday, and we loved getting to know you and Maggie. I think Tom would agree that we don't feel like we missed out on a thing. Take care of Maggie. That's a nasty cough she's got. We hope she feels better soon."

Nils waved goodbye and turned the van toward the Prairie Dawn. Once there, he parked in back and hurried around to Maggie's side of the van. He unsnapped her seat belt and she raised her head to look at him, her eyes glassy and her face red. As she looked up, she erupted into another cycle of coughs, making her whole body shudder. She looked exhausted once they subsided.

"Nils. I feel so…awful."

"I know, love. I can see."

He picked her up into his arms, relieved she had the strength to loop her arms around his neck and moved swiftly to the back door, unlocking it clumsily with his key. He quickly made his way up the stairs and unlocked her apartment door, not stopping until he reached her bedroom.

"Mo mornin'," she said softly into the crook of his neck.

"What?"

"Mo mornin'," she said again.

He placed her gently on her bed. "What about morning? Maggie, I'm going to put you on the bed. Do you want help getting your jeans off?"

"Thanks," she murmured, wheezing again.

He unbuttoned her jeans and tugged them down her hips, reminding himself that she was sick and feverish and he had no business looking at her body with lust. He had no business imagining what it would be like when she welcomed him between her thighs, what it would feel like to be lodged inside of her. Stop it, Nils. She's sick, for God's sake! He tugged the pants off her body, but left her socks on after feeling to be sure they were still dry. She curled herself into a ball on top of her comforter and he could tell she was shivering.

"Maggie, I have to move you. I have to put you under the covers."

She groaned and rolled slightly to her right so he could free the comforter, then he lifted her up and placed her gently on the sheets, covering her up again.

"So cold," she muttered, coughing again.

He felt so worthless, so helpless, watching her cough and shiver, so little underneath the down of her covers. Then he had an idea. He kicked off his shoes and unbuckled his belt so the metal wouldn't bite into her back. He slipped into bed behind her, pulling her into his arms just as he'd done for the last two nights, but this time there weren't sleeping bags between them. There was nothing between them but his clothes and her underwear and T-shirt. And while the idea of making love to her someday ranked high on his list of favorite fantasies, right now, all he was interested in was offering her warmth and comfort.

"I'm here, love. I'll keep you warm. Try to sleep."

She sighed and relaxed, scooting back just slightly until her body was flush against his, soft and settled in his arms. She didn't cough or wheeze and he was relieved when her breathing seemed to deepen and fall into a steady pattern. He was pretty sure she was asleep when she murmured something softly.

"Mo muirnín," she whispered again, and he recognized

the burr in her voice. She wasn't saying something about the "morning," she was saying something in Gaelic.

"Mo muirnín?" he repeated, a question in his voice.

"Mmm. It's what you called me. It's what you are." Her voice, soft and drowsy, tapered off as she finally fell into a deep sleep.

And Nils's heart surged and swelled with unending tenderness for the woman in his arms as he realized that when she said "mo muirnín," she was calling him "my love."

***

Maggie felt awful.

She felt worse than awful.

She felt like she'd been hit by a truck, dragged for miles in thick smoke, and left to bake under an equatorial sun. Her body felt like it was on fire and her lungs were so tight she couldn't even take a shallow breath without coughing.

"Maggie."

Nils's voice was close, and her eyes fluttered opened to look for him. He was kneeling or squatting beside her bed, because his face, etched in worry, was level with hers.

"Nils," she rasped, and the sound was so low, so labored and raspy, she could barely hear it in her own ears.

"I called a doctor. He should be here soon. You've been coughing and burning up for hours. I didn't know what else to do."

Her eyes fluttered closed. He called a doctor? Because the closest hospital was over an hour away, urgent care mobile doctors were popular in Gardiner, and house visits weren't uncommon. But was she really that sick? Every muscle ached and as she tried to fill her diaphragm, her lungs rebelled with a fierce throb of pain that resulted in a coughing attack. Yes. Yes, she was.

"Water?" she groaned in her half-voice, and a moment later Nils was pressing a glass to her parched lips.

She heard the faint knocking of her front door, and he pulled the glass away from her, setting it gently on her bedside table. "I'll be right back."

Five minutes later Doctor Garrison was in her room. He turned on her bedside lamp, illuminating her otherwise dark room. It was dark? What time was it? How long had she been asleep? Had Nils been at her place the whole time?

"Heya, Maggie."

She looked up at him without moving her head from the pillow. The effort to say hello was enough. Lifting her head felt impossible. Nonetheless, she was glad to see him. She'd seen Doc G several times at the local clinic and he was the closest thing she had to a personal physician. "Heya, doc."

"Ooo! That doesn't sound any good." He reached out to touch the nodes under her ears, which smarted tenderly from his touch, then popped a thermometer in her mouth. "103.4. That's high enough to feel pretty bad, I guess." After reading the thermometer, he checked her throat, wincing at what he saw, then reached down to take a stethoscope out of his backpack.

He turned back to Maggie. "Can you roll to your side?"

She did, but the effort it took made her start coughing again. Once the fit subsided, she felt the stethoscope pressing against her back. "Breathe in. Huh. Again. Yep. And again."

Each time she took a breath it resulted in more coughing, so it took a few minutes, but eventually she felt Nils's hand on her shoulder, easing her onto her back. He sat down on the bed beside her, as Dr. Garrison tucked his stethoscope back into his bag.

"It's not croup. Without the benefit of a blood test, I can't be a hundred percent certain, but my best guess? You've got the flu."

"The flu?" asked Nils. "But it's August."

"Flu don't care what month it is, Nils." He glanced around Nils at Maggie. "And you've got a doozy of a case. But you say the symptoms only started this morning? Well, I can give you an antiviral medication, Maggie." He rummaged through his bag again, taking out a small sleeve of pills packaged between foil and clear plastic. "Take two of these once a day. Lots of rest. Plenty of liquid. A couple of Advil every six hours. Might feel worse before you feel better, but you'll be on the upswing in a couple of days."

Nils took the sleeve of medication from the doctor and walked him out. When he returned, he helped Maggie sit up so she could take her two pills and swallow them down with a little water.

"You should go home," she whispered as he plumped her pillow before helping her settle back down under the covers.

"I'm not going anywhere," he said softly, leaning over her to kiss her forehead. "Mind if I make myself something to eat? I'll come to bed later."

"You should stay away from me," she said. "You'll catch it, too."

"I'm not worried," he said, pushing her damp hair off her forehead tenderly. "Anyway, I've slept beside you for three nights now. If I'm going to get it, I already have it." He looked like he wanted to say something else, but instead he dropped his hand from her head and stood up. "I'll come back in a little bit to check on you."

Her heavy eyes wouldn't stay open anymore, so she nodded lightly as sleep took over.

***

Nils stared at the computer screen in front of him, barely able to concentrate. He didn't want to be at the office. He wanted to be at Maggie's where he could hear her if she needed anything, but he wouldn't have been able to explain his absence. Taking Monday off made sense, since the Lindstroms generally took off the day after a tour, but by Tuesday, he had to show up at the office.

He'd stayed at her place on Sunday and Monday nights, slipping into bed behind her to hold her as she slept, to listen to her breathing and remind her to take her antivirals and Advil. She'd thanked him about a hundred times, and on Monday afternoon she'd managed to eat a little chicken noodle soup, too.

When he left her this morning, she'd smiled up at him wanly from her pillow, thanking him again for his care. "Yet again, I'm causin' you trouble."

He took it as a good sign of improvement that she was

up to teasing. He smiled at her, hating that he had to leave, even for a few hours. "Do you see me complaining?"

She shook her head, looking at him tenderly. "Nae. I dinna see you complainin'."

"Maggie, I want you to know that I..." He'd stared at her, letting his words trail off. She was just starting to feel better and they had a lot of information they still needed to learn about one another as soon as she felt better enough to resume their questionnaires. It wasn't the right time to pressure her by sharing his feelings. "I'll be back at lunchtime?"

Her eyes, which had brightened momentarily, looked away from him and she licked her lips. "I can make myself toast or somethin'. You dinna need to break up your day."

"I told you, I don't mind," he said, backing out of her bedroom door before she could protest any further. "I'll be back at noon."

He'd hurried home to shower and change before heading to the office. And the thing is? His apartment felt different when he got there. It was his house, but it didn't feel like his home. He stared at his nondescript bed as he toweled off and changed, comparing the plain navy duvet and functional hardwood frame to the white wicker and cheerful purple flowers in Maggie's bedroom. He longed for it—for the warmth of it, for the cheer of it, for the Maggie of it. And suddenly noon was far too long a wait.

He grabbed a container of orange juice out of his own fridge and on his way to the office, he stopped by her place, vaulting up the stairs but unlocking the front door quietly.

He put the juice in her fridge and walked quietly into her bedroom, hovering in the doorway as he watched her sleep.

He didn't say anything. He didn't want to wake her up; she needed her rest. He just needed to see her. He just needed to stand quietly in her doorway and drink her in, because four hours stretched out before him like a sentence without the pleasure of her flushed face and gravelly burr. When exactly had this happened? This shift from appreciating his own company to barely being able to function without hers? Was this the result of spending every waking moment with her from Friday afternoon to now? She was like an addiction to him now? A need?

That he'd loved Maggie for years with a quiet passion was indisputable, but for the first time since he'd known her, he had to consider that loving her from a safe distance and falling in love with her up close were two separate things...and as he quietly let himself out of her apartment and walked the short distance to work, he realized that there was a very good chance he was deep in the throes of the latter. Sometime between marrying her and leaving her and returning to her again, he'd started to fall in love with her. Not with the idea of her, or potential of her, but with her.

His fingers had distractedly tapped the space bar so many times, the page before him was blank. He adjusted in his seat and tried to remember what it was he was supposed to be doing. Oh, right. While Lars made calls to reconfirm the campsites, Nils was supposed to be putting together an itinerary. A big group of thirty kids and six adults from a church group in Buffalo, New York, were coming to the park for a four-day retreat, and all three Lindstrom men would be on-deck to drive vans, lead group activities and be in charge of campsites and provisions. Though they'd secured the reservations weeks ago, the logistics of such a big group took a couple of days of serious planning right before the group arrived. The tents Nils had used over the weekend needed to be laundered, they had groceries to buy and organize into coolers, not to mention the pick-up on Thursday at the airport in Bozeman would be sheer chaos until all thirty-six visitors were settled into three twelve-person vans and on their way down to the park.

And this time, there was no room for Maggie. Nils's heart lurched with the realization. He wouldn't see her for four days. Not until he returned, hot, sweaty and exhausted, on Sunday night.

"Nils, vem dog?" Who died?

Nils looked up to catch Lars's eyes staring at him. "No one."

"Something bothering you? You're scowling worse'n usual today," said Lars, eyes twinkling as his lips tilted up at the corners in a grin.

"Shut up, Lars."

Lars sauntered over from the small conference table in the front of the office and parked himself in the office chair beside Nils's desk. He glanced down at the keyboard, then back up at Nils's face, grinning with furrowed brows. "So, when did you get married?"

"What?!" demanded Nils, as his eyes shot open and his heart rocketed from zero to one hundred in a single moment. Had Lars found out? Did he know? Had he told their father? "Vad pratar du om?" *What are you talking about?*

"Whoa, brother!" Lars's neck snapped back at the tone in his older brother's voice and his smile faded as he gestured to the wedding ring Nils was wearing on the fourth finger of his left hand. "I was just kidding. What's the deal with that?"

Nils whipped the ring off, opened his desk drawer, dropped the ring in and slammed it shut. "It was grandfather's. I found—I found it when I was...I just..."

"Thought you'd fantasize about cementing things with Maggie, huh?" Lars's teasing smile had returned. "Although I haven't seen much of her lately. You two have a falling out?"

"No."

"Because while you were gone, she canceled euchre on Thursdays. Said she was too busy. Saw Beck hovering over at the café all the time."

Nils shrugged and tried to look like he didn't care while the comment sat like acid in his stomach. How much time had Maggie and Beck spent together while he was gone? And when his truce with Maggie was over, would Beck be reasserting his place in Maggie's life? As close as they'd gotten lately, they hadn't discussed their feelings at all. Here he was, falling in love with her, and he had no idea if she still had any interest in getting serious with him.

"Can we stop talking about Beck Westman and get this itinerary done?"

Three hours later, Nils was at his breaking point.

Between his short conversation about Beck's attentions toward Maggie and the ache of being away from her this upcoming weekend, he was barking at his brother more and more, barely able to focus on the itinerary they'd agreed on. Finally Lars stood up, looking at his watch.

"You're impossible today. Let's take a break for lunch. Think you could possibly find and kill whatever crawled up your ass?"

Nils clenched his jaw then nodded once. Lars was right. He was being impossible. He needed to go see Maggie. Moreover, before their interview, Nils needed to make sure that Beck was her past and he was her future.

***

For the first time since Sunday morning, Maggie was finally feeling a little bit better. She still felt stuffy and her cough wasn't going anywhere, but at least her fever and chills had subsided, taking most of the full-body ache with them.

Just as Dr. Garrison had predicted, days one and two were brutal, but Tuesday was better—thank goodness for antivirals! In fact, she felt well enough to strip down and take a long, hot shower, letting the water tumble down her back and front, easing the aches and pains of three days spent in bed. She washed her hair leisurely, smiling as she remembered Nils's outburst as they sat on the couch last Thursday night "...every time you move I smell your hair..."

Though she knew he cared for her, she couldn't have predicted the tender care he'd provided her over the past few days. From the way he'd carried her up the stairs of her apartment on Sunday afternoon to staying over every night. He'd reminded her to take her medication while she was so tired and fuzzy, she could barely open her eyes. He'd kissed her sweaty forehead, held her shivering body and made her smile as she'd finally taken sips of soup yesterday. Maggie had been with other men, of course, but she'd never known what it was to feel cherished, to feel precious to someone. Not until now.

There was no denying that they'd had a deep affection for one another for years, and over the past several months, they'd discovered a combustible chemistry, too. And now, again, Nils's actions were telling her so much about his feelings that he didn't articulate. He was falling in love with her. She'd bet her life on it. She was watching it happen.

And while it filled her heart with unimaginable joy, it didn't change the fact that secrets still lay between them. And until she knew what they were and how they'd affect the prospect of forever, Maggie still needed to protect herself.

She turned off the water and toweled her hair, wrapping it into a turban, then grabbed another towel, wrapping it around her body and tucking the loose end between her breasts. She opened her underwear drawer only to find she was out, but remembered a clean load of clothes was resting in the dryer.

As she squatted down in front of the dryer, which was tucked into an alcove in her front vestibule, she wondered about Nils's secrets, specifically as they concerned children. That was the most troubling puzzle piece. She needed answers, but she knew it wasn't the right time yet. While patience wasn't her strong suit, forcing him to answer big questions like that could make him close up, and that's the last thing she wanted.

When the lock on the front door turned, she looked up from her spot in front of the dryer in surprise to see Nils walk into her apartment.

"Maggie! You're up."

She looked at the pair of underwear in her hand and threw them back in the dryer, standing up quickly. "Nils!"

She watched his face change as his eyes dropped from her eyes to her towel, to her bare legs, to her feet and back up to her face. While she'd been sick, their attraction to one another, while not forgotten, had been secondary to his care of her and her need to be cared for. Now, it rushed back with abandon and she could feel the tension, the electricity, between them. The heat in his eyes made a flush break out on her skin, coloring it pink, not with fever this time, but with arousal, with pleasure. She liked the way he was looking at her. She liked how it made her feel.

"Y-you, uh, showered," he observed in a lower-than-usual voice.

"I showered."

"Lunch."

"Lunch?"

"I brought lunch."

"Oh," she said, wetting her dry lips with her tongue. His eyes widened as they focused on her lips before capturing her eyes again.

"You look better. You feel better?" His voice was clipped and nervous.

"Aye. A little."

His eyes darted down to the place where she'd tucked in the towel between her breasts and she saw the slight flare of his nostrils before he looked back up.

"I didn't have any clean underwear," she said, gesturing awkwardly to the open dryer door and leaning down to grab the pair she'd thrown back in.

"Oh," he said, and she saw it. She saw the thought pass across his eyes, which widened again, with raw hunger: She's naked in front of me except for that towel.

"Christ, Maggie," he groaned, clenching his jaw, adjusting the paper bag in his hands. For a moment, she thought he was going to drop it on the floor and reach for her, rip open her towel and pull her down on the floor to ravage her with his mouth, his tongue, his fingers thrusting into her until she was ready for—"Please get dressed."

Then he passed her, careful not to touch her, and headed into her kitchen without another glance. And she stood there, balled-up panties in her hand, wanting him so much, she didn't know how much longer she could wait to have him.

Chapter 16

By Wednesday evening, Maggie was finally feeling like herself again, despite a lingering cough, and things between her and Nils had resumed the rhythm they'd established before the camping trip (and her own personal sojourn in flu hell).

"Want coffee?" she called into the living room.

"Sure," he answered from the loveseat where she'd join him as soon as she finished washing up. It was the first night she'd felt up to cooking and she'd insisted that he not lift a finger after taking such good care of her during her illness.

"I know how you take it."

"Of course you do," he answered, and she grinned at the easy warmth in his voice. "Hey, did you know I didn't even like coffee that much? Not until about a year ago. That's when I acquired a taste for it."

She turned on the Keurig and peeked into the living room. "What're you on about? You been comin' into the Prairie since I got to Gardiner. That's four years of coffee."

He grinned at her as his cheeks flushed salmon.

"You came in to see me."

He nodded, shrugging sheepishly.

She turned back into the kitchen, unable to tamp down

the burst of joy she felt at his admission. They were getting closer and closer to telling each other how they felt—how they really felt—about each other. She knew it in her heart, but she forced herself to let him move at his own pace.

Returning to the living room with two cups of coffee, she settled beside him on the loveseat, tucking her legs beneath her pajama shorts and grinning at him. "Didn't like coffee."

"I swear. I hated the stuff. But you offered me a cup. I couldn't say no to those green eyes."

She placed her cup on the coffee table then looked at him, batting her eyelashes. "These?"

"Those. Tease."

Giggling, she reached for their questionnaires, handed his to him and turned to a page somewhere in the middle. "High School."

He looked down at the packet on his lap but didn't make a move to open it. "Is that where we are?"

"That's where we are," she said, sensing the change in him, the sudden tension that the words "high school" elicited.

"What do you want to know?"

Who did you date? Did you fall in love? Who was the girl in the prom picture?

"What was your favorite subject?"

"Phys Ed."

She gave him a look. "Academic subject."

He shrugged. "English, I guess, for the reading, though I didn't much like being told what to read. Would've liked it better if I could've chosen for myself. You?"

"Math, I guess. Teacher said I had a head for numbers."

"And a bod for sin," he retorted quickly. He shook his head in surprise and chuckled softly. "I heard that in a movie once."

"Stop flirtin'. We have to do this," she insisted, trying to get them back on track, despite the rush of pleasure his words provided.

"Fine. What else?"

"Did you have a girlfriend?"

His blue eyes were searing as he stared at her, and she could see the conflict behind them. He was protecting something, or someone, from the rest of the world. He was hesitant to talk about it. But Maggie wanted to know. She needed to know. She stared back, impassive, in spite of the fierce thumping of her heart.

"Yes," he finally answered in a low, measured tone, all traces of teasing gone.

The hardest thing Maggie ever did in her whole life was to not ask questions, just stare back at him and wait for him to continue. He looked away from her, clenching his jaw over and over again, and she couldn't bear it—she reached out and placed her hand on his arm. He glanced down at her hand then took it in his, lacing his fingers through hers.

"You saw, um, you saw her picture that day in my pop's attic. Veronica. Olsen. Veronica Olsen. She was a transfer student my senior year and we had chemistry together. She was my, um, my lab partner."

Maggie squeezed his hand gently, adjusting her grip,

and he looked up from their hands to catch her eyes. The pain in his made her breath catch, and she winced.

"She died," he said softly. He blinked quickly twice, but he didn't look away from her. "She died the summer after senior year."

"No," sighed Maggie, reaching for him, pulling him into her arms.He wrapped his arms around her, too, resting his cheek on her shoulder as she trailed her hands soothingly up and down his broad back. "I'm so sorry, Nils. I didn't know. I didn't know you'd lost her."

"It's why I...well, I must have looked pretty upset when I saw her picture. I hadn't seen a picture of her in a long time."

"How did..." She felt the muscles in his back tense as she started her question.

"It was...it was, um, an operation. There were terrible complications and she, um, she lost too much blood. She lost—"

"Shhh, now." Her heart twisted from the pain in his voice and her hands crept from his back to the nape of his neck which she cradled gently, softly caressing his hair. "That's enough. That's enough, now."

"I should tell you..." He started in a broken voice.

"No. I dinna want to pry or make you talk about painful things. That's enough for the interview. I shouldn't have even asked..."

She drew back to look at his face, his downturned gaze, his cheeks that were slightly slick from an escaped tear or two.

She still had questions.

She still feared that they desired different things from life.

She still worried that he would break her heart.

But if his actions told her nothing else, they assured her that he was falling in love with her, that he cared deeply for her, that he wanted her as much as she wanted him. She was finished with barriers between them. He was the man she loved. He was, in fact, her husband. It was time to be his wife, in every single possible way.

She felt him grinding his jaw against her cheek and she knew he was bottling up his emotions, just as he had last Thursday right before he exploded at her on the couch, just as he had on Tuesday when he found her in the front hallway wearing a towel. She knew it was probably terribly inappropriate for her to kiss him when he was talking about a former love who he'd lost so painfully, but she didn't know how else to offer him comfort, how else to let him channel his feelings into action.

She leaned forward and touched her lips to his gently then drew back and touched them again, lightly tracing his lips with feathery kisses. She could feel the change in him as he let go of his sorrow and was present in the moment they were sharing together, tightening his arms around her as his lips finally began to move beneath hers. His hands slid down her back slowly, cupping her backside to maneuver her onto his lap where she straddled his rock-hard thighs, scooting forward until her unbound breasts, in a flimsy sleeping sweatshirt, pressed impatiently against his chest.

Leaning back, she pulled it up and over her head, baring her breasts to him completely. As her shallow breath amplified in her ears, she looked up to find his eyes which feasted, hungrily, on the sight before him, reaching out to cup her soft flesh in his warm, coarse palm. She gasped as he bent his head and took her nipple between his lips, kissing it lightly before licking a circle around it and finally latching on to it with his mouth and sucking it into a proud red bud. She ran her fingers through his hair, trying to bear the sweet sharpness of the sensation when he suddenly changed course, taking her other nipple between his lips and loving it as he had its twin. Like a bolt of lightning from the tips of her breasts through her belly straight to her increasingly hot, wet core, the heaven of his mouth loving her so intimately made her arch her back, pushing forward against him. When she couldn't bear the building pressure anymore, she cried out his name, frantically pushing his head back so that she could crash her lips into his.

As their kiss deepened, his hands skimmed the bare sides of her torso, over her waist, and into the waistband of her pajama bottoms. Finding no panties barring his access to her soft, rounded flesh, he emitted a groan of surprise into her mouth, kneading his fingers urgently as she rolled herself over his erection. Desperate to feel his skin against hers, her hands skated down his back, slipping under his polo shirt and pushing up. He broke away from her mouth to grab his shirt behind his neck and dispatch it to the floor with a quick tug over his head. His lips found hers again as he ran his hands over the soft skin of her back, making her shiver. His muscles flexed and relaxed under her fingertips and she lingered over his shoulder blades as he kissed her, mesmerized by the hard, masculine beauty of the man in her arms.

She leaned back, still moving gently against his erection, still stroking the taut outlines of his back with her fingers. Leaning forward to touch her lips to his ear, she felt him shudder lightly as she tugged on the soft skin of his earlobe with her teeth. "Listen."

"I—I'm listening."

"I want you."

"Maggie," he groaned. "Are you sure?"

"I want you more than anythin'."

She licked his ear again and his arms tightened around her.

"I've never wanted anyone in my life as much as I want you," he murmured.

Her eyes burned with tears at the sweetness of his admission.

"Stay," she breathed.

"Overnight?"

"Aye, overnight," she said, drawing back to capture his eyes with hers, so that he'd see she had no reservations, no misgivings—so he'd know she'd have no regrets in the morning. And then—without even the slightest waver in her voice—she smiled at him and repeated tenderly, "Stay."

***

Her words were the only permission he needed to give himself over to the sweet relief of loving her body as completely as he loved her heart. And after four long years of quietly yearning for her, he carried her in his arms to her bedroom where he laid her reverently down on her bed in the darkness. Unable to wait any longer to hold her naked body in his arms, he hooked his fingers into the waistband of her shorts and pulled them down the impossibly smooth, toned legs that had tormented him for months.

"Now you," she said, lying on her back completely naked, leaning up on her elbows, as the moonlight bathed her pale body.

He unbuckled his belt, unbuttoned and unzipped his jeans, and joined her on the bed a moment later as naked as she. Gathering her into his arms, he held her, gazing into her face as his eyes adjusted to the dim light, surprised by the strength of his self-control as he allowed them to get used to the feeling of their bare bodies pressed intimately against each other.

"Maggie," he said, because she needed to know, because it was time, because he couldn't keep the words inside anymore. "I would do anything for you. Anything. No more truce. You and me…this is real."

Maggie answered in a low, raspy voice, thick with emotion. "Aye, it is."

She reached up to cup his face in her hands as he swung his body over hers, lowering his head to find her lips. She thrust her tongue into his mouth to find his, and it was electrifying to him, making all of the blood that he'd used to form coherent words, travel south to one place that throbbed, hard and aching for her, for the release he could only find by joining his body with hers.

"Would you...I mean, do you need—do you want to go slow?" he asked through a thick haze of desire, kissing a trail from her mouth to her ear, running his lips against the sensitive skin at the tip of her jaw, then resting them in a small hollow of her neck that he wanted to own, that he wanted to make his home, that he never wanted to leave, ever again. His pelvis pushed gently, rhythmically against hers, making his desires known.

"Nae," she said softly, and her voice broke with emotion as she arched up to meet him, pushing the soft folds of her sex into his. "Later. For now, I just need you."

His fingers trailed down her side, over her hip to her belly, then lower, landing on the soft triangle of hair at the apex of her thighs. She moaned lightly as his fingers skimmed lower, finding her wet and ready for him.

"We'll take it slow next time, love," he promised as he readjusted his position, bracing his elbows on either side of her head, dipping his head to kiss her.

"Please," she said, her voice breathy and urgent. "I want you, Nils. No more waitin'."

"Do we need...?"

"I'm on the pill," she whimpered, arching up against him in readiness.

"You're sure?" he confirmed, searching her eyes. There could be no accidents with Maggie. He couldn't bear it.

"Aye. I'm sure."

He swallowed, his self-control depleted as he positioned himself at her hot, slick entry. "I meant it, Maggie

May. This is real."

"This is real," she half sobbed, half moaned, reaching for his face and pulling him down to kiss her as he thrust forward, burying himself inside of her in one smooth motion and surrendering to the awesome joy of making love to his wife for the very first time.

***

"Why'd we wait so long?" Maggie asked him as they lay side by side, facing one another, hours later.

He leaned forward to press a light kiss on her nose. "We weren't ready, love."

"Speak for yourself," she answered saucily.

He looked surprised, then delighted, and he pulled her closer, close enough for her to feel that even after making love to her twice, he was ready for her again.

She chuckled lightly, feeling the velvet steel of his length push insistently against her tummy. "Though I don't know that I'd ever have been ready for this walloper... if I'd have known."

"Walloper?" he asked.

"It's Scottish for..." She pushed her pelvis forward, eliciting a groan from his lips. "Let's just say that yer a verra big man, mo muirnín."

His face fell, stricken with concern as he started pulling away from her. "Did I hurt you, Maggie? Did I—"

She threw her arm over his waist, keeping his body flush against hers. "No! No, Nils. We fit together, love. So perfectly."

"I was worried," he confessed, relaxing against her,

nuzzling her nose, pulling her closer.

"Of what?"

"Hurting you."

"I promise you gave me nothin' but pleasure," she said, her nipples beading against his chest as her inner muscles reminded her of the bliss she'd just found in his arms. Which reminded her of the joy she'd felt when he declared, "This is real."

"You meant it?" she asked. "About the truce being over?"

"That stupid truce," he muttered, rolling onto his back. "I couldn't think of another way for you to let me back into your life. For you to give me another chance. I couldn't stand the thought of you choosing Beck over me."

"Maybe I still will," she said, saucily, propping herself up on one elbow to face him.

"What?" His head whipped sharply to the side to look at her and relaxed as he examined the grin she couldn't hold back. "Don't tease me like that."

"You silly man," she said, reaching out to trace his lips with her fingertip. He caught it between his teeth and bit down lightly. "There hasn't been anyone for me...but you. Not for years."

"You sure looked chummy with him at Midsommardagen," he pouted, releasing her finger and staring up at the ceiling.

"I was angry with you." She chewed her lip for a moment before asking, "Do you remember that night right before Midsommardagen? You were goin' to help me straighten up the Prairie and instead you left me alone with Beck. Why'd you do that?"

"Same reason I left after we kissed. I thought he could be good for you. He's a lawyer. Successful. Doesn't have as much baggage as I do."

"I want your baggage, mo muirnín," she said, remembering his face as he told her about Veronica. She caressed his cheek with the tips of her fingers and he turned his neck to face her.

"Does that mean what I think it means?"

"What do you think it means?"

"Love," he whispered, as one whispers sacred things. "My love."

"Aye," she said softly. "It means what you think it means. I dinna want Beck, my love. I only want you."

He propped himself up on his elbow to mirror her. "Promise it'll stay that way."

"What're you offerin' me in return?" she teased.

He swallowed, looking down at the white sheets between them for a moment before seizing her eyes with a stark, vulnerable certainty. "My heart."

Her breath caught and tears filled her eyes as she stared back at him. "Now see...ye go an' say somethin' like that and I canna think of another thing except this..."

She leaned forward to kiss him and he gathered her into his arms, pushing her gently onto her back and proving, again, that his heart wasn't the only thing that belonged to her.

***

Four days.

He'd only be away from her for four days. Not four weeks. Not four months. Not four years. Four days. He could handle that, right?

As he drove the van toward the Bozeman Airport, farther and farther from Gardiner, he wished away the feelings of emptiness that battled with the fullness of his heart. Though Nils hadn't exactly been celibate in the years since he lost Veronica, the affairs he'd had were almost universally meaningless and brief, with the exception of Missy, who'd somehow managed to become his friend during their short time together. But certainly no one had come close to owning his heart the way Maggie did; he hadn't loved any of the others. Living his life without her now was unthinkable; after knowing the tenderness of her eyes when she drew back after kissing him, the teasing in them as she'd straddled him and rubbed herself over his lap, taunting him, the fire in them when he entered her, claimed her, climaxed in tandem with her, he'd never be able to let her go.

He'd sentenced himself to life the moment he'd carried Maggie into her bedroom, and he cursed himself for a fool now, because he hadn't been completely honest with her about his past.

He thought about the normal trajectory of any relationship: friendship or flirtation to attraction, attraction to chemistry, chemistry to dating, dating to deepening feelings, deepening feelings to commitment, commitment to sex, to love, to marriage, to a life together. He and Maggie had gone from friendship and unacknowledged attraction to marriage to deepening feelings to sex. But what about commitment? What about love? What about honesty?

Though he'd told her what they had was "real," he hadn't articulated what he meant by that, and the reality is that he meant everything: the friendship, the attraction, the chemistry, the love, the commitment, the sex, the marriage, the life together. All of it. The whole shebang. Boiled down, he wanted Maggie and Nils Lindstrom, husband and wife, together forever.

He hadn't intended to sleep with her without full disclosure, but when she'd insisted that he didn't need to say any more about Veronica, he'd taken the out, and when she'd kissed him and taken her top off, it had short-circuited his brain. Any noble intentions of honesty had been thrown completely out the window at the exact same time logical thoughts of latent collateral damage dissolved into a sea of hot, pulsing lust.

Anyway, he hadn't quite figured out how to say it.

My girlfriend and my son died on an operating table in Missoula.

Veronica was innocent and beautiful and got pregnant with my child, but we were young and foolish and she was scared to tell her aunt or her mother, scared to go to the doctor, scared to do anything but ignore the baby growing inside of her. She went into labor in the dingy room we shared in the basement of an old couple's house. After hours of screaming and bleeding, I picked her up and carried her over twenty blocks to the emergency room, where I found out they were both in severe distress. The child was so big for her petite body, the labor was obstructed. Shoulder dystocia led to the compression of his cord and a lack of oxygen, which was the probable cause of his death. The doctors broke her pelvic bone trying to get him out, but he was already dead when they delivered him, and she hemorrhaged to death anyway. My son's name was Jens and I only held him once, for twenty minutes, before they took his broken little body away.

It was my fault, he thought again, as he had a million times before. *It was my genes that created a child so big, it killed itself and its mother trying to be born. It was my fault...my fault...my fault...*

The car beside him laid on the horn and snapped Nils out of his dark memories, as he righted the van from veering into the adjacent lane. He looked up at the bright green sign. He was halfway to Bozeman.

When Veronica had finally told him she was pregnant in April, she was barely showing, and when they'd graduated in May, they'd moved up to Missoula together. He told his parents he had a forestry internship for the summer, but the truth was that he worked at McDonald's to scrape together enough money to pay for their rented room.

By July, she was huge and unwieldy, often complaining of pain, but refusing to go to the local clinic. She didn't want to give her name. She didn't want for her mother, who was still in Afghanistan, to be alerted to what she regarded as a shameful situation. Though he'd offered to marry her, the conversation had made her cry harder as she insisted she wasn't ready to be anyone's wife, anyone's mother. *Her* plan was to quietly have the baby at home and give it up for adoption at a local hospital a week or two later. She'd read that you could leave any child under the age of twelve at a hospital and they would take it, and though the idea of giving up his child upset him in theory, he knew that it was the best option. He was only eighteen years old. Like Veronica, he wasn't ready to be anyone's husband, anyone's father. Not to mention, in his teenage heart he truly believed that bringing home his illegitimate child to his god-fearing parents was an impossibility.

Veronica bought a book about home births and insisted Nils could handle the delivery, but he'd never read the book, choosing to pick up extra hours at work and bury his head in the sand of denial instead. Plus, he truly believed she'd change her mind and head to a hospital when the baby was finally coming.

He was wrong about that. She'd labored for over twenty hours, insisting—up until the moment she finally passed out from pain and exhaustion—that they could handle it without a hospital, desperate that their shameful news never be exposed.

He'd stayed in Missoula for the remainder of that summer, returning home in October. Veronica's funeral had been sparsely attended by her mother, who returned home from her tour when she was alerted by the hospital that her eighteen-year-old daughter had died in childbirth, and a few local relatives. Nils watched from a distance as they lowered the casket holding his girlfriend and son, and spent many long nights drunk and weeping by their gravesite, mumbling "I'm sorry...I'm sorry...I'm sorry" over and over again, trying to blot out the sheer horror of their death with cheap vodka.

Though people in Gardiner eventually heard the sad news about the pretty senior who died up in Missoula, she wasn't a local girl in the strictest sense, and the news had been passing at best. At one point Lars had approached him, asking Nils if he knew the sad news about "that chick you dated last year" but that was the extent of anyone's remembrances. She was a forgotten girl who'd left no imprint during her short stay.

Except for Nils, on whose heart her memory lingered, and who not only mourned her loss, but the terrible way she lost her life, and his culpability in her death and the death of their son. If only he'd insisted she go to the hospital when the labor began, when it got bad, when she first started bleeding...if only he'd insisted she go to a clinic and get checked out once or twice during her pregnancy, but he'd been a scared kid who knew nothing about girls and babies, hoping she'd have the baby and they'd go back to life and loving and feeling eighteen again.

When he told Maggie he had baggage, he meant the kind of baggage that changes your life forever. The kind of baggage that changes how you see the world and how you see yourself. The kind of baggage that you can't actually forgive, and you just hope that your life will give you opportunities to make amends. The kind of baggage that compels an eighteen-year-old kid, heartsick and paralyzed with guilt, muddy from the newly turned earth around him, to make a promise at the gravesite of his infant son:

I will never let this happen again, Jens, min son, min son, min litta son. Jag lovar dig. I promise you. I will remember what happened to you, min Älskling son, and I will never, ever let it happen again.

***

Maggie was walking on air.

She was married to the man she loved, who had finally told her—in his own way—how he felt about her. *My heart.* He'd offered her his heart, and she'd accepted it....along with everything else his body had to offer. And what a body it was. Her skin still flushed from the heat of their lovemaking, the secret place between her thighs thrumming with the memory of his length, the way he filled her so completely. She was lost in the physical sensations and in his feelings for her. When she thought of the way he moved within her, gentle and slow, rough and fast, it made her sigh with pleasure, with longing. Four days. Four bloody days apart, and she was a soppy mess of need.

"Hey, Mags!" said Paul, distracting her from the spot on the counter she'd been wiping in a slow circular motion for the better part of an hour as she daydreamed.

She looked up, a grin coming easily to greet her friend.

"Whatever you're thinking about must be pretty good."

You have no idea.

He drummed his fingers on the counter as he took a seat. "Bethany said you had the flu. Glad you're up and about."

"Sunday, Monday, and Tuesday were terrible," she

admitted, gesturing to a coffee cup and filling it up when he nodded. "Doc Garrison gave me antivirals, though, which I strongly recommend. I was feelin' better by yesterday."

"You look better than...better."

Maggie couldn't help the smile that took over her face. "I feel like myself again."

He nodded, giving her a curious look. "Guess we're not playing euchre tonight. Even if Beck would play, both Nils and Lars are in the park."

"Assumin' we could even drag you away from your laptop for a few hours!"

A few weeks ago, while Maggie had been nursing her own broken heart and spending time with Beck, she'd taken a specific interest in Paul's love life and opened an internet dating account for him. It turned out that the girl Maggie chose for him—a girl from Mystic, Connecticut, named Holly—had been a good choice. Paul had been corresponding with her regularly ever since.

"She's something," said Paul, a dopey smile—probably the twin to Maggie's—spread across his face as he took a sip of coffee. He finally looked up, giving her a cock-eyed, sheepish look. "Have I said thank you yet? For setting me up with her?"

"Aye. Somewhere between 'You're crazy, Maggie,' and 'Stay outta my love life, Maggie,' I believe you did." She pursed her lips, but she couldn't hold on to a perturbed expression and burst into giggles. "Aw, I'm glad it's workin' out. You deserve someone nice."

"You too." He sipped his coffee as she filled a to-go

order. "Speaking of you, I haven't seen Beck around much lately."

"Ah. Was wonderin' when you'd pry. You're just as bad as I am."

"And you're avoiding the question."

"Was there a question?" she asked innocently.

"What happened with Beck?"

Maggie shrugged. There was so much that Paul didn't know about her and Nils, but they'd agreed not to share anything about their relationship with friends or family until after the interview. Even then, they'd have to decide on a story. Still, she didn't want to lie outright.

"Nils came home."

"You have it bad for him."

"Aye," said Maggie, giving him a small smile. "Always have."

"Think it'll work out? Never seen him get serious with anyone."

Maggie took a deep breath and sighed. "I heard this in a movie once: 'I have no talent for certainty.' That's true. I canna say for sure. I only know what's in my heart. I only know what I want."

Paul nodded, his smile slightly concerned as he slid off the barstool and picked up his coffee cup. "Good luck, Mags. See you tomorrow."

She waved goodbye as he ducked out the door into a mid-morning rain storm, her words roosting in her head and bothering her. After what she and Nils had shared last night, shouldn't she be surer about where they were headed? And yet, she wasn't. The last time she'd shared a meaningful physical milestone with Nils, he'd left for the park for a month, and even though she trusted that things were different this time, she wouldn't feel secure until he was home again. Only then could she gauge if he was regretting their decision to sleep together, and the wait from Thursday to Sunday suddenly seemed interminable.

***

Rationally, he knew the right thing to do would be to park the van in the lot behind the office, walk home, shower and shave, send Maggie a quick text to be sure she was up for company and then head over to her place. But the second he saw the Welcome to Gardiner sign, there was only one place he wanted to go, only one place he needed to be, and almost as if he had no control over the decision, he drove right by the office and parked in the lot behind the Prairie Dawn instead. Four days without her had been enough. He wasn't interested in spending another goddamned second without her now that he was back in town.

The sun was setting on the horizon as he took a quick look at himself in the rearview mirror. Tanned and gritty from summer sun and trail dust, he was a sight to behold. For a moment, he thought about running home real quick, at least to shave the four days of stubble that was already shaping into a light beard. He ran his hand over his jaw, clenching it as he grew impatient with himself. Out of the corner of his eye, he caught the ambient light of her television through an upstairs window, and he threw open the van door, his decision made. His whole body was taut with impatience as he approached her door, wanting her, hoping that after four days she hadn't second-guessed or reconsidered their decision to sleep together, hoping that she was as much in love with him as he was with her.

As he unlocked the ground-level door, his adrenaline skyrocketed, making his heart drum like mad, as he took the steps two at a time. Just as he reached the hallway at the top of the stairs, he heard a deadbolt click and then suddenly, there she was, standing in her doorway in those skimpy little pajamas with her light red hair in two braids. All the air was sucked out of the small space between them as he drank her in, clocking the three seconds it took for him to harden in anticipation of the sweetness that waited for him in her bed.

"You're back!" she said, flashing him a beaming smile.

So overcome by the very sight of her, he closed the distance between them and pulled her into his arms, crushing her against his body in happiness and relief as he bent his head to find her lips with his.

As she backed them into the apartment, he kicked the door shut, reaching for her sweatshirt, lifting it over her head and letting it drop to the floor. Her hands grappled with his shirt, yanking it out of his jeans and pushing it up his chest until he grabbed it and tossed it over his head. His hands skimmed down to her hips and he lifted her effortlessly as she locked her legs around his waist. Pushing her up against the vestibule wall he ravaged her mouth, reaching up to cup her cheeks with his hands, his fingertips brushing over the smooth hair pulled back at her temples.

Finally he drew back and rested his forehead against

hers, panting, feeling the hard tips of her breasts brushing his chest with every forceful breath.

"I fucking missed you," he murmured. He shook his head, trying to catch his breath. "I'm filthy."

"You're my fantasy," she replied in a breathy voice, laced with sexy humor…and happiness. He could hear it and it mirrored everything he felt holding her in his arms again. Happiness. Joy. Requited longing.

"You're certainly mine."

Her fingers were laced behind his neck and her thumbs played with the short hairs on his nape as she bit her lower lip. He drew back to see the pink skin around her mouth and winced.

"I should have shaved first. I should have showered and—"

"No," she whispered, shaking her head back and forth gently and leaning down to lick and nip lightly on his bare shoulder, her breath hot on his skin. "I'm glad you came straight here. I'm glad you couldn't wait."

"It felt like dying to be away from you. I couldn't wait. I couldn't—"

"Me neither," she confessed, and then leaned back to catch his eyes in the dim light offered by the TV in the living room. She caressed his cheek gently and he closed his eyes for a moment, leaning into her touch. "But you *do* need a shower, *mo muirnín*."

"I do."

She swallowed, looking slightly nervous, before lifting her chin a touch and holding his eyes with a fierce heat. "Me too."

His breath hitched as he realized what she was suggesting. He'd never showered with a woman before. Never. Not in his whole life.

"You're going to give me a heart attack, Maggie May."

"Nope," she said, smiling at him. "There are other things I'd much prefer to give you."

She unlocked her legs from his waist, rubbing her chest against his as she slid down his front and sidled away from the wall. She reached out her hand to him and as the rest of his life flashed before his eyes, he knew that forever, until the end of his days, when she reached for him, he would follow her.

Anywhere. Anytime.

Anywhere. Anytime.

Until the end of his days.

Chapter 17

A week later, as Maggie watered the violets on her bedroom windowsill on Sunday evening, Nils came up behind her, pushing her hair aside to plant a gentle kiss on the back of her neck.

This is the way it was, now; after holding himself back for so long, he reached for her all the time. And like her violets, that soaked up the water and stretched toward the sun, she soaked up Nils's tenderness and basked in his warmth. With each passing day, she settled into a secret life with him that had been heretofore only a fantasy. But here, in her little apartment, away from their families and work and any other reminders of life except the growing love they bore one another...here, it was real. *They* were real and she wanted to trust that he belonged to her as surely as she belonged to him.

She placed the little watering can on her bureau and leaned back against him as he wrapped his arms around her, and she caught their reflection in the dresser mirror. When she looked at them together, her heart flooded with happiness because she didn't see two unconnected people, or even two friends anymore; she saw a couple. Being with him felt as natural as breathing, as sleeping, as waking up to feel his legs entwined with hers or see his face beside her, as she did every morning.

And yet, questions about their future lingered at the edges of her happiness. For all of their growing comfort with one another, they still hadn't broached the most important topic of all: what happens next?

After the interview, would they leave the safe cocoon of her apartment and face the world as a couple? Would they tell their families that they were married? Dating? Would they ever have a "real" wedding ceremony in a church with friends and family looking on? They hadn't actually addressed any solid plans for the future, and though Maggie felt increasingly certain that their love for one another was a forever kind of love, they hadn't said "I love you," yet either.

He'd agreed to join her—somewhat grudgingly—for Little Café on the Prairie story time on Wednesday night, but he'd changed the subject quickly when she asked if he'd be willing to read to the children. She noted this with frustration, but it hadn't daunted her plan: come hell or high water, they were discussing children on Wednesday night.

When he'd asked if she was on the pill last week, it had confirmed her suspicions that he was capable of having children, which led Maggie to believe it wasn't a matter of *can't*, but *won't*. And that made no sense to her since he so clearly loved his big family and his tiny nieces. Nils Lindstrom was a man practically built to be a father with his gruff voice and caring ways. She was desperate to understand his opposition to having a family of his own, and whether he wanted to discuss it or not, they didn't have the luxury of sitting on their secrets anymore. With the interview only a week away and questions about their plans to start a family almost guaranteed, they needed to discuss it.

"You're scowling," he whispered into her ear before resting his chin on her shoulder, covered with only the thin strap of her cami. He lifted the strap and pressed his lips to her skin, sending a deluge of shivers down her arm, and she adjusted her hands, lacing her fingers through his, under her breasts.

"What're you thinking about?" he asked.

She relaxed her face in the mirror, smiling into his eyes. "Us."

"Why is 'us' making you scowl?"

"Because I don't know what happens next."

He scowled. "What do you mean?"

She turned in his arms to look up at him. "The interview's a week from Thursday."

"And we'll be ready. Don't you think so?"

"Aye. I do."

"So, don't be worried. What happens next? You get your green card."

"Then what?"

"We come home."

She chuckled lightly, but it wasn't a light-hearted sound. "Home? Where's that?"

"Here."

"Here in my wee apartment? Or yours? Or neither?"

He tilted his head, furrowing his brows at her, worry seeping into his eyes. "What does *that* mean?"

She swallowed and licked her lips nervously. "I don't know our plans. Do you move in here? Do I move in with you? Or do we have to take it slower than that and not move in together at all? Do we spring the happy news on your pop? *'Guess what, Mr. L! You've got a new daughter-in-law! The weddin'? Oh, no. Nobody was invited. It was a green-card weddin' that happened to turn into somethin' more after we got flagged by immigration services.'* How's that goin' to go over? I mean, have you even thought this out? Do we stay married?" She paused and her final words came out in a strangled whisper. "Do we stay together?"

"Maggie!" he exclaimed, his brows furrowing in worry and confusion. "Stop."

"I canna. We'll finish the questionnaires by Thursday, but there are so many more questions, Nils. And they swim around in my head and I have no answers for them, and I fear you dinna either."

"I do. I do have answers. Lie down with me," he said gently, pulling her down on the bed. He kicked off his shoes and scooted back until he was sitting against the headboard and Maggie crawled up the bed to join him, resting her head on his chest, over his heart. It beat strong and true under her ear. Thu-thump. Thu-thump. Thu-thump. It was hers. He had given it to her. She could listen to it forever. She *wanted* to listen to it forever.

He stroked her hair again and again, soothingly, lovingly, and she took a deep breath and sighed. "That's so nice."

"We stay together," he murmured, his voice low, but

fierce with conviction. "We stay together because I love you. We stay together because I think you love me. We stay together because we waited too long to *be* together, and it's better than anything I ever imagined. Because I can hardly bear a minute away from you. Because I want you in my arms every morning and every night. Staying together isn't a question or a conversation. Staying together is like water or salt or sleep or air or anything else I would die without. We stay together."

She closed her eyes against the sudden rush of tears, and nodded her head against his chest. "We stay together. Because you love me and I love you, too."

"We stay married," he said softly. "Because when we took our wedding vows, I meant every word. I said I would honor you and keep you and forsake all others. I said I'd love and cherish you, in sickness and in health, for richer and poorer, until I die. And I meant it. We stay married because we *are* married. We stay married because it doesn't matter how we found ourselves saying the vows, but because we said them, because they were real from the very beginning even if we didn't know it then. Unless you don't…"

"We stay married," she murmured as her heart exploded with love for him, his strong, simple words beating back the uncertainty she'd felt only moments ago. "Because you meant every word, and I did, too."

"As for my pop and your family and our friends? I want them to know you're my wife. But I don't want to hurt them. How would you feel about us getting through the interview first and then come home and we could *start dating*?

Immediately. That night. And after a month or two, I'll propose. And yeah, of course, we'll take the vows again in a church in front of our friends and family. At Christmastime, maybe. Beck and Emma can't violate our confidentiality and Missy wouldn't. No one else knows. No one else will ever know."

At the mention of Missy, Maggie stiffened, clenching her jaw. "Missy."

The backs of his fingers skimmed the underside of her chin, pushing it up gently until she met his eyes. He bent his head and kissed her softly, lovingly. "I love *you*." He searched her eyes intensely, as his chest heaved, betraying the profound depths of his emotion. "My love. *My wife*."

She smiled at him, laughter bubbling up from a joyful place in her heart where all of her dreams were coming true. Where all of her deepest longings were soothed and relieved by the truth of his words, by the power of his love for her.

"My husband. *Mo muirnín*," she said, her voice thick with wonder and tenderness. "I love you, too."

She reached up to hold his face in her hands as he pulled her up and onto his lap.

Their kiss changed from tender to urgent as she wiggled out of her cami and let it fall beside her on the comforter. He ran his hands lightly along the sides of her ribcage as he feathered kisses near her ear, down the line of her jaw to the tip of her chin, following the curve of her neck with his lips as she still held his head lightly, guiding him through the plains and valleys of her body.

***

On Wednesday afternoon, Maggie left Bethany in charge so that she could make extra shortbread upstairs, instructing Summer to come up in an hour or so to collect the first batch. Her favorite part of Little Café on the Prairie, aside from reading the stories, was watching all of the little ones snack on her shortbread as she read. She didn't want them to have to wait until after story hour to have their treats. She wanted them to always associate reading with sweetness and pleasure, so she had Bethany and Summer offer cookies after every individual story which meant that each child had three cookies in their belly by the end of the hour.

She took the sixth batch of shortbread out of her oven and started cutting it as the phone rang.

"Maggie?"

"Aunt Janet!"

"Hello, lass. Ye're well?"

"I am! I'm makin' Gran's shortbread right now."

"Who'sa lucky devil gets to eat it?"

"Bite yer tongue. It's fer the bairns at story hour."

"That's lovely, Maggie. I willna keep ye…just callin' to say that Gingy finished his courses early. He'll be comin' across in two weeks rather'n four. If that's okay."

"Two weeks?" she repeated, wiping her hands on her jeans and glancing at the calendar. Circled in red was their appointment on the fourth. "The ninth?"

"Aye, um, nae, the sixth. I ken it's quick, but it's fer the best, Maggie. If ye're willin'."

"Oh, I'm willin'. He's in trouble? Ye *need* to send him sooner?"

"He's runnin' with a bad lot. A sorry lot."

"He's finished his course, though? The carpentry?"

"Enough o' it."

"And where's he now, then?"

"He'll be fine here for a few more days."

"Send him sooner," said Maggie, hearing the worry in her aunt's voice. "Send him now if you can."

"Nae, Maggie. Couldna get the tickets changed any sooner. The sixth is the earliest. Ye'll be ready, though?"

"Aye, Aunt Janet. Whenever he gets here, I'll be waitin'."

"Yer a good lass, Maggie."

Maggie smiled into the phone, missing her family for a moment, wishing she could tell them that she was married, that she was happy, that her life was full. Instead she asked, "How's Mum?"

They spoke for a few more minutes and her aunt gave her the details of Graham's travel plans before hanging up. Maggie wasn't sure how long someone had been knocking lightly at her door, but she answered it to find Summer standing in the hallway.

"Come in and give me two more minutes, Summer. I'm just cuttin' it up now. You can bring it downstairs and start arrangin' it in those tins for me."

Summer followed her boss into the little kitchen, leaning up against the counter as Maggie cut the sheet of shortbread into small pieces. She looked up at the pretty brunette teenager, giving her an easy smile. While she'd spent a good deal of time with Summer's sister, Bethany, she realized she didn't know Summer very well.

"I was just talkin' to my aunt. She's sendin' my cousin, Graham, over to stay with me for a while. He'll be here the weekend after next."

Summer nodded politely.

"He's about your age, you know. Maybe you and Bethany could show him around a bit?"

"Sure, Miss Campbell. We'll be glad to."

"Who knows?" She winked at the girl. "You two might suit!"

Summer grinned back. "I'm sure he's terrific, but we won't suit."

"You haven't even met him yet! Give the lad a chance!" she teased.

"Oh, no offense to him, I'm sure he's great. It's just...I've—well, I'm sort of taken."

"You've got a boyfriend? I'm not surprised, but I've never seen him hangin' about."

"No, I don't have a boyfriend, but..."

Maggie turned away from the shortbread to face Summer, curious and bemused. It was the longest conversation they'd ever had, aside from pleasantries and talk about the café. "But what, lass?"

"I'm going to marry Beck Westman."

"Are you, now?"

"Mm-hm."

Maggie chuckled good-naturedly. "Have you set a date?"

"Of course not." Summer's smile faded a touch as she

shook her head. "I'm only seventeen. I still have to finish high school and go to college. Besides, he doesn't know yet."

Maggie put her hands on her hips, staring at the girl, increasingly aware that this was not a joke to Summer, as Maggie had originally assumed. "You're serious."

"Yes, I am." She lifted her chin a notch. "Bethany said he doesn't come around anymore, which means you gave him up, which means he's free."

"Summer, lass, he's just turned thirty."

"I know that." She shrugged lightly, a small, dreamy smile on her young face as she sighed longingly. "It doesn't matter to me."

Maggie tilted her head to the side, looking closely at Summer and seeing the certainty there. Maggie thought of all the days she'd watched Nils come into the café, praying that he'd finally turn to her, finally make a move, finally let her know that "friend" was secret code for "the love of my life." How many times had she almost given up hope? And now here she was—married to him, in love with him, practically living with him. Maggie knew in her heart that nothing was impossible. Not where love was concerned.

"Beck Westman, huh?" she asked softly, grinning at Summer as she scooped the last of the shortbread into a Ziploc bag and handed it to the young woman.

The teenager's smile returned—lovely, serene, and convicted—and she nodded at Maggie, as she took the bag and headed for the door.

"He's a good man, Summer. I wish you luck. Lots of it."

Summer turned at the door, her brown eyes deep and sure as she looked back at Maggie. "Thanks, Miss Campbell. But I don't need luck. It'll happen. Someday."

"You're very sure."

"I am." She shrugged again. "Some things are just meant to be."

Maggie smiled at her again then closed the door behind her, leaning up against it. *Some things are just meant to be.* Like her and Nils. No matter what. And after tonight, there would be no more secrets between them. She pushed back on the doubts that tried to creep into her mind. No matter what secrets he held on to...no matter what, deep in her heart she agreed with Summer: some things are just meant to be.

***

Surrounded by two dozen children, including the two sharing her lap, Maggie finished the second story with a flourish.

"And then the poky little puppy curled up in a wee ball, happy to be home at last."

After a respectful moment of silence, the children clapped enthusiastically and Bethany and Summer appeared on either side of the large group, passing around the cookie tins and reminding the children, "Just one."

Maggie looked up for the hundredth time trying to catch Nils's eyes. From the moment he'd arrived, he'd kept his distance, frozen by the door, about as far away as possible from the dense circle of little bodies on the floor in front of her. And for the first time in weeks, his eyes had that cool, growly look to them that he'd always had before his month away from her in Yellowstone. He didn't look like the warm, tender man she'd come to know over the last three and a half heavenly weeks. He looked like his old self—tortured, closed and cold. Unreachable. Wary. It made her heart beat out of her chest at the thought of what she was about to do.

She finally caught his eyes and smiled at him, but he didn't return the smile. He stared back at her, his face cautious and uncomfortable...and something else. Guilty? No, that wasn't quite it. She watched him carefully and pinpointed the look. Aye, there it was again: sorry. He was sorry. For what? She bit her bottom lip, about to chicken out on her plan, but she lifted her chin and started talking.

"Children, we have a special guest with us here tonight. He's a very good friend of mine, and I know he'd like to read a story to all of you. Would that be okay?" She looked around at the little heads nodding yes. "Yes?"

She looked up at Nils, whose brows furrowed together as he set his jaw and shook his head no.

"He might need a wee bit of convincin', though."

If he could just sit with all of them—feel their innocent, eager eyes on his face as he read a story, the lovely way their warm, wiggly, little bodies clustered together hanging on the words. He would see how wonderful they were. He'd be reminded of how wonderful it could be to have his own someday.

She smiled at all of the children encouragingly, looking back up just in time to hear the bell over the door ring as the door slammed quietly shut. Her mouth dropped open in surprise to see that the space he'd occupied was empty. He'd left. He was gone.

She looked back at the children, pasting a smile on her face and blinking rapidly as her eyes watered. "I, um…"

"I don't need any convincing at all! This looks like a fine group of young students!"

As Paul Johansson broke through the crowd of parents, he caught her eyes, giving her a sympathetic smile. He'd seen it all and bailed her out, and she was so grateful it doubled her tears. He smiled at the children, waving to the younger siblings of his students as he made his way to Maggie. When he got to her, he jerked his head toward the door to tell her to go after Nils, and took her place, sitting down on the floor and picking up the book she'd chosen for the third selection.

"*Oh, the Places You'll Go?* Well, this is one of my all-time favorites! Who here saw the movie *The Lorax*?"

Maggie looked back as she made her way to the door. Paul had saved the day and the children were already engaged with the young principal, their giggles filling the café with warmth and joy. Maggie wiped the wetness off her cheeks and stepped out into the cool evening air, turning toward her apartment, only to find Nils sitting hunched on the stoop under the porch light.

***

"You shouldn't have done that," he said softly as he watched her approach.

"I guess not," she replied, standing a foot away from him, arms folded protectively over her chest. "I just thought if you could see how lovely they are, you wouldn't hate the thought so much."

"The thought?"

"Of children."

"I don't *hate* children, Maggie. I'm not a monster. I just…"

He stood up, shoving his hands in his pockets and staring at her. She looked so sad, so damn sad and confused, and it was his fault. And suddenly their love for each other, their commitment to their marriage—all of it—seemed like a sham, like nothing but a fantasy. Any fool could see how much she loved being with those kids, how much she wanted her own. He was a selfish bastard for loving her, for letting her love him, when he couldn't give her the one thing she wanted more than anything else.

"We need to talk," he said.

"Aye."

"Upstairs?" After weeks of treating her place as his own, he suddenly felt the need to ask permission.

"Sure."

She looked him in the eyes, as if to ascertain just how bad this conversation was going to be, and then swiped her hand over her worried, glassy eyes. He opened the door and she walked past him, preceding him up the stairs and into her apartment. She didn't turn on a light. She walked straight to the loveseat and sat down, tucking her feet under her, and for the first time ever, he took a seat in the chair across from her, rather than sitting down beside her and pulling her into the crook of his arm. He rested his elbows on his knees, lacing his hands together between them and bowing his head, as if in prayer.

"Tell me why," she whispered in the darkness.

"Why?"

"Why you don't want children."

He swallowed, wishing he could see her eyes, at the same time glad that he couldn't. He swallowed and cleared his throat, finally exhaling a shaky breath before speaking.

"I told you that my high school girlfriend, Veronica, died. But, that wasn't, um—the whole story. She um—she died giving birth to our son, Jens."

He heard Maggie's gasp from four feet away, but she didn't approach him, didn't cross the room to put her arms around him as she had when he told her about Veronica. She stayed where she was, her expression inscrutable in the darkness.

"The Christmas prom picture? I got her pregnant that night. We kept it a secret, and after graduation we moved up to Missoula together and stayed in a rented room. She wouldn't go see a doctor. She was scared to death of her mother finding out." His eyes filled with tears and he wet his dry lips with his tongue. He hadn't articulated this story since he'd told it to Missy five or six years ago, and saying the words aloud was just as difficult now as then. "She went into labor while I was at work. When I got home, she'd already been in pain for nine hours. She had a book and thought I could help her deliver him, but things got worse and worse. She wouldn't let me call anyone. It was only after she passed out from the pain that I carried her to the ER. His sh—um, his shoulder was, um, was stuck. They had to—they broke her pelvic bone trying to get him out, but…but…"

"Oh, my God," she whispered, and he heard the tears in her voice, the pity, the deep sorrow.

Nils didn't know where the strength came for him to keep talking, to finish the story—he only knew she deserved to know. He cleared his throat as tears streamed down his face in the darkness.

"Neither of them made it. They both died. I only got to hold him for a moment before they took him away."

And suddenly Maggie was on the floor kneeling before him, her hands on his knees, her cheeks glistening in the moonlight.

"*Tha mi duilich, mo muirnín*," she whispered, and he knew in his heart and by the broken tone in her voice, that she was telling him how terribly sorry she was.

He slid from the chair to the floor, leaning his head down until it rested limply on her shoulder. She encircled his body with her arms, pulling him into her embrace, whispering soft, comforting words in Gaelic as he wept quietly for Veronica and Jens.

***

After a while, his body stopped trembling and Maggie stood up and took his hand, leading him to her bedroom, where they got into bed together, lying side by side on their backs in the darkness.

"Your pop doesn't know?" she asked. "Lars? Your mother?"

"No one," he answered. "Just you."

"And Missy."

"Yeah." She felt him nod his head beside her. "And Missy. She was kind to me, Maggie. She was the first person I ever told. The only person."

"I'm grateful to her," said Maggie quietly, surprised to discover that her jealousy was gone, and she was telling the truth. Not only did it explain the depth of friendship she sensed between Nils and Missy, but she was thankful he'd had someone—*anyone*—to talk to about such a tragic episode in his life. "I dinna know how you kept it inside for so long..."

"What would have been the point of burdening my parents? Veronica was dead. Jens was...gone." His voice broke and he cleared his throat. "It would've broken their hearts."

She propped herself on her elbow, gazing at his strong face tenderly. "So you bore it alone."

He nodded again.

"How? You were so young. Only eighteen." She thought of Summer today in her kitchen, so innocent, so lovely and certain about her future. So full of hope and conviction. All of Nils's innocence had been stolen from him before he ever reached adulthood.

"Old enough to be at fault for what happened."

"At *fault?* Surely not. No one was at fault. You were just kids."

"No, Maggie. It was my fault."

"You were practically a chi—"

"No. You don't get it. It's *my fault* they died. Don't you

341

see? She was tiny. He was a big baby. Too big! Because of me. My genes. My fault."

The full horror of his burden started to come into focus as she listened to his words. "Oh, no. No, love. She was young and frightened. She didn't want medical care. She—"

"—would be alive today if she hadn't been pregnant with *my* baby. He broke her bones trying to be born. He—"

"Nils, stop. Please, love..."

"They died and I survived. It was my fault. Mine and solely mine."

"No," she said again, shaking her head, as more tears flooded her eyes. He had blamed himself for long enough. "It wasn't your fault. It wasn't anyone's fault."

She reached out to touch his cheek and felt his jaw clenching beneath her palm. She knew the tell. He was holding something back.

"What else?" she whispered.

"That's why I won't have any more children. It's because I made a promise. I went to his grave and I promised him it would never happen again."

"To Jens?" she asked, feeling dazed.

He nodded, tightening his jaw again, and she knew he was holding back tears.

"You promised your son you wouldn't have any more children."

"I promised him that his death wouldn't be in vain. I promised I'd never risk the same thing happening again."

Her eyes closed and she withdrew her hand from his face, rolling onto her back as the pain of realization engulfed her.

"I...oh, Nils, I..."

Her words trailed off into the darkness. She wanted to tell him that she understood—not only that she understood but that she respected his decision. However, a wave of sorrow took hold of her heart and squeezed it so hard, she thought she might faint. It only took a moment for her to realize the awful choice before her: she could have Nils or she could have children of her own, but she couldn't have both.

She didn't know how much time passed in silence before she felt his hand move silently to cover hers. Without thinking, she adjusted her hand so that his fingers lined up to lace through hers.

But it was hours before she slept.

***

The sun streamed through the windows and she squinted, burrowing deeper into her pillow and feeling Nils's arm tighten around her reflexively. She realized she was still wearing the T-shirt and jean cut-off shorts she'd been wearing the night before. They'd never even changed for bed.

An unexpected heaviness washed over her as the details of last night's conversation returned to her consciousness.

"Are you awake?" she whispered.

"Yeah," he answered, his breath warm against her neck. "Didn't sleep much."

"Me either," she confessed in a thready voice, turning in his arms to face him.

His eyes were tired and sad, as though he'd bypassed worry during the night and already surrendered to hopelessness. "I still have that tour today and tomorrow."

"I know," she answered.

"You're not coming," he said softly. A statement, not a question.

"I think I need a little…time."

He swallowed then nodded briefly, dropping her eyes and clenching his jaw. The hand covering her hip flexed and released. "Am I losing you?"

"I have to get my head around it."

"I'd never hurt you, Maggie. I'd never get you pregnant. I'd never let that happen to you. I promise."

It was then that she realized how totally out of sync they were. And though she knew it would hurt him to hear the truth, she needed to say it. She needed to be honest and know that he had heard her.

"Nils. Love. The only thing I am still longin' for in *my* life is *your* child. You wouldn't hurt me. I'm strong! I'm not scared—"

"I am."

"But I'd have medical care. As much as I needed. And we're adults. Fully grown, rational adults. We'd be—"

"Maggie." His eyes were flinty and sharp as he lifted his hand from her hip. "I can't."

"Now, that's not technically true. Technically, you *won't.*"

"I made a promise."

"When you were a kid. A scared, guilt-ridden, grieving

kid."

"I made a promise," he repeated softly, but firmly.

"I see."

"It's not about me not wanting kids. I love kids." He reached out for her again, lightly this time, but her body throbbed with relief to feel connected to him again. "We could adopt. A little redheaded girl. Like you."

She couldn't keep the sadness from filling her eyes, so she closed them, taking a deep breath and trying not to cry as her dreams died before her eyes.

"Maggie?"

She couldn't hold back the tears as she answered him. "I've never looked like anyone. I've n-never looked at someone's face and seen my own s-smile, the color of my eyes, the line of my j-jaw. I've never known what it is to belong to someone by b-blood."

"And you want that."

"Aye. I do." She reached up to wipe her cheeks with her free hand, sniffling miserably.

He abandoned her hip again, rolling onto his back and throwing his arm over his eyes. "What you're asking me to do? I can't, Maggie. It's not just about breaking my word to Jens, I can't risk it. How could I put you in danger? You, who I love more than life. Seeing you bleeding and struggling and—My God! What if I lost you?"

"Listen. Listen to me." Taking a deep breath, she rubbed her eyes, forcing her tears to stop. She was still leaning up on her elbow and she reached out, placing her damp hand flat on his chest. "Your brother has two bonnie babies. Your sister has one, too. Same genes. Beautiful, healthy children. Beautiful, healthy mothers."

He lowered his arm and looked at her, his eyes beseeching her to understand. "Please don't ask me to do this."

"I'm not askin' you for anythin'," she insisted. "I just want you to think about it."

He closed his eyes and shook his head "no."

"I'm sorry," he said quietly, rolling away from her and swinging his legs over the side of the bed. "I can't."

Tears coursed into her hair from the corners of her eyes as he left her, pulling her front door closed behind him with a firm, but quiet, thud.

Chapter 18

Maggie lay in bed for a long time until her tears subsided, and she was left with red, burning, puffy eyes.

She was sad for so many reasons: the sheer horror of Nils's story and the way he'd had to not only bear the losses by himself, but the heaviness of the memories, made her want to weep all over again. She thought of all the times he gruffly disengaged from a conversation with her, or looked away in pain when she helped a child with their hot cocoa at Little Café on the Prairie. She was sure now that her love of children was the *reason* he'd kept her at arm's length for so many years, and it hurt her. Very much.

She swung her legs over the bed and headed to the bathroom to turn on the shower. And now she knew the truth: he was perfectly capable of having children, but he wouldn't. She couldn't ask him to break the promise he made to his dead child, yet her heart twisted with the unfairness of the situation. She loved him, she wanted him, but he wouldn't give her children. It made her so frustrated and so sad, she wanted to scream.

Lathering the strawberry shampoo into her scalp, she let more tears fall as certain truths began to assert themselves. What if she let go of Nils, whom she loved as she'd never loved anyone in her life? What if she found someone else—Beck, Paul, anyone—and married them only to find out they were unable to father children? She'd be giving up the love of her life in exchange for something uncertain.

Blow drying her hair, she stared at her face in the mirror, thinking about his words: *We could adopt. A little redheaded girl. Like you.* It made her wince with pain and tenderness at the same time. She *could* adopt someone just like her. A baby who needed a home as she had. Some other woman's unwanted child whom she and Nils could love. And perhaps Maggie was even uniquely qualified to parent such a child. She would know all of the right things to say, all of the ways to soothe the aches and pains that were inevitable in the life of an adopted child.

Her eyes were dry and clear as she made her way down to the café, sucking in a deep breath of fresh air as she rounded the building. It's not that she wouldn't have to grieve the demise of her own deep-seated dreams and desires, but as she unlocked the café door, she knew that her decision wouldn't be as difficult to make as she'd originally imagined. In fact, deep down, she'd known all along what her decision would be.

Nils finally belonged to her.

There was no way she'd be giving him up.

Not for anything.

***

Nils led the way down a familiar trail with a group of six young couples following behind, but he was distracted by his thoughts and his usual nonstop commentary felt somewhat stilted.

"Mr. Lindstrom? Did you say there were wolves in this area?"

He looked beside him to find an attractive blonde falling into step beside him.

"Yep. My brother's been tracking them."

"Well, we're not in any danger, are we?"

Nils shook his head, glancing at the way her breasts spilled over the top of her skimpy shirt. He felt for the canister of pepper spray hanging from a belt loop at his hip. "Nope."

She reached out and touched his arm, giggling conspiratorially. "So, we're all trying to figure out...are you married or...not?"

He furrowed his brows, looking down at her upturned face. If he wasn't sure before, he was now. She was flirting with him. He glanced back at the man she'd arrived with; he was a good deal smaller than Lars, huffing and puffing like the trail they were hiking was a lot more exercise than he was used to.

Nils gave her a look.

Giggling again, she continued, "It's just that we're out here in the woods for a couple of nights and I thought..."

"You're here with someone."

She batted her eyes and shrugged. "Who? Andy? We have an...understanding."

"Well, I don't."

"Oh. So, you *are* married. You don't wear a ring," she pouted.

"Ring doesn't mean anything."

"To your girlfriend or your wife?"

He let her words tumble around in his head before answering. Either? Neither? His heart was so heavy, he didn't know how he kept putting one foot in front of the other. Maggie deserved so much—she deserved a baby that looked like her, was as beautiful as her. She deserved the family she'd always wanted. She didn't deserve some damaged bastard who'd never be able to give her what she wanted more than anything, who'd already had his shot at fatherhood and lost it.

And yet.

The idea of giving her up made him want to die. It was that simple. After knowing the sweetness of holding her, making love to her, reaching for her whenever he wanted to, life wouldn't be worth living without her in it. It'd be a marginal existence living in shadow and sorrow, so what was the point?

"Wife," he answered gruffly, hoping to God she still wanted to be.

"Just my luck," said the blonde, shrugging before falling back to walk with one of her friends.

***

Maggie spent Thursday evening cleaning the small, sparsely furnished apartment beside hers that hadn't been used as someone's permanent residence since Jenny Lindstrom vacated it a few years ago. She'd used it for café storage and the occasional visitor to Gardiner, but it would be a nice little place for Gingy. She could keep her eye on him without compromising her own privacy.

On Friday evening, she made a trip up to the Target in Bozeman for a new loveseat slipcover, a small flat-screen TV, fresh linens and towels in a deep, masculine forest green, and a few small decorations to make the place feel homier. While the timing of his visit wasn't terrific, she couldn't deny how glad she would be to have her cousin near her again.

Unlike the rest of her dark-haired family, Gingy's hair was a shock of red he'd inherited from his father, not wholly unlike Maggie's strawberry-blonde, and they were both covered with freckles from head to toe. People could easily assume she and Graham were, in fact, blood relations, and it had always drawn her to him in a special way. It was probably part of the reason she had felt so close to him, closer than she did to anyone else in her adoptive family. That and she had spent a good deal of her early adolescence caring for him after her father's death, his toddler antics cheering those dark days. She would always have a special place in her heart for him, though she didn't fool herself that he wasn't trouble.

Which made her wish Nils was home so she could talk to him all about Graham's visit. He'd offered, a while back, to take Gingy under his wing, and Maggie realized what a relief it was to know that she wouldn't be alone in his care. Her husband could help her figure things out, and according to their plans, she and Nils would be "dating" by then, so there wouldn't be a need for secrets or sneaking around.

And at no point during these thoughts did Maggie's

eyes well up with tears or did she feel the sharp sorrow she'd felt on Wednesday night when she realized she'd never have a biological child with Nils. Sometime between then and now, she'd come to terms with her decision to adopt with him, and though she'd always feel a little wistful about not having a baby of her own flesh and blood, she'd never regret the man standing beside her, so strong, so tender, so loving.

"Penny for your thoughts, Mags," Paul said on Saturday evening, sidling up to the bar and sitting down.

"Mine are dead dull," she responded, checking her watch. Eight o'clock? Where had the day gone? Her brows furrowed. Nils's tour should've been back a couple of hours ago, yet he hadn't stopped by yet. She tried not to read too much into that. She'd been the one to ask for space, right? "Penny for yours instead. How's Miss Mystic?"

Paul shrugged. "Good, I guess."

"You guess? Trouble in paradise?"

"Mystic's a long way away."

"Aye. It is. You want coffee?"

Paul nodded. "Espresso, please. Holly's so amazing. In a million years I never thought I'd meet the girl of my dreams on the internet. It feels like it should be impossible that I have feelings this strong for her without ever having met her in person."

Maggie slid the piping hot mug to him with a smile after fashioning a heart in the foam with a butter knife. "There isn't one right way to fall in love with someone. Sometimes the route is long and windy. Sometimes it includes a proxy marriage or a secret plan to escape an ex-boyfriend. Or meeting someone on the internet. Meeting someone like Miss Mystic."

He grinned at her as the front door opened and a young woman dressed in pajama pants, a Boston College T-shirt and a baseball hat stepped into the café. After looking around for a minute like Alice in Wonderland or Dorothy in Oz, she eased onto a barstool two down from Paul. Turning to face them from under her cap, her eyes looked tired…and a little wary.

"We have a visitor, Paul," said Maggie lightly, catching the girl's attention. "From Boston, no less."

It turned out her name was Jane and she'd just spent the day with Lars, getting ready for a magazine photo shoot in Yellowstone next week. She was, in fact, the personal of assistant of Samara Amaya, the famous supermodel, who, in an unexpected twist, was her cousin, too. After exchanging pleasantries about her job, Paul shifted the conversation back to his love life, which made Maggie wonder about her own. She checked her watch again then glanced at the front door, as though wondering about Nils's whereabouts would suddenly make him appear.

Jane suggested that it was time for Paul to visit Connecticut and Maggie jumped back into the conversation, not wanting to appear distracted. "Aye, the lass has some good advice, I think."

Deciding that she'd be distracted by Nils's absence for the rest of the night if she didn't go find him, Maggie signaled to Bethany, who was cleaning tabletops.

"Do you play euchre, Jane?" she asked the visitor,

thinking that it was time to reinstate their Sunday and Thursday night games, and add some normalcy to things again. "With Lars workin' so hard on your group we need a fourth tomorrow."

"Who's the third?" she asked.

"Lars's brother." Maggie felt the flush in her cheeks as she said his name. "Nils."

"His brother?"

"Aye. 'Twill be fun. Tomorrow night. Seven-thirty, and all the warm milk you like."

"Thanks, I'll be here," said Jane, hopping down from her stool and waving goodbye.

Bethany set her spray bottle and rag on the bar and Maggie turned to her. "Can you close tonight? I thought I'd head home."

"Sure, Miss Campbell."

Maggie smiled at the young woman, taking off her apron and folding it quickly. Last time Nils came back from a tour, he had raced to her side. They hadn't been able to keep their hands off each other. She was starting to feel worried that he hadn't come to see her. Maybe he was putting some distance between them? Well, she'd be damned if she'd let that happen. She'd waited too long to be with him. She wasn't losing him now.

"You think she's right?" asked Paul, as Maggie passed him on her way to the door.

She stopped and turned to face him. "About what?"

"You think I should do it? Buy a ticket? Go visit Holly?"

She shrugged. "I think you have to follow your heart."

And then she sailed out the door, determined to take her own advice.

***

When he'd peeked into the Prairie Dawn, she'd been chatting with Paul and a tourist at the bar, looking warm and relaxed, and suddenly Nils couldn't approach her. Couldn't watch her face change from easy to fraught. He'd arrived back in town hours ago but had purposely avoided the Prairie. He couldn't bear the idea that she'd had some time to think and might have decided that her life would be better off without him. It made for the possibility of such a stark and terrifying future, it was actually making him reconsider his choices.

Was there any way to honor the loss of Veronica and Jens while still having a baby with Maggie? Was there a doctor good enough to guarantee her safety? He half hated himself for even considering it, but he couldn't help it. She'd called him *a scared, guilt-ridden, grieving kid* when he'd made that promise, and her words had resonated with him. But did his age or mental state at the time make his word any less binding? It didn't. Not to mention, his fears for Maggie's health and safety were looming and large when he even considered getting her pregnant.

That said…entertaining the fantasy of having a child of his own? With Maggie? That had been a slippery slope, too. Once the idea had settled into his mind, it was more viscerally appealing to him than he could ever have guessed. Despite what had happened to Veronica and Jens, despite his promise to them, despite his very real fears that his child could hurt Maggie as it had Veronica, there was a small part of him that fell a little bit in love with the idea of a child that was half his and half Maggie's. So much so, that even now, sitting on her stoop, waiting for her to come home, he could feel a slight shiver of longing down his back before shutting down his thoughts and turning them in another direction.

"Nils?"

He looked up to see that direction standing in front of him.

"What're you doin' here?"

His heart fell as he stood up, towering over her. Did she not want him here?

She searched his eyes then stepped closer to him, slipping her arms around his waist and resting her cheek against his chest. "Why didn't you come into the Prairie to let me know you were home?"

His eyes fluttered closed as he put his arms around her, pulling her closer, his relief so overwhelming that he forgot to breathe and finally gulped in a bucket load of air to make up for it.

"I didn't know if you'd want to see me. I didn't know how you'd feel, after—"

"I don't have all the answers yet. But I know this for certain, Nils Lindstrom..." She leaned back and looked up at him, the setting sun over the river making a halo around her head. "...I love you. We stay together. You're my husband..." She searched his eyes and it dawned on him that she was waiting for him to respond, to finish their self-created vows.

He clenched his jaw and his voice was full of emotion as he murmured, "We stay married."

Maggie smiled at him, her brave smile, as her eyes brightened with tears. "That's how I feel."

"That's how I feel, too."

Then he crushed her against him, burying his face in her hair, overcome by the love that seemed to unendingly multiply for the woman in his arms.

After a few moments, she pulled away from him, unlocking the door and taking his hand to lead him upstairs. "Tell me about your tour."

He grinned, staring at her adorable backside as she preceded him up the stairs. "It was awful."

"Awful! Why? They were awful? The tourists?"

"City folks. Three couples."

"Rude? Demandin'?"

"Lonesome."

"Who was lon—"

She turned and faced him, tilting her head to the side like all of the Lindstroms and giving him that loving look that made him feel hot and tender and protective and fiercely grateful all at once.

"I can't always go with you, you know."

"I wish you could. My tent felt empty."

Giving him a saucy look, she unlocked her door, flicking on the light as they stepped inside. "It better have been."

"Not that one of the girls didn't try…"

Maggie spun around at the speed of light, her eyes wide open and her cheeks flushing pink. "Try? Try for you?"

He shrugged, trying not to grin and failing.

As the door closed behind him she stepped forward, poking a finger into his chest. "You're not available anymore, laddie."

"But I am irresistible." He snaked an arm around her waist, pulling her up against his chest, all the blood in his body funneling straight to one place. "Apparently."

"And big-headed," she said tartly.

"And big…" he teased glancing down at the bulge straining against his jeans.

"Aye. Ye're big there too." She arched her back to push her breasts flush against him and he leaned down to kiss her, but groaned when she turned her face away, grinding her pelvis into his, but denying him a kiss. He clasped her tighter and she bowed her back, leaning against his arms.

"So what did you say when the bloody tramp…*tried* for you?"

"I told her I had a wife," he said, bending down to brush his lips against her forehead. "A beautiful, redheaded wife…" He felt her go slightly slack and pressed his advantage, taking her earlobe between his teeth and emitting a throaty chuckle when he heard her quiet gasp. "…who would not be happy…" His hands slid down to her backside and he squeezed, pushing her tightly against his erection. "…if I took up with another woman."

"Good answer," she murmured in a breathy voice as he trailed his lips along the curve of her neck. "And what did she say?"

"She said I didn't need to tell you," he said against her skin, stopping at the soft plane behind her ear, half mad with wanting her.

"And you..." Her voice trailed off in a breathy murmur. She trembled in his arms and he moved his hands to her hips, lifting her easily and trying not to kill them both as he walked back to her bedroom in the dark with her legs wrapped around his waist.

"Maggie May," he said tenderly as he lowered her onto the bed and covered her body with his, kissing her forehead, "I told her I..." and then her nose, "am with..." and finally her lips, "you."

She grabbed his face, threading her fingers through his hair, frantically kissing him as he trailed his fingers down her sides, pushing at her shorts. Her fingers moved to his waist, unbuckling and unzipping him before wiggling out of her own shorts beneath him. When they were both naked from the waist down, without asking, unable to wait another moment, he thrust forward, a strangled groan released from his throat as her fingernails raked across his lower back. He plunged his tongue into her mouth, and she sucked on it eagerly as his strokes became deeper and more urgent.

When she cried out beneath him, calling his name, he thrust inside of her one final time as deeply as possible, pulsing, trembling, falling apart and finding himself put back together, surrounded in every possible way by the strength of her love.

***

They lay spooned together the next morning as the sun slowly rose, illuminating Maggie's violet room with morning light. They hadn't slept much, loving each other until the early hours of the morning, but feeling fully satisfied and sated physically didn't mean they'd broached the topic of children, which lay unspoken and unresolved between them.

"Maggie May," said Nils softly, running a hand soothingly along the ridge of her side to rest on her hip lightly.

"Mmm?"

"I thought about it."

"About…"

"Kids. Having them. Our own."

Her eyes widened and she turned slowly in his arms.

He swallowed, meeting her eyes before looking away. "I just…I wanted you to know I thought about it."

"And what did you think?"

"I'd have to break an important promise."

"Aye, you would."

"It'd be terrifying."

"Aye. You'd be worried."

"You could be hurt."

"Aye. There's always a chance."

"You're not helping," he said, brows furrowing as he bit his lower lip.

She felt her face soften as she gazed at him, at this man who wanted to give her everything. Could she live knowing she'd pressured him into something he didn't really want? Would it slowly chip away at the fabric of their relationship?

Would he resent that she'd pressured him into doing something he hadn't wanted to do?

"I thought about adoption," she said.

"You did?"

She nodded. "I remember what it felt like. At every age. At five and at ten and at sixteen. I'd always know what to say to an adopted child, how to make it better."

"But an adopted child might not look like you."

"That's true." She thought about the pictures she'd seen of the unwanted children who'd grown up at the Magdalene houses. "But I was chosen. You canna know what that means to me, the comfort it's always given me. Someone chose me and gave me a home."

"Not with a bunch of crazy Swedes."

"A child could do far worse than to wear the Lindstrom name, *mo muirnín*." She tilted her head, anxious not to break the fragility of the moment, but feeling overwhelmed by their exchange—by the possibility of it, the tenderness wrought from compromise. "Why don't we both keep thinkin' about it?"

"I can't promise anything, Maggie. I wish I could."

"I know."

"You deserve—"

"You. You're all I want."

"Better," he murmured, as though she hadn't spoken. "You deserve better."

Then he leaned forward to claim her lips with his, leaving words behind to show her, once again, that he was a man of action.

Chapter 19

The day of the interview dawned misty and murky, and Maggie couldn't help but wonder if it was an omen of things to come. That, and the fact that everything that *could* go wrong seemed to be going wrong.

First, she misplaced the letter with the address for the USCIS office in Billings and they had to scramble around on Google, looking for the street address online. Her pantyhose—which she hated with the heat of a thousand fires, but felt were necessary for a polished appearance—ran after she snagged them on a splinter of wood sticking out from one of her kitchen cabinets, so she threw them away but felt uncomfortably casual without them. Nils forgot his suit jacket at home and had to run back for it, hoping not to run into Lars who'd have a million questions about why Nils was dressed for church on a random Thursday, and then the whole area was covered in a blanket of fog. When they finally did hit the road, Nils drove cautiously, worried about hitting elk, sheep, deer or other wildlife as they headed north toward Livingston.

In short, they were both frazzled at the very moment they needed to feel calm and connected, and their nerves weren't exactly in check. While both felt the strong bond they'd forged over the course of the last month, defending their fledgling marriage to a trained immigration agent made them both feel edgy.

Maggie suggested that they drill each other with questions on the way north and Nils turned to her.

"Mother's name?" he asked, adjusting and readjusting his hands on the steering wheel nervously.

"Britt Askeland."

"Yup. Father?"

"Carl Lindstrom."

"Born?"

"Here. To first generation Swedish immigrants."

"Yup. Now you ask me."

"How many windows in my bedroom?"

"*Our* bedroom," he reminded, giving her a look. Saying "my" and "mine" would be flagged. "Two."

"Aye. What food gives me hives?"

"Strawberries."

"Aye. And what kind of tampons do I use?"

His neck and cheeks flushed red as he answered softly. "Playtex."

A feeling passed through Maggie as she watched his reaction—humor and affection, yes, but something else, something subtle and nagging that she didn't have time to explore right now.

"Aye. Who woke up first this morning?"

"You did."

"I didn't, Nils. You did."

"I *spoke* first," he answered, looking over at her and

grinning for the first time all morning. "But you were awake first. I could tell when I woke up. You feel different in my arms when you're already awake."

Maggie's heart drummed with love for him. How could they fail when they could give answers like that?

"I love you," she whispered.

"I love you, too," he answered, reaching for her hand.

"How did you ask me to marry you?" she asked.

"At the Roosevelt Arch. With bagpipes playing on my iPhone and white-frosted cupcakes."

She squeezed his hand. Wherever possible, they'd agreed to use real bits of their own history to fill in the gaps.

"And when did you first see me?"

"Behind the counter of your aunt's café. She was in a book club with my mother, and I already knew she was dying. And I was sorry for that. You were the prettiest thing I'd ever seen in my whole life. And I had no idea what to do about it."

"And you were the handsomest," she answered, trying to feel confident, trying to keep the impending melancholy at bay. She felt fragile and foolish, sure that the interviewers would see through their practiced answers and fail to see the real love that existed between them. "Why did we get married in a lawyer's office?" This was a tough one for them to fudge, so they'd decided to answer it with a half-truth. "We were already engaged, and then your visa ran out. We decided to accelerate the process of getting married."

"Aye," she said, squeezing his hand as butterflies

whizzed furiously in her belly.

"When did you first tell me you loved me?"

"I told you with my eyes about a million times before I ever said the words," she answered without thinking.

"Good answer," he said quietly, flicking his glance to her before raising her hand to his lips for a kiss. "What are our plans for a family of our own?"

She took a deep breath. Since last week, they'd avoided the subject, but it had hovered between them—the unspoken elephant in the room, the one thing that kept them from truly lacing their lives completely together. "We've discussed it, but we aren't sure what to do. We've discussed having our own and we've talked about adoption. Right now, we only know that we want a family someday. We don't know how. Yet."

"Yeah," he murmured, and she could hear it in his voice—the regret, the apology, the conflict, the sorrow—in that one small syllable.

"What's my favorite movie?" asked Maggie, trying to break the tension.

"*The Quiet Man*," answered Nils, releasing her hand and clenching his jaw before turning away to look out his window.

After that, they rode in silence.

***

As they walked hand in hand from the parking lot to the short, squat, brick federal building, Maggie looked up at him and Nils hated the worry on her lovely face. He stopped walking and leaned down to kiss her, drawing her into his arms and holding her close. When he leaned back, she still looked worried, but at least her face had softened a little.

For the thousandth time, he wished he'd done everything differently with her—dated and courted her, asked her to marry him, allowed himself to fall in love with her and trust that they could overcome whatever challenges befell them. He wished that she'd never gotten that initial letter from USCIS, or that when she did, they'd already been married for a year or two. What a lot of time he'd wasted

"It'll be okay," he said softly, pushing her hair off her face, and caressing her cheek. He wished he could ease her fears, but their reality—convincing immigration officers that their marriage was legal and legitimate—was too serious for sugar-coating. Besides, he knew that well-meaning platitudes would only make her more nervous.

"Just quickly, Nils...what if it's not? What if it's not okay?"

Her green eyes were bright and anxious as they searched his. He flipped over his wrist and looked at his watch. They had eight minutes before their appointment. Finding a park bench set under a dogwood tree near the building's entrance, he pulled her down beside him, putting his arm around her shoulders.

"We need to think positively. We're Maggie and Nils Lindstrom. That's who we are. That's who we've become."

"What if we can't convince them?"

"We will."

She swallowed, and he reached over to take her free hand as her eyes swam with unshed tears. "If I get sent back to Scotland—"

"That's not gonna happen."

"Please, Nils."

"Okay." He took a deep breath. "If we fail and you're sent back to Scotland, we'll still figure it out. Being deported doesn't mean we're not married anymore."

"It could be years."

"Then I'll earn a lot of frequent flier miles flying back and forth."

Her shoulders rolled forward a little with despair and he dropped her hand to tilt her chin up with his finger. "Maggie?"

"I love you," she whispered with tears spilling out of the corners of her eyes.

"We stay together," he answered. "You're my wife."

"We stay married. No matter what."

She gave him a brave smile and took a deep breath, accepting his handkerchief to dab her eyes.

"Come on, Mrs. Lindstrom," he said, standing up and offering her the hand that wore his grandfather's wedding ring. "It's time."

***

"Miss Campbell…"

"Mrs. Lindstrom, please. Or Maggie."

The interviewer, a surly, attractive man in his early thirties, nodded curtly. "Mrs. Lindstrom. I'm Officer Galvez. We're going to jump right in. This is the Stokes interview to ascertain the validity of your marriage. I'll ask questions. You answer them. If you don't have an answer, respond 'Skip.'

Shall we begin? Good. What kind of toothpaste does your husband use?"

Maggie flattened her cold hands on the serviceable conference table. Other than the two chairs she and Officer Galvez occupied, it was the only furniture in the small room. No windows. No clock. Just a security camera in the corner. Her eyes flicked to it.

"Mrs. Lindstrom. His favorite toothpaste, if you please."

"C-Crest."

"Does your husband wear briefs or boxer-style underwear?"

"Boxers."

"Do you use birth control?"

"A-aye." She knew she would be asked these sorts of questions, but the rapid fire manner in which she was being interviewed was jarring and the question embarrassed her. It felt invasive, intrusive, inappropriate.

"What kind?"

"W-what?"

"Birth control. What do you use?"

She wrinkled her brows for a moment before answering. "I'm on the pill."

"Does your husband have any tattoos?"

"Aye. Two small crosses. Over his heart. Here." She touched the skin over her breast gingerly, but Officer Galvez didn't look up.

"Your husband's cell phone plan?"

"What?"

"Is it the same as yours? Are you on a family plan?"

Maggie glanced away from Officer Galvez's bent head, feeling panic overtake her. She had no idea. She had no idea what cell service Nils used.

"I'm assuming you see the bill come in from time to time?"

"I don't pay his bills."

"His?"

"*Our* bills. I don't pay our bills," she repeated meekly and then she added, "Skip."

The immigration officer looked up sharply, holding her eyes for a moment before looking back down at his clipboard and marking something. Maggie's pulse started racing, which is why she made a very bad decision when it came to the next question.

"And how does your husband pay the bills, Mrs. Lindstrom? Online or via mailed paper checks?"

She had no idea, but she couldn't bear to say "skip" again…

"Checks."

…so she guessed.

***

"Mr. Lindstrom."

"Nils, please."

The older gentleman glanced up from his clipboard and nodded briefly. "I'm Officer Sherwood. This is the Stokes interview to ascertain the validity of your marriage to Margaret Leslie Campbell. This interview is being recorded via closed circuit camera. I'll ask questions. You answer them. If you don't have answer, simply respond 'Skip.' Any questions before we begin?"

"No, sir."

"Does your wife have any allergies?'

"She gets hives from strawberries."

"Who does the grocery shopping?"

"It depends on who's making dinner."

"*You* make dinner?"

"Yes, sir." Nils nodded. "Sometimes."

"Does your wife's place have cable television?"

"*Our* place has cable television, yes."

"What kind of shampoo does your wife use?"

"Strawberry."

"Ironic," said Agent Sherwood dryly.

"She's not allergic to the smell."

"Does she have any tattoos?"

"No, sir."

"Was your wife born in Scotland?"

"No, sir."

"Where was she born?"

"Ireland."

"What part?"

Shoot. Nils looked down at the table where he'd folded his hands. It began with a C. Or a K? A C or a K. Damn it. Cork? Was it Cork?

"Cork."

The interviewer looked up from his documents, raising an eyebrow.

"Kerry?"

"There's only one right answer, Mr. Lindstrom."

Nils's palms started sweating. Fifty-fifty chance. "Kerry. She was born in a convent in Kerry."

Agent Sherwood cleared his throat, marking the form on the clipboard.

"Does your wife suffer from menstrual cramps?"

Nils's eyes widened, thrown off by the intimacy of the question. As his heart picked up speed, making him feel panicky, he realized he didn't know. They certainly hadn't discussed it. She must have kept her time of the month private because he didn't remember her having it, let alone complaining of discomfort.

"Mr. Lindstrom. Does your wife suffer from menstrual cramps?"

He looked up, feeling like a deer in the headlights, his face flushing uncomfortably hot as he tried to think about something other than Maggie having her time of the month.

"I…I mean, I…um, skip."

Agent Sherwood took a deep breath and sighed as he marked his clipboard again.

"Do you have a joint checking account?"

"Not yet, sir."

"Who pays the common bills?"

"I do."

"Via check or an online bill pay?"

"It's all automated, sir. I don't even own a checkbook."

"Do you plan to start a family?"

"Maybe."

"Maybe?"

"We're not sure yet." Nils unfolded his hands, placing them flat on the table and trying to sound confident and self-assured.

"Did you discuss children during your courtship?"

"We…I mean, we *do* discuss it."

"I see."

He thought of Maggie's face when he told her he didn't want to get her pregnant, didn't want biological children. He thought of the sadness in her eyes when she shared that she'd be willing to adopt. Her brave smile. And suddenly he couldn't bear to discuss it with a stranger drilling him on shampoo brands and joint checking accounts. It was none of their business. It was none of their goddamned business.

"So…you *did* discuss children during your courtship?"

He looked up and before he could stop himself, he growled, "Skip."

***

Maggie had been sitting in a chair in the hallway for several minutes when Nils finally joined her, lowering his body down beside her and reaching for her hand immediately. She didn't think that was a very good sign.

"How did it go?" she asked.

He shrugged, looking down at their hands.

"Nils? How did you do?"

"I skipped a few," he muttered.

Maggie swallowed back the lump in her throat.

"You?" he asked.

"I skipped a few, too."

"How many?" he asked.

"Five or six," she answered.

"You?"

"Four."

"And I guessed on two," she confessed.

"Beck said never to guess."

"How do you pay bills?" she practically whispered.

"Online," said Nils, looking over at her.

She nodded miserably, forcing her face to remain impassive. There was no point in letting him know she'd been wrong. It was too late, and her heart plummeted as she realized that more likely than not, she wouldn't be returning to Gardiner with Nils tonight. She'd be deported. She dropped his hand, standing up with her back to him and crossing her arms over her chest.

From his seat on the bench behind her, his voice was soft and gentle, but utterly devoid of hope. "Whatever happens, Maggie, we'll figure it out."

Tears flooded her eyes and she nodded, unable to turn around and look at him. All of the hours they'd put into studying hadn't been enough. They'd each skipped more than two. They'd almost certainly failed.

Suddenly she felt his arms circling her waist and she couldn't hold back the tears anymore. She spun around to lay her wet cheek against the crisp white Sunday shirt covering his chest, breathing in the fresh soap, slightly spicy smell of him.

This is where we belong, screamed her heart and her mind in unison. *This is where I belong. Here with him!*

Nils ran his hands soothingly up and down the back of

her simple summer dress as her shoulders trembled with silent tears of exhaustion and fear and sorrow, until she finally got a hold of herself and he led her back to the chairs, pulling her down beside him. She leaned her head on his shoulder as he put his arm around her, gently massaging her shoulder. "Whatever happens, we'll…"

His voice trailed off and she heard the sound of a door opening down the hallway. She looked up, drying her eyes quickly to see Agent Galvez and an older man smiling and nodding at another man, whose back was turn to them. Maggie rose slowly, realization kicking in at the same time Beck Westman turned around and made eye contact with her.

"Beck…" she whispered to herself, confusion making her voice breathy and unsure.

Beck offered Maggie an easy smile, keeping his eyes trained on her as he approached, followed by the agents.

"Heya, Lindstroms! I was just talking to Juan Carlos and Frank here. JC and I were in law school together and when he realized I was the officiating lawyer for your wedding, he gave me a call. Since I was here in Billings today, anyway, I thought I'd stop by and say a quick hello."

Maggie's eyes flicked back and forth between Officer Galvez and Beck. "You're friends?"

Beck turned to his friend and chuckled. "Loved watching that Stokes interview back at U of M. Eh, JC?"

Officer Galvez grinned. "Just enforcing the law, Becker. You know me."

Beck smiled back at his old school friend. "I meant to

ask…how's Collete?"

Maggie hadn't realized that Agent Galvez had teeth—she certainly hadn't seen hide nor hair of them during the interview. "Pregnant with number four."

"Law ain't all you're enforcing, brother."

Officer Galvez slapped Beck on the back with a thundering chuckle then looked to the older agent standing beside him. "You go to lunch, Frank. I got this. I'll wrap it up."

Frank shook Beck's hand and gave Nils a brief, thoughtful nod before turning and heading back down the hall.

Officer Galvez turned to Maggie and Nils. "Come on back inside, folks. We'll finish this up quick and then we'll go grab a burger, Becker. You can fill me in on small-town life."

"Good enough. I'll meet you out front."

As Beck passed by Maggie, he winked before continuing down the hallway.

Once they were seated in Officer Galvez's office, he tapped on their file.

"Frank and I agreed that you were borderline. I recommended that we fail you, but Frank said he thought you were legit. Because we were split, we would have had to comb through your answers before meeting with you together. Or we might've had you come back tomorrow. At any rate, it would've been a long couple of days."

Maggie swallowed nervously, reaching for Nils's hand under the table. He laced his fingers through hers quickly, squeezing her hand.

Officer Galvez opened the file and pulled out the form on top, signed the bottom, then took a stamp from his desk drawer and stamped the form three times.

"But I've known Becker Westman since we were twenty-two years old, and I wouldn't'a made it through law school without him. Stroke of good luck for you he was doing some court filings up this way today. He says you're legit? I guess you're legit. But I can't give you this form unless you answer one final question for me, Mrs. Lindstrom."

Maggie leaned forward in her seat, staring at Officer Galvez like her life depended on it. He narrowed his eyes at her. "How does your husband pay the bills again?"

"Online," she answered quickly.

"You know you said checks? When I asked you in the interview?"

Maggie held up her free hand which visibly trembled. "Nerves, Agent Galvez. It's been a nerve-wrackin' day."

He glanced at her hand then looked lazily back to her face, nodding, as he slid the approved form across his desk.

"All right, then. Welcome to America, Mrs. Lindstrom."

***

All Nils wanted to do was grab Maggie and kiss her until they were both dizzy and breathless, but Maggie pulled Nils down the hall as soon as they left Officer Galvez's office, walking at a clip.

"We have to find him!"

"Find who?" asked Nils.

"Beck!"

She was walking so briskly, he doubt she realized that she'd dropped his hand, surging ahead, out the doors and into the sunshine, leaving Nils behind.

He stopped in the hallway, a few feet from the door, and put his hands on his hips, watching as she threw herself into Beck's waiting arms. He couldn't hear what she was saying, of course, but when Beck—*finally*, thought Nils, with a grimace—released her, she smiled that beautiful, brilliant, happy smile that he loved so well. Nils looked down at the tiled floor, biting his lower lip.

Nils knew in his heart as he stood there that Beck's presence in Billings today hadn't been a coincidence. Of course he would have known the date of their interview and Nils was sure he'd made sure he was local just in case Maggie needed him, which, in fact, she had. Without Beck, they may have failed. With his help, Maggie was free to stay in Montana.

And suddenly Nils felt uncertain about the rest. It was almost as though the combination of passing the interview, Beck's ninth-hour help and Maggie's desperation to thank her ex-boyfriend snapped Nils back to reality—specifically, to the reality that preceded their truce. The reality where Nils had run away from Maggie, propelling her into Beck's safe and loving arms. He thought about them holding hands in Beck's conference room the Sunday evening five weeks ago when Nils had arrived to discuss the issue of their impending interview. In Nils's absence, Maggie had chosen to be with Beck.

He looked down at the ring on his fourth finger,

slipping it off and tucking it into his pocket. Maggie hadn't *chosen* Nils. Maggie had been *trapped* into a marriage with him. Now she was free. And her first order of business was to race into Beck Westman's arms.

They chatted in the sunshine, Maggie occasionally looking uncertainly back at the building, maybe wondering why her husband hadn't followed her out yet. Beck's handsome face softened with tenderness as he spoke to her, and it twisted Nils's heart, but his love for Maggie forced him to face the truth: What exactly was he, Nils, able to offer her, other than his name and his love?

Not a lot. And certainly not what she wanted most in the whole world: a child of her own.

He stood at the glass doors, watching as she smiled and laughed with Beck, her red hair shining in the sun. She pushed it off her face and Beck's shoulders rolled as he chuckled at something she said. He was still crazy about her, that was obvious, and he'd been her "someone" before the mechanics of the truce had forced Maggie to quickly accept Nils as her "husband."

Nils's fingers curled into fists as he realized that Maggie deserved the chance to decide who she wanted to be with. Now that she was free, now that she didn't need Nils, now that she was no longer frightened, she deserved the opportunity to make her own choice. It was the very least he could do for her: set her free.

He pushed through the doors and Maggie looked up to find his eyes, her smile more brilliant and beautiful than any work of art, any natural miracle, anything he'd ever seen.

Nils offered his hand to Beck as he approached. "Thanks, Beck. Thanks for everything."

Beck's expression cooled appreciably, but he took his rival's hand. "Glad it all worked out for Maggie."

Maggie turned her face to Nils, and that beautiful smile lost a little bit of its shine as she searched his eyes, her forehead creasing momentarily in question.

"We did it," she said encouragingly, reaching for his arm.

"Beck did it," said Nils, stepping back from her. "He saved the day."

Nils gave Beck a tight smile before gazing down at the confusion in Maggie's upturned face. He tasted the bile at the back of his throat as he clenched his jaw so tightly he feared it might snap. How would he let her go if she chose Beck? How would he bear it?

He would. He would bear it because he loved her. He would bear it because she deserved to be happy.

"I'll let you two, uh…" Nils gestured dumbly, nodding at each of them before turning toward his car.

***

Maggie watched Nils walk away, her chest tightening with that old feeling of fear. Her stomach flip-flopped, making her momentarily nauseous, and she hated the doubt that crept into her head and into her heart. He'd thrown their truce out the window the first night they'd made love, but suddenly she felt like the fantasy of their safe little glass bubble was shattering around her. Now that they had passed the interview, their truce was over: Nils was free to go back to the life he'd had before the pressure and fears that accompanied the interview.

"Still not sure of him, huh?" asked Beck.

She turned to look up at him and he searched her face with his kind, brown eyes.

Maggie smiled at him, suddenly thinking of Summer, of how lucky Summer might be one day if her prediction came true and she married Beck Westman.

"I'm sure of me," she answered softly for Beck's benefit, to make it clear that nothing had changed between them. Then, remembering Summer's words, she added, "Some things are meant to be."

"Like you and Nils."

She nodded.

"Well, I wish you luck, Maggie Leslie. Can't deny I've been nursing a wounded heart these past few weeks. Been missing your smile."

"I've missed you, too," she sighed, putting her hand on his arm. "But there's someone wonderful for you, Beck. I know it."

"Okay, Maggie." He chuckled lightly, his cheeks turning a little pink. "If you find her first, send her my way, huh?"

"Promise me you'll be patient?" asked Maggie with a grin, doing the quick math that Summer needed *at least* five years before she'd be ready to sweep Beck off his feet.

Beck furrowed his brows, giving Maggie a quirky half-smile. "Do you actually have someone in mind?"

"Might just. But give it a little time." She leaned in and kissed his cheek just as Nils pulled up curbside to wait for her. "Tell me one thing. Were you in Billings on purpose today? Just in case?"

"It doesn't matter," he said, and she knew he was releasing her from the possibility of any debt. Damn, but he was a good man.

"You made the difference," she said, unable to resist the urge to hug him again. "Your friend Officer Galvez said as much."

Beck shrugged, squeezing her tightly just once before patting her back and pulling away. "Take care of yourself, Mrs. Lindstrom."

Maggie smiled then turned and made her way to the curb, where Nils was waiting. She got into the car, sat down and shut the door behind her, immediately aware of the awkward silence between them where tenderness and communion had existed for the past five weeks. He pulled away from the curb and her heart sunk as she decided to wait him out.

After he'd been driving in silence beside her for over an hour, she couldn't bear the simmering tension between them anymore.

"Let's have it."

He looked surprised, flicking his glance to her, then back to the road. "Have what?"

"Whatever's goin' on in your head."

"Let's just get home first."

"No. That doesna work for me," she answered, terse and worried. "I need to know now."

"You were pretty anxious to celebrate with Beck.

Kissing and hugging him."

"That's what this is about? Jealousy?" She crossed her arms over her chest. "You think I'm pinin' for Beck? What have we been doin' these past five weeks, then? Because I could have sworn it was your body next to mine every night and every mornin', you horse's arse."

"Maggie…"

"You think I want to be with *Beck*? He's my *friend*. He deserved our thanks and lots of it. That's all."

"Maggie…"

"Dinna 'Maggie' me. You're suggestin' I'm interested in some other man when I'm your *wife*."

"But you don't have to be," he blurted out. "My wife." He paused and she could hear him swallow beside her. "You got the green card. You don't have to stay married to me."

He surprised her by jerking the wheel and pulling over to the side of the highway, as her jaw dropped, and tears brightened her eyes.

When the car stopped, he flexed his hands on the steering wheel, staring out the windshield, speaking quickly. "I trapped you into that truce, saying I wouldn't help you unless we acted married. You had no choice. I made it so that if you wanted my help, you had to *be* my wife. But I won't hold you to it, Maggie. Not if you want out."

"Do you love me?" Her quiet, gravelly voice, infused with pain, cut through him like a knife.

He finally turned and looked at her. "It doesn't matter how I feel. I want you to be free to choose what you want. Beck could give you children—joyfully, with a clear conscience. He could give you a family of your own, children who looked like you. If you stay with me, you're giving up too much, and I can't guarantee—"

Furious, she couldn't stand to listen anymore. Her hand cracked across his face like a whip and he stopped talking, staring at her with his mouth open, stunned and frozen.

"Enough," she growled. Her whole body trembled as she stared at him, her hand burning from the sharp contact of the slap. She blinked furiously, trying to hold back the hot tears, but they poured from her eyes anyway.

"I. Belong. To. You," she finally whispered.

"Maggie—"

"Do you hear me? I love *you*. I'm *your* wife. I *belong* to *you*. Dinna you understand what that means? It means *you* matter more to me. More than any childhood dreams. More than any unborn child. *You*. You, who saved me and cared for me and—" Her voice broke as uncertainty washed over her. "L-love me."

He clenched his jaw, staring at her with naked love written all over the strong contours of his face. The cheek she slapped was bright red and angry and as she reached for it gently, he flinched, which squeezed her heart, but she lay her palm against it tenderly. His eyes closed and he took a ragged breath, leaning into her, his heat warming the cool skin of her hand.

"Unless you have *stopped* lovin' me, don't you ever suggest to me—not ever again, Nils Lindstrom—that there is another option for me other than you. Don't you *ever* insult me like that again."

"I feel like you weren't given a choice. I just want you to be sure. To be happy." His eyes opened, light blue and uncertain.

She released his cheek as a sick feeling unraveled in her gut, making her dizzy and nauseous for the second time in a single day. Was it possible that this wasn't actually about her even though he insisted it was? She thought of all the times over the years they'd gotten too close to one another only for him to back up, back off, run away. This is what he did. It's just that their "truce" had made it possible for him to relax into a temporary status quo and stay put for a while.

But now what? Now what? Would he choose her? Choose to be with her, love her, stay with her? Or would he run again?

"I don't think this is about me," she said quietly, staring at him gravely. "Because you've known from the beginnin'— aye, from that night you walked me home after May Day. I've gone over it in my head a million times. I told you how I felt about you that night, didn't I?"

He winced, then nodded slowly.

She smiled, a little bitterly, before looking down at her hands, neatly folded in her lap, the right one stinging much less than her heart. "You knew then and you know now. I've already chosen you. You're it for me, baggage and all. I've wanted you for as long as I've known you. But I dinna know that you can say the same, because even though you love me, you willna give yourself permission to be happy with me. You willna forgive yourself for somethin' that happened fifteen years ago, for the terrible, tragic thing that you canna undo and canna forget."

His eyes watered as he looked down. She swallowed the painful lump in her throat as hot tears coursed down her face.

"But, my love, *mo muirnín*, I canna do *this* again. I canna watch you pull away from me and break my heart again. You say you're doin' it *for* me, but I dinna think it's true, and even if it is, I canna bear it."

She reached over and touched the back of his hand, running her fingers over the springy blond hairs that covered his tan, weathered skin. That same hand had held his child for a few minutes before saying goodbye, before turning his whole life into an act of penance, a shadowed memorial.

"Maybe you're terrified to love someone again. Maybe you feel like you dinna deserve happiness. I understand that. Love is scary. No matter how much we love each other, we're goin' to fight sometimes and hate each other sometimes, and I'm not goin' to live forever. Happiness is scary, too. You can only know heartbreak if you've known joy. But I canna wait for you anymore, Nils. Either we return to Gardiner and start our life together...or not. It's up to you, love. I belong to you right this minute and you need to decide whether or not you belong to me. Today. Before tomorrow dawns. And whatever you decide, you need to commit to that decision, and you need to live with it. In the simplest possible terms, either you belong to me— completely, Nils—or you let me go."

Sometime during her speech, her tears had stopped and though her voice was soft and low, it was strong with conviction and truth. Every card she had was now laid out on the table before him. She had nothing else to add, nothing more to say or show. His eyes, red-rimmed and dazed, gazed back at her, but the rest of his face remained expressionless.

Breaking through the almost-sacred quiet of the car, Nils's phone rang on the console between them. They both glanced down at it to see Mr. Lindstrom's picture pop up on the screen. Nils swiped at his eyes, as if waking up from a dream and looked up at Maggie, silently asking her if he should answer. She nodded.

"Pop?...Uh-huh. Where? Okay. The supermodel. Yeah. I'm an hour away. I'll go get her. Yeah, Pop. Bye."

Nils pressed the end button and Maggie raised her eyebrows in question. "Lars broke down coming back from a photo shoot in the park and he's waiting for a tow. Pop's in Bozeman for a pick-up, so I need to get the supermodel back to her cottage."

He turned the key and merged back onto the highway.

Maggie took a deep breath, rubbing her burning eyes and looking out the window, feeling utterly exhausted. Before opening the Prairie for the evening crowd, she was going to take a long nap, probably preceded by a deluge of tears. After everything she'd just said, he hadn't responded. He hadn't said a word. She could almost hear her heart breaking. She could certainly feel it.

As he pulled up in front of the Prairie Dawn, she turned to him.

"I love you, Maggie," he said, and she could see in his

eyes that he was telling the truth.

"I know you do," she said softly. "But I need more than your love for this to survive. I need all of you."

Then she opened her door, swung her legs out of the car and walked away from him without looking back.

Chapter 20

Nils watched her walk away then backed out of her driveway, heading south toward the park. Based on where his father said Lars and Samara Amaya were stranded, he had about a forty-five-minute drive in front of him. He loosened the tie he'd been wearing for the interview, pulling it out from under his collar with one hand and unbuttoning the top two buttons of his shirt. He turned off the air conditioning in the car and rolled down the windows as he zipped under the Roosevelt Arch, taking deep, restoring breaths of fresh air.

Damn it if Maggie wasn't right.

About everything.

He ran his hands through his hair as he picked over her words:

You willna give yourself permission to be happy with me.

Maybe you're terrified to love someone again.

Maybe you feel like you dinna deserve happiness.

He rubbed his eyes as the truth of her words sank in to the hilt, slicing his heart into pieces. For fifteen long years, he'd punished himself for what had happened to Veronica and Jens, blaming himself alone for their loss. But he realized as he drove deeper and deeper into Yellowstone that blaming himself wasn't only about having the strength to take responsibility, it was also about fear; it was the perfect way to protect himself from ever being hurt again. As Maggie pointed out, if he didn't know joy, he couldn't know heartbreak. And yes, of course his heart wept for what had happened to his girlfriend and tiny son...but did he honestly believe that Veronica or Jens would have wanted his life to be nothing more than a shrine to theirs?

He thought of Veronica's bright green eyes, laughing behind light green chemistry goggles. She'd been full of innocence and life, ready with smiles and giggles and an open heart. She wouldn't have wished for him to stay frozen in time, emotionally truncated at eighteen years old. She would have wanted him to keep living, no matter the risks to his heart.

A tear tumbled out of the corner of his eye, whipped back into his hair by the rushing wind, as he remembered the slight weight of his dead son in his arms. And little Jens. He didn't demand any promises from Nils. All these years later, Nils thought of the promise that he made at Jens's graveside as a mutual agreement, but there was nothing mutual about it. Nils realized, shamefully, that the promise had very little to do with poor Jens, actually. It was about Nils protecting himself from ever having to live through that sort of loss again. If he never loved a woman, never got her pregnant, he'd never have to face the abyss of loss.

And that worked fine for him for years. Living his life as a memorial to Veronica and Jens felt right—even more, felt righteous and respectable. But that's only because no one had come along to reach through the layers of pain and suffering to touch his heart. No one had challenged his fear.

He hadn't counted on Maggie.

Maggie had shaken him from his status quo, forced his heart to open, patiently demanded—in tender, quiet ways—that he make room in his life for her. Hearing that she loved him, telling her he loved her back, feeling her body moving against his like a prayer—all of these steps had led him to today. Today. Where he knew in every fiber of his being that his love for her was endless.

Could he take the final step?

Could he give himself permission to love her completely?

Could he take the risk that loving her with his whole heart, whole body and whole mind meant that the same love could also snap him in half if ever lost?

Could he decide that his fears were outweighed by the bounty, the blessing, the sheer, stunning, irrevocable beauty that Maggie's love brought to his life?

Could he, after more than a decade of dusk, surrender to the bright morning light of joy?

His eyes stopped burning and his lips wiggled, trying to tilt up, as he felt the answer move through him. And almost as though Veronica and Jens were finally waving farewell to him, he took the first conscious step forward without fighting, ready to leave his past behind, ready for a new life to be reborn.

***

By seven o'clock he wasn't back, she hadn't heard from him,

and despite an unexpectedly long nap, Maggie was a bundle of nerves.

Was it possible that he'd really decide to let her go? Was it possible he'd really believe that it was in her best interest to be set free? How exactly did that look to him? She'd get her green card, they'd get a divorce and they'd go their separate ways? Could he possibly think that a life that didn't include him would be bearable for her?

But from the beginning he'd kept her at arm's length. Certainly during their friendship, but even later, during their truce—when he'd offered to sleep on the ground during their camping trip, when he hadn't stopped in at the Prairie after sharing the story of his tragic past. He always seemed to be offering her an out she didn't want. Always arguing with her that she deserved more, deserved better, than him. Even when he said he loved her, even when he said they'd stay married, still she had worried deep down in her heart because until he *gave himself permission* to love her—all of her, with all of him—she would always wonder if he would someday choose to walk away from her again.

The bell over the door jingled and her head snapped up to see Paul walking in. She waved hello from the table she'd reserved for their game in the back corner of the café, trying to calm the fierce thumping her worried heart. He sat down and she handed him a deck of cards and he started shuffling. Not even a moment later the bell rang again, and Jane walked in.

Poor Jane, who had somehow managed to fall head over heels for Lars Lindstrom while he managed the details for her cousin's magazine shoot, didn't look very happy.

"Jane! You're here!" said Paul as Maggie waved her over to the table.

"I'm here," Jane answered, glancing glumly at the empty chair. "Where's Nils?"

Where indeed, thought Maggie, trying not to panic, trying to trust that whatever was between them was good enough, strong enough for him to choose it with his whole heart. Good enough and strong enough for him to show up tonight and tell her that he'd chosen her, not just for now, but forever. She twisted her Claddagh ring nervously. "I don't know if he's coming. He had to go get Lars."

"Go get him? Is everything okay?" Jane asked.

"I guess he and your cousin broke down in his truck on the way back to Gardiner," said Paul.

Jane's eyes filled with tears and Maggie reached for her new friend's hand, furious with the Lindstrom brothers for torturing the hearts of good women. Paul tried to convince Jane that Lars, who had hooked up with Jane prior to her cousin's arrival, was not interested in Samara. But Jane wasn't having it.

Unable to convince her that Lars still cared for her, Jane changed the subject and they talked about Paul's infatuation with the internet girl from Mystic, but all the while Maggie's belly swarmed with flutters.

What if he didn't show up?

What if she should've been more patient with him and given him more time to decide how he felt and what he wanted?

She'd essentially given him an ultimatum in the car, and if she'd learned nothing from *Cosmopolitan* magazine over the years, it was that ultimatums rarely worked out in a woman's favor. She tried to stay present in the conversation she was having with Paul and Jane, but as the seconds ticked by she became tenser, sadder, and was losing hope.

Suddenly the bell over the front door jingled and Maggie's breath caught in her throat as she looked up slowly to see Nils walk into the café. His face didn't give much away as he looked around for her, seizing her eyes and heading for their table.

"You're here," Maggie murmured, unable to look away from him, stunned by his presence, even though she'd been praying to see his face as every long, lonely minute passed in agony.

She searched his eyes, reading such a great deal in them: conflict, longing, love. And—*oh my God, there it was*, her heart thrilled, leaping and dancing—*surrender…and hope.*

"You're here," she whispered again, almost inaudibly, her voice breaking with emotion.

Trembling and overwhelmed, she looked down quickly to hide her tears from Jane and Paul. She wanted to get up and leave. She wanted to take his hand without a word, run upstairs to her apartment and make him say the words over and over and over again: *I choose you. I choose us. I belong to you.* But if she looked up at him, she'd start weeping, so she kept her head down.

***

"I'm here," he said softly, staring at her bowed head. He

could tell from her posture that she was on the verge of tears and trying to control herself. He decided it would be best for now to help her by deflecting attention away from her. He flicked his glance to Paul. "Did you deal yet?"

"We were waiting for you. Everything okay?" Paul slid the deck toward Nils as he put his coat on the back of his chair and sat down beside Maggie. Every cell in his body longed to reach for her, to touch her, to pull her onto his lap, to grab her hand and race upstairs. He shuffled the cards instead, the thin cardboard in his hands a terrible substitute for having his wife back in his arms.

"Long day. Finally get back to Gardiner and I have to pick up Lars and drive Miss Amaya back to her cottage. Then I got to pick up that nervous, sweaty fella from the motel and take him over there to keep her company. These famous types sure are a lot of work." He looked up and caught Jane's eyes, looking away quickly. Maggie still hadn't raised her head. He shifted slightly in his seat so that his knee grazed hers. Just that tiny bit of contact quieted his nerves, filled his heart. She belonged to him, and he…

He had shuffled the deck about ten times. He looked up at Jane and took in her surprised, and vaguely amused, expression. No matter what her cousin was like, Jane seemed like good people. Not to mention, he'd never seen Lars so upside-down about a girl. "Uh. Sorry, Jane. No offense. Present company excepted."

"Oh, I'm not famous, Nils. No offense taken. Samara Amaya's a terrible person. Say whatever you like."

A little startled by Jane's comment, Nils dealt quietly,

the dueling tensions at the table fueled further by Maggie's silence. He watched as she placed her hands over her cards and slid them closer to the edge of the table. Was she crying? Was she okay? Did she regret what she'd said to him in the car? Was she waiting for him to say something? Declare himself? Right here? Right now? A bead of sweat popped out over his brow and made a slow journey down the side of his face.

"How's Lars?" Jane asked, flicking her gaze up to Nils and distracting him from his thoughts.

"Fine. But his truck's dead for now. Arranged for a tow. He won't be back in Gardiner for a while."

"Poor, disappointed *Miss Amaya*," Jane observed, dryly.

Now this was a curious response. Nils looked up at Jane. "How's that?"

"She'll have to wait for this evening's company."

No, thought Nils. *She's got that sweaty fella from the motel at her place to keep her company.* "What's that got to do with Lars?"

"Lars is screwing my cousin," Jane offered matter-of-factly.

Nils stared at her, surprised by two things: the coarseness of her declaration and the fact that it hadn't made the slightest impact on Maggie. Not a gasp, not even the slightest bob of her head to look at Jane. He swallowed nervously. Was she going to stay frozen until he said it? Was he going to need to say "I belong to you" right here in front of Paul and Jane?

He cleared his throat. "I guess that'd be his business if it were true."

"I guess so. And it *is* true. We could be family one day, Nils. My cousin. Your brother."

"We could be family one day, I guess. But, it won't come about like that."

"Why not?" asked Jane.

He really looked at Jane now, and realized that she was holding back tears like he'd seen Jenny and Maggie do about a million times. She was hurting. Bad. He gentled his voice. "There ain't no chance on God's green earth that Lars is sleeping with that woman."

"Really?" challenged Jane, her eyes brightening with tears and flickering with hope. "My information says otherwise."

"Then your information's bad, Jane."

He adjusted his knee, rubbing it against Maggie's, hoping for any reaction at all, but she stayed stock still, hands over her cards, neck bent. She had said that she wanted all of him. And he sensed this was the final test: he was going to need to figure out a way to confess his feelings for her in public. Could he do that? How? Saying those things to her in private was one thing...

"Is that right?" asked Jane.

"That's right."

"And why is that?"

The moment had arrived. He knew it. He felt it in every fiber of his being and someday he would thank Jane for pushing the conversation to this place where he had an opening, where he could say what needed to be said.

Nils arranged his cards in a neat pile and folded his

hands on top of them, in a mirror image of Maggie beside him, then he pushed his knee meaningfully into hers, feeling the slight pressure of her pushing back. It was time.

He looked at Jane. "Because Lars is taken with *you*. And if you're taken with someone…if you feel that they—in fact—*belong* to you…" He shifted toward Maggie, leaning his face toward her, his lips a breath away from her ear and spoke in almost a whisper with words only for her, "…it's *impossible* to let them go."

Maggie lifted her face slowly, her bright, glistening eyes capturing his as her mouth opened softly in pleasure, in tenderness, in love and surprise, as she held Nils's gaze with a primitive, aching intensity.

If he thought there was a chance in hell of ever walking away from Maggie Campbell Lindstrom again, for as long as he lived, it died right there. Right there at a table in the Prairie Dawn, his life unfolded in front of him and not one portion of that blank sheet from corner to corner and end to end included a moment that didn't have Maggie's hand touching it, and her heart imprinted upon it.

She didn't flinch as she stared at him, but her face turned pink under Nils's unwavering scrutiny, and in a role reversal, she clenched her jaw twice, as though trying to be sure that he was certain, sincere and true. He stared back at her, and then turning toward her just slightly, to be out of view from Paul and Jane, he mouthed the words, *I belong to you.*

Maggie blinked her eyes rapidly and bit her lower lip, flicking a quick glance at Paul and Jane, then she stood up and headed to the door without a word. He knew where she was going—to the heaven that was the violet bedroom—and she knew that he would follow her now, as he would forever. And as far as Jane, and especially Paul, were concerned, tonight would be the night that Nils and Maggie "happened."

He took one moment to process what had just happened, privately and publicly, overwhelmed with emotion as his heart swelled and his breathed changed, almost panting with love for her, with the want of her. And then he stood up, scraping his chair loudly across the floor as he grabbed his coat. Shrugging into it without a word of explanation to Paul or Jane, he followed his wife home.

Chapter 21

Happiness is like its own beautiful virus. Once infected with it, it systemically affects everything in your life.

When Nils finally allowed the last barriers between them to come down, Maggie's life quickly changed in ways that left her spellbound, wearing her love for him on her sleeve, in her eyes, saturated in the tone of her voice when she spoke to him. She was a sap for it, a slave to it, mesmerized by the miracle that the man she loved unreservedly loved her unreservedly in return.

Maggie sighed, yawning as she daydreamed with her elbow propped up on the counter, her breasts aching and her body sensitive and throbbing as she remembered making love with Nils last night. The protective tenderness she'd always sensed in his friendship for her had been seamlessly transferred to their marriage, and she never felt it more strongly than when they were making love. He was careful—almost reverent—in the way he loved her: no touch wasted, all infused with the full depth of his feelings for her. And when they climaxed together, he would invariably remind her of his love, bellowing her name like an oath, with hunger and possession.

And afterwards, as she lay in his arms, they spoke of the little and big things in their lives, laughing about the reactions they were getting from family and friends, marveling in the fact that they had finally found their way. It was joy that ruled over those precious hours where the pain of their longing for one another was requited. It was joy that claimed their hearts and made their eyes soften with tenderness.

It was joy.

Even Graham, who'd arrived two weeks ago as planned, only added to Maggie's happiness. He was challenging in the way all young adults are challenging...keeping his eyes hooded and his answer monosyllabic, playing the loner despite Bethany's attempts to include him in her various activities...but, he didn't make trouble.

He kept a low profile at work, helping whenever Maggie asked and otherwise working diligently on building her a deck before the cold weather set in. The only glimmers of spirit she noticed were around Nils's visiting cousin, Julie, to whom Graham seemed to have more than a passing interest. Maggie caught his well-concealed longing glances, the way he stared just an extra beat longer than necessary when the pretty blonde came in for coffee. But, Graham, with his spiky hair, tattoos and piercings, wasn't even on proper Julie's radar. Which was probably for the best...while Maggie could share the great joy of loving a Lindstrom, she didn't get there without a healthy dose of heartbreak first. Still, she loved having her cousin close to her again and even Nils had to admit that despite Graham's rough urban appearance, his behavior was—if not warm and friendly—

irreproachable.

The Lindstroms and Paul had accepted Nils and Maggie's new dating relationship with open arms and knowing smiles, kidding that it was "about time" they finally got together.

Indeed, it seemed love was everywhere, even for Paul, who was spending lots of time with a mysterious visitor who'd arrived in Gardiner a few days ago. Despite his online infatuation with a girl from Connecticut, this new stranger certainly seemed to be capturing his attention, and as long as he didn't get hurt, Maggie was anxious to see what would happen between them.

Honestly, there was only one fly in Maggie's ointment and it worried her in quiet moments: since the interview two and a half weeks ago, she been increasingly tired all the time and it wasn't getting better, it was getting worse.

At first, she'd chalked up her midday drowsiness to the fact that she and Nils weren't getting much sleep, waking each other up several times every night to press up against one another with urgency until they found their release together. But, even on the mornings when she actually got six or seven hours of sleep, she was *still* wiped out by mid-morning and mid-afternoon. Add to this—or perhaps because of it—she'd recently come down with a light stomach virus that made her feel nauseous off and on throughout the day. Between the two symptoms, she was always tired and had almost no appetite, which also meant she'd lost a few pounds. And though the moments she spent with Nils were fully electrified, at other moments of the day, she worried quietly that something more significant could be wrong with her. After lots of internet research, she decided she might be anemic and she made an appointment with Doc Garrison for next week, just to run a blood test and be sure, and in the meantime she'd picked up some iron supplements, hoping they would help.

She glanced at her watch as the minute hand drew closer to three, her heart quickening as she wondered if he'd stop by, as he often did once Bethany and Summer arrived for work after school, to grab her hand and race up to her apartment. Once the girls walked into the café, she could barely conceal her anticipation, trying not to look over at the door, trying not to be disappointed if he got too caught up in work today to—

Before she could finish her thought, the door opened and there he stood, his blue eyes searing and hot with lust as he raised his eyebrows, asking her a silent question...to which the answer was "Hell, YES!"

Maggie felt her insides coil tight with need and she circled the bar, pulled toward him like a magnet. "I'll be back in a few minutes, girls."

She took his hand and they sprinted around the building, Maggie's giggles mixing with his panting breath as he pulled her up the stairs, barely getting inside the door of her apartment before he had her up against the vestibule wall, her panties torn off from under her dress, his pants around his ankles as he thrust frantically into her welcome heat.

"I missed you." His eyes fluttered closed and his

breathing was shallow as he thrust upward again. His hands were fisted against the wall behind her as her legs draped over his muscular forearms. "God, I miss you every second I'm not with you, Maggie. I can't get enough."

She grabbed his head and pulled him down violently to kiss him in response, her tongue slipping into his mouth where he sucked on it, swallowing her whimpers and quickly bringing them both to a shattering climax.

With only a few minutes before they both had to return to work, he carried her back to her bedroom and they fell onto the bed together, still panting, half-dressed, tangled together.

"I love you," he murmured from beside her, his hand flat on her belly, over her dress.

"We stay together," she answered, rolling onto her side to face him. "I belong to you."

"We stay married," he said, leaning up and smiling at her. "I have to get back."

"Me too."

"I'm making dinner tonight."

Her stomach gurgled at the thought and she grimaced, sitting up slowly, and covering her nausea with a weak grin. "*Svenska Kottbullar?*"

"Is that a request?" he asked, looking down at her as he pulled up his jeans and tucked in his shirt. His eyes swept over her face and his brows creased in worry. "Hey, are you feeling okay? You look tired."

"Maybe I ate somethin' off." She didn't want to worry him.

He leaned down, dropping a kiss on the tip of your nose. "Poor Maggie May. Why don't you rest for a while? Let the girls take care of things."

She smiled up at him as her stomach settled, and he pulled the comforter over her, watching her lingeringly, love softening his Arctic blue eyes.

"Reminds me of when you were sick. Hey," he said, pushing her bangs off her forehead and kissing her forehead gently. "You want me to stay?"

"No need," she yawned, already half asleep. "See you tonight."

When she woke up, it was dusk. She reached for the clock on her bedside table, knocking her birth control pill pack to the floor in the process. *4:56 p.m.*? She'd been asleep for almost two hours?

Sitting up gingerly, she waited for the familiar nausea to overtake her, but it didn't, and she breathed a sigh of relief. Maybe the little bug she'd had was finally gone. She bent over to pick up her pills. The cover had been knocked open and she looked distractedly at them before snapping the lid closed in her hand.

The sudden realization of what she'd just seen was like a gathering storm in her brain.

She whipped the plastic container back open again.

She bought her pill packs three at a time at the Target in Bozeman and when she got home, she labeled them all at once. This was the second pack of three packs, and she stared down in horror as she realized that the next pill was for Tuesday.

Which would have been fine, except for that today was Thursday.

"Oh, my God," she whispered. The tiredness and nausea? Her extremely sensitive breasts? "Oh, my God."

Reminds me of when you were sick…

Her eyes fluttered closed as she snapped the pill pack shut and her stomach rolled over. She barely made it to the toilet in time to heave the contents of her lunch into the bowl, and it all came together in a flash. Over the two days she was sick with the flu several weeks ago, he'd woken her up to give her Advil and antivirals, but there were two small pills she'd missed during her illness because he hadn't known to give them to her and she was too sick to remember. And she'd been so caught up in their truce and falling in love with him, she hadn't noticed before now.

She sat back against the tub on the bathroom floor and lifted up the skirt of her dress, looking down and placing her hand over her bare belly. A breathy smile turned into a giggle, turned into laughter as she covered her abdomen carefully with both hands, processing the miracle of what was happening inside her body.

In that second, that moment, that pause in the endlessness of time, Maggie fell in love for the second time in her life. A surge of happiness—of pure, unadulterated joy—made her eyes flood with tears as she realized she was almost definitely carrying Nils's child.

Nils's child.

Her laughter tapered off…

Nils's child.

...but her hands remained protectively over her tummy...

Nils's unwanted child.

...as her face fell.

***

Maggie was acting weird. *Super* weird.

He noticed it as soon as he got home. Instead of greeting him at the door with a kiss and smile, he found her on the couch, an open magazine on her lap and a faraway look on her face.

"Maggie?" he asked, once he was standing in front of her.

She lifted her eyes to him, giving him a small smile. "Hi."

"Heya. You feeling any better?"

She shrugged, closing her magazine and walking into the kitchen. She set the little table with two plates, two glasses and two napkins.

"I thought we'd have pizza," she said. "I know you were going to cook, but I've been craving it lately..."

He watched her: the way her eyes didn't quite connect with his, as though she were avoiding him somehow, even though he was standing right there. That was weird enough, but she was almost standoffish, too. Cooking dinner together every night was their way of reconnecting with each other. If it was his night, she'd sit on the counter, teasing and heckling him as he prepared their food, and at least half of the time, they'd end up going at it on the kitchen counter or floor before he even got a chance to finish. If it was her night, he'd sit in one of the kitchen chairs, remarking on the way she moved her body around the kitchen, all the ways she was turning him on. And finally, when she'd had enough, she'd walk over to the table and straddle him in his chair, kissing him deeply, burning the dinner and giggling later as they ate charred chicken breasts or overcooked pasta.

"That's fine," he said carefully, wondering what was up. Had he done something wrong? "Want me to go pick one up?"

"Had it delivered." She gestured to the oven. "Keepin' it warm. Will you put it on the table and pour the drinks? I'll be right back."

He watched as she left the kitchen, hating how detached he felt from her. Where was her warmth and teasing? The way she was acting was the behavioral equivalent of the dreaded "I'm fine." He must have done something wrong, but he couldn't think of what. Heck, he'd just been here a couple of hours ago having intensely awesome afternoon sex. Maybe that was it? Maybe she didn't feel cherished because that had been such a slam-bam-thank-you-ma'am style interlude? But she had seemed as into it as him, and she knew he loved her. She knew that. Didn't she?

He took the pizza out of the box and filled their glasses with beer.

She walked back into the kitchen dressed in sweatpants and a T-shirt, not her usual short-shorts and camisole.

"You never answered me before," he said, staring at her as they both sat down. "Are you feeling better?"

She took a piece of pizza, biting into the slice and

sighing. "Mm-hm."

Sipping his beer, he took a slice and put it on his own plate. "At least you got your appetite back."

"I guess so," she answered, without looking up. She was staring at the beer. "But, best not to try a beer. Might come back up."

She took it to the sink and poured it down the drain, refilling the glass with water.

"Maggie," he asked, his appetite all but lost and his insides in a twist. "Is everything okay?"

She turned around, the glass still touching her lips. He searched her face to figure out what was going on with her, but she didn't seem angry or sad. Just...detached. Distracted. "Mm-hm."

"Is Graham giving you a hard time?"

She sat back down across from him, drawing her knee up to rest one foot on the seat of her chair and taking another sip of water.

"Nae. He's still on his best behavior. Though I think he might have eyes for your cousin."

"For Julie?"

Nils wasn't sure how he felt about this. For all of Graham's tattoos and smart mouth, he hadn't been any trouble to Maggie, and Nils could tell how much she loved having him around. Many times, Nils had caught her tousling his hair, or staring at him from the bar as he bussed one of the café tables. In fact, as long as Graham continued to behave himself, Nils was all in favor of Maggie having her cousin around, and since Bethany and Summer were back in school, he was glad Graham was there full time to give her a hand when he wasn't working hard building the outdoor deck.

"Mm-hm." She took another bite of pizza.

"I don't know if that's a good idea. Julie's pretty innocent. She's lived a sheltered life."

"And Graham's so experienced at nineteen?"

"I didn't say that." He looked down at his plate, feeling off kilter. They were chit-chatting like friends, like two people who weren't madly in love with each other, and it felt cold. It felt strained and he hated it. "But yeah, actually...he has experienced a lot more of life."

"Sometimes opposites attract, you know. Look at Sam and Jenny."

"Or you and me."

"We're not so opposite," said Maggie, looking at him thoughtfully. "Though I suppose we're not on the same page about everythin'."

He picked up his beer and took a long sip, considering her words.

Is that what this was about? Children?

He swallowed, wondering if he should share his more recent thoughts with her. How much his heart had softened toward the idea of having a baby with her. Somehow he felt as if Veronica and Jens had released him from any debt, and his heart felt free to belong completely to Maggie. If he could only overcome his fears for her health, for a safe preg—

"Anyway, I'm not sure he'll do anythin' about it. She

snubs him every chance she gets," added Maggie, chuckling lightly as she finished her pizza and reached for another slice.

"Smart girl," said Nils, trying for humor, but he couldn't carry it off, and he ended up sounding like he didn't like Graham.

She looked up at him with brows knitted and hurt in her eyes. "He's not so bad, Nils. He's tryin' to fit in. You could try a wee bit harder too."

Was that it? She didn't think he liked her cousin?

Damn, that wasn't true at all. Sure, he'd been initially apprehensive about Graham being a handful or sucking up all of Maggie's time, but he'd been fine. He mostly kept to himself, just making a smart-mouthed remark now and then. But Maggie loved him and despite his rumored past and tough appearance, Nils didn't have any actual problem with him.

"Oh, I know. I didn't mean anything. It's great for you to have him here." She didn't look up and he reached for his pizza, taking a bite, but his appetite was all but gone. "Maggie, are you sure that everything's—"

"You know Paul's Miss Mystic?"

Did she purposely cut him off and change the subject so he couldn't ask about her? "Yeah. I mean, I know *of* her. The whole town knows *of* her."

"Speaking of the town, she's here. She's in town."

Nils's eyes darted up to meet Maggie's. "What? No! Holly's *here*?"

"Her name's not Holly, it's Zoe."

"Zoe? No," said Nils. "I met Zoe. Gave her a ride in

410

from the airport on Saturday."

"And Paul brought her to the Prairie last night. Took me a beat before I recognized her, but it's her. Holly. Zoe. Actually, her name is Zoe Holly."

"Well, I'll be…" said Nils, distracted from Maggie's strange behavior by this new bit of information. "She looks nothing like her picture."

"She was in a bad accident some time ago. Changed her hair and wears contacts now. But it's her, all right."

"Paul must be on cloud nine," he said, reaching for her hand. "To have his girl here, finally."

She slid her hand away and picked up her water glass, taking another sip. His hand sat limp and alone on the table, and his stomach flipped over with worry.

Was she pushing him away? Why? And why didn't she just come out and tell him rather than torturing him like this?

"Paul doesn't know," she said softly.

"Doesn't know?"

"Like you said, she doesn't look a thing like her picture. She doesn't know how to tell him."

Nils took another sip of beer, considering this. "Won't go well if she keeps lying to him."

Maggie's eyes whipped up and she looked like she was about to say something. She looked away, polishing off the last bite of her pizza and standing up to put her plate in the sink.

"Maggie, have I done someth—"

Her eyes glistened as they held his for a moment. "Sometimes the truth is messy and you dinna know how

411

to...well, I—I hope they figure it out. They love each other."

Then she picked up her glass from the table and placed it carefully in the sink, keeping her back to him.

"I know. I—I hope so, too," he said softly to her back. "I can't say anything right tonight."

He couldn't stand it anymore. Standing up, he moved quietly to stand behind her, putting his arms around her, trapping her between his body and the counter. He dropped his lips to the back of her neck, relieved when she relaxed, leaning back into his chest. "Should I be worried?"

She took one of his hands and drew it up to her face, pressing her lips to it.

"Dinna be worried," she whispered against his skin, but her voice wasn't reassuring. It was quiet and tense.

"Are you upset with me?"

She turned in his arms, her eyes still glassy and a little bit sad...or concerned...or, damn it, he didn't know what, but not happy, not relaxed and not like his carefree, loving, teasing, tender Maggie.

She shook her head, blinking her eyes like she was about to cry. "I'm just tired."

"I want you to see a doctor tomorrow," he said. Maybe that was it. If she was under the weather, it might explain some of her strange behavior tonight.

"Maybe I will."

She reached up and kissed his lips briefly then wiggled out of his arms, leaving him confused and alone.

***

She hadn't meant to act so weird last night.

The secret she was keeping from him was so big and so life changing, every time she uttered a word, she worried she'd blurt it out. He kept asking her if everything was okay, and the reality was that everything was *not* okay. Her mind was buzzing with about a hundred different thoughts and questions, and most of all, she was anxious to start figuring out the answers to them. She wanted to jump online and research pregnancies. She wanted to call her OB/GYN in Bozeman and get an appointment. She wanted quiet time alone to figure out how to best share the news with Nils. And she could do none of these things while Nils was home.

So, as bad as she felt to see the concern creasing his face as he said "goodbye" and as much as she would miss him while he led a three-day tour over the next few days, it was a relief to have a few days to herself.

The first thing she did was call her doctor and book an appointment for tomorrow.

She explained that she only had a short window and was grateful when Dr. Sweetwater managed to slip in an appointment tomorrow afternoon. She'd close the Prairie for a few hours, and without Nils in town, no one would even notice. She shared some of her concerns, including what limited information she had about Veronica Olsen's pregnancy, but her doctor was reassuring.

"Careful monitoring will tell us the size of your baby as you get closer to delivering and we'll assess whether or not you're a candidate for a cesarean section. But let's not worry about that now. We'll keep a close eye, Maggie. You'll both be fine."

Maggie hadn't realized how concerned she was until tears popped into her eyes at the doctor's optimism and confidence.

"Oh, one other thing…we'll do a transvaginal ultrasound. If you're right about the conception date, we might get lucky."

"Lucky?" asked Maggie, her heart pounding and her mind a blank.

She heard the smile in her doctor's voice. "The heartbeat. If you're right around six weeks from conception, that would be eight weeks pregnant. We have a good chance of hearing it. It's early, though, so cross your fingers."

For the rest of the day Maggie waffled between wanting to laugh out loud with thunderous joy, and wanting to weep with uncertainty.

Tomorrow was like a little visit. She'd see her wee tiny bean of a baby and maybe even hear his or her heartbeat. She massaged her belly tenderly, overwhelmed with feelings of protectiveness and love.

But then her mood would shift, and her eyes would glisten with worry, not wonder.

What if Nils couldn't bring himself to love the baby? What if he felt trapped or tricked into fatherhood? Would he turn his back on her? On them? Not to mention, in the eyes of his family and their friends, they'd *just* started dating a couple of weeks ago. For Lord's sake, how were they going to explain it in a month or two when she started showing?

On the long ninety-minute ride to Bozeman the next day, these questions circled endlessly in her head and by the time she got to her doctor's office, she felt no closer to answering them. She filled out her paperwork, peed in a cup and waited, restless and nervous, in the waiting room until her name was called.

Dr. Sweetwater was able to confirm her pregnancy with a quick pelvic exam, but then she took out a wand and turned on a machine by Maggie's head.

"Shall we take a peek? Lie back. Just relax; this might feel a little cold."

Despite the slight awkwardness she felt from the ultrasound wand, she felt excited and centered. Turning to the small screen beside her, she was mesmerized as a black kidney-shaped mass came into view, and in the middle of the black, a smaller kidney-shaped mass of gray, wiggling slightly as she watched.

"That's your baby," said the doctor softly, pointing at the small gray shape. "Let's see if we can…"

And then, with the flick of a switch, Maggie heard it: the *whoosh-a, whoosh-a, whoosh-a* of her baby's galloping heart.

"…and there's the heartbeat."

Tears streamed down her face as she stared at the screen and a mix of peace and excitement filled her heart with a love so strong and so pure, she knew that nothing in her life would ever be the same again. Different than belonging to her adoptive family or belonging to Nils, she belonged to this tiny being in a way that transcended everything she knew about love. And in that moment, she was sure, with the faith and fierceness of a new mother, that the strength of her love would overcome any uncertainty, reassure any fears, override any doubts in her husband's heart.

Eventually. First she needed to figure out how to tell him.

Chapter 22

Nils couldn't stop thinking about Maggie. And mostly, he couldn't keep from wondering if he was losing her. And it felt a little bit like dying to wonder it at all. Because life—his life, his heart, which had surrendered wholly and completely to his love for her—wasn't even worth contemplating without her.

As he often did, he fingered his grandfather's ring, slipping it onto his ring finger in the privacy of his jeans pocket and remembering the times he'd worn it publicly: during their weekend in the park with the Skinners and at the USCIS interview. Not very much. Not much of a public declaration of their marriage and their feelings for each other.

He furrowed his brows as he filled jug after jug of water at the camp pump. Could that be it? They'd only been "dating" for three weeks, but could Maggie doubt his intentions? She still wore her little Claddagh ring, but he hadn't given her a ring as a public testimony of his feelings for her. Could that be what was bothering her?

Because honestly, it bothered Nils too. He was getting sick of pretending that she wasn't his wife when, in fact, she was and had been for months now. He wanted to claim her. He wanted the whole world to know that she belonged to him and he belonged to her. Despite the fact that their original timeline had him "proposing" around Thanksgiving, he didn't want to wait that long. Was it possible that she felt the same way and was just waiting for him to make his move?

A few of the women on his tour—a dozen older ladies from a larger group called The Blazin' Grannies—passed him as they returned from the gift shop adjacent to the campground.

"What do you think, Mr. Lindstrom?" asked one gray-haired lady, holding out her wrist where a gold bracelet sparkled in the dying sun. "Pretty?"

"Very nice, ma'am."

"That shop isn't cheap, but they sure do have some lovely things. Think your dad will like it?"

"Maybe he'd like it on his bedside table!" exclaimed one of her friends and all of the ladies tittered.

They were a surprisingly rowdy bunch and kept shocking Nils and his father with such forward comments. Nils's father had become the reluctant object of affection for at least five of the ladies on the tour, all of whom were just about old enough to be his mother. Nils rolled his eyes, shaking his head at them as they wandered up to the campsite, leaving him behind, no doubt in hot pursuit of his father.

He capped the last jug and carried all six back to the campsite, dropping them on the picnic table where his father had just started preparing the evening meal with Zoe's help.

"Pop, you okay here for a bit?" Carl Lindstrom looked

slightly wide-eyed as two of the ladies sitting by the campfire wiggled their fingers at him and one licked her wrinkled lips suggestively.

"Sure could use you around camp, son," he said, a might desperately.

"I need to get to that gift shop before it closes," Nils said. "Have to get something. For Maggie."

Zoe nudged his father in the side. "I'll keep you safe, Mr. Lindstrom."

His father grinned at Zoe gratefully then looked at Nils. "Just hurry back, eh?"

Nils winked at Zoe in thanks and turned back toward the cluster of shops and camper services, walking at a clip to make it to the shop by seven o'clock. If they had expensive bracelets, surely they'd have expensive rings, too. And it was about time Maggie Lindstrom had a ring of her own.

***

If Jenny was surprised to hear from him, she didn't let on, which was impressive, since her oldest brother was calling her for advice as he stared blankly at six rows of rings with various colored stones.

"Green, Nils. I'm telling you," she insisted.

"Damn it, Jenny, I should be buying her a diamond from a jeweler, not some green stone at a gift shop."

"Nah. Maggie's not diamonds. You're doing this right. Simple. Something local from the place she chose to call her home. That's what'll suit her best."

Nils stared at the row of semi-precious stones set in sterling silver and ten-karat gold, cradling the phone between his shoulder and ear as he plucked one out from the velvet pillow. It had a bright green stone that the shopkeeper helpfully identified as Wyoming jade.

"Local artisan makes those. He finds the stones over by Copper Mountain. Don't sell very well, though. Too pricey for tourists."

Nils nodded at her, fingering the ring, appreciating the setting that looked like tree branches holding the bright green stone in place. He imagined it on Maggie's finger and had to admit that Jenny had a point. It would look right.

"Did she say jade?" asked Jenny.

"Yeah," answered Nils, slipping the little ring on his pinkie and holding it up to the light.

"Nils," said Jenny gently. "Green jade means calmness, balance, and love."

Nils grinned at the ring and asked for the clerk to price it. He inhaled sharply at the price, but nodded, answering he'd like for it to be wrapped up in a little box. A few minutes later he turned toward the shop exit.

"It's not a little…um, quick?" asked Jenny. "You know, to be asking her to marry you? You've only been dating for a few weeks, and I just—"

"Jenny, of all people…" He started, letting his voice, thick with censure, trail off.

"Right, right. It can definitely happen fast. I know," she answered, no doubt remembering her own whirlwind courtship. "You're sure she'll say yes?"

"I'm sure."

"I was just getting used to the fact that it finally *happened* for you two. A wedding so soon, though?" She paused, and Nils braced himself for more criticism. "I love it."

"Me too, Jen," he answered, smiling lightly with happiness and relief, and holding the door for a pretty blonde woman and the three blond children who trailed after her. He watched them follow their mother like ducklings and his heart clutched. "Jenny, *kan jag ställa en fråga*?" *Can I ask you something?*

"Of course."

"When you had Erin…" He paused, taking a deep breath. "Was everything o-okay?"

"What do you mean?"

He swallowed. This was uncomfortable ground for him for two reasons: first, because he and Jenny didn't talk about this sort of personal, mysterious "women" stuff, and second, because he was scared about what he might hear.

"Was everything, um, normal? From the beginning?"

"You mean…with my pregnancy?"

"Mm. Was it, um, okay?" A bead of sweat trailed down his cheek.

"Yeah," she answered, and he could hear the warmth and surprise and curiosity in the single word. "It was fine. She was healthy at every appointment, perfect with every scan. I mean, I felt a little tired and sick in the beginning, but that's to be expected."

"Erin wasn't…I mean, she wasn't too big? You know, for you?"

"Oh." Jenny laughed softly and, in his mind, he could see her cheeks turning pink. "Well, yes, in fact, she was."

"She—she was?"

"Nils, she was ten pounds, four ounces. That's a big baby. That's why I had a cesarean."

"You did?"

She chuckled. "Yeah. Why do you think I was lying in bed that afternoon that you all came to visit?"

"Oh, I…I didn't know. I guess I just…I mean, I came after that part, I guess. Pop didn't mention it."

"That's *Pappa* for you. I'm surprised you're so curious. Come to think of it, this is an awfully spur-of-the-moment engagement. Have anything you want to share with your little sister?" she teased.

"No!" he exclaimed. "Maggie's not—I mean, no, she's not—No. No, not at all. I'm just…curious."

"You know Kat had a C-section too, right?"

His mind whirled. Both Jenny and his brother Erik's wife, Kat, had needed operations to deliver their babies? But they both looked fine and the babies looked fine and nobody had ever even mentioned it to him.

"No," he said softly, feeling a little overwhelmed. "I didn't know."

"Those girls were over eight pounds each, which is really big for twins. We're not small people, Nils, but it's nothing to worry about. Someday, if you and Maggie have a baby, maybe she'll be okay delivering naturally or maybe she'll need a C-section, too, like me and Kat. Either way, she'll be absolutely fine. Before and after." She chuckled softly again. "Sam wants three more."

"And you weren't…scared?"

"Well, sure, a little. I mean, it's surgery and it's childbirth and something could've gone wrong. But, it didn't. It's such a routine procedure at this point. And Nils...Erin is the best thing that ever happened to me and Sam. She's half him and half me, and that makes her a miracle. That makes her perfect. And that makes me the luckiest woman in the world." She paused. "There's nothing more joyful in the whole world than having a baby."

He listened to the calm certainty in his sister's loving voice. Joyful. His experience had been anything but joyful, but he felt the shift in his heart as he reviewed her words and thought about her experience. She and Kat had both had C-sections, and they were both healthy with three healthy little girls between them. It was certainly a reassuring thought.

"Speaking of Erin, here she comes, all wrapped in a towel like a present. Sam just gave her a bath." Jenny's voice changed, soft and maternal, and he knew she was reaching for Erin. "Time for bed, baby? Time for bed, *älskling*?"

"Jen, I'll let you go…"

"Nils!" she said, and he put the phone back up to his ear. "Good luck! *Elsker deg Største.*"

"*Ja*, Jen. *Elsker deg også.*"

***

Maggie paced her apartment, wringing her hands and trying to calm down a little.

She glanced at her watch again; Nils had texted her thirty minutes ago saying he was almost home. She patted the envelope in her back pocket that held two things: the ultrasound picture of their baby and a brief letter from Dr.

Sweetwater outlining the plan for Maggie's pregnancy. Monthly visits for the first two trimesters, then segueing to weekly visits with ultrasound monitoring as necessary. She twisted the acupressure band around her wrist, grateful that it had helped knock out some of the morning sickness and then slipped her hands under her shirt, flattening them over her belly lovingly.

"He's goin' to be here soon, my wee bairn, and we're goin' to tell him. And he's goin' to love you just as much as I do. I know it. I just know it. Dinna worry."

But the reality was that she didn't know it for sure and she was worried. She was trying to stay as positive as possible, but honestly, she had no idea how Nils would react.

Would he be angry with her? Angry at the baby? Her hands flexed and flattened over her warm skin protectively. She didn't want to choose between them. She loved her baby. She loved her baby's father. She didn't expect him to be excited at first, but if he could just share a tiny bit of her joy...if he could try to find room in his heart and his life for their child, try to trust Maggie and her doctor, it would be the answer to every prayer her heart had ever made. She closed her eyes, quickly adding another: *Mary, Joseph and all the saints, please let Nils love our baby.*

Her eyes opened as she heard the key slip into the lock of her apartment door and she rushed to open it, falling into his arms as he held her close, burying his face in her hair.

"I missed you," he said gruffly.

"I missed you more." Her words rushed out as her lips brushed against his neck. "I'm sorry I was so strange the night before you left."

He didn't move from the doorway, still holding her tightly. "It's okay. It was good. It was a kick in the pants. I don't know what in the world we're waiting for."

Finally he drew back, and she realized that he was clean-shaven and smelled fresh from the shower.

"You went home first?" she asked.

He nodded. "I wanted to clean up a little for you."

"Cleanin' up *with* you is one of my favorite things," she pouted, feeling a little cheated.

His eyes caught fire and he pulled her up against him, lowering his mouth to claim hers for a deep, slow kiss. His hands slipped beneath her shirt and he flattened them across her back, spanning its width, his fingers curling around her ribs. She loved the size of him and the strength; she loved that he could easily hurt her with his body, but wielded his power with tenderness and love for her. It made her feel safe. It made her feel loved. Her heart twisted with a powerful longing that his tenderness would be transferred to the little life growing within her, and she drew back from him.

He rested his forehead against hers, panting lightly. "I want to take you somewhere. Come with me."

"What? Where?"

"Trust me," he whispered, running his lips down the side of her face to catch her earlobe lightly with his teeth. "And then we'll come home and pick up where we left off."

A shiver ran down her spine with the deliciousness of that promise, but she felt conflicted. She had wanted to tell him her news as soon as he got home, but he'd showered and changed and clearly had a plan of his own. If he had something important to say or do or show her, she didn't want to upstage him with her news quite yet, plus her curiosity got the better of her. She let him pull her out the door and down the stairs, wondering where in the world they were headed.

***

As they arrived at the Roosevelt Arch, he felt a ridiculous flare of nerves.

The little white cupcake, identical to the one he'd offered her the first time he proposed, waited in the back seat in a box, covered with his jacket. It felt like déjà vu, except for the important difference that this time, instead of a half-assed agreement to bail her out of a tough situation by getting married, he was going to *ask* her to share her life with him the way she deserved to be asked.

Her eyes searched his as he cut the engine and turned to her, grinning and giving her a quick peck on the cheek before opening his door. He rounded the car and opened her door for her, grabbing the cupcake box when her back was turned and holding it behind his back.

"What's goin' on here?" she asked him, her bright eyes keen with anticipation.

"Go sit at the picnic table."

She shrugged, tossing him a nervous smile and she made her way a few feet to the table. Once she was perched on the bench, he followed her, a cupcake in one hand and a small gift box in the other.

Her eyes widened as he offered her the cupcake, which she accepted with a giggle, swiping a bit of icing on her fingertip and licking it before setting it gingerly on the table behind her. "This is just like—"

"Not *just* like," he corrected, falling to one knee before her.

Tears immediately brightened her eyes and she gasped as he held the little box out to her. She searched his face before taking it gently from his palm and unraveling the yellow ribbon with trembling hands.

"We're already married," she murmured, her voice breaking as she opened the box to see the bright green stone set in shiny gold.

"But I never *asked* you. Not the way you deserved to be asked."

"It's so b-beautiful," she said, with tears streaming down her freckled cheeks. "You didna n-need to do this."

"I did. I do," he said, taking the ring out of the box.

She changed her Claddagh ring from her left hand to her right and held out her trembling fingers to him. He slipped the jade ring on her fourth finger and dropped his head to kiss it, without breaking eye contact with her. When he leaned back up, he started speaking in a low, measured voice.

"I am the proudest man in the world to call you my wife and it's time for the rest of the world to know. Every good thing in my life is better because of you. Every dark, lonesome corner has been reborn with your love and warmth. I want to fall asleep next to you every night and wake up to you every morning and make you chicken soup when you're sick and watch you read *Cosmo* and sneak away from work at three o'clock to make love to you and be the only man who gets close enough to smell the strawberries in your hair. I want to bed you and wed you and be your best friend and your only lover. And I know we're already married, but I want you to marry me again because I love you, because I will always love you…" He swallowed, looking down briefly, and he could feel the hot tears in his eyes when he looked back up at her. "…because someday, when we're ready to have children of our own, I want to have them with you."

She gasped softly and her shoulders rolled forward, shaking with sobs. He quickly shifted from his knee to sitting up on the bench beside her, and pulled her into his arms, whispering tenderly into her ear.

"I love you. We stay together. You're my wife. We stay married. You belong to me and I belong to you. Marry me all over again, Maggie May. I'm lost without you."

Her body shook in his arms as she finally murmured against his neck, through tears, "Y-Yes."

He squeezed her a little tighter, passionately kissing a path from her ear across her cheek to her lips, which he claimed with the certainty of a man whose heart was lost and now is found, was broken and now is mended, was hopeless and now is flooded with joy. He moved his hands to the back of her head, tilting it lightly so he could seal his mouth across hers, brushing her wet cheeks with his thumbs as his tongue danced with hers. Her hands cradled his jaw and her little fingers curled into his cheeks as she moaned into his mouth, making him harden instantly. All he wanted was to jump back in the car, race to her apartment, pull her up the stairs and into the bedroom where he intended to have his way with his wife all night long.

But Maggie pulled back from him, and it took him a moment to realize he was looking at an odd mixture of hope and worry on her beautiful face. He swiped at her tears with his thumbs then dropped his hands to his lap, where she caught them, lacing her fingers through his.

She took a deep breath, about to say something, and then hesitated, biting her lower lip as she looked down.

"Maggie?" he whispered, trying to combat the dueling needs of his desire for her body and the strong pull to understand what was happening in her head.

When she looked up again, she seemed more determined. She clenched her jaw once then smiled at him, but it was her brave smile and didn't reach her eyes. She was nervous about something and it made his heart race with apprehension.

"You're freaking me out," he said softly, trying to keep the edge out of his voice and readjusting his fingers through hers. "What's going on?"

"Did you mean it?" she asked quickly. "You want to have children with me?"

Relief coursed through him like a warm breeze and he exhaled, nodding at her before giving her a reassuring smile. "Yes."

She exhaled, too, and her shoulders, which had

bunched up around her ears, lowered with her rush of breath. She closed her eyes and that brave little smile changed into one that looked relieved and confident...and more—hopeful.

Tears burned his eyes again as he watched her, realizing again how much it meant to her for them to have children of their own. And although Nils still had some residual nerves, her reaction encouraged him too, made him feel lucky and blessed and excited. Someday they'd have a family of their own. Someday.

He grinned at her, caressing her face with his fingertips. "I talked to Jenny and she told me a lot about her pregnancy, and Kat's too, and it did a lot to reassure me. I'm getting there, and yes, someday I do—I want for us to have a baby. I'm going to do some research and work on my fears. I'm going to do whatever it takes to get there, Maggie May. I promise."

She bit her bottom lip. "You may want to get started on that research."

He smiled at her, chuckling lightly at her eagerness. "I will. I promise. First, we'll tell everyone about our engagement and talk to the reverend about—"

"No. Nils. Listen." Her eyes had gone wide and worried again and her tongue flicked out to lick her lips. "I mean you might want to start that research now. Like, *right now.*"

He stared at her, eyes widening, as his brain worked to process exactly what she was trying to tell him.

She squeezed his hand and smiled encouragingly at him.

"Remember when I was so sick with the flu? And

you'd wake me to take my Advil and antivirals? Well, there were, um, a couple of pills that I missed durin' those two days. Two very important pills, in fact. And, um…" She pulled her hands away from him and reached into her back pocket to take out an envelope, smoothing it nervously in her fingers as she held it on her lap.

"Maggie, are you saying you're…"

"*We're.*"

"We're…"

She raised the envelope, offering it to him and he glanced down at it, then back up at her face which had exploded in the most beautiful smile he'd ever seen in his entire life.

"We're havin' a baby," she said softly, still holding his eyes.

"Maggie," he gasped, feeling his face contort as he pulled her fiercely into his arms, his arms vise-like around her small body. His heart pounded like crazy and tears wet his face, and she ran her hands soothingly up and down his back.

"It'll be okay," she murmured. "I'm goin' to be okay, and our baby's goin' to be okay. I've already been to the doctor, and everythin' looks good, and she said…"

He leaned back, loosening his grip. "Am I holding you too hard?"

"No," she said through tears and laughter, shaking her head back and forth.

"Show me," he said, staring at the greenest green eyes God ever made.

She opened the envelope and took out a grainy black and white picture, showing it to him. "Nils, meet Bean."

"Bean," he sighed, staring at the little gray bean-shaped baby that was growing inside of Maggie right this minute. His son or daughter. His child.

He lifted his eyes to hers, blinking away the tears that made everything blurry. His eyes flicked to her belly. "Can I?"

"Of course!" she said, her own tears mingling with laughter as she raised her shirt so he could flatten his giant palm against her skin.

"Hey, Bean," he whispered, unable to process the overwhelming deluge of emotions as he stared at his rough, tan hand against the smooth white perfection of her still-flat tummy. "You saw a doctor."

"Mm-hm. While you were gone."

He took a deep breath, desperately trying to keep the panicked part of him at bay. "And she said?"

"She said everythin' looks perfect. Me. Bean. Everythin'." She placed her hand over his. "I heard the heartbeat, Nils."

His eyes rose to hers. "The heartbeat?"

She nodded as more tears spilled out of her eyes. "It was strong. It sounded like a gallopin' pony. It was the most amazin' thing I've ever heard in all my livin' life."

"I want to hear it," he said, leaning his head down as though pressing his ear to her belly would produce the sound.

"Then come with me to my appointment next month."

His blood went cold as his neck whipped up to look at her. "Next month? I thought you said everything was okay?"

"Oh, my love," she said gently, reaching up to cup his cheek with her hand, love and compassion and understanding softening her eyes as she gazed back at him. "I have to go once a month. For checkups. It's standard. And as we get closer, I'll start goin' once a week." She swallowed and looked away from him for a second before taking a deep breath and continuing. "I told Dr. Sweetwater about Veronica and Jens."

"Good," he breathed, his hand still molded protectively over her abdomen.

"But I'm goin' to be fine."

He looked up at her, finally dropping his hand from her belly and pulling her against him gently, as he would a fragile or beloved thing. His eyes closed as she laced her hands behind his neck. "I love you. I love Bean." He leaned back to open his eyes and look into hers. "But I'm not going to lie. I'm worried, too. It's going to be a long nine months."

She tilted her head to the side like all of the Lindstroms and smiled gently through tears. "Then it's a good thing you only have to wait seven."

"April?" he asked, doing the math quickly in his head.

"May Day. Where it all began," she said with a grin.

And because words weren't nearly enough to express the fullness of his heart, he pulled his wife snugly into the loving haven of his arms as their baby grew safe and strong between them.

EPILOGUE

Maggie looked around the hospital room, smiling as she realized that visiting hours really didn't apply to the Lindstroms, who'd arrived an hour ago and looked as if they intended to stay the day, treating the event of Britt Lily Lindstrom's birth like a reunion.

She looked over at Nils, who held baby Britt as he chatted with his father, Carl, who stood with his arm around Graham.

We didn't do things the conventional way, she thought.

Most people see each other, say hello, start datin', become friends, fall in love, get engaged, get married and start a family.

Next to Graham, Jenny held a wiggling Erin, while Sam talked to Erik. Beside him, Kat carefully transferred a sleeping Dagmar to her stroller while Jane, who was sporting a shiny new engagement ring, bounced Dagmar's twin sister, Heidi, on her hip, and looked like she was just about ready for a baby of her own.

We saw each other, fell in love, said hello, became friends, got married, started an accidental family, got engaged, got married and had the most beautiful baby girl who ever lived.

All out of order. All perfect.

Lars stood beside his fiancée, talking to Paul, who had

his arm draped around the shoulder of his wife, Zoe.

Family. My family, every single one of them.

As her eyes roamed around the room, Nils caught them, whispering something to his father before coming to her side, careful not to bump the stitches in her still-tender abdomen as he placed their sleeping daughter in the crook of Maggie's arm. He leaned down to press his lips to the baby's downy red hair before shifting slightly to kiss Maggie.

Sometimes, Maggie thought, when he looked at her and Britt as if God had given him a second chance at life, she loved him so much it hurt a little bit, in the most wonderful way.

He squatted down beside the bed, eye level with her. "Tired? You want me to get rid of everyone?"

Maggie shook her head. "I love them. All of them. I want them to stay."

She was a part of this family. She didn't just belong to Nils or Britt. She belonged to all of them and all of them belonged to her. And all because of the man hovering beside her, who had figured out how to open his heart to love again, even after it seemed he'd lost all hope.

"I love you," he whispered.

"We stay together," she murmured, glancing at Britt as the wee baby sighed in her sleep. "Forever, *mo muirnín*. We're a family."

THE END

ALSO AVAILABLE
from Katy Regnery

a modern fairytale
(A collection)

The Vixen and the Vet
Never Let You Go
Ginger's Heart
Dark Sexy Knight
Don't Speak
Shear Heaven
At First Sight

THE BLUEBERRY LANE SERIES

THE ENGLISH BROTHERS
(Blueberry Lane Books #1–7)

Breaking Up with Barrett
Falling for Fitz
Anyone but Alex
Seduced by Stratton
Wild about Weston
Kiss Me Kate
Marrying Mr. English

THE WINSLOW BROTHERS
(Blueberry Lane Books #8–11)

Bidding on Brooks
Proposing to Preston
Crazy about Cameron
Campaigning for Christopher

THE ROUSSEAUS
(Blueberry Lane Books #12–14)

Jonquils for Jax
Marry Me Mad
J.C. and the Bijoux Jolis

THE STORY SISTERS
(Blueberry Lane Books #15–17)

The Bohemian and the Businessman
The Director and Don Juan
Countdown to Midnight

THE SUMMERHAVEN SERIES

Fighting Irish
Smiling Irish
Loving Irish
Catching Irish

THE ARRANGED DUO

Arrange Me
Arrange Us

ODDS ARE GOOD SERIES

Single in Sitka
Nome-o Seeks Juliet
A Fairbanks Affair
My Valdez Valentine

STAND-ALONE BOOKS:

After We Break
(a stand-alone second-chance romance)

Braveheart
(a stand-alone suspenseful romance)

Frosted
(a stand-alone romance novella for mature readers)

Unloved, a love story
(a stand-alone suspenseful romance)

Under the sweet-romance pen name
Katy Paige

THE LINDSTROMS

Proxy Bride
Missy's Wish
Sweet Hearts

Choose Me
Virtually Mine
Unforgettable You

Under the paranormal pen name
K. P. Kelley

It's You, Book 1
It's You, Book 2

Under the YA pen name
Callie Henry

A Date for Hannah

ABOUT THE AUTHOR

 **New York Times** and *USA Today* **bestselling author Katy Regnery** started her writing career by enrolling in a short story class in January 2012. One year later, she signed her first contract, and Katy's first novel was published in September 2013.

Several dozen books and three RITA® nominations later, Katy claims authorship of the multititled Blueberry Lane series, the A Modern Fairytale collection, the Summerhaven series, the Arranged duo, and several other stand-alone romances, including the critically acclaimed mainstream fiction novel *Unloved, a love story.*

Katy's books are available in English, French, German, Hebrew, Italian, Polish, Portuguese, and Turkish.

Check out Katy's Website here:
http://www.katyregnery.com
Sign up for Katy's newsletter today:
http://eepurl.com/disKlD